M
14

The
Husband
Test

This Large Print Book carries the
Seal of Approval of N.A.V.H.

The
Husband
Test

Betina
Krahn

Thorndike Press • Waterville, Maine

Published in 2002 by arrangement with Bantam Books, an imprint of The Bantam Dell Publishing Group, a division of Random House, Inc.

Thorndike Press Large Print Romance Series.

The tree indicium is a trademark of Thorndike Press.

The text of this Large Print edition is unabridged.
Other aspects of the book may vary from the original edition.

Set in 16 pt. Plantin by Myrna S. Raven.

Printed in the United States on permanent paper.

Library of Congress Cataloging-in-Publication Data

Krahn, Betina M.
    The husband test / Betina Krahn.
      p. cm.
    ISBN 0-7862-4129-2 (lg. print : hc : alk. paper)
    1. Nuns — Fiction. 2. Nobility — Fiction. 3. Large type books. I. Title.
PS3561.R227 H87 2002
813'.54—dc21   2002019915

To the memory of Regina Maynard,
with all my love

One

"Heaven save me from that wretched girl!"

The abbess threw down her quill and slid from the tall stool at her writing table. As she kicked aside the voluminous skirt of her black woolen habit and headed for the door of her solar with both her elderly assistant and her informant in tow, she glanced skyward and issued Heaven yet another command.

"And while you're at it, you'd best save *her* from *me*."

Tension spread in an expanding wave across the enclosed green and through the open doors that faced the peaceful garden heart of the convent. The sisters of the order and their young female charges heard the scrape of feet on gravel and the muffled whispers rising in the abbess's wake, and a number left their stitchery, looms, and tutoring to join a growing tide of curiosity at her back. A storm was brewing, and in a restrained and tautly run community of women there was nothing so fascinating as a vehement discharge of passion.

It was well past midday, not long until the

bells would ring None, but the long wooden dining tables were bare and the chapter dining hall was deserted. Wisps of smoke hung in the air near the kitchen steps and grew steadily thicker as the abbess and her party descended through the passage. Smells of burned onions and fish and charred flour, overlaid by something like a tincture of "wet dog," caused her curious followers to hesitate, wince, and clutch their noses. The abbess, however, charged through the stench with veil billowing and determination hardening. There was no question now that dinner would be late, and the abbess had no doubt about who was to blame for it.

Baskets of turnips, bags of flour and oats, and willow ricks of vegetables were stacked everywhere, some still bearing aromatic traces of damp earth from the underground cellars. The three long worktables in the center of the great stone chamber were cluttered with crocks, pails, wooden trenchers, and the ash-covered remains of what was once edible fish. Both the tables and the floor were covered with flour, and at the far end of the chamber, plumes of gray smoke boiled from various parts of the great stone hearth.

Sister Boniface, the convent's head cook,

stood to one side with her wimple wilted and sooty, her eyes stony, and her brawny arms crossed over her bosom. Clustered behind her, eyes wide with expectation, were her kitchen staff: a pair of aged nuns, two novices assigned to the kitchens, and half a dozen orphaned scullery maids and pot boys from the nearby village.

Through the haze, the abbess's piercing gaze fixed on the singular soot-covered figure standing between the worktables and the roaring, overheated hearth. It was a young woman in a worn novice's habit. As she turned in response to the gasps and whispers in the doorway, her gaze locked with the abbess's and she froze.

"What in the blessed name of Heaven do you think you are doing?" the abbess roared.

Eloise of Argent shoved behind her back the iron skimmer she had been using to rescue some charred fish from the coals, and she felt her blood draining to her feet. She had seen that look in the abbess's eye before . . . when she improved the well and they had that little cave-in and the convent had to go without water for a day or two . . .

"Helping Sister Boniface," she answered, her throat tightening the way it most certainly would if the abbess could get her fingers around it.

"Helping her to do what?" the abbess roared, flinging a finger at the smoking hearth. "Burn down the kitchens?"

"No, Reverend Mother, I was only showing her how to fit a few more things on the . . . to improve her use of the . . ."

"*Improve?*" The notion stopped the abbess's breath. "You've scorched, toppled, and collapsed your way through every corner of this convent in the name of *improvement.*"

"But if people would only listen to what I suggest —"

"Listen? To your harebrained ideas? And bring yet more disaster down upon our heads? As if we don't suffer enough during Lent!"

The abbess lurched for the aisle between the tables, and if her aged assistant hadn't been standing on her long skirt, Eloise would have felt her wrath firsthand. By the time the head of the convent wheeled and set the old sister off her garment, Eloise had dropped the skimmer and backed out of reach.

"I'll clean it all, Reverend Mother, I promise."

"You'll do no such thing!" The abbess advanced around the table and Eloise found herself backed against a huge stack of grain barrels she had insisted would be more accessible beside the tables and would save the kitchen sisters steps. She glanced between the glowering kitchen sisters and the curious faces in the doorway. Fully half of the convent was present to witness her fate. There was no escaping it. Doomed now, she braced to meet whatever punishment the abbess would see fit to inflict. A true leader, she told herself, always took responsibility for her actions . . . be they successes or failures.

"Reverend Mother!" a frantic voice called from the throng clogging the stairs and doorway. "Riders — men-at-arms!" A rotund little nun barreled her way through the crowd and headed straight for the abbess's side. She was panting from her run and the smoke and stench caused her to gasp and sway against one of the burdened tables. "In— inside the gates — inside the court!" she managed to get out between coughs.

The news galvanized everyone in the kitchens.

"An armed force?" The abbess wheeled on the messenger. "Dearest Lord, in the Holy Season? Have they breached the cloister gate?"

The little nun shook her head vigorously as she clutched her side and struggled for breath. "Still . . . in the court . . . demanding to . . . see you!"

Faced with the potential for far worse than a late dinner or a sooty kitchen, the abbess tossed a fierce glare at Eloise.

"You — go to your chamber and stay there until I send for you! See she gets there, Sister Archibald," she ordered her assistant. Then she headed for the stairs, sweeping the air with her arms like an agitated mother hawk urging her nestlings into flight. "The rest of you — into the chapel and onto your knees. Go! *Now!*"

The scramble that followed was rescued from the throes of panic by the determined example of the older and more experienced nuns. When the sisters and their female charges reached the cloister walk leading to the chapel, the elders slowed and began to pray loudly and emphatically. The clamor of scuffing feet and the girls' cries of distress were slowly engulfed in a measured drone: "Hail Mary, full of grace . . ."

Next to rampaging plague, armed men at the gates — *inside the gates* — were the most serious threat a cloistered community of women could face. Church lands and holdings, particularly wealthy ones like the Convent of the Brides of Virtue, too often became contested prizes in the bloody power struggles between noble houses. And once the gates of a convent had been breached, the appetites of war frequently reduced its occupants from Heaven's handmaidens to the spoils of battle.

Eloise felt Sister Archibald's hand on her elbow, tugging. "Come away, girl. We must hurry. Kitchens are the first place they raid."

Eloise jolted into motion, but not toward the door leading to the secondary residence, where the novices were housed. Sister Archibald, who refused to release her, was dragged along in the abbess's wake.

"Eloise, ye cannot do this," the venerable Archibald declared, alternately teetering along and bracing to resist, trying in vain to prevent their progress. "The abbess —"

"May need help," Eloise said, undeterred by the certainty that the abbess would welcome help from the Devil himself before accepting it from *her*. Behind her she could hear Sister Archibald groan.

"Don't interfere, Eloise. She has enough trouble on her hands."

"I've got to see." Eloise paused to allow the old lady to catch her breath. "How will I ever learn to be abbess if she won't let me see how she does things?"

Another groan. "Ye'll never live to be even

a full nun, if ye don't stop this madness and go straight to yer chamber and down onto yer knees to ask for forgiveness."

"Forgiveness? For wanting to help?" Eloise peered around the corner of the chapter house and looked toward the chapel, from which wafted the sound of female voices in unified and fervent prayer. No one was left in the court or cloister. Freed from the fear of discovery, she took a deep breath and pulled Sister Archibald toward the steps at the end of the main residence and then down the upstairs hallway.

"Forgiveness for being headstrong and disobedient," the old sister said, scowling at her. "Ye're proud and stubborn and ye lack much in the grace of sufferance."

"I am not disobedient," Eloise protested.

"Look at ye . . . disobeying right now!"

"I'm doing as the reverend mother says." Eloise took the old nun's hand and pulled her along. "I'm just doing it *slowly*."

Even as she spoke, they reached the gallery that ringed the upper range of the convent's reception hall, and Eloise pulled her aged superior along toward the narrow, leaded window overlooking the courtyard. Pressing against the wall, one on either side of the window, they could make out the sounds of voices outside and the occasional snort of a horse. With a finger pressed to her lips for silence, Eloise reached for the handle of the window latch and turned it. The creak of rusted iron hinges and the appearance of two heads peering over the sill went unnoticed by those participating in the drama unfolding below.

The abbess stood before the cloister gate, drawn up to her full imperious height, with Bendick the stable hand, armed with a shovel, and Old Rupert the gardener, brandishing a wooden rake, at her back. Before the abbess, filling the dusty courtyard with horseflesh, heat, and an air of menace, were more than a score of seasoned knights and men-at-arms arrayed in a rank behind a nobleman dressed in light armor.

The nobleman dismounted and strode forward to face the abbess. She was not a small woman but this lord, in his great leather boots, battle-scarred breastplate, and forbidding hawk-shaped helm, towered well above her.

"I've come for a woman," he declared, his powerful voice reverberating through the stone-walled court like the report of a cannon.

Then something caused him to twitch with irritation and shoot a dark look over his shoulder. After a pause and a tightening of the sun-creased eyes visible inside his polished helm, the lord flexed his gauntlet-clad hands in irritation. Behind him, at the center of his cordon of men, the silk pennant bearing his coat of arms snapped sharply in the breeze.

"A wife. I've come for a *wife*," he amended his demand.

That word, even intoned in the lord's booming voice, sent a trickle of relief through Eloise and Sister Archibald, who had been holding their breaths as they stared at the battle-hardened force invading their home.

"A wife?" The abbess's voice was oddly choked. But a moment later, she slid her arms up into her sleeves in a gesture of resolve that Eloise and Sister Archibald instantly recognized. She openly assessed the scarred and hot-eyed soldiers behind the glowering monolith who stood with his legs spread and braced and his fists propped on his hips.

"Who are you, sir, and what do you mean by riding into our convent with an armed force? I warn you — our order and this holy establishment are under the protection of the Bishop of Rheims and His Highness the Duke of Avalon."

There was a pause as the lord assessed the

authority and the demeanor of the woman who administered the property and affairs of the abbey.

"I am Peril, earl of Whitmore, loyal subject of Edward of England. I've come to secure a wife."

She flung a finger at his armed contingent. "In the holiest of seasons . . . with swords and axes and men-at-arms?"

"The axes are not raised, the swords are not drawn." He sounded somewhat indignant at her objection. "I have journeyed a long way through perilous precincts, and when I am done here, I must return on the same path bearing a bride. My intentions are honorable and peaceable . . . else I would not have a priest in company."

He turned, grabbed the priest hiding behind him, and dragged him around to face the abbess.

The abbess studied the man, the wincing priest, and the situation.

"A priest is no assurance," the abbess declared. "Many lords raid and make war with the church hard by their side."

The priest, who shrank like frying bacon under the heat of the abbess's suspicion, turned to the earl and spoke in quiet, anxious tones. The lord didn't seem to like what he heard and they argued in whispers. Then the earl drew back with a snarl, unsheathed his sword with one hand and his dagger with the other, and took two long strides toward the abbess.

Sister Archibald's knobby hand clamped over Eloise's mouth as she rose to cry out. Together, they stood upright in the window, watching him hurl the dagger into the packed earth of the court, near the abbess's feet, and then plant his sword, point first, beside it.

"There they will stay," the earl declared, "until you return them to me yourself."

The action clearly had an impact on the abbess.

"Then you have indeed come to acquire a wife." Her voice seemed abnormally thin and high. He nodded sharply and after another moment of silence, the abbess announced her decision. "You and your priest will be welcome to enter our gates and partake of our hospitality" — she raked his men with a resentful eye — "as soon as your men have withdrawn to the village."

The earl looked none too pleased by this final obstacle, but soon turned to his second in command and nodded. The knight turned his horse and raised an arm in a silent order for the others to follow him. As the sound of their hoofbeats faded, the abbess took a deep breath, ordered the stableman and the gardener to close the outer gates, and beckoned the earl and his priest inside.

Eloise stood for a moment, transfixed by the sight of the dagger and sword. The gleam of the polished metal in the early spring sun sent a chill up her spine.

As the sound of the three entering the reception hall drifted up from below, Sister Archibald grabbed Eloise's wrist and gestured frantically toward the side hall. Eloise delayed just long enough to glimpse over the railing the abbess leading the earl and his cleric into her private reception chamber.

"Do you think perhaps we could . . ." She glanced longingly at the door as it closed.

"No!" Sister Archibald whispered. "Come, child."

"Did you see her?" Eloise said as they hurried down the side passage toward the stairs. "The way she stood up to them. Now *that's* an abbess. I'd give anything to be able to hear how she —"

"What ye'd give, Eloise of Argent, if ye were caught, is every chance ye have of taking yer final vows. The abbess was furious today and rightly so. She's told ye time and again to mind yer own work and keep

19

yer nose out of others' bailiwicks. But ye just don't learn."

"Oh, but I do, Sister Archibald. Every time I help someone in the convent with their duties, I learn a great deal. I've learned how to card wool, spin, and weave . . . how to dye cloth, make patterns, and stitch garments . . . how to store grains and preserve foods . . . how to plant and harvest crops. I can repair roofs and judge cattle and shear sheep and milk goats and run a dairy. I can read the scriptures and canon law . . . write wills and interpret them . . . plead cases at law, draw up marriage documents, and judge tenant property disputes . . ."

"Ye also know how to dry up a well, make a house unlivable with yer 'flea smoke,' and char fine, plump chickens past all recognition."

"But those are little things." Eloise halted so that Sister Archibald had to pause, too. "Don't you see . . . I'm doing my best to learn and prove to the abbess that I would make a good assistant now and an even better abbess in the future."

"All ye've proved, my girl, is that ye lack discipline and obedience. The abbess would never trust the convent's affairs to such a headstrong creature."

They descended the steps and hurried

along the edge of the cloister, to the novices' dormitory. Eloise's shoulders rounded as the truth of the old nun's words settled over her. Even seen through sympathetic Sister Archibald's eyes, her latest attempt to demonstrate her capability was nothing short of a disaster.

She couldn't hide her misery, and as she opened the door to her small, sparsely furnished room, Sister Archibald put a hand on her shoulder.

"There, there, my girl. 'Tis Lent. Pray for guidance an' ask for forgiveness. Ye may have worn out yer grace with the abbess, but th' Lord has promised ye seventy times seven an' then some."

Eloise's eyes filled with tears and the old nun patted her cheek before backing out of the chamber and closing the heavy door.

She sat down on her narrow pallet and drew her knees up into her arms. It had all gone wrong. Again. What was it about her that wouldn't — couldn't — leave well enough alone? What was wrong with her?

What if she were one of those people not suited to taking holy vows? The abbess called her thoughtless, undisciplined, and disobedient, and she had probably been guilty of each charge on one occasion or other. It wasn't that she didn't love God, and it certainly wasn't that she didn't want to serve others. It was just that she felt her way of serving others meant finding them better ways of doing things. Was that her true calling or was that merely the subtle-but-deadly whisper of the sin of pride?

And if it were her true calling, where did that place her in the church? Where did she belong? She had known since she was twelve and newly come to the convent that she didn't have the beauty, the patience, or the domestic nature required of a candidate for matrimony. Now it was beginning to appear that she didn't have the humility, discipline, or selflessness required of candidates for membership in the blessed order, either. Where did that leave her? Was she one of those flawed and pitiable creatures doomed to spend the rest of her life suspended in the barren regions that lay between being a bride of Christ and the bride of a man?

"Very well, Your Lordship, what sort of bride do you seek?" The abbess came straight to the point as she studied the intimidating hawk-shaped helm resting on the heavy oak table that separated her from the earl and his priest. It was her standard opening question, meant more to uncover the nature of the man than the nature of the bride he desired.

The nobleman straightened and looked around the richly appointed audience chamber of the convent . . . at the linenfold paneling, the well-tended tapestries, and the embers glowing in the hearth.

"A good one," he answered gruffly, shifting his large, booted legs and tightening his grip on the empty scabbard at his side. Clearly, being without his weapons bothered him.

"Perhaps you could be a bit more specific. We here at the Convent of the Brides of Virtue like to think that all of our maidens will make good brides. Even so, there is considerable variation."

The earl glowered. "A *very* good one."

"What he means to say, Honorable Abbess" — the little cleric ventured a correction that drew a black look from his patron — "is that he seeks a maid of great purity, great honor, and great virtue."

The earl eased and nodded. "A *great* bride."

"I can see you've given the matter much thought, Your Lordship." The abbess produced an inscrutable smile. "May I ask why you've come to us?"

"Everyone knows the best brides come

from the Convent of the Brides of Virtue," he declared with the wave of a still gauntleted hand.

It was truth, not flattery. Wives acquired from the Brides of Virtue were pious, accomplished, pleasing, well mannered, and learned in all the household arts and management . . . widely renowned as worthy keepers of the keys in houses both great and small. Their one deficit — and not an inconsiderable detraction in the ranks of the nobility — was their lack of dowries.

The maidens on deposit with the Brides of Virtue were nobility's lesser daughters, made motherless or orphaned by a scourge of pestilence, born into a family burdened with overabundant female offspring, or simply the victims of mismanaged or failing fortunes. Thus, it was a credit to the clever and conscientious management of the abbesses of the convent that their charges were not only esteemed and sought-after as wives, but that the grateful donations they generated amounted to quite a tidy profit.

"The duke of Worcester, the king of Westphalia, and the protector of Lower Saxony . . . they all got brides from here." The earl of Whitmore took a fortifying breath. "And I must have a bride 'filled with the highest virtue.'" He glanced at the priest, whose lips were moving as he stared intently at the wooden cross lying across his frayed cassock. Praying. The earl winced.

There was a covert air of anxiety about the pair that intrigued the abbess. She had a nose for desperation, and these two positively reeked of urgent nuptial need. None of her charges were capable of bringing a fat purse to a husband's coffers; the earl must surely know that. There was a story here; she was sure of it. And where there was a story, there was an opportunity. She smiled.

"Tell me about your lands, Your Lordship. Where are they?"

"South of London. My holdings are not vast, but they have always been sufficient."

"Have been?" The abbess pounced on his wording. "They are no longer?"

"No." The earl answered sharply, but not before dismay flitted through his features for an instant. "They are sound as ever. All is well."

The abbess caught Whitmore's eye and held it in her famous "inquisitor's gaze." She searched him ruthlessly, prying and prodding, but he held his ground and met her demands with a stubborn refusal to be bested by a woman . . . even an abbess. For a long moment they sat locked in visual combat, neither giving ground. Then some-

25

thing, some noise from the priest . . . a choking sound . . . caused them both to withdraw slowly, neither having conceded victory.

"All is as well as can be expected," the earl conceded, his tautly held shoulders lowering ever so slightly. "I am a warrior, a leader of men. Since I returned home from the wars to take up my late father's mantle . . . well, I am no plowman, nor much of a clerk. A fine lady wife would set my house to rights and free me to attend to my lands and my king." He couldn't help a glance at the priest. "Or so I am told."

"Told?" The abbess leveled a piercing look on the priest. "By whom?"

"My advisors." The earl shifted uneasily. "Father Basset, here. My steward . . . my housekeeper . . . my second in command —"

"We *all* wish for a worthy lady" — Father Basset nervously interrupted that litany — "to complete His Lordship's happiness and bring a new era of peace and prosperity to Whitmore."

The abbess scowled. "A woman may indeed be capable of bringing peace to a man's house and even his heart. But peace *and* prosperity to a whole shire? You don't want a wife, Your Lordship, you want a saint. And I must warn you, saints are a very

26

dear commodity these days."

There it was. The point on which this entire bit of nuptial commerce turned. The donation. The earl looked to the priest, who lowered his gaze to the wooden cross he was squeezing as if trying to wring a blessing from it. The earl would have to grapple with the matter of financing his bride alone.

"I am prepared" — he leaned forward, narrowing one eye — "to provide a tithe from my estates to the abbey for the next ten years."

"A tithe?" The abbess sat back with a huff of a laugh. "Over *ten* years?"

"It is not an uncommon way to make such a donation." The earl's face reddened furiously.

"At lesser abbeys, perhaps. We are the sisters of Virtue," the abbess declared flatly, "not the sisters of Charity."

The earl lurched to his feet and dropped his huge, armored fists on the table with a smack.

"It is *consideration,* not charity," he declared through hardening features. "Such an arrangement would benefit all concerned. As the income from my holdings increases under the diligence, wisdom, and care of this 'saintly' wife, the abbey's portion will also grow. Who knows what riches we both may reap" — his gaze probed her like a physician's fingers — "in addition to the fruits of the Holy Spirit — which are, after all, the church's prime concern, are they not?"

How she hated it when the laity turned religious on her! The abbess stared closely at the hot-eyed warrior who dared match nerve and wits with her, even knowing that she held his matrimonial fate in her hands. More there than met the eye, she told herself. Clearly penniless. But not without worth.

She rose and reinserted her hands into her sleeves.

"It is my grave and holy burden to care for this abbey. I am entrusted by God and the families of our maidens with their honor and their futures. I must spend time in prayer and deep contemplation before I can render such a weighty decision. You will stay with us until I receive direction from above." She clapped her hands and an aging nun in a worn gray habit appeared through the arched doorway behind them. "My assistant, Sister Archibald, will see you to your quarters."

Two

Sister Archibald led them through the reception hall and out into an arched stone colonnade that was densely covered with the leafless vines of last season's wisteria and morning glories. Across the open ground of the rectangular green, the earl and his priest could hear the sound of feminine voices gathered in earnest prayer. It was a sweet sound . . . a soft feminine hum . . . that caused them to look at each other in discomfort.

"Here you are, Your Lordship, Father." At the end of the colonnade, the old nun tugged open a formidable iron door and motioned them inside. As they entered the building, unfamiliar smells of soap, sweet herbs, and a subtle feminine musk caused both men's steps to momentarily falter. This community, devoted as it was to the ripening of femininity, was nothing short of foreign territory for men accustomed to the exclusive company of their own sex. They trod more tentatively down the short passage to where the venerable sister waited beside an open door.

The convent's guest quarters contained a

glazed window, two raised beds furnished with feather ticking, a heavy iron brazier, and a thick mat of woven reeds that cushioned their footsteps and lent the air a fresh, linenlike scent. They stood looking around them, shifting from one foot to the other, while the elder sister explained the convent's daily schedule, meal times, and Lenten chapel etiquette. Then she gave them directions to the stable, where they would tend their own mounts, and wished them a peaceful stay.

As soon as the door closed behind the abbess's assistant, Peril of Whitmore expelled a heavy breath and leveled an accusing look at his priest.

"I said this would be a waste of time." He tossed his helm onto one of the beds and jammed his thumbs into the low-slung belt that held his empty scabbard. "You saw her. You heard her. She's never going to give me a bride."

"She is an abbess," Father Basset said, fingering his cross anxiously and glancing at the door. "We're lucky she didn't have our ears for supper."

Peril strode toward the priest and lowered his head and voice. "*She's* lucky I didn't charge in here with blades drawn and take my pick of her precious 'maidens.'"

"A harsh jest, my lord!" Father Basset crossed himself and glanced frantically around them. "For you would never, *ever* violate a house of God." His voice grew louder. "You are too good and righteous a lord."

Peril stared at him. "I am, am I?"

"Yea, verily." The priest continued to speak in emphatic tones. "You have naught but your people's welfare at heart. You will do whatever is necessary to secure their well-being . . . including seeking a bride of great piety and virtue to be their lady."

"Including spending my last farthing to cross the Channel on a mad quest for something to pacify their —"

"Longing for a lady!" Father Basset declared loudly. "Troth — the abbess is a fair and insightful woman. She will see the worth of your sacrifice and find you a fine and virtuous bride."

Peril sensed something was happening, besides the fact that the priest was losing every last shred of his wits. The fellow was often anxious and unsettled in Peril's presence . . . tripped frequently over feet and tongue . . . and always —

Suddenly, in a bold move, the little priest grabbed him by the sleeve and pulled him to the middle of the chamber, where he low-

31

ered his head and voice in a way that insisted Peril do the same.

"The walls of abbeys have ears, my lord. Guard your tongue while here."

"What? They listen at doors and lurk at open windows?" Peril straightened, impatient with Basset's air of intrigue, and ran a hand back through his damp hair. "These are nuns, Basset. Holy women."

"Women, nonetheless," Father Basset declared, still sotto voce. "And abbesses are archwomen . . . the worst of the lot . . . clever, contriving, suspicious, treacherous, and learned in ways forbidden to women for good reason. There isn't a bishop alive who isn't wary of them."

Peril recalled his visual contest with the abbess in their interview and felt a perverse trill of satisfaction. That shameful hint of pleasure told him he had been away from battle too long; he was testy and spoiling for a fight. He stared at Father Basset with something akin to amusement. Imagine a woman that might match him will for will and word for word. Not that such a creature existed . . . but if one did, it would doubtless make for an interesting encounter — rather like seeing that two-headed calf that time in Lisbon. It made a body both desirous of seeing and desperate to look away . . .

With a sardonic smile, he shook free of those thoughts and removed his breastplate, tossing it onto the bed.

"I didn't come here to parry words with a nun, even one who has ears for supper. I came to get a woman, a *virtuous* woman" — he paused in the midst of propping a foot on the bed to unbuckle a shin guard and shot the priest a dagger-sharp look — "to rid my lands of a *harlot's* curse."

"Aghhh!" Father Basset hurried to his side, motioning for silence. "Please, my lord — do not speak of that within these walls," he whispered.

"What? Now you would have me not speak of the thing that you and everyone on my estates have plagued me with for months on end? The thing that has hounded me from my hearth and home and forced me to spend my last farthing on this fool's errand of a journey?"

"Pleeease, my lord!" Father Basset squirmed with discomfort. "Pray never let the abbess hear you say such things. All women consider matrimony a serious undertaking . . . but for her it is a calling, a mission, a sacred charge from the Almighty Himself."

Peril leaned over the priest with a wicked smile. "Is that so? Then perhaps I should lay out the entire story for her and enlist her cunning aid in finding a bride that will break the curse." He stroked his stubbled chin with muscular fingers. " 'Pray, good abbess, which of your fair maidens might be up to the task of breaking a fiendish spell and rescuing my lands and people from a terrible blight? Eh?' " He cupped his ear. " 'The nature of the curse, you ask? Oh, just a jealous woman's ranting — a fetching mistress overthrown for a horsey bride with a heavy dowry, who decreed that until love triumphed over greed and a bride of great and surpassing virtue again held the keys of Whitmore, naught would grow, naught would be completed, and none in Whitmore would know peace.' " He sobered, thinking how uncannily those oft-quoted words described the true state of affairs in his domain. His next words were uncomfortably close to his real sentiments.

"They say 'No one rejoices more in revenge than a woman.' And that witch, it seems, has quite a bit to rejoice about."

Father Basset moaned and crossed himself, then threw himself onto his knees and into prayer with heroic intensity.

Peril squeezed his eyes shut against the sight. He hated it when Basset despaired of reasoning with him and threw himself headlong into the Almighty's arms. It made him feel cruel and irredeemable and more than a little ashamed of himself. Baiting a priest. Basset couldn't help that the Lord had given him a far larger task than he had the constitution for.

There came a knock at the door and Peril called out permission to enter. A young nun peered around the edge of the door, and seeing Peril seated on one bed and Father Basset on his knees, deep in prayer, opened the door farther to reveal two more black-clad sisters bearing linen, a bucket of water, and coals for the brazier. The trio huddled together like frightened chicks and moved almost as one, scurrying to fill the brazier and the bowl and pitcher on the shelf under the window. They laid out linen toweling, then backed out of the room with heads bowed, bobbing and mumbling something like "Your Lordship."

Peril shook his head. They behaved as if he were some flesh-eating ogre. In that, they weren't too different from the rest of womankind. Females who couldn't avoid his presence altogether generally cowered or simpered. Peril sighed and rubbed his dusty, bristled chin as he reflected on the effect he had on women. Not without reason, this time; he must look like the very Devil himself.

It was a mistake, he saw now, to leave his squire at home and insist on traveling fast and light. He should have brought a full retinue; a serving woman or two in the company would have made his suit appear more civilized. He sighed heavily.

Why was it that he always thought of such things too late?

The abbess straightened from the niche in the stone wall, lowered the burlap curtain to cover the opening through which she had listened to her guests' conversation, and paused to set what she had heard to memory.

"Lands and fortunes blighted by a curse that can only be lifted by a virtuous bride. A lord who must be forced to marry by his people, who demand it as a remedy for their suffering." She scowled. "Little wonder he does not seek a bride among the local nobles. Who would send a daughter into such a marriage?"

And how could she, in all conscience, send one of her precious charges into such conditions? Even the most stalwart and capable among her maidens would soon find herself overwhelmed by such expectations . . . not to mention the indifference of the lord himself. He was a seasoned warrior, huge and intimidating in the extreme, who seemed to have no personal interest in a marriage. Matrimony, even a marriage of necessity, required some degree of personal agreement and consideration between the parties involved.

In truth, there was little about him to recommend him as a husband. No fortune, no tenderness, no gallantry, no desire for closeness or companionship or even heirs, from the sound of things. His own priest was frightened of him.

No, she decided reluctantly, he would not find a bride among her charges.

She made her way through the barrels and baskets stacked in the storeroom. Outside, Sister Archibald waited and kept watch for her.

"Well?" Sister Archibald asked as they hurried along the deserted colonnade toward the abbess's private quarters.

"He is a proud, powerful, and difficult man." The abbess scowled. "Not at all suited to matrimony, I fear. But the Lord has not delivered him into my hands for nothing. Given time, I shall find some goodly use for him."

The guests' meals were delivered to their quarters that evening, and when they emerged from the chamber to tend their horses, they discovered the aged Sister Archibald waiting to escort them through a deserted cloister to the stables. She informed them that there would be someone outside their door, all night . . . on the off chance that they might need something.

Nuns keeping watch outside their door? Peril looked questioningly at Father Basset, who gave him an I-told-you-so look and muttered: "Let thy speech be better than silence, or be silent."

Had they somehow heard his irritable discourse? Peril closed his eyes and groaned. He'd just given Basset the perfect excuse to pummel him with proverbs for days to come.

The next morning, the abbess again sent old Sister Archibald to fetch Peril. She no doubt expected that the aged nun would be less of a temptation to rapacious warriors and randy priests, Peril thought sourly.

There was some activity in the middle of the cloister court, and Peril slowed to study the bevy of maidens collecting there and chattering excitedly. There was at least a score of them, dressed in the soft colors of autumn wildflowers, their long hair shining in the sun, and their cheeks blushed becomingly in the brisk morning air. As he watched them, wondering which one would be his, something in his stomach lightened and fluttered strangely. *His.*

He scowled and his shoulders tightened and swelled defensively.

The young girls, the bolder of whom had been casting curious glances his way, saw the change in his countenance and their interest turned to anxiety. Their chatter subsided to uneasy whispers and they began to move to the far end of the court. When he turned to continue on with Sister Archibald, the old nun was watching him with a discerning eye. She had seen both his reaction and theirs. He groaned silently and followed her to the great hall.

The abbess met him at the door. "I have sent for you to beg a favor, Your Lordship." She was smiling, and Peril experienced a palpable sense of foreboding.

"Whatever service I may render," Peril said, with a courteous half-bow. "You have only to ask."

"I hoped you would agree, sir. Our girls have so little opportunity to practice."

The abbess sailed past him toward the courtyard and he had to retrace his steps — back to the very group of young girls he had just frightened. They had been joined by a number of older girls and several severe-looking nuns in black, and were now gathered around a table on which sat a basin, linen, and implements of some sort. Beside the table, in the midst of that sea of untouched femininity, sat an empty chair. He swallowed and felt his stomach slide lower in his belly.

"We endeavor to prepare our charges for the customary womanly duties . . . including the personal care of husbands and male members of the household. Since you did not travel with a squire" — she looked over his bristled face and tousled hair — "we will provide you that service and gain practice all at once."

"A shave? They're going to shave me?" His first reaction was embarrassment at how grizzled and unkempt he must look to a bevy of sheltered maidens. His second didn't occur until he removed his tunic and stood bare-chested in the cool air . . . before two dozen curious and covertly avid stares. It was then he saw at close range the bright eyes and rosy lips and smelled the mellow linen-and-lavender musk that spoke arousal to every particle of his being. As he watched the dozens of slender white hands touching each other and gripping shoulders and waists and locks of that soft hair in trepidation and excitement, his skin began to heat.

Sweet, holy — he had to clear his tightening throat — what had he gotten himself into?

Under a drone of instruction, first one, then another of the older girls approached him, reached for the soap and water . . . then lowered her head and withdrew with shame-stained cheeks. Several aborted attempts later, one young girl managed to wet and soap his face and another picked up the razor, stropped it awkwardly, and poised it to make the first stroke.

It had taken nearly every ounce of his battle-honed self-control to ignore the slide of those cool, slippery fingers over his cheeks, lips, and throat. But when he saw the way the hand holding the razor was trembling, he had to reach down into his deepest reserves, grip the chair arms tightly, and force himself to submit. After all, it was just a morning shave. How bad could it possibly be?

Then he looked up and spotted the old gardener standing not far away, leaning on his rake handle, giving him a smile that contained a sardonic bit of sympathy. It was then that Peril noticed that the man bore dozens of tiny scars, some clearly fresh, on his weathered face.

Eloise opened her eyes as she bent over

her prayer bench, shifted her aching knees, and then closed her eyes again, forcing herself to complete yet another prayer of supplication. Not that any of them were working, as far as she could tell. She was confined to her chamber, forbidden to take meals with the rest of the order, and had not yet been assigned the enormous mass of recitations for penance that she was certain was coming. She might have thought the abbess had forgotten all about her . . . except that she knew the abbess never forgot anything.

It was the worst punishment that could be inflicted on her: idleness and solitude. The combination in significant amounts could be lethal. But she had to endure it, had to learn obedience and the grace of suffering if it killed her.

A gentle tap occurred on the door and she sprang up from the prie-dieu and hobbled to the door with aching knees. In slipped a somewhat older nun with a flushed face, who hurriedly closed the door behind her and then hugged Eloise.

"I've been so worried about . . ." Sister Mary Clematis drew back to examine her bedraggled friend. "Look at you." She brushed at some of the flour lingering on Eloise's skirt, and then wetted the tip of her own veil with her tongue and used it to rub one of the stains on Eloise's bodice. "You look like old Sister Mary Dunne's dishclout after she finishes wiping down the tables."

Mary Clematis, on the other hand, always looked as if she had arrived in the world fully grown and perfectly groomed. Her black habit and white wimple — which fitted snugly about her face and then pooled gracefully about her neck and shoulders in the manner of their order — were always immaculate. She was constantly cheerful, charitable, helpful, and modest . . . never willful or out of sorts. She was the epitome of nunlike virtue and decorum, in spite of all of which she had become Eloise's dearest friend in the world.

When Eloise arrived at the convent Sister Mary Clematis had been assigned to oversee, instruct, and correct her . . . which may have accounted for at least some of Eloise's perceived shortfall as a novice. Dour solemnity, sternness of judgment, and zeal for inflicting discipline on others were simply not a part of Mary Clematis's constitution.

"What does it matter how I look, when I'm stuck away in here?" Eloise said, stilling Mary Clematis's hands. "Do you have any idea of how long I'm to be punished, Clemmie? Has the abbess said anything about me?"

43

"She is busy with other things, just now," Mary Clematis said, lowering her eyes and stooping to tidy the hem of Eloise's habit. It was evasion, pure and simple, and Clemmie did it so seldom that she was horrible at it. She hadn't a prayer of ever becoming an abbess.

"What things?" Eloise asked, urging her friend to her feet. "Those men — that lord and his soldiers — is it them?" Mary Clematis winced and Eloise knew she was on to something. "What's happened? Have they caused trouble?"

"I don't believe so . . . at least, not any more than the abbess has caused for them." Mary Clematis's sigh had an unburdened quality. She always felt greatly relieved when she didn't have to keep a secret.

"What did she do? Tell me. Everything."

"Well . . . the lord and his priest stayed in the guest quarters last night, with Sister Archibald keeping watch, and this morning" — Mary Clematis paused to savor Eloise's suspense — "the abbess is using the lord for shaving practice."

Eloise blurted out a laugh. "Surely not. I mean, the man may be heavy-handed and arrogant and domineering and rude . . . but no man who wields a sword for a living deserves to have his face whittled off by

44

twelve-year-old girls."

Rewarded by Mary Clematis's burst of surprised laughter, she grinned. Her face, which had been forced for the last several hours into a penitential frown, ached with relief. "How did she persuade him? What did she say?" She moaned, feeling well and truly punished. "A perfect opportunity to see her bring men of power and influence to their knees, and I'm missing every bit of it."

"I have no idea how she convinced him. She simply appeared with him minutes ago and set him down in a chair in the court." Mary Clematis shook her head. "I doubt he'll get a proper shave. The girls are too frightened to go near him."

Eloise expelled a huff of disgust. "Cowards."

"But you should see him, Elly. He's . . . well, he's . . ."

"What?" Eloise stared at her, noting the brightness of her eyes.

"He's just so big and so . . . bare."

"And handsome?" Eloise asked, striking to the heart of the matter.

"Oh! I wouldn't know about that. I didn't —" To say she didn't look would be a lie. Mary Clematis never lied.

Curiosity boiled up in Eloise, hot and urgent, not to be denied.

"I have to see." She grabbed Mary Clematis's hand and dragged her toward the door.

"Ohhh, no!" Mary Clematis dug in her heels.

"Come on. I'll be there and back before you know it." Eloise pulled her to the door and peered out.

"If the abbess sees you, you'll be locked in your quarters *forever.*"

"She won't see me. I'll be hiding behind you. Besides, she will be too busy watching His Lordship's lesson in humility."

They crept down the passage and out onto the cobbled path, then around the novices' dormitory to the cloister court. Eloise led and kept an eye out for the sisters, while Mary Clematis mumbled prayers of intercession under her breath and allowed herself to be drawn along. Suddenly they were at the edge of the colonnade and peering at a tense gathering of nuns, novices, and maidens, all of whom were riveted by something in their midst.

Eloise wilted briefly with disappointment. She couldn't see a thing.

Over Mary Clematis's frantic whispers, she darted toward the rear of the group and stretched up onto her tiptoes to see. A dark male head was just visible at the center of a tight circle of nuns and maidens. One of the

46

older girls, Alaina — it would have to be the beautiful but sharp-tongued *Alaina* — was struggling with how to set the razor to his intimidating face. One of the older nuns could be heard advising her.

Desperate for a better view, Eloise tiptoed around the group and popped up again and again, hoping for a better vantage point. The earl wore an expression of steeled endurance, and from what Eloise could see, not much else. Through glimpses here and there, she began to see what had reduced Mary Clematis to speechlessness and the girls trying to shave him to jitters. The earl was large and sun-bronzed, and he radiated a disturbing sort of heat that she could feel even through the others gathered around. She could scarcely take her eyes from him.

Odd, she thought to herself as she found a break in the group and edged forward, she had never been this interested in the sight of Bendick or old Rupert naked as Adam in the Garden.

"We shall be here all day, at this rate," the abbess's voice boomed out over the gathering, startling Alaina and causing her to nick the earl's chin. The head of the convent stepped into the middle of the gathering with her hands tucked up her sleeves. She obviously had something in mind.

Eloise suddenly found that the shifting of the people in front of her had not only left her with a clear view, it had also left her appallingly visible. As the abbess leveled a piercing gaze on her, her breath stopped in her throat.

"We must have someone who is accomplished finish the task. Eloise!"

A murmur arose as the group followed the abbess's gaze to its victim. The others scuttled to distance themselves from her, leaving her to face the abbess's wrath alone. She swallowed hard, wishing just once she would listen to Mary Clematis and save herself these wretched situations.

"Yes, Reverend Mother?" She felt her throat tightening and face heating.

"Finish shaving His Lordship."

"Pardon?" She could scarcely believe her ears. No screeching, no tirade? Just "shave the man"? Relief flowed through her. "Oh, yes, Reverend Mother."

"No need," the earl declared irritably, peeling his fingers from the arms of the chair and reaching for the toweling. "I've lost enough blood for one day."

"No, no, Your Lordship." Eloise darted forward and seized the other end of the linen, surprising him and jerking it away. This was her chance not only to obey, but to show the abbess she could hold her own when dealing with a nobleman. "Stay seated," she ordered, enforcing it with both hands on his shoulders as he started to rise. "You'll lose no more blood, I assure you."

He seemed somewhat confounded by her air of command and her bold physical contact with him. She was a bit surprised herself at the pluck she showed, but desperate times called for desperate measures. A chance to redeem herself in the abbess's eyes didn't come along every day.

"I said it is not necessary," he grumbled.

"You cannot go about half shaved, Your Lordship. Be still and I shall make quick work of it."

He glowered.

She glowered back.

It was only then that she surveyed his face and the damage already done. He was formidable indeed: large face, chiseled features, broad but well-shaped mouth, dark eyes under thick dark brows, black hair . . . and several small but bloody cuts on his cheeks and chin. Her hand was a bit less steady as she re-soaped his face, took the razor from the trembling Alaina, and set her hand on his temple to position his head.

Telling herself that he was simply old Rupert in disguise, she made her first stroke of his cheek with the razor and, to her relief, no blood appeared. The second stroke was easier and by the third, she was back to her usual form. Using her thumb and finger to tighten his skin she managed to clear his cheeks without further bloodletting and then raised his chin to begin on his neck.

He jerked his head down and glared at her. She glared back and shoved his chin up.

Each stroke of the razor up his throat caused him to flinch. When she paused near the end to strop the dulled razor and returned to make two final strokes, he caught her wrist and held it. She met his glare and for a moment sank into the dark pools of mystery visible through those windows on the soul.

A host of impressions assailed her: pride, anger, determination, frustration, and pain. A deep and diffuse pain that seemed to have been there well before the maidens of the Brides of Virtue started to slash their way across his chin. In that moment, which seemed to go on forever, she felt a curious tug of response in the depths of her stomach.

Gasps and murmurs from the nuns gathered around them finally registered in her senses and she withdrew from that unsought intimacy with chagrin.

"I am nearly finished, Your Lordship. If you will be patient . . ."

Her voice sounded forced in her own ears, but he relented, released her, and, after drawing a deep breath, raised his head to again give her access to his throat. With the final stroke, he gripped the arms of the chair tightly.

"Finished." She dampened the toweling and wiped his face, pressing hard on each of the several small cuts he had sustained. "Hold still. A press of the finger will soon stop the bleeding." She held her thumb over each of his several wounds and they did indeed stop bleeding. As they did, she began to feel the warmth of his skin under her hand . . . the firmness of his jaw . . . the power of the underlying muscles . . .

The abbess clapped her hands, startling everyone. "Lesson completed. Back to your studies and duties," she called, unleashing an eruption of chatter from girls and nuns alike. In moments, the court was mostly empty and the abbess stared intently at her novice nemesis, this time with an inscrutable smile. "Thank you for your help, Eloise. Back to your duties as well," she said.

Eloise backed away from the earl. The abbess made a dismissive gesture in the direction of the novices' quarters, and Eloise dipped with respect and turned away smiling, the words *thank you* ringing in her ears.

The abbess watched her go, then suggested to the earl that he might wish to see to his horses before returning to his chamber to await her decision.

"I have it, Archie," the abbess said with a broad smile as she swept ahead of her assistant into her private solar. She stood in the middle of the chamber and opened her arms, welcoming the sunlight streaming in through the open window. "And it's brilliant, if I do say so myself."

"What is brilliant?" Sister Archibald asked, closing the door and wondering at her friend's expansive mood. "What do ye have?"

"A solution to the earl's problem and to mine."

"Which problem?"

"The one that has been a thorn in my side for years now. And I shall need your help." She went to her writing desk, took her perch on the stool, and pulled out a fresh piece of parchment. She dipped her quill in the inkwell and poised it at the top of the blank sheet. "You must help me make a list of all the highest and best qualities a husband can have."

Sister Archibald looked bewildered. "Me? How should I know? I've never had a mortal husband."

"Nor have I," the abbess said with a calculating glint in her eye. "But that doesn't stop me from having firm opinions on what one should be. Now, what shall we start with?" She tapped her lips with the tip of the plume, then began to write. "Ah, yes. 'Pious.' "

Sister Archibald went to peer over the abbess's shoulder at the parchment, and curled her nose. "If t'were my list, I would start with *clean*."

Three

The next day Peril paced his borrowed quarters, feeling caged and frustrated and oppressed by the ever-present air of "woman" that hung about the place. What did this cursed abbess want from him? He shot a hard look at Father Basset, who, upon being caged up with him, had taken to using unceasing prayer as a shield against his volatile moods. The little priest did seem to have been right about the abbess, however; she clearly enjoyed wielding her power.

He rubbed his chin briefly, wincing at the several cuts that an entire day later were still tender to the touch. It occurred to him: once wedded, would he be expected to present his face regularly for such mutilation? He snarled quietly, picked up his empty scabbard, and headed for the door and the stable beyond. At least his horse wouldn't pray at him or try to bleed him.

Halfway across the stable yard, he was hailed by the aged Sister Archibald, who brought him a summons to the abbess's private reception chamber. The abbess, it seemed, had finally finished consulting with

Heaven and was ready to announce to him their joint opinion.

As he strode along, well ahead of the abbess's creaking messenger, his mind conjured up the bevy of maidens he'd seen, and he wondered if he would be allowed to choose for himself and just how a man went about determining whether or not a maid would make a good wife. More importantly, how could one tell if she were filled with "surpassing virtue." He scowled thoughtfully, supposing that he could rely upon the abbess to have a few ideas on that. But then — he nearly tripped on the thought — how could he be certain that she was giving him a maid of great virtue and not one of her sluggards or dolts?

"I have a decision for you, Your Lordship." The abbess greeted him and waved him onto the bench beside Father Basset, who had been summoned as well. When he was seated, she fixed him with a somber look. "I cannot in all conscience hand over a tender young maiden into your hands . . . on such short acquaintance and with no more security than you offer."

"But — but —" He rose with a hundred protests leaping to mind. "I've told you —"

"*However*," she said succinctly, waving him back down onto his seat, "I believe

Heaven has provided a way for you. You are to be given a test. A *husband* test."

"A what?" He was halfway down, but sprang up again. "A test?"

"To decide if you will be a suitable husband and, of course, if the circumstance into which you will take a bride is suitable to a young woman of delicacy and breeding. I have decided to send home with you our convent's husband judge." She sat back and waited for the impact of her words to be felt.

"Husband judge? To judge *me?*" He thumped his chest with clenched fist. "I'm to be inspected and judged by some nun on whether I will make a suitable husband?"

"And on whether your home will be proper for a young and tender wife," the abbess said calmly.

"That is absurd . . . insulting!" he thundered, jutting across the table toward her. "How dare you presume to —"

"I dare because I am the abbess of this convent and the head of this order!" The abbess was on her feet in a trice. "*No* maiden is given in marriage here without my permission. That is especially true when the potential husbands are noblemen of dubious refinement and even more dubious fortune."

"You think me paupered and unworthy

because I will not make you a fat donation?" he demanded. "Did it never occur to you that I will not part with hard-earned coin without being certain of the value I shall receive for it?"

The abbess crossed her arms and fixed him with a fierce look.

"I would never allow any man — even one who offered me a chest filled with gold — to carry off one of my charges without a thorough assessment of his character and situation. You, sir, arrived here with an armed escort and without reference or even the most basic of servants and civilized comforts. I have every right and obligation to question your fitness as a husband and provider." She raised her chin to look down her nose at him. "Your willingness to cooperate with the requirements I place upon you will go a long way toward proving your character. If you find my conditions unreasonable, there is the door. Be done with us and go. Take a bride from your own precincts." She smiled icily. "If you can."

"Please, my lord," Father Basset pleaded, grasping his arm. "This is no terrible hardship. It is perhaps your best chance to have what will satisfy your people and restore the peace and prosperity of your household . . . as well as delight your fine and noble heart."

He swallowed hard as Peril turned a heated glare on him. "For it is surely only a formality; you will no doubt win this husband judge's favor quickly. A boon, in fact — for once at home on your estates, you can see to the spring planting while preparing for your bride's joyful arrival at Whitmore. A fortnight's delay, at worst."

The earl turned on the abbess.

"And when I have proved to this 'husband judge' that I am a suitable plow for your precious furrow . . . then what?"

"Then I shall send your bride to you."

"How do I know you'll send the right bride? How do I know she will be diligent and wise and, above all, virtuous?"

"That, sir, you must trust to God and to me. I will attend carefully to the report our husband judge writes. She will state your nature and needs most clearly. Therefore, I suggest that you listen carefully to her words and provide assistance to her in all matters."

"I will not buy a horse in a blanket," he declared forcefully. "I must have some assurance that the maid will be acceptable."

The abbess met his determination and gave his words some thought before conceding: "Very well, I can promise that I shall send to you one of the maids whom you have already seen . . . one of the ones who helped to shave you this morning."

He scrambled to recall their appearance and manner and was mollified by the realization that every one of that group was fetching and probably had the requisite amount of "virtue." Any one of them would probably be acceptable for his purposes. He looked at Basset, who nodded eagerly, and took a troubled breath.

"Very well. I will take this 'husband judge' to my home with me. But you must send me a bride as soon as you receive her report."

The abbess's expression thawed slightly.

"I shall indeed."

"I am to do what?" Eloise said, struggling to calm her pounding heart. In answering the abbess's summons, she had run all the way to the head of the convent's private solar, where she had found the abbess and Sister Archibald waiting with a small stack of documents and a mission for her.

"To function as the convent's husband judge in the matter of —"

"But I've never heard of such a thing. I didn't know we had a 'husband judge.' "

"We don't always," the abbess said with a forbidding glance at Sister Archibald, who seemed as if she might speak. The older nun scowled, folded her gnarled hands, and held her tongue. "Only when it is necessary. And now it is necessary. His Lordship, the earl of Whitmore, needs a bride, but I cannot send one of our maidens to him until I know that his home and his person are suitable. That will be your task: to judge His Lordship and His Lordship's home for suitability to matrimony."

"But I haven't the slightest notion where to start. I know nothing about husbands, good or bad."

"A condition you must remedy if you are ever to become —" She halted and seemed disconcerted by what she had nearly said. Eloise's heart skipped as she pounced on that telling slip. "Never mind your lack of experience." The abbess gave a dismissing wave, then let her hand fall to caress a leather-clad sheaf of documents on the table. "We have well-established standards for husbands. All you need do is assess each quality and circumstance listed in these documents and send a report back to me. When I have read your description of the earl's personal qualities and situation, I can choose the proper bride for him."

Eloise still had difficulty grasping the scope of the mission she was being given. A long journey was required, travel to a far-flung land . . . in the company of the irascible earl. . . .

"I cannot help but think that someone else would be better suited to such an undertaking." She fidgeted, eyeing the documents. "To making such weighty judgments . . ."

"Eloise of Argent," the abbess said sharply, "this is no time to develop a scourge of humility. I selected you because —" She paused to check her ire, and watched Eloise lower her gaze and hold her breath. "Because you have applied yourself diligently to learning virtually every task in this convent. Who better than you — our most *relentless* student of good management and husbandry — to judge whether or not an estate is sound and a house properly run? Furthermore, your loyalty and tenacity are unparalleled in our order. I believe we could trust you to ferret out the truth even if it were hidden in the king's privy."

Such praise! Eloise felt a little dizzy at the sudden change in her fortunes.

"But I am only a novice."

"So you are." The abbess's agreement strangely put her more at ease.

"Surely one of the elder sisters —"

"The elder sisters all have other duties. I believe I may say with confidence that once this task is complete, you will not be a novice much longer." The abbess rose and rounded the table slowly. "We have had more than a few trials, you and I, as we have sought your proper place here." Her voice lowered. "I believe we may have at last discovered what our dear Lord has had in mind for you all along."

Eloise's eyes filled with tears even as her heart filled with hope.

"I did not doubt your wisdom in giving me this great charge, good abbess, only my ability to carry it out. But now that I see your faith in me . . ." She sank to her knees before the abbess and reached for the abbess's hand. "Thank you for entrusting me with so important a task. I will not fail you."

"I know, child." The abbess gave Eloise's bowed head an awkward pat, then disentangled herself and stepped back. "I am certain that you will be fair and thorough in your judgments. Above all, you must take sufficient time. Do not judge the man or the situation too quickly. Remember always that what is easily seen is often misleading. You must delve beneath the surface of both the man and his circumstance to discover that which is true and lasting — a task which will require at least a month of close observation . . . perhaps two . . . even three . . ." She paused to clear her throat and slide her hands up her sleeves.

"Now, as to arrangements. You will wear our order's full habit."

"Me? A full habit?" Her heart all but stopped.

"We have discussed this, Sister Archibald and I, and though it is unusual, we feel it would be better protection for you in the outside world. And you are to take another sister with you, someone older and more settled, for aid and companionship. Go now, and see good Sister Montgrief about your new garments. You must prepare quickly." She handed Eloise the documents. "The earl is eager to be on his way."

Clutching the leather folio to her breast, Eloise rushed to throw her free arm around Sister Archibald for a tearful, wordless hug of gratitude for whatever part the old nun had played in securing her turn of fortunes, then dashed outside.

The abbess began to smile. And as her smile grew to a grin of satisfaction, she looked at Sister Archibald and found the old lady staring at her with one eye narrowed.

"Not a word from you, Archie." She shook a finger.

"You didn't tell her about the curse."

"We don't know for certain that there is a curse."

"The priest seemed to think it real enough," Sister Archibald declared.

The abbess snorted. "He's a hedge-priest. And you know how these lack-Latins are. They see Satan's plotting behind every bush."

Sister Archibald canted her head with a look of reproof, but not even her best friend's disapproval could dim the pleasure the abbess felt.

"I did what had to be done." She sat down on her window seat and leaned back with her arms crossed and tucked.

"It was either her or me."

Eloise rushed along the colonnade and through the outbuildings to the weavers' house, where Mary Clematis was finishing a loom-winding lesson for some of the younger girls. She was buoyant as she swept Mary Clematis up into a hug and danced her around the lint-littered floor between the looms.

"Stop — stop, Eloise!" Mary Clematis dragged her breathlessly to a halt. "What's come over you?"

"We're going to England, Clemmie. You and I. I'm to give His Lordship the 'husband test,' and you have to help!"

It was late that evening before the pace of preparation slowed long enough for Eloise to look through the documents that the abbess had given her and realize that her mission, while a great honor, was far from an easy one. There were pages upon pages of qualities and characteristics to be evaluated, and the more she thought about it, the more overwhelmed she felt.

Who was she to sit in judgment on a nobleman, deciding whether he was worthy of a bride or not? Then chagrin crept over her. The abbess had finally found her a task that made use of her hard-won knowledge and natural abilities and she was quailing in the face of it.

Get hold of yourself, girl, she heard old Sister Archibald's chiding in her head and it stiffened her resolve. This was her chance to show the abbess just how valuable she could be. When she came back, having successfully discharged her duty, the abbess had all but said that she would be allowed to take her vows. And once she had taken her vows she would have years ahead to prove to the abbess that she would make a worthy successor.

After Matins, she crept into the chapel by

the light of a lantern near the chancel door and a small bank of intercessory candles on a side altar. Alone in the peaceful dimness, suffused with the familiar scents of lingering smoke and incense, she went down on her knees at the altar railing. So many fears, so many expectations, so many blessings . . . her heart and mind were so full it was difficult to speak. For the first time in years, she felt that she had a task to do and a valuable place in the order. The abbess finally had taken note of her efforts, and now counted on her to perform a task that would determine the matrimonial fate of a young maiden and an important English nobleman.

"Thank you for bringing His Lordship to our convent," she prayed, "and for providing me this chance to prove myself. Help me to see His Lordship fairly and compassionately and to do Your holy will with regard to his bride." She winced as she added: "And if it's possible . . . let him live somewhere that doesn't require climbing aboard a horse."

The stone of the convent's courtyard had been washed a dark gray by the light rain that had fallen through the night. The thick damp and early spring chill caused sounds to echo thickly: the creak of leather harness, the mutters of mounted men-at-arms, and the restless snorts and stamps of horses un-used to the peculiar strain of idleness. At the center of the earl's waiting horsemen stood an aged wooden cart bearing a basket of provisions and two small trunks. The old stableman, Bendick, was fussing over a har-ness he had already checked a dozen times, while whispering exhortations to the fat, brindle-colored donkey assigned to pull the cart. Snatches of "behave" and "none of your heathen willfulness" reached the men nearby.

Peril turned his face from the sight with a silent groan and his gaze met that of his second in command, Michael of Dunneault, who rolled his eyes. The bells of Tierce had rung some time ago, but the entire place was still on its knees fingering beads and mur-muring prayers. The day would be half gone before they rolled out the gates, and by the time they reached the shore, they might have missed the tide. If they couldn't find accommodation, it would mean camping in the wet and mud, and no doubt this "hus-band judge" would hold it against him. He would start her "husband test" with black marks already against him.

Spring, he grumbled, glancing up resentfully at the low clouds scudding by. It was nothing but rain and sucking mud and fish — endless fish — for supper. He couldn't for the life of him understand what made people look forward to —

Voices came from the doorway and he straightened, training his gaze on that opening. Suddenly, nuns dressed in a bewildering array of faded black and worn gray habits came streaming out into the courtyard, their attention focused on two figures in stark, fresh black being shepherded along by the abbess. She led the sisters straight to him.

"Your Lordship, I would have you meet our husband judge, Sister Eloise."

He blinked. The nun was far younger than he expected — not that he had known quite what to expect — and as she dipped with respect, he felt something seemed familiar about her. He nodded, trying to read in her surprisingly smooth face some hint of the rigors he would be forced to endure on her account. But she lowered her eyes to her bead-wrapped hand and he was forced to turn his attention to her companion.

"And Sister Mary Clematis, her aide and companion. They will be your guests for the near future. I must ask your word that you will guard and care for them as though they were your most cherished relations. They, sir, are the key to your matrimonial future."

She was asking for his oath that the two would come to no harm? Did she think him a total heathen? It took a moment for him to stifle his first impulse and replace it with something more civilized.

"I shall guard them with my life," he said, from between clenched teeth, his eyes hot with indignation. But his ire found expression with his next breath. "I assume that cart" — he gestured to it with a disapproving look — "is intended for them. It won't be necessary. I will provide them mounts so that we might make better time on the journey."

"A cart is our customary mode of transport," the one designated as the husband judge — What was her name again? — declared.

"They do not ride?" he demanded of the abbess.

"We are sisters of a cloistered order," Sister Husband Judge answered before the abbess could speak. "We have no need to ride."

Pricked by her high-handed attitude, Peril waved irritably to one of his younger men and ordered him to dismount and drive for them.

"That won't be necessary," Sister Judge declared crisply as she climbed into the cart and settled herself on one of the small trunks. "I am quite competent at the reins."

She looked up as he stalked toward her, and their gazes met. For a moment there was utter silence in the courtyard. He stopped near the cart, studying her face and voice and erect posture, and suddenly recalled her. A groan of dread crept up his throat. The bossy one. The one who had manhandled him and made quick work of his tortured whiskers. The one who apparently knew her stuff where men were concerned. From the steady look in her clear blue eyes, she already believed she had the upper hand. By the saints' beleaguered knees, he'd show her she was wrong!

"What are you doing up there?" He turned on the young soldier who had already relaxed back into his saddle. "I told you to dismount and take the reins," he roared. Then he mounted his own horse, nodded to the tight-mouthed abbess, and charged out the convent gate with his arm raised, as if heading into battle. His second in command barked an order and the men fell into a column as they exited behind him at a brisk pace.

Eloise found herself confronted by a lanky

young soldier with an apologetic expression and an outstretched hand. Grudgingly, she allowed him to climb aboard and take the reins. The next moment she was engulfed by a tide of arms and faces crowding the cart, hugging her and Mary Clematis and wishing them a tearful "Godspeed." It was an outpouring of belonging and affection that caused Eloise's heart to swell and Mary Clematis's eyes to mist.

In spite of the crush, Bendick managed to turn the donkey toward the gate and give the driver a nod. With a slap of the reins, the donkey leaned hard into the harness and the wooden wheels groaned into motion.

But after three paces the animal stopped dead.

"Come on now, wretched beast!" Bendick hurried to the donkey's head and began to pull on its halter, while the soldier frantically flapped the reins and muttered threats against the beast's future offspring.

The animal leaned and heaved again, and again the cart rolled three paces before grinding to a halt. The problem was now abundantly clear. The animal was not to blame; the cart was simply too heavy with the earl's man in it.

Eloise folded her arms and cast an irritable look through the gates, where the arrogant earl's column was already disappearing over the first rise. So much for husbandly foresight and consideration.

"Truly, I can manage the reins," she said, touching the soldier's sleeve. "It would lighten the load and you can return to your mount."

He looked as if the temptation to do as she said horrified him.

"I have my orders, Sister."

"Well, don't just stand there, the lot of you," came the abbess's anxious voice. "Give it a push!"

With a burst of excited chatter, nuns and novices alike rushed to the rear and began to push. In no time, the cart was through the gate and rumbling along the rutted road toward the coast. Eloise and Mary Clematis hung on to the sides of the cart with one hand and waved with the other. The farewells of their sisters continued, fading softly, as they proceeded up the incline of the first hill, going slower and slower until they came to a complete stop.

The soldier snapped the reins and barked commands, but the donkey knew the impossible when he felt it and refused to try further. Behind them, at the gate, the abbess watched with widened eyes.

"They'll never make it up the hill without

help," she declared loudly.

Half a dozen of the younger nuns rushed out of the gate and up the road to the stalled cart, tucked their skirts, and set their shoulders to it.

That was the way Peril found them when he rode back to see what was keeping them: his man sitting red-faced and stiff with mortification in a cart being pushed up a hill by a passel of nuns with their legs bared and muddy and their faces red with exertion. A burning sensation began in the pit of his stomach and he ground his teeth together as he watched them struggling up the rise.

On the downward side of the hill, Peril constrained his horse to a walk and rode with his back rigid and his face stony. Behind him, his man walked beside the cart, holding the reins, while a clutch of bare-legged nuns stood on the hill waving and loudly beseeching God's care upon the husband judge and her plump-cheeked cohort. *Sister Eloise.* That was her name.

When the calls of the sisters finally ceased, he hoisted himself in his saddle to look back and found the husband judge sitting with her back straight, her arms folded, and her features sharp with disapproval. Everything about her bristling posture and narrowed eyes said that he was in for a bad time of it. He turned away and felt her stare boring a hole in his well-armored back. A moment later, he felt the first raindrop. Two moments later the skies opened and his last bit of sufferance for this journey dissolved in the ensuing downpour.

Four

"This isn't so bad," Mary Clematis muttered, rearranging her posterior against the floor of the cart yet again. "We could have driven the cart ourselves and been soaked to the skin and half frozen."

Eloise raised her head and caught the glint of her friend's eyes beneath the heavy felt cover they had tented over the cart for protection against the rain. Mary Clematis, ever one to make the best of a bad situation, was wrong. It *was* bad. Miserable, in fact. The two of them were curled over and around their trunks on the cramped floor of the cart, trying unsuccessfully to get some sleep after an entire day of being rattled bone from joint.

They had arrived at the coast just before sunset. Low clouds and heavy mist shrouded the water from view, but the tang of salt in the air and the sound of breaking waves made their location unmistakable.

"We've missed the tide," the earl declared as he rode up, wiped his wet face, and scowled down into their comparatively dry transport. "We'll camp here for the night and cross at dawn." He glanced over his shoulder at the men waiting for him. "I have to go into the village to arrange for passage and food."

"We will go as well." Eloise had thrown back the felt blanket and turned to climb down the open rear of the cart. "It would do us good to stretch our legs. And there may be a chapel saying Vespers."

With a quick spur, he put his horse across the end of the cart to block her exit.

"Basset, there, can hear your prayers." He pointed over her shoulder toward the priest, who was trudging toward them on foot, holding his waterlogged cassock up out of the wet with both hands. When she turned back to the earl, he was already riding away and signaling to his men to follow.

"Good sisters, if you will be patient" — the priest winced at his employer's brusque manner — "the men will build a fire. After you've bestirred and warmed yourselves and have partaken some food, we can recite from the Psalter together."

But there had been no fire and no Vespers. Within minutes of Father Basset's offer, the sky opened up and rain came pelting down again. Eloise and Mary Clematis, who had barely had time to stretch their legs and an-swer nature's call, went dashing for the cart and spent the balance of the evening, huddled and shivering, under a sodden tent filled with the scents of hot breath and wet wool.

"Wretched man," Eloise grumbled, "dragging us thither and yon without so much as a by-your-leave. Just imagine what living with him would be like. 'Stay in the cart, woman. Say your prayers by yourself, woman. Where is my supper, woman?' It won't take a month to know that life with him would be pure Purgatory."

"Well, perhaps he has just gotten off on the wrong foot with you. Perhaps he has other, *better* qualities," Mary Clematis suggested.

"Such as?" Eloise crossed her arms irritably and frowned.

"Well, he's obviously strong. And his men seem to obey readily enough. And he has . . . um . . . good teeth." Mary Clematis stiffened at Eloise's laugh.

"I don't believe 'teeth' are on the order's list of requirements for husbands. It is his character I'm here to assess — his honesty, charity, judgment, and consideration. And thus far he's — what are you doing looking at his teeth, Mary Clematis? Blessed Heaven!"

She turned her back sharply, punched her

cloak that was folded up to cushion the hard wooden floor, and tried to purge the thought of the earl's admittedly fine teeth from her mind. But the very effort of trying to banish them perversely broadened the memory until it included his full lips and hard, sun-bronzed cheeks . . . smoky eyes . . . broad shoulders that had drawn her gaze again and again that day as he rode doggedly ahead, impervious to both her glare and their discomfort.

Arrogant creature.

But in her mind Clemmie's words melded with the abbess's. She must not be hasty in her judgment. . . . Give the earl a chance. . . . He undoubtedly has better qualities. . . . It will take at least a month . . . perhaps two or three. . . .

Somewhere in the darkness and discomfort she must have surrendered to sleep, for the next thing Eloise knew, she was being jolted awake by the lurching of the cart and the sound of male voices. The earl's men, the coast . . . She could hear the crashing of the waves and sat upright, her heart thumping.

Rolling up onto her aching knees, she raised the felt cover to look around. The wind caught it and yanked it out of her hands. Hanging onto her precious new veil with one hand and the jostling cart with the other, Eloise called to Mary Clematis, who was struggling to right herself in the bottom of the bouncing vehicle. Then she looked out through the moisture-heavy dawn and glimpsed the sea for the first time in nine years.

It was nothing short of terrifying. Wind-driven waves rose briefly into polished gray walls that slammed into the rocks and shattered into glittering spray. Her throat tightened as she watched new waves rising in relentless succession to take the place of those that broke against the shore.

The rain had stopped, but the clouds were low and swirling. Powerful winds buffeted them from one direction and then another as they rumbled along a rutted path down the side of a cliff toward the water. She could make out a cluster of rough stone cottages, byres, and sheds huddled on the cliff overlooking the beach. Just beyond was a narrow stretch of sand on which a motley assortment of fishing boats rose and fell on the encroaching waves. Offshore were two much larger ships that rolled heavily in the white-capped water, and a smaller longboat that was trying valiantly to reach them.

"What are they doing?" she asked of the soldier handling the cart's reins.

"Loadin' up," he said without looking back at her.

"Now? In this weather?" It wasn't quite a storm . . . more of a vicious wind just now. But a quick look toward the heavens told her that rain could come pouring down at any moment.

Memories of her last trip across the Channel assailed her: the howling elements, the tossing ship, the agonized prayers of the aged uncle charged with delivering her to the convent, the feeling that she was about to die . . .

Fighting a rising panic, she located the earl amongst his men, hip deep in surf on the beach. As soon as the cart reached the beach, she jumped down and hurried across the waterlogged sand.

"Your Lordship!" He either didn't hear or didn't care to acknowledge that he had heard her. "Whitmore!" she yelled with all the force she could muster and he finally turned, scowling. "What do you think you are doing?" She had to grab up the skirt of her pristine new habit and scuttle backward to avoid being soaked by a wave. He came splashing toward her through the water, his face set and his eyes dark under the visor of his helm.

"Preparing to board those ships" — he pointed to the beleaguered boats — "to cross the Channel, and to continue on to my estates."

"In this maelstrom?" She drew herself up to meet his glare, sensing that to quail now would be to diminish whatever authority she possessed. "We surely must wait until the storms cease."

"We have no time for that." He propped his large, bare fists on his waist, and his already broad shoulders seemed to grow. "It could be days before the sea calms this time of year. The captains are eager to sail, and most of the men and horses are already aboard."

As he spoke, she heard a whinnying cry and looked out to see a horse being lifted out of the churning water in a sling and hauled aboard one of the ships. It was then that she noticed two more horses in the water . . . swimming for their very lives. Her horror must have been visible on her face.

"Don't worry, Sister," he said with a hint of a sardonic smile. "We won't make *you* swim for it." Before she could vent her indignation, he scooped her up and carried her through the surf toward a longboat.

"Wh-Whitmore!" She gasped and sputtered, shoving against his thick, heavily armored chest. "How dare you set hands to a sister of —"

81

"Be still or I'll drop you."

"You wouldn't dare!"

A moment later, however, he did just that — onto one of the longboat's weathered wooden seats. Then he waded back through the surf toward the cart and the quaking Mary Clematis. Having learned from Eloise's example, she meekly accepted the earl's assistance from the cart and, when they reached the water, his muscular transport to the boat.

After depositing Mary Clematis on the seat beside Eloise, he paused for a moment with his wet hands on the edge of the boat.

"I have vowed to safeguard your person against all perils," he said sharply, aiming it right between Eloise's eyes. "And I always keep a vow."

That, Eloise thought, holding on to the splintery seat with cold numbed fingers while the longboat pitched and shuddered seaward through the incoming waves, remained to be seen. By the time she was seated in the canvas sling, being hauled upward, and banging against the side of the ship each time the vessel rolled, she was fairly certain that his standards for safeguarding her person must consist of keeping her poor corpse in one piece.

Once aboard the ship, she and Mary Clematis were ushered to the rear part of the main deck, seated on a raft of barrels that had been lashed together, and admonished by a burly sailor not to move. When the captain finished flogging his crew with threats, he paused to give the two of them a severe look and an order not to move. Then the earl climbed over the rail, surveyed the disposition of his men and horses in the open hold, and strode over to reiterate: "Don't move."

If only someone would tell her stomach, Eloise thought irritably, clutching her middle. Her inwards were now imitating the tumultuous rising and sinking of the sea and from Mary Clematis's face, she was experiencing the same reaction.

She swallowed repeatedly, clasped the chaplet of beads wound around her wrist, and tried desperately to recite the Our Father. But closing her eyes only made the upheaval in her stomach worse, so she opened them, grasped Clemmie's free hand, and focused on recalling just how long it took to cross the Channel. The answer provided no reassurance whatsoever. *An eternity.*

Between the low, swirling clouds and the tilting deck, it became increasingly difficult to tell backward from forward and up from down. As the ship got underway, the square sail overhead filled first one direction, then another. The captain shouted continuous orders above the roar of the wind and water, frantically turning the wheel to starboard, then just as frantically turning it back to port. With each change of wind, the ship swayed, creaked, and groaned as if it might be crushed under the strain. Eloise's fear reached a higher pitch as large waves began to crash against the hull and break over the deck, washing everything with icy seawater.

Eloise and Mary Clematis clung to their seats and slowly adjusted to the successive drenchings and dire digestive upheaval as the vessel remained afloat and wallowed through the heavy seas. It was of little comfort to them that the earl's men climbing up out of the hold were a bit green in the face as well. True warriors, they looked to their iron-nerved leader, swallowed their stomachs back into place, and refused to head for the railing.

Their iron-nerved leader, however, was little better off. Peril, earl of Whitmore, disliked open water . . . had too often encountered trouble at sea to ever be truly at ease aboard a ship. But he had an example to set and he had the husband judge's approval to secure. He had to be strong and show her he was in control of the situation; she would respect no less. As the wind and waves both increased, he glanced ever more frequently in her direction. There she sat, her skirts and feet soaked, struggling to remain upright, with her chin raised and her eyes closed. Praying, he realized. His groan was audible, but mercifully the sound was carried away on the wind.

He made his way to the hatch by hanging on to stacks of cargo and ropes that had been strung across the deck, and he shouted orders to his men in the hold to secure and calm the horses as best they could. Then, following the side railing, he made his way to the wheel where the captain was struggling to negotiate the volatile weather and threatening sea. They would be all right, the old salt shouted above the roar, if the wind didn't get any worse.

Peril removed his helmet and stowed it in a coil of rope, and stood looking out over the length of the ship. The sight of the modest vessel battling its way through the massive waves was deadly sobering. For a moment, he almost repented his insistence on sailing that morning. It *was* urgent that they return to his estates as quickly as possible. But the threat of unknown calamities and of the interference of a greedy, overbearing neighbor wouldn't matter if they were all dead and lying on the bottom of the sea. The ironic possibility of them all becoming fish food during Lent caused his stern expression to crack briefly.

Just then, the ship pitched wildly and some of the cargo stacked on the wet deck began to slide, including the nuns' cart, which had been overturned and stowed on the forward deck for transport. Two crewmen scrambled for the cart, but couldn't reach it before it slid to the railing and smacked hard into the posts. Peril was in motion, grabbing for a rope and heading to the cart, intent on tying it down, when a monstrous blast of wind broadsided the ship, ripping the sail and rolling the ship hard to one side.

He was thrown back against the railing and could only watch in horror as the ship tilted farther . . . farther . . . and still farther. With the deck approaching vertical, the cart tipped onto its wheels against the balusters and rolled over the railing. He watched it disappear beneath the churning waves only to bob to the surface a moment later, already some distance away. A scream reached him through the roar and he looked up to find barrels, crates, and the husband judge sliding straight for him.

Panic shot through him as he watched her

careening across the deck, her arms flailing for something to grab as she plunged straight for the mid-ship opening where the cart had gone overboard. He released the rail and lunged for her just as she neared the water at the edge of the deck. His momentum carried them just past the opening, where he was able to drag her against him and wedge his feet between the posts in the railing.

The yardarm dug into the waves and the ripped sail filled partly with water, holding the ship on its side for what seemed an eternity. Icy seawater poured over and around them. The pressure of the rail posts around his feet and the feel of her body against him were all his cold-stunned senses could register.

Then just as suddenly as it had risen, the deck fell away toward horizontal and they followed it down with a thump. Both they and the ship shuddered and groaned as the vessel rolled back into its keel. It was a moment before the captain and the crew recovered enough to take stock of the damage and scramble up the ropes and haul down the ripped and sagging sail.

Eloise found herself sprawled over the earl's prone body, her face buried in his chest, her fingers digging into the flesh of his thickly muscled arms. She was unspeakably cold and wet everywhere but where her body was in contact with his. His arms twitched around her and she raised her head to find him staring at her with what seemed to be great relief. As he struggled up, she fought a fierce urge to cling to him. Then the deck swayed again and she spotted one of the trunks they had brought from the convent sliding toward the break in the railing.

"My trunk!" she cried as she peeled her aching fingers from him to point.

She was dumped unceremoniously on the deck as he scrambled to intercept the doomed chest. She sat up just in time to see him divert the wooden box to the railing, where it lodged until the deck swayed the other direction and he was able to shove it to a more permanent place of safety.

She looked to the raft of barrels she and Mary Clematis had been seated on and her heart all but stopped. Through the lashing wind and spray, she made out that several stacks of cargo had been washed overboard with the cart, and Mary Clematis wasn't to be seen. She lurched to her feet, calling to her friend.

Huge arms closed around her and she fought to remain on her feet as she was dragged back to the shelter of the stacks of cargo lashed to the deck.

"Sister Mary Clematis!" she cried, frantically trying to free herself. "She's been washed overboard!"

"I'll find her!" came his reply. "Sit! And hold on!"

The earl pushed her down onto the barrels and she instinctively sank her hands beneath the ropes lashing the barrels together. She watched him stalk carefully across the pitching deck to the open hold and saw him drop to his belly and shout to his men below deck. Shortly, a dark object flopped over the edge of the hold and he seized it and pulled. A head popped up — two huge, dark eyes rimmed with white and black. Clemmie!

"I tried to come after you but I slid and f-fell into the hold," Mary Clematis declared tearfully as Eloise met her and caught her in a fierce hug. "I landed on a horse and got kicked . . ."

A thundercloud loomed over them. The earl.

"You don't have the sense God gave an onion, between you!" he roared, pushing them down onto the few barrels remaining on the deck. *Sit! And for God's sake, stay!*"

The storm had blown itself out and the

sea was much calmer when they reached England's shore. The same, however, could not be said for Eloise's temper. She and Mary Clematis had finished the voyage on a windy, wave-scoured deck, encased in layers of icy, waterlogged woolens that provided precious little protection from the biting elements. Over and over in her mind, she kept hearing him compare her wits unfavorably to an odiferous vegetable, and her pride was nettled more with each repetition. By the time they were hoisted over the side in the sling seat and lowered into a longboat, Mary Clematis was blanched with cold and Eloise was an ominous blend of blue cold and crimson fury.

The ships had made landfall on a sheltered stretch of sand dotted here and there with clusters of large rocks and boulders. On the low cliff overlooking the beach were several gnarled and windswept trees, beyond which were mostly winter-brown fields with an occasional tuft of greening vegetation. As her longboat approached the shore, Eloise fixed her gaze on the tall, commanding figure shouting orders through the confusion of the horses arriving on the beach. The minute the boat scraped sand, she climbed over the side and plunged through the cold surf while holding up her waterlogged skirts with icy fingers.

"Wait, Elly!" Mary Clematis called from the boat. "We must give thanks for our deliverance!"

Growling, she turned back to help Clemmie out of the boat and knelt with her on the first bit of dry sand they encountered for a quick Paternoster. A heartbeat later, she was on her feet and charging toward the earl just ahead of Mary Clematis.

He turned, spotted her approaching, and pointed to some large rocks just down the beach, ordering her in that direction. She held her course and planted herself before him, tossing her skirts to the sand with a wet plop.

"Never, in all my born days, have I encountered such disregard for life and limb," she declared hotly.

"We made it through, didn't we?" He glowered back.

"Barely!"

"I told you that I vowed to keep you safe, and I always keep a vow." He edged backward, but then halted and jammed his fists on his waist. "I caught you, when you were sliding off the deck, didn't I?"

"You expect psalms and laurels for that, when it was *you* who put me in peril in the first place?"

"You wouldn't have been in danger if you'd stayed where you were told." He shoved his face down toward hers. "What the Devil did you think you were doing, up and wandering around the deck like that?"

"I was not *wandering.* I saw where you were headed and I intended to help you —"

"I didn't need your interference." Anger flashed briefly his eyes. "And I surely didn't need your *help!*"

She jerked her chin back, suddenly aware of him all around her, filling her sight with his intense, dark-centered gaze and her every breath with his heat and salty male scent. She took a step back, feeling her cheeks beginning to burn with something more than just anger and embarrassment.

"Rest assured," she said through a humiliating tightness in her throat, "it will not happen again."

"Good." He snapped upright, averted his gaze, and gestured down the beach toward some large rocks. "Now, if you will be so good as to do — whatever it is women need to do — and prepare to mount up."

"Mount up?"

"We lost the cart. One of you will have to ride the donkey. The blasted beast made it through without a scratch." He looked toward the animal standing stoically among the horses. "The other will have to ride double with my lieutenant or myself, at least until we find a village and secure another mount."

"Leave? Now?" She glanced around at the way his men were drying and saddling their horses, preparing to depart. It finally dawned on her that he expected them to climb straight aboard four-legged beasts for another punishing round of travel. "But it's nearly dark."

"A full moon will be rising; we will have plenty of light. The storm blew us off course. We have to get moving if we are to find the nearest village, arrange for provisions, and be ready to start at daybreak."

Her disbelief dissolved in a renewed surge of anger.

"In a pig's eye," she said with an adamance that would have been a credit to any abbess. "Sister Mary Clematis is chilled to the bone and I am not far from it. We must warm ourselves and dry our clothes before one or both of us fall ill."

His mouth drew into a grim line as he studied her waterlogged clothing. "Very well" — he made it sound a major concession — "we will arrange for a fire and a place for you to sleep as soon as we reach a village. Dunneault!" he roared for his second in command. A pleasant, thick-set fellow of middling years and thinning hair responded from the midst of the men and horses.

"Yea, milord?"

"Bring the ladies some blankets."

She stared at him with incredulity. Blankets? That was his solution?

"We are not *ladies,* Your Lordship, we are sisters of the Brides of Virtue whose task — need I remind you — is to assess your fitness as a husband. We shall not budge from this spot until we've warmed ourselves and dried our garments."

"Perhaps I haven't made myself clear," he began in a strained attempt at a conciliatory tone.

"Unfortunately for you, sir, at this moment you are more than clear to me. Come, Sister." She put an arm around Mary Clematis and the two made their way down the beach under the earl's glowering regard.

The longboat carrying Father Basset came ashore moments later, and the cleric hurried up and down the beach looking for the sisters. Unable to locate them among the men and horses, he confronted Peril and demanded to know if they had been drowned when the ship nearly capsized.

"They're cold and wet, but otherwise well," Peril reported irritably. "They went off down the beach to see to their needs before we leave." When Father Basset started off in their direction, Peril called him back. "Wait — take these with you." He shoved the blankets Michael of Dunneault had located into the priest's hands and then jerked a nod to allow the priest to continue.

Some time later, Father Basset hurried back down the beach with his cassock raised and his knotty knees churning. "Your Lordship!" The urgency of his call caused Peril to come to attention. "You'd best come!"

Peril motioned to Michael to accompany him and headed down the beach to intercept Basset.

"What's happened?" Peril demanded as they seized Basset between them and headed for the rocks where the nuns had disappeared.

"They are . . . they mean to . . . stay . . ."

Dread tightened Peril's gut as they approached and rounded the boulders.

Sitting beside an irregular circle of stones was the husband judge's assistant, her cloak, kirtle, and veil shed and spread over nearby rocks. It was something of a jolt to see the nun in a wrinkled wimple and linen shift, wrapped haphazardly in the blankets he had sent. At her feet was a small pile of driftwood. Hearing the approach of footsteps in the sand, he looked up from the wood straight into the husband judge's imperious blue glare.

"I imagine you must have within your company someone who is adept at making fire," she declared, proceeding straight to the pile of wood to drop the pieces of driftwood in her arms. "If not, you need only provide me with tinder and a fire steel, and I shall manage on my own."

Astonishment gave way to heat that was part embarrassment, part anger.

"I t-told you —" he sputtered, "we are riding to find the nearest village."

"You are entitled to come and go as you please, Your Lordship. I, however, do not intend to set foot from this spot until Sister Mary Clematis and I are warmed and our garments are dried."

Peril stalked toward her searching the pale oval of her face in the gray dusk. She stood her ground, her steel blue gaze unwavering.

"You will accompany us to the nearest village," the earl ordered, stepping closer, looming, coercing with his physical presence and proximity.

"Dragging Sister Mary Clematis and me — not to mention your own men — aboard ships in the middle of a howling storm betrays an appalling lack of judgment," she declared irritably.

"My men are battle-hardened and well accustomed to such conditions. They are not easily inconvenienced." He slid his gaze over her in a way that made it clear he did not consider her to be cut of the same stout cloth.

"But the good sisters, being of the fairer sex and an unworldly occupation" — Basset inserted himself between them — "must surely have found such a misadventure disturbing."

The father was an ally, Eloise thought, or at the very least a useful influence. Indeed, he seemed more anxious to secure their favor and the earl a bride than the earl himself was.

"So distressing" — she aimed her agreement at the earl like a hammer — "that the thought of mounting horses and riding off into the chill of night is unbearable."

"But of course it is!" Basset wrung his hands and turned on his patron with undisguised horror. "My lord, we must give the good sisters a chance to recover before continuing. A night's delay and a good fire are the very least we can do." When the earl still hesitated, the priest added one last persuasion: "Remember, milord: 'He that hath a head of wax must be careful not to go out in the midday sun.' "

The earl's face darkened and shoulders swelled with reaction. With a mutter that Eloise was grateful not to have understood, he stalked back around the boulders and began shouting orders for his men to make camp.

The only thing more puzzling than the earl's haste on this journey, Eloise thought as she sat warming her bare shins by a crackling fire, was his lack of courtesy and cooperation. Sheltered from the wind and set apart from the others by a number of large pillars of rock, she and Mary Clematis had removed cloaks, kirtles, veils, and even wimples, and spread them across the rocks. Their shifts they dried by standing before the fire and turning slowly, and as the circulation returned to their limbs, they wrapped up snugly in their blankets and settled onto quilted pallets provided by the amicable Michael of Dunneault.

Why would the proud, determined-to-the-point-of-arrogance earl go to such trouble in seeking a bride and then balk at complying with the requirements for acquiring one? He had done nothing to commend himself to her as a husband. Did he truly not want a bride? If not, why had he come to the Brides of Virtue in the first place? The hope of dower lands and an advantageous marriage settlement were out of the question, which left primarily the business of heirs — a reasonable motivation, though not necessarily a compelling one for seeking a bride. She knew enough of the world to know that men got heirs all the time without the holy sacrament of marriage. With a canny bit of legal maneuvering, bastards could and indeed had become dukes, bishops, and even kings.

Once again the earl's memorable eyes and sun-bronzed face appeared in her mind. Somehow, she couldn't imagine him sowing bastard children like so many groats of summer wheat. Her eyes narrowed. That would require making himself agreeable to *women*.

But Clemmie had been right, she continued her analysis, glancing over at her friend huddled on a pallet not far away. His men followed well and willingly. They certainly trusted his judgment enough to obey when he ordered them to climb aboard ships in the midst of a howling gale. She considered that for a time. He and his men had done battle together, no doubt formed bonds of loyalty based on endured hardship and shared experience. He was capable of forming bonds, then. Perhaps he was just reluctant to form one with a woman. It was the sort of double-mindedness that the abbess would have sniffed out like a blooded hound on a fox's trail. It was probably what had caused her to invoke the rarely used "husband test" in the first place.

She raked her fingers through a damp clump of her hair, separating the strands as she thought of the young women being prepared for matrimony at their convent. She couldn't help wondering which girl would be selected for — sentenced to — life with the earl.

The scrape of leather against stone and a sudden shower of sand and gravel caused her to start and look around in alarm. On the low cliff behind her stood two male figures cloaked in gloom. She sprang up and pulled the blanket tighter around her as she recognized the earl and his second in command.

"Don't be alarmed, Sisters," Michael of Dunneault called as he descended the bank toward them. She sagged with relief when she saw that his arms were filled with driftwood. "We bring fuel for your fire."

He was halfway down the bank when the earl, whose arms were also full of wood, started down with long, sure strides that did not falter even when the sandy soil gave way underfoot. As he approached the firelight she saw that he had discarded his armor and padded doublet. Clad only in a tunic, hose, and boots, he took on more human dimensions.

When he paused to drop the wood in his arms onto the pile Michael had begun, the sound alerted Eloise to the fact that she was staring fixedly at him. She lowered her gaze only to have him drop straight into it again as he squatted by the fire to tent several pieces of the wood over the wheezing red coals.

"This should be enough to last you the night," Michael said by way of explanation when the earl remained adamantly silent.

"It was kind of you . . . we shall say a novena in thanks," Mary Clematis said when Eloise remained uncharacteristically quiet. When Eloise looked over, she found her companion had pulled her blanket up over her head and held it together under her chin. "Consideration is a most admirable trait, is it not, Sister Eloise?"

"Most admirable," Eloise echoed, pulling her own blanket higher and finding her heavy tresses blocking it from rising to cover her head. Her face suddenly felt hot. "I'm afraid we must impose further on your hospitality, Your Lordship."

He rose without glancing in her direction, and dusted his hands.

"Why does that not surprise me?" he muttered.

"Our trunks. The one that was rescued and the other one. We need them."

"One is all there is. The other was lost overboard."

"What? But you —"

"Apparently missed rescuing one while I was busy rescuing you." He started to turn away, but his gaze darted back and caught on hers. Dark eyes. Luminous. Intense. She could scarcely take a breath.

"My vow of protection did not extend to your possessions," he declared, and he strode off around the rocks to his own camp.

Five

Eloise's anxiety melted moments later when Michael of Dunneault and another of the men brought them the remaining chest and she opened it to find her own spare shift and wimple folded on top. Beneath them she could see the kirtle of her old habit, her boar-bristle brush, her nightcap, and her prized possession: a pair of sturdy boots she had used while walking and working in plowed fields. Sinking to her knees, she reached inside for the precious leather sheath of husband-judging documents . . . which trailed a trickle of water across her knees as it emerged. Staring at the ominous gray drops on her shift, she felt her heart skip a beat. She grabbed the side of the chest; as it tilted, she heard liquid slosh. She stared in horror at the brine covering her parchment, her horn of ink powder, and her precious quills. The entire bottom of the chest was filled with seawater!

Frantically, she untied the cord binding the documents, and her hopes sank when the sheaf didn't spring open in her hand. She pulled back the leather cover, and her worst fears were realized. Her instructions for administering the husband test were now just soggy sheepskin on which most of the ink had dissolved into unreadable dark streaks. She tried to separate the pieces and found them stuck together in a gluey mass, except at the center where a few pieces of the cheap, ill-cured parchment had not yet been soaked by seawater. Hang the abbess for always trying to save the order a coin or two!

Desperate to salvage whatever might be undamaged, she pried apart the pages and discovered there were only a few words, here and there, left unblurred.

"Grave and holy duty . . . charity no less than dis— *something* . . . humble judgments . . . submit our ques— *something, something, something* — our dear Lord . . ."

Her blood drained from her head in a rush. All that was left were the meditations and admonitions the abbess had written to accompany the standards. Panic gripped her. Why hadn't she paid more attention when she looked over the documents at the convent? She squinted at the swollen pages and strained to recall the qualities and virtues named in the husband standards. There were several *p*'s — patience . . . piety . . . plenteous something. Quite a goodly number of *c*'s — courage and charity and, of course, consideration. She scowled. Did she remember that because she had read it in the standards or because Clemmie had just mentioned it?

In the standards there had been dozens — *pages* — of qualities to observe and evaluate, and she could only think of *five*.

What was she going to do? It was too late to turn back to the convent. They had already crossed the Channel, and even if she could summon the courage to relive that nightmare of a voyage, she could just imagine the earl's reaction to a request that they climb back aboard ships . . . after she had berated him for forcing her to make that trip in such weather in the first place. He seemed driven to return to his home as quickly as possible; he would never agree to return to the convent, even if she could swallow her pride to ask it of him. She chewed her lip, thinking. Perhaps if she asked for a messenger to go and send word of the accident to the abbess, asked for another set of standards . . . *The abbess would declare the mission a disaster and never permit her to take vows.* She groaned and closed her eyes.

"What's the matter, Elly?" Mary Clematis asked from nearby.

Eloise started and squashed the leather-clad sheaf to her chest.

"Nothing. Why? Do I look as if something is wrong?"

"You look like you did . . . that day in the kitchens."

Mary Clematis was her best friend in the whole world, Eloise thought. Surely she would understand. . . .

"It's all right, Elly. I don't mind that my trunk got lost. I'll make do."

Over the open trunk lid Eloise glimpsed Mary Clematis's doleful expression and clasped a hand to her mouth. "Oh, Clemmie, I'm so sorry. I forgot about —"

"There's nothing to be sorry about. I'm glad they saved your trunk. I just said a hymn from the Psalter in gratitude." She smiled in a loving, beatific way that made Eloise feel like a snake in a garden. While she had been panicking and plotting, Clemmie had been *praying*. "You're doing so splendidly. The earl is a beast and you have stood your ground and made him reckon with you. You've proved the abbess's faith in you." She crept over on her knees to put her arms around Eloise. "She couldn't have chosen a better husband judge."

Clemmie honestly believed that. Eloise stewed in guilty desperation as she returned the hug and privately girded herself to judge a man on the basis of . . .

She couldn't tell anyone about this . . . not even Clemmie . . . especially not Clemmie. Sharing her problem might make her feel better temporarily, but wouldn't change anything; she still would have to judge the earl's husbandly qualities and she still would have nothing to guide her. As Clemmie released her, she studied the guilelessness of her friend's face. If Clemmie knew what had happened, sooner or later it would come out; secrets made Clemmie physically ill.

Then it occurred to her that no one knew what was in those documents but her and the abbess. And only she had access to both the standards and the earl himself. That meant no one — not even the abbess herself — could question her judgment of whether or not the earl would make a proper husband. It was all up to her.

Relief and fresh panic contended inside her. How could she possibly judge a husband when she had not only not been married, but had seldom even met a married man?

Mary Clematis got up to check their garments, and when she came back to the pallet, she was holding her kirtle and scowling.

"I'm so sorry about your things," Eloise said, thinking she should offer Clemmie the use of her own spare garments. Not that she would accept. Even Clemmie's old things looked like new. Then a whiff of something unpleasant caused her to sit up and look around for the source of it, scowling.

"It's just that it would have been nice to have my novice habit" — Mary Clematis winced as she held up the damp hem of her kirtle to the fire and the odor bloomed in the air — "to wear until I can finish cleaning the horse manure out of my clothes."

On the other side of the rocks, Peril lay on his pallet by the fire, stiff as a poker and wishing he could close his eyes against the sight of its golden flames and not see an all too similar red-gold flame inside his head.

He had gone out earlier with his lieutenant, Michael, intending to clear his thoughts and regain his equilibrium while Michael collected wood. He found himself picking up fuel as well, feeling somehow that a piece of his composure returned with each hunk of weathered wood he gathered. On the way back to camp they had paused on the low cliff overlooking the nuns' campfire, and he felt his renewed balance eroding just as the sandy bank was doing under his feet.

There, in the firelight, stood one of the nuns in a halo of red-gold hair that merged astoundingly with the light of the flames behind her. It was as if she stood in a ring of living fire that reached from the top of her head to below her hips. He had never seen such hair. And to see it on a nun — one of the nuns in whose good graces reposed the success or failure of his fortunes! — was too much for him. He had known that he was in trouble, floundering for composure, but stalked straight down the bank toward her anyway. He had to see her at close range, to verify the sight with his own eyes or — he clung to the faint hope — disprove it and dispel the sorcery that had settled over his senses.

But when he approached and stood beside her, the strange effect of the firelight somehow lingered. To his dismay, it was the husband judge herself who stood in the center of that silken flame, her cool blue eyes a stunning counterpoint to the visual heat simmering around her. He found himself incapable of speech and set about stoking the fire to cover that alarming disability.

Somehow he made it back to his camp, back to his men, and back to his solitary soldier's pallet without betraying his distraction. But he hadn't come alone. The sight of her had come with him, seared into his mind. And now, when he closed his eyes . . .

"*Jesus. What have I done to deserve this?*"he muttered irritably, not realizing that he spoke aloud.

"What is the matter, my son?"

He started up at the voice and bumped into Basset, who was kneeling by him with a look of priestly expectation.

"Do you need to confess?"

"I simply cannot!" Mary Clematis whispered to Eloise the next morning as they stood wedged between their cart donkey and the earl's intimidating destrier. She was wide-eyed and pale and she was trembling, and Eloise knew from experience there was no use in arguing with her.

"Very well." She handed the donkey's reins to Michael of Dunneault, who stood by waiting to help them mount. "Sister Mary Clematis will ride the donkey and I shall walk."

"The devil you will," the earl's voice rolled over her from above. "Pull her up behind you, Dunneault."

"That won't be necessary." She struck off on foot, headed inland. She felt certain that if she were headed the wrong way, someone would correct her course.

"Please, milord!" Father Basset's whine could be heard above the roar of the waves of the incoming tide. "It would be most unseemly for her to *walk*."

"Fine. Throw her up behind Basset, there," the earl snapped.

"Oh, no, milord. For a man of the cloth to ride so with a woman —"

She kept walking toward the lowest part of the cliff and the path visible up the face of it. If she walked briskly and made it up the cliff, there was a chance —

"Dammit, Basset!" the earl roared.

He swore! And at a priest! Tension prickled the hair on the back of her neck. She felt as much as heard the movement behind her; it was all she could do to maintain a steady pace. Suddenly a huge, snorting war horse planted itself in her path and she was forced to halt.

"Really, Your Lordship!" She looked up and felt her breath catch in her throat. Hawklike helm, breastplate, gauntlets . . . eyes like burning coals . . . he was as formidable a knight as ever sat astride a horse — which, fortunately, meant he still had a way to go before matching an abbess. And she was an abbess in training.

"If you think you're walking all the way to

Whitmore, Sister, you are badly mistaken." He looked up from her to someone approaching on foot. "Throw her up here, Dunneault!"

To his credit, the earl's lieutenant hesitated before setting hands to what he must have supposed to be her waist. Eloise sputtered and shoved at his hands, but quickly found herself being boosted by the seat and simultaneously dragged by an arm up onto the rear of the earl's monstrous horse. She flailed for a moment, then, with the intimate assistance of a hand she was relieved not to be able to identify, she managed to part her knees and straddle the beast so that she sat just behind the earl's ornate saddle.

There were a few muffled laughs from the men mounted and moving into position behind them, and a gasp of "Milord, please!" from Father Basset. But the deed was done; she was seated behind the arrogant earl and there was nothing to do but endure it. She held on to the cantle of his saddle, but nearly tumbled off the rear when he kicked the horse into motion. An arm lashed back just in time to keep her from falling.

"Hold on, dammit," he snarled.

"I'm trying." Her fingers kept slipping off the hammered metal designs.

"I mean to me!" He grabbed her wrists

112

and pulled them around his waist, jerking her hard against his back. Allowing a moment for her to find a grip on his belt, he gave his horse the spur and it lunged forward eagerly.

It was intolerable . . . her arms were filled with an overheated nobleman, and her body was pressed intimately against his broad back, while every dent and rivet in his armor wore deep impressions in her cheek. And to top it all, she was forced to endure the discomfort of riding astride. Her muscles were stretched and screaming and her bottom was being pounded as if it were a tough side of beef. In desperation, she finally balled a fist and gave his shoulder plate a savage thump.

"Slow down!"

To her surprise, he did. As the horse slowed to a trot and then a walk she was able to sit straighter and collect her wits enough to demand: "What could possibly be so urgent at your home that you hazard life and limb to return there at such a mad pace?"

She watched his shoulders rise and fall heavily, but he remained silent.

"I know of only two things that can drive a man to such reckless haste," she continued, sensing that he was listening. "Love and fear."

Still he said nothing.

"Which is it, Your Lordship?"

There was a long pause before he answered.

"Neither."

"Ah." She drew back and hooked her hands once more on the cantle of his saddle. "Then I am forced to conclude that bashing and barreling headlong through life are simply your natural way. A finding that leads me to a number of other time-saving conclusions on your character: thoughtless, feckless . . . inattentive, immoderate . . . ill-mannered, ill-considered . . ."

She saw him stiffen and for a moment wondered if she had overdone it.

"I have lands to oversee," he said tersely.

"As do all men of title. And?"

"I have spring planting to do."

"You have a steward and a head plowman, do you not? What else?"

"This is an important planting."

"To those who wish to eat, every planting is important. What else?"

"I have . . . interfering . . . neighbors."

She noted his choice of words. English nobles, she had heard the abbess declare more than once, made stealing a neighbor's land their prime occupation.

"*Greedy* neighbors," she interpreted.

"What nobleman doesn't? What else?"

"God's teeth — isn't that enough?"

"No. Not enough to risk life and limb, or the possibility of losing an excellent bride." She leaned slightly to the side to glimpse his face as she readied her final thrust. "Unless, of course, you don't truly *want* a bride."

She very nearly tumbled backward off the horse's rump as he kneed the animal sharply to a gallop.

By the time they reached the village, she was willing to ride a horse, a mule, a donkey — even a large dog, if it meant not having to suffer the earl's temper and intolerable proximity. While he inquired about any animals that the cottagers might be willing to part with, Eloise and Mary Clematis wobbled on twitching legs around the cluster of stone buildings, greeting the villagers and enduring the boisterous fascination of the villagers' children, who had never before seen a real nun. The little ones picked at their sleeves and peered under their veils, and the youngest stuck their heads under the hem of Eloise's kirtle to discover if she had real feet. She and Mary Clematis soon escaped to one of the larger cottages where a rough-hewn bit of planking had been set up outside the door to feed the visitors.

Settling her aching bottom on a bench near a number of the earl's men, Eloise listened to their banter and realized there was more than one way to learn about a man's character. She began by asking them their names and how long they had ridden with the earl.

Sir Simon, Sir Ethan, Richard, Pascoe, William, Terrence — each nodded respectfully and weathered with good humor the information his fellows provided concerning his strength and skill as a soldier and his personal circumstance. Three were full knights, not one of them wedded . . . several, mostly younger men, were mounted squires awaiting a chance to prove their valor and earn their spurs . . . several identified themselves as sons of yeomen who had been drafted into training as soldiers and had excelled. All participated in the talk and jests, though clear deference fell to the knights when the talk of battle arose. Apparently, a man earned the right to recount such things as well as to participate in them.

"And the earl . . . where did he earn his spurs?" she asked. "What is the story of his colors?"

There was a brief silence while most attended their bread, curds, and beer, and the knights looked to the tall and courtly Simon of Langdoc to speak.

"Lord Peril earned his spurs early, Sister. He was fostered in a northern house whose lords are known for their combative natures and fighting prowess. He crossed the Channel to fight in France, Spain, and Italy before he was thirteen, and had his spurs even before he reached his full height. His colors are those of his father's lineage." He gave her a wry, evaluative look. "Crimson for the blood of men . . . blue for the tears of women."

She sensed several layers of meaning in that information.

"A grim meaning for such lovely colors," she observed, glancing at the pennant driven into the ground by the picket line of horses, "is it not?"

"A straightforward meaning for fighting men," Simon said, as if to challenge her to dig deeper into it. "Where there is bloodshed, there will be tears. A knight who takes the field of battle accepts that. The women who remain at home must accept it as well."

"His arms." She squinted toward the banner. "What is that on his shield?"

Sir Simon looked at the others and they smiled, anticipating the story.

"Spurs, Sister. They are his own device, chosen because he won his spurs so young

117

and because he strikes hard and fast, goading the enemy to desperate action. In his first campaign as a full knight the enemy dubbed him 'the duke's spur.' The name stuck."

For the next few minutes, they recounted for her a list of their lord's campaigns and victories, including two harrowing escapes where his quickness and cunning meant the difference between life and death for several of them. The meal and the stories ended with Sir Simon's gaze directed toward the horizon.

"He's never so content, Lord Peril, as when he's just set out upon a campaign. I heard him sing once, on the road. He's not a half bad balladeer." The others laughed as they left their seats and warned Sir Simon in genial mutters that he had best keep such observations to himself.

Moments later the earl himself appeared, glowering, and ordered his men to prepare to move. The few left at the table quickly abandoned it to return to their mounts, and he addressed Eloise without looking at her.

"I found you a horse." He strode straight past her, heading toward his men, adding under his breath: "Of sorts."

"But I don't want a horse." Eloise stopped dead, calling after him: "A donkey such as

118

Sister Mary Clematis rides would be more than sufficient!"

"It would be an insult," Michael of Dunneault advised quietly as he fell in beside her and urged her forward. "Ladies don't ride donkeys."

"I'm not a 'lady,' I'm a sister bound to poverty and humility. Donkeys are perfect for us . . . the Blessed Virgin rode a donkey to Bethlehem."

"Whitmore," he observed cryptically, "is a long way from Bethlehem."

The men were clustered around something, but parted as she approached. She heard a few muffled laughs as she passed and felt her face reddening. Then ruddy, thickset Sir Ethan of Horne stepped aside, and there was His Lordship, standing beside a horse standing as high as his head, with feet the size of bushel baskets. She halted, feeling every eye on her, knowing that her first reaction — blind terror — must not be allowed to escape.

"I could not possibly ride something so . . . so . . ."

"Old?" the earl finished for her, his face reddening. "These people have nothing else to spare. It is this horse, or the rear of my mount. You choose."

She forced her gaze to focus past the size

of the beast to its hairy, withered mouth, swayed back, and pendulous belly. It was an old plow horse. A *very* old plow horse. The beast reached down for another mouthful of grass and then raised its head to look at her with huge, wizened brown eyes. Something in that steady, gentle gaze started the icy knot in the middle of her melting.

Then she looked up and found the earl staring at her with a look that said she could plead poverty and humility all she wanted, but he knew her real reason for demanding a cart or a donkey. She was afraid. And how dare she presume to judge him if she could not rise to the challenge of simply riding a horse?

She spotted Father Basset wringing his hands nearby and abruptly sank to her knees, pulling Mary Clematis down with her.

"Bless this horse for us, Father," she said.

"Eh?" Basset seemed to choke on something.

"Bless this beast to heaven's holy purpose," she reiterated, "as you do the animals on a Rogation Sunday."

"R-Rogation?" Basset seemed confused.

After a moment's pause, the earl's voice issued from just out of sight.

"Dammit, Basset — bless it, so we can be on our way!"

Eloise tugged on Michael of Dunneault's arm, urging him down beside her, and as he went down with a thud onto one knee, the rest of the earl's men looked at one another and took a knee as well. Soon the earl and Father Basset were the only ones left standing. The father looked a little bewildered as he made the sign of the cross and tried to think of something suitable to say.

"Thank you, dear Lord, for this . . . goodly . . . beast. We give You thanks for . . . its . . . past service and for . . . the new service into which You in Your infinite wisdom have called it. May it . . . um . . . carry the good sister wherever you would have her go. And may she . . . always . . . ummm . . ."

"Not fall off," Peril prompted in irritable tones.

"Not fall off," Basset echoed on an indrawn breath, adding on a relieved exhalation: "Amen."

Prayers were answered that day, on the road west. The horse, whom Eloise dubbed Sir Arthur, proved to be a rather gallant old fellow who lowered his head and plodded doggedly up hills and then trotted gleefully down the other side, setting Eloise to bouncing wildly, but never once unseating her. Several times, she was spotted leaning forward and patting the beast's neck and

121

murmuring to it. And when they dismounted that evening to make camp just outside a small milling village, she insisted on feeding and tending the animal despite her fatigue and the fact that she was walking as if she had a barrel between her knees.

Peril watched her from the corner of his eye, unable to fathom her suddenly reasonable mood. He had just given her an insult of a mount that had jounced her along through twelve miles of rolling terrain, and she behaved as if she were quite content. One minute she fainted and whined for special treatment, the next she proved a game and stalwart traveler. Not that he cared how she traveled, except that he was grateful that she wasn't hanging on to him bodily anymore.

It had taken all of his self-control, that morning, to keep from dropping the nosy little shrew right on her sanctimonious buttocks. He had found himself staring all too eagerly at her when she first emerged from behind the rocks that morning, looking for some trace of that hair that had caused him such torment during the night. But she was once again tucked and wimpled and woolen . . . all nun and all business. And before ten words had issued from her mouth, she had declared all-out war on both his sovereignty and leadership. He could have cheerfully strangled her. Then she dragged his whole company down onto their knees to bless the old scrub he had provided her and then climbed aboard it as if it were royal transport.

If he lived to be a hundred, he would never understand females.

Not that she was a real female, as she took great pains to remind him.

Wending his way to where she was giving the old turf-turner a drink of water, he watched her running a hand down its withers and regarding its massive feet with a frown.

"I see you survived your first day on horseback," he said.

Standing in the shadows of an aged elm, a leather water bucket in her hand, she turned and scowled at the sight of him. "He's got foot problems, you know."

Peril stiffened and braced. Here it came . . .

"I count four and he seems to be upright and walking on them," he declared tightly. "How is there a problem?"

"His hooves are overgrown. He could rock babies to sleep while standing still."

He stared at her, startled by something akin to humor in her, then looked down at the animal's hooves. Sure enough, the beast's hooves were overgrown and some-what bowed, which accounted in part for his jerky gait.

"What would you know about horses' hooves?" He propped his fists on his waist and gave her skeptical look.

"Just because I don't ride horses doesn't mean I can't know something about them. In preparing to become — for my work at the convent, I've studied all of the agricultural arts: the growing of field crops, beekeeping, dairying, orchard and flax cultivation, and the husbandry of diverse animals."

"Including human husbands?" He studied her face . . . her direct and confident gaze . . . those fine blue eyes . . . "How does one become a judge of husbands when one lives in a cloister of women?"

Those fine eyes narrowed ever so slightly. "The order has very detailed standards for such things . . . the combined wisdom of years of observation and assessment."

"Then I should like to see these 'stan-dards.' " He crossed his arms.

"Impossible." She backed up, bumped into the horse, and turned to busy herself with the brush in her hands.

"How so? I believe I have a right to know on what accounts I am called to answer." He stepped closer.

"It is our practice not to divulge our husband standards," she said shortly, "lest some unscrupulous applicant contrive to appear to be that which he is not."

"You prefer to tyrannize the applicant with endless scrutiny instead."

"We prefer to observe firsthand and make our own fair and proper judgments," she asserted, brushing harder and faster. The old horse nickered appreciatively.

"So, you hold me up to these precious standards of yours and measure me . . . What if I come a bit too short in some area or a bit too long in another? What if I don't fit your precious ideal? Does that mean I am not fit to marry? Look at my men — some are tall, some short . . . some are powerfully framed, some slight of limb . . . some are reticent, some affable. I can tell you, it would be a dangerous error to assume that the shorter or slighter or more affable are less effective fighters." Irritation crept into his voice. "If there is variation in the ranks of good warriors, what makes you think good husbands must all wear the same face and bear the same nature?"

"We do not require that husbands look alike or have the same nature, Lord Whitmore. But there are aspects of character known to be common among good husbands, and it is our God-given charge to use discernment in choosing mates for our maidens. Marriage is, after all, a sacrament. And meant to last a lifetime."

"I've been all over the world, Sister, and I've seen what passes for marriage in a hundred different lands. Most places, more care is given to buying a camel than to acquiring a wife. And yet they manage to bump along."

"Well, if you would be content with a wife worth less than a camel," she snapped, refusing to look up, "then, by all means, go and get one."

"Would that I could. It would certainly make my life easier!"

She paused mid-stroke and turned a look on him that made him feel like a parboiled beet about to be peeled.

"If you are of such a mind, why did you journey all the way to our convent seeking a bride? Why haven't you just married the first passable, serviceable female you met? Better yet, why haven't you married the best dowry available? You wouldn't be the first to make his fortune by making a maid a wife."

"I cannot," he declared, trying to contain the frustration that both she and his accursed situation produced in him. "I must have an excellent bride — a bride *filled with the highest virtue.*"

"Who says so?"

"My people say so."

"Your people? What have they to do with your marriage?"

"They would have a lady worthy enough to . . . They insist that . . ." He halted, feeling himself teetering on the edge of a precipice. She wouldn't think a lord who allowed himself to be coerced into marriage by a few villeins and cottagers was much of a lord. He flexed his jaw.

"They insist what?" she prodded.

He looked down, desperate for a way to finish his unthinkable statement, and his gaze fell on the old horse's feet.

"Those hooves are indeed bad. Terrence is skilled with a farrier's knife and file — I'll send him to you." He turned abruptly, heading toward where his men were settling in around a campfire.

Eloise felt a curious weakness in her knees as she watched him striding off to summon his men to look at Sir Arthur's hooves. He was so tall, so clean-limbed, so strong . . . and so utterly filled with conflict. What was it he was hiding from her? Did he honestly think she couldn't see it in him?

In short order he and his men had shouldered her aside and were lifting, cleaning, and trimming the old horse's unwieldy hooves. Unable to assist with the trimming or to pursue her conversation with the earl, she retreated to the fireside, where Clemmie was standing by herself, warming her hands.

As she approached, one of the men — Pascoe, the fire-maker from the night before — jumped up and offered to make her and her companion a fire of their own. She declined to make more work for him, but he and the others insisted. Then, as Mary Clematis hurried over to stand by her, she noted that each man Clemmie passed drew back his chin or averted his face. It was only when she and Mary Clematis stood before the fire together that the reason for those strange looks became apparent. The warmth of the fire released the lingering scent of horse manure from Mary Clematis's still besmirched clothes.

There was nothing to be done about it until they reached a place where they might secure some fuller's earth and clean her habit properly. Without comment, Eloise offered Mary Clematis a blanket and, when their separate fire was ready, steered her to a seat on a log beside it. Wrapping up in a blanket herself, she sank gingerly to a seat beside her friend and sighed.

"Are you as sore as I am?" she asked, rubbing her bottom.

"I feel like my bruises have bruises," Mary Clematis said, biting her lip.

"The only thing harder than that saddle is His Lordship's head."

"Don't make me laugh," Mary Clematis said holding her side. "It hurts too much." After a few moments she grew more thoughtful. "His Lordship is a hard one. Even Father Basset seems wary of him."

"Small wonder. His Lordship is not an especially reverent sort — regarding marriage or religion." Eloise looked to the edge of the trees to where the earl and his men were still working on her horse's hooves. "What puzzles me is that he clearly doesn't want a marriage, but feels compelled to take a wife."

"Duty?" Mary Clematis offered, scowling and sniffing to the side for a moment before dismissing the perception as a phantom and returning to her thought. "He has a duty to his estate . . . all noblemen do. They are bound to secure proper lady-wives who will run proper households and, of course, give them proper heirs."

"I suppose. But I cannot help feeling there is more to it than that."

When Father Basset came to their fire for evening prayers, she quizzed him.

"Why does he feel compelled to seek a bride he doesn't want?" she asked.

"Oh, no, Sister, you are mistaken. He is most eager to have a lady bride . . . to take her to his home and . . . begin a new life and . . . produce many fine children." As he spoke those reassurances, Basset nervously fingered the wooden cross he wore and forced a smile so thin as to be transparent. "Why else would he have undertaken such a tiresome and expensive journey?"

"That was what I was hoping you would tell me."

"Please understand, Sister . . . His Lordship is blunt and harsh spoken at times, but deep in his heart he truly desires a fine and virtuous woman."

Evening prayers were exceedingly short and Father Basset kept losing his place and repeating himself. Eloise watched the priest scurry back to the men's fire and thought to herself that it was little wonder the earl disliked him so. Father Basset was a liar.

Six

For the next three days they traveled from sunrise to sunset along roads lined with newly tilled fields and greening pastures. The sun came out strongly each afternoon to warm them, and with the sky a rich blue, the clouds pristine white, and the roadsides a brilliant new green, the countryside was a treat for the senses. Time and again, Eloise let Sir Arthur plod faithfully forward while she closed her eyes and raised her face to the lavish sunshine. If it weren't for the dull ache in her lower half and the earl's ever-shortening temper, she might have believed she was close to Heaven itself.

In truth, what she was close to was Whitmore. And Whitmore was — as Michael of Dunneault might have said — a long way from Heaven. The closer they came to the earl's estates, the more tense and irritable the earl became. He refused Eloise's help in negotiating a lesser toll across the earl of Sussex's land. He nearly burst a vessel in his temple when she helped the men consolidate their remaining supplies and repack their provisions. And he all

131

but snapped her head off when she insisted on helping him purchase oats and dried apples from a canny farmer and beer from a duplicitous village victualer. In each case, when she fell to her knees to pray for guidance, the earl's frustration erupted mightily.

After each confrontation, Father Basset sought her out to mollify her with excuses and assurances. But even he was at a loss to adequately explain the earl's behavior. Worse still, the earl's distemper seemed to be spreading through his men, darkening their countenances and stifling their customary banter. They rode increasingly with rigid backs and solemn faces, and took their evening meal with few words and even fewer smiles. This, Eloise observed to Mary Clematis, was not the behavior of men anticipating the pleasures of home.

She was so focused on the changes in their company that she scarcely heeded the subtle but significant changes in the countryside. It was only when they stopped two days later, at midday, that she noticed the untilled fields, the depleted and sagging hayricks, and the unused appearance of the road. There was less greenery here and the tree buds were not even swollen for leafing.

She sought out Michael of Dunneault for an explanation, but he was nowhere to be found. She looked for Father Basset; he was missing as well.

"Where are we?" she finally asked Sir Simon.

The tall, usually droll knight looked a bit pained.

"We just crossed onto Whitmore land."

"This?" She looked around at the countryside — the brown fields, the scrubby roadsides, and the slumbering trees — and blinked. "This is Whitmore?"

"It is." The earl's voice crackled with tension as he approached them from behind. "Simon, I'll have a word with you." Sir Ethan and Pascoe, who happened to be nearby, were summoned by the earl also.

As he led them away, she waded through some dry brush and climbed to the top of a nearby knoll to have a look. It wasn't an especially inspiring sight. Brown to the left and gray to the right . . . a colorless patchwork of inactivity. She frowned. The weather was warming daily. Where were the plowmen, the children picking rocks, the sowers, the flocks and herds grazing, the new lambs frolicking? She looked down at the tufts of weedy brown grass under her feet, then up at the thickening clouds overhead. Where was spring?

Peril watched her standing on that knoll,

her hand shading her eyes as she surveyed his holdings, and felt his stomach sliding toward his feet. The day of reckoning was finally here. He had left orders to see the hall and manor cleaned and freshened for them; he had sent word for the cottagers to tidy the commons and lanes just outside the manor's walls; and, when they were close enough, he had sent Michael, Father Basset, and now Simon, Ethan, and Pascoe to make sure all was in readiness. But he couldn't do anything about the land itself or the lack of warmth and resilience that seemed to affect nature itself within Whitmore's borders.

The curse, his tenants and villeins called it. To a man, they were convinced that Whitmore struggled under the yoke of a single spiteful utterance proclaimed more than a score of years ago. Every difficulty, every misfortune, every loss was attributed to it. And in the two years of his tenure as lord, he had been unable to dent, much less dislodge, that vile belief. In a moment of desperation, he had finally agreed to seek a bride who would end the curse. But instead of a bride filled with the highest virtue, he was returning to his blighted home with the very opposite: a nun, whose sworn duty it was to judge every aspect of his life and person, and who disliked, disregarded, and at every turn disobeyed him!

Every way he turned she was meddling, intruding, prying, or assuming. She kept busy every minute she wasn't on horseback: inspecting the food and supplies he purchased, declaring them "off," and marching them back to farmer and brewer; butting in while he was negotiating tolls; dropping to her knees at the slightest provocation; running Father Basset about as if he were *her* errand boy instead of Heaven's — the latter being something of a mixed blessing, since it kept Basset from haranguing him with hope of Heaven and praying at him.

He slowed the pace as they wound their way through his fields and orchards, giving his men as much time as possible to prepare for their arrival. He forced himself not to look back at her. He remembered his own first glimpse of the hall and manor house too clearly to nurse the hope that she would find it pleasing.

The manor, built as it was on the highest ground in the area, commanded first attention. A sturdy stone wall surrounded a sizeable enclosure, which was dominated by a tall but unfinished stone keep. Around that structure, huddled like goslings to a mother goose, were a number of what appeared to be temporary wooden buildings and one more permanent one made of cut stone and timber. From a distance, the manor had the aspect of a castle under construction. At closer range, the still-exposed timbers were revealed to be well weathered, and enough generations of weeds had sprouted and grown through the unplaced stones to completely cover many of them.

Outside the walls, along the road, were a number of cottages, byres, and sheds. Beyond them in each direction was the commons, on which several cows and sheep competed for the few remaining tufts of brown grass. To the east were fields that had not yet seen plow or harrow, and not far to the west stood a sizeable copse of trees that was connected to a substantial forest by a narrow band of what appeared to be a much newer planting.

It had rained earlier in the day, and the road had become little more than a muddy swath between the cottages. The scents of mud and manure from the nearby pens, the smoke of burning peat, and the smell of moldy straw hung heavy in the air.

Home, Peril thought to himself. Unfortunately, just as he remembered it.

His home, Eloise thought as she studied the sturdy wall and unfinished keep within it, noting its air of neglect and of unaccomplished goals. It was not at all what she had expected of his lordship's estate. So proud a nobleman would surely have a home and estate to justify that pride, she had thought. But then, outward appearances could be deceiving. Perhaps more care had been taken inside the hall and with the stables and working houses of the manor.

She quickly turned her attention to the people lining the road leading to the manor gate and those running from the common and the fields beyond to greet their lord. A few, mostly children, called a welcome and waved. The adults, most poorly dressed and shoeless, clumped together whispering and lowering their heads in respect when the earl turned their way. There was precious little joy on Whitmore at its lord's return.

They entered through the gate and wound their way up the rise to the front of the stone tower where a number of people awaited them. She was pleased to see Sir Michael, Sir Simon, Sir Ethan, and the amicable Pascoe among that party. But it was an aged man in a velvet robe and steward's chain of office, leaning on a crutch, who came forward with the first hand of welcome as the earl dismounted.

"Yer Lordship!" He squinted as he

lurched forward — well to the right of where the earl stood. "Welcome back, sarr. Safe an' sound." The earl darted left to intercept the old fellow and clasp his shoulder.

"Sedgewick!" The earl fairly shouted into the old fellow's ear, turning him back to the main body of visitors. "How are things here?"

"Beer? Ye want beer?" The old fellow turned to issue an order.

"No, no — I don't want beer — I want to know if things are all right."

"Right as rain, sarr. Except" — the old man's face fell — "yer father's dead. Poor soul, he died in his —"

"Yes, yes, two years past," the earl shouted. "Is everything all right?"

"It is, seigneur." An elderly woman using a young girl's arm instead of a cane or crutch hobbled forward to answer in a French accent. She wore a velvet smock and immaculate wimple and veil, but her eyes were hooded by folds of skin, most of her teeth were missing, and her hand trembled enough to shake the girl's arm. "No deaths. No maiming. No great misfortunes."

To Eloise's surprise, the earl took a deep breath of relief, acknowledged the woman with a nod and an *Et bien, madame. Merci,* and then came to help her and Mary Clematis to dismount.

"This be yer bride?" Old Sedgewick wobbled over to give Eloise a looking-over. He peered at her and drew back, startled. "Troth! Looks like a nun to me."

"She is a nun," the earl said through clenched teeth. "This is Sister . . . Sister . . ."

"Eloise," she supplied.

"Ye gone an' married a nun?" The old man was truly horrified — as were the other householders as the words "married" and "nun" flew like a contagion through the household servants. Several of the women dropped to their knees, crossing themselves, and the men began to talk all at once, demanding to see Father Basset.

"I'm not married yet. Sister Eloise and Sister Mary Cockleburr, here, have come with me to help prepare for my bride's arrival."

It took a moment for the words to sink in, but instead of allaying confusion they unleashed another round.

"But we have already prepared, *mon seigneur,*" the old lady declared. "Worked day and night . . . night and day . . ."

"So, ye be a nun, eh?" old Sedgewick said to Eloise, thrusting his nose against hers in an effort to see her better. "One o' them holy women."

"I am . . . from the Holy Order of the Brides of Virtue," she responded, careful of her wording, and was rewarded with a gasp.

"Ye hear that?" The old man staggered back. "A bride of virtue! 'Is Lordship's brung home a *bride o' virtue!*"

Silence descended suddenly, allowing an intrepid young voice from the back to float prominently out over the court.

"Who's this 'Virtue' feller and why's the earl got 'is bride?"

The scarlet-faced earl looked to be on the verge of an explosion.

"I haven't married anyone yet!" he shouted. "Least of all one of these sisters!" Volume, he apparently had decided, was the only way to deal with the situation. Then, after seeing his words take root, he seized the old lady's free hand and dragged her toward Eloise.

"Our keeper of the keys, Madame Fleurmort." Then he gestured to the old man still inspecting Eloise at uncomfortably close range. "My steward you've already met. Sedgewick. He was my father's steward and his father's steward before that . . ."

And probably Noah's steward on the Ark, Eloise thought, as she escaped the steward's even more personal inspection by accompanying the earl and Mary Clematis through

140

the open doors into the great hall. They moved first through an antechamber with a stone floor and an iron chandelier, up several broad stone steps, and into a huge, dimly lit hall. Everyone was talking at once, all in loud voices, and enhanced by the echoes off the stone walls, the effect was nothing short of deafening.

Overwhelmed, she paused with Mary Clematis to cross herself and offer a prayer of gratitude for their arrival, then focused on what she could see rather than hear. The hall, the walls of which were formed by the base of the unfinished tower, was exceedingly tall and braced with massive timbers overhead, from which hung what were once colorful banners. They, like the thick stone walls, were darkened with soot that seemed to absorb what modest light was admitted by the high-set windows.

The air was stale and smelled of old grease, decayed food, and mildew, despite the apparently new rushes underfoot. The torches in the iron brackets around the hall smoked prodigiously, and there were few furnishings that didn't look as if they were formed by planks propped together.

The earl mounted the dais and sent his household back to work, just as a pack of hounds came rushing in, jumping, yapping, barking, and gleefully defying the hound boys' and house women's attempts to corral them and drive them back outside.

Eloise found herself trapped against a bench against the wall by two enormous hounds bent on licking her within an inch of her life. Sir Simon and Sir Ethan seized and tossed the beasts aside and Sir Michael led her to a seat near the hearth on the dais. Mary Clematis was rescued next, and they sat together in shock as the hall was purged of all boisterous four-legged beasts and all but a few of the two-legged variety.

"Dammit, Michael, I sent you ahead to make certain everything was ready," the earl ground out as the last yelps, barks, and shouts faded.

"I'm sorry, milord. I told them . . . We told them all . . . They just —" Michael halted and straightened as Sedgewick wobbled up.

"Damned hellhounds." The old steward managed a toothless grin and a thump on the arm for his earl. "Glad to see ye, I reckon . . . jus' like the rest o' us. I 'spect ye'll be wantin' to wash the dust from yer throats."

When Eloise and Mary Clematis asked for barley water instead of beer, it was brought, and as soon as they had finished it, the earl insisted they accompany Mme. Fleurmort to their quarters.

They followed the wheezing, doddering old housekeeper up a broad set of spiral steps at the corner of the hall near the dais. Twice they had to pause to allow the old Frenchwoman to catch her breath. But eventually they reached a musty chamber in the tower above the hall, where new straw pallets on old wooden cots awaited. The chamber contained a crude table, a tallow lamp, an unshuttered window in which swallows had made a succession of nests, and plenty of spider webs and undisturbed dust.

The old lady looked around as if she herself had never seen the chamber before, and said she would send up water and linen. She showed them the passage to the garderobe and advised them to use it, since the household was short of chamber pots. When she was gone, Mary Clematis sat down on one of the cots with a pinched expression and folded hands.

"Well, it's certainly . . . large," she said, her customary optimism reeling.

Eloise went to the window to peer down on the thatched and wooden roofs leaning against the wall and the main courtyard below. For a moment words failed her, and she told herself that was probably a blessing. The abbess had warned her against hasty judgments, no doubt with just such an experience in mind. Their arrival and introduction to the earl's home had been something of a disaster. But, she reminded herself, it might also have been worse.

"It will seem better when we've had some dinner and a good night's rest," she said, hoping to convince them both. "We are just tired and a bit overtaxed."

Mary Clematis nodded, lay back on the dusty ticking, and sneezed. And sneezed.

But a hearty dinner and a sound night's rest were not easy to come by at Whitmore, Eloise soon learned. She and Mary Clematis were summoned to their first meal at Whitmore by a wary, long-faced woman in ripe-smelling garments over which had been placed a new linen apron. She insisted they walk ahead of her and stared expectantly at them, crossing herself and muttering, as they descended the steps to the great hall.

Planking tables had been erected on the main floor of the hall and on the lord's dais, but all remained undraped. Light was provided by the torches on the walls, the tallow candles on the tables, and a fire in the hearth behind the lord's chair. But the sooty hall was still dark and unadorned, and there was still that odd, moldy odor about the place.

The earl was speaking with his men on the main floor when she and Mary Clematis arrived, and his men drew back, acknowledging them with nods as he turned to greet them. She stared, dumbstruck by the sight of him dressed in his best garments: a quilted velvet tunic with a standing collar and slashed sleeves, matching hose, a belt overlaid with gold tracery and semiprecious stones, and soft deerskin boots that wrapped his muscular calves nearly to his knees. His dark hair was damp from washing, and his several days' growth of beard had been scraped away. He looked more than civilized; in other circumstances, she would have deemed him courtly — until she met his gaze and the intensity of his mood sent a shiver down her spine. His determination to prove himself and his household suitable was etched into every stubborn line and combative curve of his countenance.

"Sisters." He approached with both hands extended and bowed courteously when they responded in kind. "Allow me to welcome you to Whitmore in a more proper fashion. Will you have some wine before we are served?"

Eloise felt her face heat as he held her hand on the way to the table on the dais while motioning for a young manservant to bring them cups of wine. Another shiver went through her as his hand dragged across hers when he released her. Ordinarily she would have refused wine, but she could see that Father Basset, seated not far away on the dais, was imbibing. And she was shivering, no doubt from the drafty hall. Thinking of the long chilly night ahead in their drafty tower room, she supposed it wouldn't hurt her or Mary Clematis to have something to warm their bones.

She accepted, took a sip, and instantly regretted it. The wine had a harsh vinegary rasp that made her eyes water with every sip.

Fish was the first thing served, since it was Lent. Smoked fish and stewed fish and roasted fish stuffed with leeks . . . all of which was dry and salty and as tough as leather. Next came bowls of peppery pottage into which sundry root vegetables had been cut. A soup, of sorts, she might have said, except that it was served in piles on bread trenchers that had the color and consistency of wood. Then came pies made of the strangest combinations of fillings Eloise had ever seen: curds and cured herring; yams and pungent goat cheese; onions, cabbage, radishes, and dried plums. All around the hall, the earl's men were closing their eyes and filling their mouths. She managed a few bites of each, picking out things she recognized from the leathery, half-charred crusts.

Then came the main course, a roast capon . . . served up with the news that Father Basset had given them a special dispensation to roast it in honor of their guests, even though it was Lent. Charred on the outside but still red and raw inside, the bird looked scarcely edible. Mindful of the earl's gaze on her, Eloise picked through the carcass and selected a sliver of meat. But in the end, she couldn't make herself eat it.

Eloise exchanged suffering looks with Mary Clematis and buried her nose in her vinegary wine hoping its astringence would scour the tastes of the food from her mouth. When she looked up, she found the earl staring fixedly at her, his gaze dark and his manner intense in a way she had not seen it before. Their gazes met in a glancing blow and both looked instantly away. She felt a sudden flush of warmth, which she gratefully attributed to the wine.

There was little talk after the platters, trenchers, and cups were cleared away. Tension hung over the hall like a shroud until the earl asked the burly William of Wright to play some melodies on his lyre. William, eldest son of Whitmore's plowwright, blustered good-naturedly and protested his ineptitude until the earl barked an order for him to get on with it. He was surprisingly agile at the strings; his big, thick-fingered hands were magically transformed into agents of harmony. His songs were simple country ballads, but his deep voice lent a depth and resonance to the music that rendered it truly enjoyable.

When an argument over lyrics broke out — aggravated by the quantities of beer consumed — Eloise rose, holding her head, and excused herself and Mary Clematis to evening prayers. The earl rose, stone-faced, and ordered Father Basset to accompany them.

"That won't be necessary," she demurred, watching the well-wined priest struggle to rise from his seat. "Just tell us which way to the chapel."

"Take your prayers in your rooms tonight," the earl ordered. "You can visit the chapel another time."

Eloise would have protested his high-handed treatment, but she was not eager for yet another disagreeable incident before reaching her bed. Bidding him have a "goodly night," she picked up one of the tallow candles, and together she and Mary Clematis climbed the winding stairs.

Peril watched the husband judge and her companion flee his hall and his company, feeling as if he were hanging above a bottomless pit by a very thin rope.

This homecoming had been every bit the nightmare he had feared. His steward had slipped even further from reason and his housekeeper now complained endlessly of her rheumy joints and seldom left her pallet. The preparations he had asked for had been poorly carried out and he dreaded the ordeal that lay ahead as he showed the husband judge around his holdings. He had watched her taking in every detail of the hall and refusing most of the unpalatable dinner, and realized her critical gaze would miss nothing.

She was going to see every decrepit, disheveled, ill-tended, and unproductive inch of his estate. He tossed back another sizable draught of sour wine, grimacing. And there wasn't a thing he could do about it.

Upstairs, in their room, Eloise and Mary Clematis prepared for sleep much as they would have at the convent . . . removing their outer garments, washing their faces and hands, and kneeling side by side to say their evening prayers. Eloise finished first, as she always did, and removed to her narrow, wood-framed cot to pull out her brush and drag it through the uncoiled mass of her hair.

When Mary Clematis finished, she came to help.

"Let me," she said, prying the brush from Eloise's hands. "I haven't had to do this in quite a few years. I confess . . . sometimes I rather miss it."

"Well, I won't," Eloise said holding up a handful of her thick, reddish gold hair and scowling at it. "I'd cut it all off this minute, if I could."

"Elly!" Mary Clematis was scandalized. "You mustn't even think such a thing. You must have all your long hair to give as a sacrifice the night you keep your vigil and take your vows. The longer and more beautiful your hair, the greater the gift it is to God." She paused mid-stroke. "And you have such glorious hair. I wish mine had been so thick and soft . . . and such a beautiful color."

"Well, it's a nuisance to me." Eloise reclaimed the brush and dropped it into her trunk. "I can't wait to be rid of it."

Mary Clematis sighed as she transferred to her cot, donned the nightcap Eloise had loaned her, and wrapped up in her blankets. "If you couldn't be a nun, Elly, what would you do?"

"Don't be silly, Mary Clematis. I'm a nun already in everything but vows."

"I know, but if you couldn't —"

"Don't ever say such a thing!" She answered more sharply than she intended. "I'm the order's husband judge. I am going to take vows as soon as I return, and someday I'm going to be an abbess." She blew out the light and jerked her blankets from the cot to wrap up in them.

But once she lay on her bed, staring up into the dark shadows of the beams above, she repented the harshness of her tone.

"I'm sorry, Clemmie. I didn't mean to snap," she said into the darkness. There was a long pause before Mary Clematis answered.

"It's all right, I understand." Her sigh turned to a groan. "I think His Lordship's welcome dinner isn't so welcome in my stomach. That awful capon . . . I took too much and then I couldn't just leave it there with the earl staring at me like that. Did it make you queasy, too?"

"I didn't eat any of it," Eloise said, putting her hand to her stomach as she recalled the unappealing sight of the meat and the earl's glower of resentment as she refused it. It was a wonder that the residents of the manor survived such food.

"But I thought with Father Basset's dispensation it would be so good," Mary Clematis said with a whine.

There apparently was such a thing as too much faith, Eloise told herself.

"I doubt the archbishop himself could have blessed that bird to an edible state," she said. "I'm heading for the kitchens tomorrow, first thing. Perhaps I can suggest a few improvements . . ."

Some hours later, in the dead of night, Eloise was awakened by a groan and a rustle. She turned onto her side and snuggled deeper into her blanket, but the sounds came again, and again. Another groan, louder, and a scuffle suggesting movement. Awakening fully, she looked over her shoulder to see Mary Clematis rising from her cot, holding her stomach in distress and pacing.

"What's the matter?" She threw back her blankets.

"Ohhh, I feel awful — I think I'm going to be sick!"

"Where is the . . ." They didn't have a chamber pot, she recalled as she rushed to put an arm around Mary Clematis. "To the garderobe, quickly!"

Without a light, she had to fumble for the latch and then half carry her friend out into the landing. The stairs were visible to the right, and the narrow passage leading to the garderobe lay to the left. Across the way, a door she hadn't noticed before stood ajar, shedding a much-needed slice of light onto the landing.

"Ohhh, Elly —" Mary Clematis clamped a hand over her mouth.

"Hold on, Clemmie — you can't do that here!" As Mary Clematis's knees buckled, Eloise struggled to keep her staggering toward the garderobe in the darkened passage. From the far end came a flash of dim light that illuminated a human form in the passage . . . just as Mary Clematis crumpled and slid from her grasp.

"No, Clemmie — please help us," she called to whoever had just emerged from the garderobe. "Sister Mary Clematis is ill and I need help to get her to —"

A sensation of heat struck her as she was shouldered aside. She heard Clemmie's moan and a man's faint groan as her friend was being lifted. There were a few footsteps, which she followed frantically, then a pause, in which she bumped into her helper.

"The door," he ordered tautly. And she knew beyond a doubt the identity of their Good Samaritan.

She felt along the passage wall and found

the door's wooden handle. A streak of light fell across Mary Clematis's limp form as the earl ducked inside, set her on the planking bench, then backed out. Eloise darted in past him and shut the door behind her.

Mary Clematis was cold and clammy and weak as a willow twig. Eloise stayed with her as she was sick, holding her forehead and rubbing her shoulders.

There came a knock on the door.

"Are you all right?"

"Fine," Eloise answered the first time.

"Well enough," she responded to his second query.

"I think I need help," she admitted after Mary Clematis failed to rouse.

The door opened and the earl lifted Mary Clematis and carried her out. He had to walk sideways with her down the narrow passage, then paused on the landing to wait for Eloise.

"In here . . ." She brushed past him to push open the door to their room. Using the moonlight coming through the window, she located Mary Clematis's cot and pulled back the blanket for the earl to lay her on the bare ticking.

"We need light," she said, feeling Mary Clematis's forehead and trying not to let her fear show. They were leagues away from the convent and Sister Bernice's potent herbal nostrums. If only she had spent more time learning the aged sister's healing arts. . . .

The earl located the candle and carried it out the door. Moments later, as Eloise tucked the blankets snugly around Mary Clematis and rubbed her limbs, he returned with the candle lighted.

"What else do you need?" he asked, holding it aloft for her.

"More blankets . . . from my bed, over there." She nodded in that direction as she stroked Mary Clematis's pale face. "She's beginning to chill."

The earl ripped the two blankets from her bed and brought them to her.

"What's the matter with her?" he asked.

"It's hard to say." She spread and tucked the blankets. "She's easily chilled, and since we left, she's been cold all the time. She's ridden for four days . . . she's exhausted . . . and she's eaten all manner of strange foods . . ."

"What else can I do?" he asked, then paused. "You only have to ask."

She shivered and rubbed the tops of her arms through her shift.

"Some coals for the brazier would help. It is cold in here."

"It's damned well freezing in here." He

searched the room and stalked back with the empty pierced-metal box. His voice filled with suppressed anger. "They didn't bring you coals for the night?"

Before she could answer, he was out the door and tromping down the steps. While he was gone, she located her cloak and pulled it around her, shivering.

"I'm sorry, Clemmie," she murmured, uncertain that her friend could understand. "I'm so very sorry I dragged you into all of this."

The earl returned with not only a brazier of coals, but a warming pan for the elder sister's feet. As Eloise tucked the warmer inside the blankets, he disappeared again and returned moments later with an additional candlestick and a low stool, insisting she sit rather than kneel on the cold floor.

"Thank you, Your Lordship." She settled onto the padded seat. For the first time since he had come to their rescue, she looked up, straight into his eyes. They were filled with genuine concern. The light flickered over his striking features, which seemed somehow different; not so much hard as strong, not so much arrogant as determined.

"Water," Mary Clematis said weakly.

"Oh, Clemmie." She came back to her patient with a start. "Are you all right? Where do you hurt?"

"Stomach . . ." she whispered with effort. "Water . . ."

The earl checked the table, where he found only an empty pitcher, and stalked out of the chamber, muttering furiously. A moment later, he was back with a pitcher of water and a cup, a metal basin, and several lengths of linen toweling. He poured water and helped Eloise lift Mary Clematis to drink.

"Time is the thing now," Eloise said, her voice hushed with anxiety. "If it is just a bit of bad food, we should know by morning."

"If it is of any comfort, the damned food didn't sit well with me either," he said, sinking onto one knee beside the cot.

She gave a wan smile, but then looked back at Mary Clematis's drained features and prayed that her sickness would quickly pass.

"I probably shouldn't have insisted she come. But she is a devoted sister of the order and always a source of wise counsel." She felt tears welling and looked down, hoping he wouldn't see. "No, she's more than that, she's my dearest friend. When I entered the convent she was my guide, my teacher, my elder sister. She helped me through Latin recitation . . . through setting the Psalter to memory . . . through Father Elias's religious instruction and Sister Mary Stephen's rules of conduct . . . through vigils on my knees and fasts and saints' days and feast days . . ." She tried to swallow the lump in her throat. "She was always there."

"At your back."

It seemed an odd thing to say, until she realized he had interpreted her experience through his own as a warrior.

"Yes, I suppose you could say that," she murmured.

She dared a glance at him and found him studying Mary Clematis with a thoughtful expression. His dark hair was tousled from sleep, he had a crease from bed linens on one cheek, and his eyes glinted darkly in the candlelight. He was clad simply in hose and an oversized shirt that was untied at the neck and revealed part of his muscular chest.

She had never encountered a man in so intimate a context before. Her first response was to distance herself and reestablish her role as his examiner. Her second and more compelling urge was to explore this rare opportunity and absorb all she could of this new experience, to let it inform and deepen her growing knowledge of him.

Her gaze slid down his nose, across his cheek, and circled back to fasten on his mouth. Bold, firmly bordered lips that until now had always seemed thinner and hard with resolve. Now, in the middle of the night, by the light of the candles, he seemed so much more approachable ... more accessible ... more intriguing. ...

Her breath caught and a flush of warmth bloomed in her face as she realized she was staring. She turned and leaned abruptly forward to check her patient, who seemed to be sleeping more restfully.

Peril watched her sudden movement and the way her cloak slid down her shoulders to unveil that torrent of unruly gold-kissed hair, and his breath stopped. With every small motion she made, more of it appeared, until she reached for the basin on the floor beside the bed and dipped a piece of clean linen in it to wipe her friend's face. As she rose slightly, one side of her hair slid from her shoulder and hung between him and the candle on the nearby table. The light infused those strands, setting it aflame. It was once again living fire. And when she drew back from the bed and matter-of-factly seized that lock and tossed it back, part of it tumbled onto the hand resting on his knee.

Which came first — the curl of her hair

around his hand or the curl of his hand around that lock of hair — he couldn't say. But suddenly he was winding her hair around his fingers . . . stroking it with his thumb . . . mildly surprised that he wasn't burned by its silken heat. Then she felt a tug on that lock of hair.

He met her surprise and searched the depths of her dark-adjusted eyes, glimpsing the warmth and passion that lay behind the cool blue waters of her daylight gaze. He leaned toward her, memorizing each sensation, savoring the anticipation . . . holding her spellbound by the force of his own fascination. He sank his hands into the waves of liquid fire rippling down the sides of her head. It was pure and exhilarating sensation, a cloud of sensual heat that engulfed his perception. He moaned softly and closed the distance between them.

Her mouth neither resisted nor yielded to his. It was as if shock prevented her from responding to her own perceptions. He gentled the pressure of his lips on hers and began coaxing, kneading, teasing . . . showing her a range of sensation and pleasure. And she began to respond.

Tentatively at first, she tilted her face to complement his and lifted her chin, seeking him, then joining with him in a bone-melting kiss. He dragged his hands through her hair, filling them to overflowing with that sensory feast, and then abruptly pulled her from the stool onto her knees, facing him.

But the jolt of her knees against the floor was too sharp a sensation. It jarred her back to her senses and back to her customary sound reason — in which kisses were not expected, not desired, and not allowed.

She jerked her chin back, shoved against his shoulders, and, when she was free, scrambled back up onto her stool. Then, still reeling, her eyes widening with horror at the recognition of what had just transpired, she jumped up and staggered back enough to put the stool and Clemmie's sickbed between them. Kissed. He had kissed her, and — the Devil take him — she had let him!

He was on his feet in a single movement, staring fiercely at her, his face dusky, his eyes dark with the passions he was struggling to master. Then, before her eyes, a new passion emerged to narrow his eyes and clench his hands into fists.

Under his narrowing glare she realized she wore her only bare shift and wrapped her arms protectively around her middle. Her throat tightened, forbidding speech.

But he quickly backed out of the chamber and swung the heavy door shut with a thud.

When she could gather breath, she clasped her heart and felt it hammering as if she'd run a race. And indeed she had. A race against the lush and destructive temptations of the flesh! She covered her burning cheeks with her icy hands. A race against the wicked maneuvering of a desperate and unscrupulous man. A man who would kiss and importune a woman under his protection, intending to persuade her to concede her office, if not her honor, to his callous desires.

She had been warned in the convent about the workings of the world and about the way men of power would use every foul device to secure their ends. But she had not believed until now that the earl of Whitmore was one of them.

Peril stood on the landing for a moment, staring at that heavy wooden door, feeling molten and volatile and utterly bewildered by his own behavior. What the hell was he thinking — sinking his hands into her unbound hair and kissing her?

He stumbled back into his chamber across the landing, slammed the door, and stared at it as if he feared two sets of ironbound oak and a world of prohibitions might not be enough of a barrier between them . . . at least between him and his own unthinkable fascination with her.

But was it *her* he found so enthralling, or just *her hair?* He wobbled to his great wooden bed and began to once more shed his boots and shirt. Twice now that stunning fall of hair had become his own personal burning bush . . . seizing his senses and bringing him to his knees before the revelation of his own carnal nature and his dangerous susceptibility to the tempter's snare. He shook his head to clear it, then snorted with disgust at his reversion to Basset's admonitions on the soul-sullying lure of the flesh.

The tempter's snare indeed. More like the *tester's* snare.

He halted in the midst of peeling off his hose and began to tense from his scalp all the way to his feet. She was the husband judge, the one who knew men: their strengths and most especially their weaknesses.

He had walked right into her little test . . . using her companion's "illness" and her own female attributes to test his integrity and moral fiber. Diabolical female. Until now he had no inkling that she herself might be part of the husband test. But what else could she be, with that ensorcelling banner

163

of hair that defied every churchly ban on womanly vanity?

He lay back on the bed with his hands behind his head, his body rigid. He might have failed her first test, but he was damned if he was going to fail another. Henceforth, the husband judge would find him anything but soft, unsuspecting, or susceptible.

Seven

Eloise kept her vow of going to the kitchens early the next morning. Mary Clematis had awakened at dawn with a clearer head and calmer stomach. After morning prayers, Eloise emerged from their chamber and paused on the landing across from what she supposed must be His Lordship's chamber. It probably ranked as a minor miracle that the door's wooden planks didn't burst into flames as she stared at them. Continuing downstairs with the intent of ordering her companion some Flemish broth, she paused for a moment in the great hall.

Reminders of a night ill-spent were draped over the planking tables and slumped against the walls on benches . . . still wearing their best tunics and hose and snoring loudly. A sour smell emanated from the far end of the hall, but she doubted that the earl's men were too ill to remove to their usual sleeping quarters. They had simply continued to celebrate their homecoming long after she and Mary Clematis retired. She scowled as she noted that the bowls, platters, and trenchers from the night before were still present as well. Shaking her head, she spotted a set of stairs on the far side of the great hall, leading downward.

The reason for the continued disarray in the hall was suggested by the several bodies sleeping on mats of straw along the sides of the steps. The house servants were still abed as well. It was past time for Tierce; half the day was gone and they had not yet roused. Where was the housekeeper, Madame Fleur-pot? Where were the steward and the cook? And was His High-and-mighty Lordship still abed as well?

As it happened, Peril had been up and about since dawn and was now standing in the stable door between his horse-master and his head plowman, holding a fistfull of each one's shirt and struggling to keep them from seizing each other by the throat.

"Dammit — stop this — the both of you!" he thundered as he strained to hold them apart.

"I won't give up a single one o' my horses to pull no plow," the horse-master declared, swinging at the farmer but reaching only air.

"I have to have good, strong animals t' pull them iron-edged shares. If'n I don't, all yer fancy horseflesh'll starve, come winter!" The plowman lunged and swung frantically at his opponent, eager to demonstrate that a plowman's fist would have the same impact on a nose as a stableman's.

"Then get somethin' fittin' for a dumb farmer," the horse-master sneered "Get an *ox!*"

It was Peril's fist that landed the first blow — on the horse-master's jaw. As the farmer eagerly sprang to finish what his lord had started, he ran into the earl's other fist and went sprawling.

"You!" Peril ordered one of the stable-boys. "Bring me a rope! A long one."

With a bit of help and the threat of a second blow, he dragged his groggy horse-master and head plowman together so that they were sitting on the ground, back to back. Then he bound them together with a long coil of rope, and stationed a water bucket and a stable-boy beside them.

"Give them water whenever they ask for it," he ordered, keenly aware of workers from both stable and field standing nearby, watching dubiously. He leaned down and whispered into the stable-boy's ear, "And come and get me when one of them has to piss."

The boy frowned, then widened his eyes and nodded with a grin. Peril ruffled his hay-mop of a head, then strode off toward the great hall. It had worked when there was conflict between soldiers on campaign; there was no reason such a tactic shouldn't work here as well.

If only he could use it on the husband judge. . . .

He was greeted in the antechamber of the hall by one of the older house women, Milla, who said he was urgently needed in the kitchens.

"Go find the madame," he responded.

"She's there, milord."

"Then what are you troubling me for?"

"I mean *she's* there." Milla gave him a meaningful look, crossed herself and clasped her hands as if in prayer. He knew instantly the identity of the person those motions identified.

Her. In his kitchens. He groaned and rubbed his neck, anticipating the pain that was about to strike it.

There she stood, when he arrived, in the midst of the cooking chamber, her arms folded and her countenance stormy. Before her in a determined phalanx stood the aged head cook, Ethel, backed by her two bare-armed assistants, Tweet and Hessie. A number of young girls and small boys were collected just outside the open fourth wall of the chamber, peering in through the smoke and steam. And two much older women sat culling dried beans, their attention riveted on what was happening between the nun and the cooks.

"What in the Devil is going on here?" he demanded irritably. But even with fair warning, he was unprepared for the full force of Sister Eloise's disapproval when she turned on him.

"I simply said the soup was already burned and they might as well toss it out and start over. No use throwing good food after bad and making people sick in the bargain." She strode past the sputtering cooks to the huge black iron kettle hanging from a hook over a roaring fire, grabbed an iron ladle, and scooped some of its contents. "See for yourself."

He strode over to take the ladle from her and sample the day's stew. Before it reached halfway to his nose, much less his mouth, he smelled the acrid, burned-fish smell and spotted the flakes of blackened who-knew-what floating on top of the murky liquid. In a stubborn good-faith gesture to his cooks, he made himself taste. It was like fishy-smelling pitch. He refused to gag; he would not give *her* that satisfaction.

"Not" — he glanced at his trio of cooks — "one of their best efforts."

"Not" — her glare could have boiled the grease from goose feathers — "even palatable. Furthermore, half of the foods from your root cellar are spoiled. Your beans and lentils are full of weevils, and something's gone wrong with your leaven." She raised her chin. "Your wooden trenchers are half rotted, your cups are befouled by layers of grime, and your bowls and spoons all need replacing. But worst of all" — she stalked closer, her eyes narrowed in disgust — "not one person in your kitchen has the faintest notion of how to make a Flemish broth."

He looked to his cook Ethel, who shrugged. Tweet and Hessie scowled and copied that fateful motion. Heads wagged all around the kitchen as he looked from one person to another. Red-faced, he turned back to his inquisitor.

"What is so special about a damned 'Flemish broth,' anyway?"

"It settles the stomach and assists healing. It is indispensable in a proper household."

"We've gotten along fine without it."

"Fine?" Her voice and eyebrows rose as she gestured to the dilapidated kitchen around them.

"Very well." He crossed his arms. "Then show us how it's done."

It was a challenge she dreaded, never

having actually made Flemish broth herself. But she had to show his high-and-mightiness that she was competent at more than just being a critic, or risk losing whatever respect she commanded.

"Eggs," she demanded, turning to the cooks. "*Fresh* ones."

It was something of a challenge for the cooks to come up with the things she required, including a clean pot of clear water and a bit of white wine that hadn't gone bad. Then the challenge was hers: to crack the eggs and beat the whites until they were like sea foam, to then add a trickle of wine in just the proper proportions . . . drizzle the mixture into heated water over the fire, stirring all the while . . . taste and add salt and sugar in just the right amount. She held her breath, praying that it wouldn't clump or curdle and that she hadn't used too much wine.

Soon it was poured, perfectly blended and nourishing, into a clean bowl and set with a clean metal spoon upon a tray draped with a bit of clean linen.

"That, sir, is a proper Flemish broth," she declared, regarding it with no small pride. It was her first independent culinary feat.

He pushed off from the table he leaned against and strode over to stick a finger into the bowl and then into his mouth. His dubious expression faltered.

"How are we to know how it should taste?" he demanded.

She looked up into his face and watched the centers of his eyes darken as he dipped his finger in the bowl a second time and sucked the broth from it.

"Is it warm and slightly sweet and easy to swallow?" she asked.

"*Some* might consider it so." At that moment Peril was finding it difficult to swallow at all. Those blue eyes staring up at him . . . that soft skin . . . those rosy lips caressing every word . . .

"It has nourishing ingredients and is soft and comforting on the palate," she said, her voice oddly breathy, "which, of course, is the essence of a healing food."

Something in the way she said the words "soft and comforting" sent a tremor of excitement through the skin of his belly. Then a flash of light streaked through and heated his thoughts . . . the shimmer of candle flame in a torrent of red-gold hair . . . His entire body flushed with heat.

Her eyes widened and she stepped back.

"The benefits are doubled when earnest prayers are stirred in during the making," she said crisply. Then with cheeks reddened and back rigid, she picked up the tray and hurried for the steps.

He stared after her as that prim reminder of her identity and her first allegiance doused his hot response. *Prayers.* Of all things. What the Devil was the matter with him, letting her invade his thoughts and responses like that? Hadn't he learned anything last night?

Crimson-faced, he turned to Ethel and found her ready to burst with indignation.

"New trenchers, spoons, and bowls. See the woodcarver about them. And —" He picked up a greasy, fire-blackened wooden spoon and tossed it onto the packed earth floor. "— get rid of this filth." As he strode out, he turned back and pointed furiously at the cook and her minions. "And don't let me ever hear of you stirring prayers into my food!"

Mary Clematis was sleeping peacefully when Eloise left her later that morning, intent on inspecting the rest of the house. In truth, she needed to be alone for a while to purge her heart of the shame of her reaction to the earl. What was she thinking . . . letting him stand so close . . . looking up into his deep, tawny colored eyes . . . feeling her mouth water as she watched him lick the broth from his finger . . .

The burning in her face spilled over into her pride. Clearly, he was still plying her with his disgraceful carnal tricks, still hoping to sway her judgment and bend her to his will. She narrowed her eyes as she trudged along the path around the tower. If he thought she could be either lured or coerced with a few kisses, he had another think coming.

The stone structure that hugged the tower obviously had been intended for use as the main house of the manor. Inside, she discovered a number of chambers that included a lovely but ill-kept chapel. The beams that supported the chapel's arched ceiling were carved, and the walls were finished so finely that they appeared to be polished stone. Religious motifs involving vines and lilies and roses were carved into each stone corbel and all over the wooden panels framing the chancel. But weeds sprouted from between the floor's flagstones, and the chancel was completely bare of altar furnishings. Adding to the forlorn feel of the place was the layer of dust and cobwebs that coated all but one kneeler and the carved wooden cross at the front.

From there, she explored a number of well-constructed but sorely neglected chambers . . . two with large carved stone hearths, and one with a set of three matching glazed windows in a nook above a bench that commanded a fine view of the estate to the east and south. Then she came across a set of steps that mounted into the open air — and stopped as precipitously as the building itself, above a set of half-completed foundation walls.

Who had begun such a marvelous building and then stopped with so much already completed? There must have been a reversal of fortunes before the earl came home to take the title. If so, what had caused it?

She found her way outside and strolled purposefully around and through the nearby outbuildings and workhouses. There were several large storehouses, a dairy, a carding house for wool, attached to a generous weavers' house . . . a laundry, complete with vats for dyeing and bluing . . . a communal oven that appeared to be sound but was completely cold.

Disorder was everywhere; in each house, shed, and building. Tools were left strewn, exposed, and unmended; materials from wood to iron to bales of raw wool were stacked in careless piles edged with crust, rot, and rust; and rubbish littered the footpaths between buildings.

At length she came to the smithy, which was tended by two strapping but listless youths who were all but ignoring the fact that the fire in the raised brick hearth was almost dead.

"What's happened here?" she asked, fixing the pair with a disapproving look. "Where is your master?"

"Ailin'," one of the youths answered with a sullen curl to his lip.

"And why aren't you tending the hearth and working?"

They glanced at each other, then looked at her as if she must be a bit daft.

" 'E ain't told us what to do."

"Well, what was the last task he assigned you?"

"Poundin' iron flat," one answered, rubbing his sooty hands down begrimed breeches.

"Fer shoein' horses," the other added, gesturing to a pile of iron bars pounded unevenly and bent into crude curves.

"They were made apprentices just a few months ago," came a voice from behind her. When she turned, the earl was standing just under the roof of the smithy shed with his hands on his hips, looking very large and very annoyed. "They've not had time to master the art of making horseshoes."

"Nor of tending a fire, it seems," she said, folding her arms. "The coals are nearly out."

He strode to the hearth and scowled as he held his hand over its ash-covered contents to test her statement.

"The first tenet of smith work is that you must maintain a proper hearth and sufficient heat," she declared for the earl as much as the errant apprentices. "You must befriend the fire and bend it to your will before you can ever begin to bend the iron."

"And what would you know about *fire,* Sister?" the earl demanded, turning on her. "What would you know about heating a rod of iron until it is searing hot . . . pounding, stretching, shaping it . . . forcing that lump of cold, defiant metal to your will . . . sweating and straining to produce something of value?"

Every word seemed to be aimed at nerves just beneath her skin. Her face caught fire as he towered over her with eyes suddenly like hot Baltic amber . . . tantalizing her, testing her . . . making her recall the heat that had risen between them in the darkness . . . making her face the heat that even now was rising in her.

"I — I —" She stumbled backward and

was stopped by an anvil. She clenched her hands at her sides. "I've spent long hours in a smithy, learning what makes a proper forge. I know how most tools and household goods are made, and even how to patch armor."

He seized her hand and pried open her fingers to inspect her palm.

"But you've never plunged a rod of iron into glowing coals, yourself." His voice lowered to a pitch that vibrated her skin. "You've never wielded a hammer over and over, pounding the same stubborn piece of metal until your arms and back — your whole body aches. These hands" — he stroked her soft palm with his callused thumb and his words grew thick and velvety — "have never tamed a white-hot iron."

She suppressed a shiver and tugged her hand, but he refused to release it.

"The fact that I have never done a smith's labor does not mean I cannot judge the quality of a smith's efforts. A man is known by his work."

"So, Sister Judge, is a *woman*."

He relinquished her hand, this time, as she pulled it away. Her heart was pounding and her knees were quaking as she turned and strode from the smithy.

Cursed man. Every word he spoke

seemed stuffed with excess meaning. She pressed her icy fingers against her burning cheeks. How dare he presume to judge her? How dare he imply that because she hadn't done every task on the demesne that she couldn't know how they should be done? How dare he insinuate that because she hadn't instantly rebuffed his kiss, that she was somehow unfit to judge him?

Shamed by the feeling that she was fleeing him, she halted to take her bearings and spotted the weavers' house. Desperate to retreat into the familiar and comforting company of women, she headed for the building.

Peril watched her stride up the path and pause to look things over before entering the weavers' house. She was inspecting his home, bit by bit, passing judgment on him and his beleaguered holdings. Arrogant female . . . insisting she knew a right bit of ironwork when she saw it and declaring his forge a disaster . . . all while flashing those blue eyes at him, reminding him of his lapse of self-control last night.

Determined to confront and combat her disapproval, he struck off after her. When he stepped inside, he found her standing over his head weaver, Edythe of Lyon, quizzing the woman and her assistants on the work in progress there. She scowled when she spotted him in the doorway, and she strolled around the loom to examine the sagging braces, worn heddle, and crude treadle mechanism.

"It is remarkable," she said to Edythe, straightening, "that you manage to produce much of anything from such an aged loom."

"We used this loom since me great ma were a girl," Edythe said anxiously. "Ye get used to a thing's queer ways after a bit. Ye make do."

"A bit of wisdom that applies to more than just plying a shuttle back and forth," Eloise said evenly, strolling around to the front of the loom. "Even so, I am certain you could do better with a better loom."

"It looks fine to me," Peril declared, inserting himself between the women and looking over the cloth that was emerging on the loom. Dismay filled him as he spotted the tiny knots and threads that covered the heavy bit of weaving. He could feel her scrutinizing his reaction and savoring his chagrin. "I'm certain it will look better when it's . . . completed."

"You know nothing about weaving, do you, Your Lordship?"

He reddened. "I know enough to judge the hand of a velvet or the comfort of a tunic. That is all I need know."

She studied him for a moment with an arch look, then pulled him with her to the side of the loom. Her fingers traced the yarns wound onto the wooden header, then pointed out the various steps of the process.

"This yarn forms the weft, the basis and structure of the cloth. The yarns or threads that form the warp are tied to a shuttle and woven through the weft as the threads are lifted according to the pattern. Then they are joined . . . tightened . . . tamped into place with the heddle. It is a tedious and painstaking process."

She beckoned him to the back of the loom and pointed, ordering him down to peer through the loom at the underside of the cloth being made. Even in the dimness, he could see that it was devoid of the knots and excess threads and strings he had seen on the top.

"Weaving is much like life, Your Lordship . . . filled with twists and turns. The shuttle, like a human soul, flies back and forth, parting the cords of the weft as it carries the yarns, weaving in and out, unaware of the pattern it is making. Even the weaver sees only a partial image of the true weaving . . . one thread, one color or thickness of yarn at a time. And the quality and beauty of the cloth are not revealed until the weaving is completed and it is turned over."

She looked at him intently as she ran her fingers across the weft yarn as if it were a lute. Her blue eyes were darkened and her voice softened.

"That is why women make better weavers. They are used to working guided only by faith and hope, with an eye to the future. Cloth and children and homes . . . all are made by one pass of the shuttle at a time."

He realized he had drifted, leaned closer to her with every word. He could see the light reflected from deep in her gaze, could feel the moist heat of her breath stirring the air around him. With a turn of thought he could almost feel those slim, delicate fingers dragging across the skin of his chest. He swallowed hard, watching those lips speak of weaving . . . in and out . . . parting the cords . . . joining . . . tightening . . . Then those rosy lips pronounced the one word that could halt his warming thoughts midstream.

"Just like a marriage," she said, "which also is made one day, one bit of trust, one gift of sharing at a time. You would do well to remember that."

He froze, feeling an alarming chill creeping over him. What the Devil was he doing? Watching her intently, listening to her lulling voice, staring into her eyes . . . plodding straight into her trap?

God's teeth, these nuns were a conniving lot!

"There is another lesson here, Sister Judge," he said, his jaw hardening so that he spoke through clenched teeth. "You cannot fairly judge the worth of a cloth if you insist on looking only at its *wrong* side."

He shoved to his feet and strode out, leaving her to rise and smooth her skirts and exit the weavers' house with her face burning.

Wretched man. Disparaging her fairness and objectivity even as he sought at every opportunity to sway them. Well, she wasn't the one being tested here; he was. And until she saw considerably more evidence of his capability, his industry, and especially his integrity, she would never recommend the abbess send him a bride. Not even the spoiled and haughty Alaina.

She continued her walk through the outbuildings, letting her annoyance fade as she sought out and stored impressions of Whitmore's suitability as a home. Sadly, the manor sank dismally against every standard she applied. It would take years to bring the place back to its previous glory . . . months to make it merely functional again.

Spotting the stables over the brow of the rise, she headed for them. As she hoped, the stables were in much better condition than the rest of Whitmore. There also seemed to be more activity in that area, or at least more people, for no one seemed to be doing much of anything. It was as if they were all waiting, watching for something. Then she came to the edge of the wooden corrals and the main stable door, in front of which two men were seated on the ground and tied firmly back to back. Beside them on the ground were a bucket and dipper and a young boy sitting on his heels, watching expectantly between them.

"What on earth has happened here?" she asked some of the people standing with their arms folded or leaning on a broom, rake, or curd paddle. "Are these men thieves or poachers?" One by one, each person or group she approached lowered their heads and stepped back, unwilling to explain. She went straight to the heart of the situation and demanded an explanation of the men themselves. They were so far sunken into stubbornness or misery that neither responded. The boy, however, responded to her question of who had tied them up together.

" 'Is Lordship."

"This isn't even a proper set of stocks." She was beginning to feel she was the only sound-witted soul on the manor. "How long are they sentenced to stay like this?" The lad just shrugged. "How long have they been here?" Another shrug.

She turned to the men propped against the nearby corral fence.

"If you cannot or will not speak, then be so good as to loosen that rope so that they may at least breathe properly." They stared at her anxiously, but not one man moved to obey. Her frustration mounted.

"Where is His Lordship now?"

"Right here," came his irritable voice from behind her. She whirled and found the earl striding down the slope from the main house with determination resounding in each footstep.

"What is the meaning of this?" She indicated the two men on the ground and braced for a confrontation. He continued storming toward her until she thought he meant to run her over, but he halted a hair's breadth short of her hem.

"This is the means to end a problem I do not intend to suffer ever again."

"What sort of problem?" she demanded. "Poaching? Thieving? Short-weighting? Drunkenness? If the latter is the charge, then every man in your garrison should be sitting in a courtyard wearing a coil of rope."

"A problem that does not need your attention or *interference*. I shall see you in the hall. Later."

He was dismissing her as if she were a troublesome servant. She drew herself up straight and looked him in the eye.

"May I remind you —"

"I need no reminder of your place here, Sister." He leaned to within an inch of her nose. "But perhaps *you* do."

Flushing crimson, she stepped around him, jammed her hands up her sleeves, and stalked toward the great hall. She hadn't fallen for his despicable bit of cozening last night or this morning, and now he intended to make her pay for it. Well, they would see who —

She was nearly bowled off the path by several of the earl's men rushing from the hall to the stable-yard. They looked newly wakened, donning tunics and belts and raking back recently wetted hair.

"Sister!" Michael of Dunneault caught and steadied her. "Begging your pardon. We just heard that the earl —" He looked past her to the scene in the stable yard and a grin nearly split his broad, genial face. "It's true,

186

then. And it looks like we're in time for a few good wagers."

"Three deniers says the plowman goes first," Sir Ethan declared.

"The Devil he will. Five says the horseman has a bladder like a titmouse's," Pascoe countered.

There was raucous laughter, which sobered markedly when they noticed the astonishment on her face. "Sorry, Sister," Pascoe said, lowering his head.

"You're wagering on . . . I . . . I don't think I understand," she said, looking from Pascoe to Sir Ethan to Sir Michael as several others slipped past them on the path to continue to the stable-yard.

"It's an old soldiers' tactic, Sister," Sir Simon explained as he looked past her to the men bound back to back. "Men in battle must be able to depend on each other. If there is deep conflict between two men, a commander has been known to tie them back to back, on their arses, and give them plenty of water. And if they are to avoid wetting themselves, they must help each other stand and move. They learn the hard way to put aside their differences and work together."

"And those two men?" She glanced back at them and at the earl standing over them with crossed arms, waiting with ruthless patience.

"Our horse-master and the earl's head plowman," Michael put in. "If I had to guess, I'd say somebody needs horses and somebody won't give them up."

She murmured thanks as she struck off again for the hall. But just before reaching the kitchens, she paused and looked back to the stable-yard, where bets were being placed enthusiastically and just possibly a lesson was being taught. She scowled. A rather crude bit of teaching . . . a man's sort of lesson. But she could see that it would likely be an effective one. And, played out before the entire populace of Whitmore, it might well prove instructive for more than just the two men involved.

Turning back and bracing to enter the hall through the hostile realm of the kitchens, she huffed irritably. Why hadn't he just told her what he was doing? Did he think her too simple to understand? Or did he just consider himself to be above having to explain his actions to anyone?

Accursed man. This was probably just the way he would treat his poor, unfortunate wife.

As she trudged up the winding steps to the tower chamber she shared with Mary

Clematis, she heard voices and scuffing sounds coming from above and raised her skirts and ran up the rest of the stairs. There on the top step sat Mary Clematis in her shift, with blankets wrapped around her. Her eyes were red and watery, her nose was swollen, and she leaned limply against the stone wall for support. But she had been on the mend . . .

"Clemmie, what's happened? Are you all right?" She flew to wrap her arms around her beleaguered friend, who nodded wearily.

"They're cleeding da chaber," Mary Clematis said through a blocked nose. "Th' dust an' such . . ."

Sure enough, as Eloise entered the room, she made out — through a prodigious cloud of dust — two women with brooms sweeping furiously.

"Stop!" she called, clapping a hand over her nose and mouth, refusing to breathe in. "What are you doing?"

They froze at the sight of her.

"You're just sweeping the dust and filth into the air so it can settle down again onto the floor and walls. Come out of here, this minute." She whirled and exited onto the landing, where she sucked a huge breath. When they didn't follow, she stuck her head

189

back into the chamber. "Did you hear?"

"Th' earl hisself sent us. Said fer us to clean," one ventured with a cough.

"He did, did he?" The dust had begun to settle, so she stepped back into the chamber and stood near the door. The women eyed her warily and edged closer together. "Well, if you don't do it properly, it will just be to do over."

"It'll be to do over anyways," one muttered, fingering her broom handle. "This place won't never be clean."

"This were *her* chamber," the other said in a voice just above a whisper, with a wary look around. "Her what caused it all. The curse."

"Curse?"

They shushed her frantically, hurried across the chamber, and pulled her out the door. They muttered apologies as they brushed dust from her habit.

"What curse?" she asked.

"Hush, Faye," one warned the other.

"She'll learn sooner 'r later, Milla," the one called Faye said irritably.

"Not from me," Milla said stubbornly, clamping her lips together.

Faye jerked a thumb over her shoulder toward the open door. "That were 'is mother's chamber. Her what caused it all by marryin' 'Is Lordship's father. If she hadn't married 'im, he might 'ave wedded Mistress Ann an' she wouldn'ta cursed the land an' folk."

"Not sayin' we blame 'er . . . Mistress Ann," Milla put in, eager to be a part of the tale now that it was out. "A right fine woman. An' breedin' in secret with the old lord's babe. He went an' got himself a rich, fancy bride" — she glanced with disdain at the unfinished tower — "fer money to build 'is fancy castle."

"Made her fit to tie, Mistress Ann," Faye continued. "One stormy night . . . her big with child . . . she come to the castle to see 'im and tell him about his babe. And his wife, that wicked French witch, made 'im turn her away."

"Her bearin' his babe and he wouldn't even see her."

"Broke 'er heart." Faye nodded vigorously. "That's when she done it."

"Laid on the curse," Milla clarified, then paused to recall it from memory. " 'Until love means more than money, until a bride filled with the highest virtue holds the keys to this wretched house . . . nothing will grow, nothing will prosper, and nothing will ever be finished on Whitmore land.' "

They stared at her, waiting for a reaction, and when it came they were clearly disappointed.

"Well, curse or not, there are better ways to get the dust out of a chamber. Faye, go and fetch some very fine wood chips from the carpenter's shop and get some oil from the larder to make a sweeping mixture." When they just stared at her, confused, she gave the talkative Faye a nudge toward the stairs. "Go on." Then she turned to Milla. "And you . . . you'll need a bucket of water and vinegar and a good stout brush to get the bird lime off the floor and window ledge."

When the women were gone, she sank onto the step beside Mary Clematis, who had heard most of what was said.

"You dink it's drue? Dere's really a curse ober Widmore?" she asked, sniffing hard but taking in no air through her swollen nose.

"I have no earthly idea." Eloise clasped her hands and put them between her knees. "Curses are a grave business. The church takes them very seriously. They have special priests who —" She halted, her thoughts flying as she put one and one together and came up with two thousand. "That's why he wants a bride!" She straightened, her eyes searching the dimness of the stairwell even as her mind searched her experience. She grabbed Mary Clematis by the hands. "Remember I said that His Lordship felt bound to acquire a bride, but didn't really want one? There was more to his motive than just a sense of duty? I'll wager this is it. He doesn't want a bride, he wants a curse-breaker. 'A bride filled with the highest virtue' — he used those very words!"

Her elation at solving the puzzle of his attitude deflated quickly as the problem it posed became all too clear. If he wanted a bride as a curse-breaker, what sort of husband would he be? Would he marry a woman, install her in a dusty tower room, and forget about her? She thought of the maidens at the convent and imagined them, one by one, sitting in this pile of stones feeling overwhelmed and unwanted. It was a fate she wouldn't even wish on *Alaina*.

How dare he presume to apply to the Brides of Virtue for a bride that he intended to use and then neglect? The abbess had been wise indeed to send the husband judge instead of a bride home with him!

"Where are you going?" Mary Clematis called after her as she hurried down the stairs.

She retraced her steps, helped Mary Clematis to her feet, and ushered her down the stairs.

"I'll find someone to build you a fire in

the hall until they've finished cleaning the room," she said, her jaw setting with determination. "I've got to find Father Basset."

After considerable squirming and dissembling, Father Basset confirmed both the women's story and Eloise's worst suspicions. Peril of Whitmore sought a bride primarily to break the curse his late father's mistress had placed on the estate when she was overthrown in favor of a wealthy French bride. The earl had journeyed to their convent, using the last of his coin, because of the fine and virtuous reputation of their maiden wards . . . but also, Basset admitted, because none of the earl's acquaintances and neighbors — knowing his family's history and circumstance — would consider wedding a presentable daughter to him.

Refusing to be mollified by the priest's entreaties, she headed for the stable-yard to find the earl and render her verdict on both his ignoble intentions and his suit for a bride. The earl, however, was not in the stable-yard. He had been called away from the duel of the stubborn bladders to tend to some other urgent business. Just where, no one seemed to know.

Growing more irritable and indignant with every step, she strode through the rest of the walled area of the manor — past dilapidated animal pens, the large cow byre, the dairy badly in need of a whitewashing, the spring house, the granaries, the carpentry yard, the barns, the plow shed, the brewing house, and the armory — and could see nothing but negligence and decay. Witnessing such widespread blight made it easy to believe the place was under some sort of curse.

The few people she encountered as she went pulled their forelocks, mumbled something approximating respect, and shook their thickly thatched heads when asked their lord's whereabouts. Finally, an old lady seated by a cottage door, just outside the gates, mentioned that she had seen the lord race by on a horse a while past. Eloise thanked her and turned in the direction the old woman pointed, but found her sleeve caught fast in the old woman's hand.

"Pray fer me, Sister," the old woman entreated.

"Be assured that I will." Eloise turned again, but was stopped again by that grip on her sleeve. She looked back to find the old woman staring at her expectantly. "You mean, now?" The old girl grinned, baring toothless gums, and slid from her stool onto her knees with a grunt of discomfort. Eloise expelled a sigh and sank to her knees. She prayed for the old woman's soul and safe-keeping, and — upon prompting — for her aching bones and worthless husband, wher-ever he was, and dutiful son and grand-children.

"An fer 'Is Lardship," the old girl prompted just as Eloise was finishing.

"And for His Lordship the earl," she added to the prayer.

"That 'e find a good an' vir-tius wife."

Eloise looked up to find the old lady peeping at her through one heavy-lidded eye. It was not the prayer of her heart, but she told herself she could at least pass it along.

"That he find a virtuous bride."

"Like his mother . . . bless 'er soul."

"Like his mother . . . bless her soul." Eloise looked up. "His mother?"

"I were 'Is Lardship's nurse, many a year ago," the old woman whispered in an aside. "His mother were a fine and noble lady. French, true, an' a bit hot-tempered. But alwus good to the babe an' me." Then she lowered her head, indicating they should get back to the business at hand.

"An' pray 'Is Lardship come to peace . . . in his troubled heart an' in 'is poor, beset house," the old nurse said in rising and descending tones that hinted it might be her last supplication.

"His troubled heart?" Eloise echoed, glancing up and thinking that she wasn't even certain the man had one.

"Ahhh . . . poor lad." Another whispered aside. "Had naught but trouble since he come home. The curse, most likely. It weights heavy on 'im. He has a good heart, that boy. Jus' needs a proper vir-tius bride to put 'im right."

It would take a good bit more than one woman, however virtuous, to put the earl of Whitmore right, Eloise thought. But she bowed her head to comply with the old lady's wishes so that she could get on with her search.

"And may His Lordship come at last to peace in his heart and in his house," she said quickly, glancing up at the old woman, who nodded, pleased.

"Amen." Eloise stood and helped the old woman back onto her stool.

"That way." The old woman pointed toward the fields to the east. " 'E rode that way." When she lifted her skirt and started off, the old woman's voice called her back yet again.

"What now?" Eloise demanded. The old lady didn't seem to notice her shortness, but beckoned her over with an arthritic finger.

"This is fer the sister what's sick." She put something on Eloise's palm and bent Eloise's fingers around it. "A bone from the finger of Saint Peter hisself. It has a healin' way."

Surprised by the woman's claim, she opened her hand and looked down to find herself indeed holding a bone . . . a chicken bone. She looked up, thinking the old woman had lost her wits, but when she saw the hopeful expression in the woman's face, what came out of her mouth was: "Thank you, good mother. Sister Mary Clematis will cherish it as she treads the road back to health."

She was ready to screech when the old lady called her back yet again.

"Sister!"

"What?"

"Ye'll need a horse."

Eight

Everyone on Whitmore seemed to have gone a little mad, Peril thought to himself as he stood in the middle of a cart path between what should be oat fields, surrounded by a score of angry plowmen and sowers and his hotheaded bailiff. Why else would everyone required for spring planting be coming to blows with the very people with whom they most needed to work? Planting madness. Spring fever. If it didn't stop soon, he himself was likely to be its next victim.

"I told him not *this* field." His thin, choleric-looking bailiff, Hadric of Hyde, pointed emphatically here and yon. "*That* field is the one to plow — this one's for fallowing. You see, milord, how the lout refuses to listen!" He glared at the veteran plowman, Hugh of Often. "Clean the wax outta yer ears!"

"This one fallowed last year." Hugh leaned hard against Peril's restraining arm. "Anyone with two eyes can see th' old clover. Yon is the one needs fallowin'."

"It won't make no difference which ye plow and which ye leave," another plowman, Ned Alder, declared as he stretched out a hand filled with seed from the bag by his feet. "The seed's gone bad — molded and half rotted. It were stored in th' damp!" He was seconded by half a dozen workers with harrowing rakes in their hands, who also glared accusingly at Bailiff Hadric.

"An' whose job is it to mind th' seed, eh?" put in a third plowman standing nearby and holding the reins of a double hitch of oxen.

The men lunged at each other and Peril had to intervene fast to prevent blows from landing. He shoved the bailiff back, then turned on his plowmen with his body tensed and sword half drawn.

"Hold there or suffer!" he roared, feeling his limbs trembling with rising anger. "I'll have no more of this — do you hear? You have planting to do — all of you! And every day you waste with this sniping and brawling puts us all one day closer to a hungry winter!" He could see in their faces that his anger and his threatening gesture had an effect.

"I stored that seed grain proper, milord!" Hadric declared, straightening his tunic and glaring at the plowmen challenging his authority. "It was no fault of mine that the roof began t' leak. It was the damned cur—"

Peril's big hand closed on the neck of the bailiff's tunic, cutting off the rest of that word as well as much of the fellow's breath. He was yanked to within an inch of Peril's livid face.

"If you value your position, Hadric, as well as your hide, you'll take care never to utter that word again. Not in my presence, nor even outside of it." He gave the reedy bailiff a bit of a throttle. "Do you hear me? There is no damnable curse! There never has been!"

"Yea, m-milord," Hadric sputtered.

"Your Lordship," came a voice from above and behind him that blended so completely with the bailiff's whine that it was almost indistinguishable. It was only when Eloise repeated, more forcefully, "Your Lordship, I would have a word with you . . . about this 'curse' of yours," that he released the bailiff and turned.

There she sat, erect on her swaybacked old horse, her black veil moving softly in the breeze, and her eyes as hard and blue as deep winter ice. God's holy knees. The damnable curse. She knew about it.

"This is not the time." He jerked a desperate breath in hopes of restarting his heart. "Can't you see that I am busy, woman?"

"I would say this is the perfect time, since, unless I am mistaken, you are dealing with the effects of this wretched 'curse' right now."

Every person present had a opinion on that and expressed it instantly and at the top of their all-too-healthy lungs. The resulting burst of noise startled even the stoic oxen waiting nearby, who took off across the field dragging a plow, while several young boys ran after them yelling. The bailiff and plowmen were suddenly nose to nose again, pushing and ready to trade blows. As he tried to separate them, Peril looked up to see Eloise's mouth moving and her expression scornful as she took in the chaos.

"Milord, help! We need help!" came frantic voices from the path leading from the village. Even through the tumult around him, he heard enough to make him listen harder. He moved to intercept them . . . a man and a woman, cottagers from the village outside the gates.

Panting from running, they pushed through the arguing workers to reach him and he caught the woman just as she collapsed.

"Please, Yer Lordship — my boy — he's gone!" she said, grasping his sleeves as she sank to her knees.

"Samuel, milord." The man dragged his cap from his head and recovered breath enough to speak. "I keep yer bees. Me an' my boy was out settin' beekeps at th' edge of the west fields. We saw some bees an' followed 'em to see if there was a honey tree. I got busy an' when I looked up, he was gone. I called and called . . . my woman Dora an' me looked everwhere." The man's face twisted with the effort of containing his grief. "He's a good boy, milord. Our Tad's never been no trouble."

"Help us, milord," Dora choked out through her sobs.

Peril felt his blood draining toward his feet. Again. Another one. He wasn't quite aware of the sudden silence until he looked up from the couple and heard his own thoughts expressed aloud.

"Jus' like Ellis's boy," someone said with horror. "And Molly Bane's before that."

"Took by wolves," came another frightened opinion.

"Or spirits," said yet another.

"Please, milord, please . . ." The anguished mother clung to him, sobbing.

He felt as if someone had driven a stake in his gut. Anger, outrage, fury — no reaction would be strong enough to vent the misery flowing from the woman's breaking heart into his own. It was now, as when Ellis the Tanner's boy disappeared three months past, that he himself fell prey to the vile superstition that had wrecked his father's life and now threatened to destroy his own. Nothing — no disappearance of sheep or spoilage of seed or failure of crops, not even a decimating plague of hail — had been able to make him doubt his desperately held reason and trusted skepticism. But then his people's children began to disappear . . .

"Hadric!" Peril grabbed the bailiff's arm and ordered, "Go to the stables. Tell Sir Michael and Sir Simon to mount up and bring every available man to the west edge of the fields." He pushed the bailiff to send him on his way, and then turned to Samuel. "Show me where he disappeared."

Refusing to look at the still mounted Eloise, he grabbed his horse's reins and strode with the distraught beekeeper down the cart path toward the west fields. The plowmen and sowers hurried along after him, anxious to see what would happen but wary of setting off into the woods themselves. Samuel showed him the place and, after a brief search for tracks at the edge of the forest, Peril was somewhat relieved to say that there was no evidence of wolves. Then he looked up at the manor and caught sight of Eloise, watching from nearby.

"If I wait for them, I'll waste daylight." He checked the position of the sun and then the edge of the still-bare forest and made his decision. "I'm going ahead. Tell Sir Michael and the others, when they arrive, that I've gone straight in at this point. They're to take forty-yard intervals and move straight in, keeping within calling distance of each other. Can you do that?"

Samuel nodded. In a flash, Peril had mounted his horse and was pointing to the ground behind him. "Right here, Samuel. Start from right here."

The grieving father nodded and he managed a look at the mother.

"We'll find him. Don't worry."

He plunged into the tall grass at the edge of the trees and did as he said he would — forged straight ahead into the thickening stand of forest. With a habit born of old, he pared away the perception of expected sounds — the swish of small branches and the muffled thuds of his mount's hooves on the cold, moist earth — and set his hearing to detect noises from outside his immediate vicinity.

He wasn't very far into the forest when he heard movement off to his right and raised higher in his saddle, straining to see through the twiggy, gray undergrowth. Dammit! Michael and his men knew better than to make that much noise. Then his entire body tightened at an unmistakable flash of black and white moving through the trees about forty yards off.

"You!" he shouted, glancing desperately around to mark his location, then turning his mount perpendicular to his course in order to intercept her. "What the Devil do you think you are doing?" He crashed through the whiplike branches of old undergrowth to plant himself across her path.

"Helping you search for the boy," she declared, raising her chin.

"The hell you are," he snapped. "I've got a lost child — I don't need a lost nun as well. Turn that horse around and go back the way you came." Then he managed to pull his anger under control. "If you're so damned set on doing something, go say a few of your prayers. Or if you really want to be useful, go comfort the boy's mother."

"I've already sent up a flight of prayers, thank you. Now move out of the way. We're wasting daylight."

"I'll not be responsible —"

"Two pairs of eyes are better than one. And who said you were responsible for me?"

"I did."

In that moment, in the winter-weary gray of a still-slumbering forest, Eloise saw the strain in his face and both heard and felt some part of the weight of responsibility he carried on his shoulders. For the first time, she truly understood that his constant orders and determined command of his surroundings involved more than just male pride. She had seen the devastation in his face as the woman clung to him and pleaded for help in finding her son. She had watched the bleakness that was unmasked in his soul when he was reminded that other children had disappeared. He truly cared for these people. His people. Something in the middle of her chest began to soften.

"Well, you needn't fear for me," she said calmly. "I will be forty yards on your right with my eyes peeled and ears alert. I will be nothing but helpful. Think of me as . . . your right hand."

He shifted in his saddle, glowering, torn visibly between his desire to be rid of her and his desire to get on with the search. As she hoped, the boy's plight took precedence.

"All right, dammit. But if you get lost, I won't come looking for you until after I've found the boy." He reined off and plowed back through the underbrush to the area he had abandoned earlier. But as they moved deeper into the forest, he kept looking her direction, checking to see if she was still there.

Determined to be a help and not a burden, she began to call for the boy and then pause to listen for a response. He must have sensed that her calls were as much to reassure him of her whereabouts as to help locate the boy, for when he paused to spot her through the trees, he had relaxed enough to acknowledge her with a nod.

As the forest grew denser and the going harder, she found herself forced by a ridge of rock outcropping to veer left and move closer to his course.

"Is there a place hereabouts where boys might come to hide or idle away hours?" she called. "A special stand of trees, a cave, a brook?"

"I have no idea," he responded sharply.

"But surely when you were a child here —"

"I never lived here as a boy. I was fostered early." There was a pause before he continued in a less strident tone: "I had not returned here until two years ago, when my father died and I inherited."

"Never?" She was genuinely surprised.

"Never." He spurred his mount and surged ahead for a time.

She thought of the emotion in his face as

he learned of the boy's disappearance and laid down orders for a search. He seemed to take it so personally. She would have thought he had lived here all his life and was devoted to the welfare of these people. Did he truly care about them, or was it just that he hated the idea of losing something that belonged to him?

"Is it true that this isn't the first time a child has disappeared?" she called as she worked her way closer to him. There was a noticeable pause.

"Yes."

"How many are missing?"

"Three, now. One just over a year ago. We searched everywhere, thinking he might have been taken by thieves or gypsies . . . or wolves. We found no trace. Not even bones. Then it happened again, just three months ago."

"What do you think happened to them?"

"It's not the damned curse, if that's what you're asking."

"You don't think there is a curse?"

"What I think doesn't matter. At least not to them." He reined up and waved a hand behind him to indicate the people of Whitmore. "They're convinced that every little thing that goes wrong on Whitmore land is a part of some great evil visited upon them by a scorned woman's anger. One woman. How could words uttered by one woman more than a score of years ago be responsible for so much misunderstanding and misfortune?" He shook his head, his features hard with frustration. "I don't believe it."

"If you don't believe it, then why did you come to our convent seeking a bride filled with 'the highest virtue'?"

He looked over, his eyes hard and defensive. But after assessing the earnestness in her expression, he eased in the saddle.

"They need a bride . . . a woman . . . a lady to give them hope. For if I have learned anything in my rootless, battle-scarred life, it is that if you think you're defeated, you're defeated."

He spurred his mount and plunged straight ahead, driving deeper into the forest to search for the boy. But his words stayed with her. "To give them hope . . . rootless, battle-scarred life . . . if you think you're defeated. . . ." Once again, he applied to his life at Whitmore lessons that his life as a soldier had taught him. It seemed an odd fit at first, but as she thought more about it, she realized that wisdom — however, wherever gained — was wisdom. And the very essence of wisdom was to be able to apply one's learning from one situation to another.

He truly wanted the bride . . . not for himself, but for his people.

A wave of warmth and insight washed over her.

There was more to the earl of Whitmore than she had thought.

Darkness now tinged the sky overhead and cold shadows lengthened, stealing light and warmth from the increasingly gloomy forest. Again and again they had heard leaves rustle and twigs crunch, but were always disappointed to find only small animal tracks or diggings around a winter burrow or a small stash of nuts. They called again and again for the boy. Their voices echoed eerily off the hard, bare trunks of trees and came back empty.

Then suddenly, ahead of them something started and raced headlong through the trees ahead of the earl's horse. Out of habit, he spurred his horse and went after it. Eloise tried to keep up, but had to settle for following the trail he blazed through a stand of snags and younger saplings. A blur of something dark darted in and out of the shadows. As she urged her old horse to an ungainly trot, she heard a furious squeal as the creature fled and realized it was a boar. Disappointed, she slowed Sir Arthur to a walk and fastened her attention on the place in the distance where Peril had disappeared between the trees.

She hadn't realized just how damp and chilled the air was growing until the moment the earl had ridden out of sight, and in the next breath she heard an ominous grunt from nearby. Coming to attention, she searched the shadows and weedy underbrush off to the right. But her heart didn't start to race until Sir Arthur, the least excitable horse in the kingdom, picked up his ears and feet and began to prance anxiously. There was another grunt to her right and suddenly an answering one on her left. Boars! More than one of them!

Scanning the shadows, she glimpsed one closing in on her — yellow tusks protruding from a piglike snout, vacant black eyes, and a large porcine body with ribs prominent. After the long winter, foraging was poor and the beasts were ravenous. Hungry boars, she recalled the workers on the convent lands had said, took chances with anything on foot . . . including horses and men.

She kicked the nervous Sir Arthur into motion and kept banging him with her heels until he reached a full gallop. Over the pounding of his hooves and the rasp of her own panicky breaths, she heard the snapping of twigs and the thrashing of under-brush to both the right and the left. Grunts and squeals of outrage seemed to come from all directions as the beasts gave chase. She had no time to think of what might happen when she reached the earl — if indeed she could find him. Her overpowering instinct was that her only safety lay with him and his battle-quickened responses.

Suddenly, through the trees, she glimpsed a flash of pale gray and blue . . . his horse and tunic. She screamed his name.

"Lord Peril!"

She saw him turn briefly to locate her and knew that he must have seen that she was galloping full-tilt toward him. But he turned back to whatever had claimed his attention and suddenly dismounted.

"No! Don't!" she screamed. "Boars! Wild boars!"

Then, in a bizarre confluence of time and event, motion seemed to slow and actions became labored and larger than life. She was piercingly aware of Sir Arthur slowing . . . of the boars rushing in on both sides . . . of the earl on foot with his sword and dagger drawn. She spotted the boy and the boar in the same moment.

Panic gripped her throat as she realized that the two boars following her were now focused on the enraged squeals of the boar crouched between the earl and the boy clinging to a fallen trunk that had wedged at an angle between two narrowly spaced trees. The boy wasn't high enough to be completely safe from the boars and could climb no higher; there were no branches on the other trees low enough for him to reach.

Their only hope was for the earl to distract the beast or kill it. And it might have worked — until she arrived with two more beasts, each as large and hunger-crazed as the one he faced. She had led them straight to him. She watched in horror as the tusk-laden beasts that had chased her charged on into the small clearing. Peril of Whitmore was caught in the center of a deadly triangle.

He looked up and for one brief moment met her eyes with a look that was beyond eloquent. It was a compression of such pain and determination, such hope and duty, such recognition and acceptance . . . and yet a longing so intense that it seared through her paralysis and scored itself into her very heart.

"The boy — get the boy!" he called as the first boar rushed him. And there was no more breath to waste on words.

The cornered boar charged with a scream that was both unearthly and all too real. The earl dodged at the last minute, aiming a blow at the beast's neck as it passed. The blow glanced and the beast turned to charge again . . . but not before another had already bellowed and rushed in, tusks slashing. The boy wouldn't have stood a chance with one of the beasts. Peril of Whitmore, even with two blades and a lifetime of fighting experience, faced three.

The boy! Eloise ripped her gaze from the battle to locate him. He was crouched as far up as he could get on the leaning tree trunk, terrified and crying for help. With the boars focused on the earl, she might be able to circle around behind the boy and have him jump through the crux of the trees and into her arms. It was the only way, and she was the only one left to do it; the earl had ordered her — *trusted her* — to finish the rescue.

It seemed to take forever for Sir Arthur to pick his way through the brush surrounding the small clearing. "Tad! I'm coming to get you, around the back! Climb up between the trees and get ready to jump! Tad — listen to me!" She had to call several times before the boy began to respond. But as she reached the far side of the trees, she heard the aged trunk cracking ominously and saw that the end wedged between the trees was badly decayed and ready to break apart.

As she worked Sir Arthur through the brush — giving thanks for the trampling of his huge feet — she called to the boy, telling him how brave he was and that it would be all right. The earl was a great knight and a powerful fighter. . . . His mother would be so happy to see him. . . . He would have honey-sweetened wafers when they all reached home. . . .

The cracking, splintering sound came too early — she was too far away. She could only hold up her arms and yell, "Jump!" He hesitated, terrified. Then as the rotted wood gave way, he extended his arms to the trees on either side and managed a push that carried him beyond the falling trunk.

He hit her with enough force to knock her from Sir Arthur's back, and together they went tumbling through the leaf-bare undergrowth. In a heartbeat, she recovered her senses and scrambled to her feet. Pulling Tad up with her, she rushed for the horse and was halfway there when one of the boars found them.

A deafening silence descended. The grunts and bellows on the far side of the trees had abruptly stopped. There was no way to tell who had won the fight. But there was no doubt that, without weapons or a head start, she and the boy would never win this one. Facing the same decision the earl had made moments earlier, she thrust the boy behind her and backed toward Sir Arthur.

"Listen to me, Tad. When we reach the horse, I'll boost you up. The moment you hit the saddle, you grab hold and hang on. Do you hear?"

"Yea," came the boy's terror-constricted whisper.

It happened all at once. The boar pawed the ground, readying a charge. She whirled, scooped the boy up, and lifted him high enough to throw his legs over the saddle. Knowing she could never reach the stirrup in time, she gave the old horse a desperate smack on the rump and he bolted off through the trees.

She heard a porcine squeal and whirled, scrambling back at the sight of the boar bearing down on her. It would go for her legs — they crippled their larger prey with those tusks, she thought wildly. If you were out in the forest and came across a boar, she heard in her head, *climb* ... the boy had been right ... protect your legs ... maybe her skirts would —

There was a rush of movement, a glint of light in the deepening gloom, and then thrashing and heaving. It took her a moment to realize that the boar hadn't reached her — was, in fact, defending itself against the earl. He had leaped onto its back and was digging his dagger into it as it rolled and tried to scrape him off. Again and again the dagger flashed and the boar screamed. Then, suddenly, all was still.

Peril lay atop the last beast, panting for air, half blind with bloodlust and pain, and feeling a deep primal cry of survival welling up in him. They were dead and he was alive. He had taken them down, one by one. Fighting hand to hand, fang and claw, he had defended his land, his place, his kind. Staggering to his feet, he filled his lungs, threw back his head, and let out a cry that reverberated powerfully through the dark forest. At that moment he was pure element and impulse. His every breath was a bond with the pulse of nature itself. His every heartbeat was a prize won by his own strength and cunning.

Then he turned with his arms thrown wide and his victory cry on his lips . . . and looked straight into the widened eyes of the husband judge.

For a moment he just stared at her with his chest heaving. Then he lunged at her, snatched her off her feet, and whirled her around and around and around. She clung to him laughing, sobbing — it was hard to say which.

It was some moments before her demands that he put her down registered in his brain. He stopped, weaving drunkenly, dizzy with victory, and let her slide down his front. The astonishment in her face and the smear of red on the white of her wimple pulled him back down to reality with a crash. And the reality was he was alive and standing with his arms around her in a darkened, isolated forest . . . and he had never in his life wanted to kiss a woman so desperately or to love a woman so intensely.

His head lowered, but just as he neared his objective . . . it moved and sound came pouring out.

"You're bleeding, Your Lordship."

He halted, and after a moment, he glanced over at his shoulder where dirt and blood were ground together in a smear across his tunic. When he looked back at her, the moment and the unexpected intimacy were gone.

She pushed back and he let her go. Trembling but determined, she set about inspecting his arm and shoulder. His wounds were less than critical, she announced, pushing him to a seat on a log and ripping fabric from under her habit. Then, as he wiped the blood from his dagger on a tuft of dry weeds, she discovered another nasty gash on his left leg and tended and bound both injuries. She worked in silence, hands quaking, glancing up at him each time her fingers brushed against his damaged skin.

"The boy?" he asked, watching the shadows play over her features. When she glanced up, her eyes were glistening, and the tightness in his loins refused to subside.

"There wasn't time — I put him on my horse and sent him off."

Finished with his wounds, she got to her feet and looked off into the darkness, searching for his horse. As he pushed to his feet and tested his leg and arm, they heard movement around them, something approaching. He drew his dagger and stepped in front of her, scanning the dim outlines of the bare trees.

Out of the gloom a pale, hairy muzzle appeared, then huge hooves, and a swayed back with a small, crouched figure clinging to a saddle.

"It's him!" Eloise rushed to peel the boy from the saddle and he screamed and struggled as she dragged him into her arms. "Hush, now. You're safe. The earl has killed them all. He saved us, just as I said he would. Didn't I say he would?" The boy stopped fighting, and as the fact of his safety became real to him, he looked up at the earl and nodded through his tears. Then he threw his arms around her neck and wouldn't let go.

As Peril went to retrieve his horse, her image and her words lingered in his mind. *"He saved us . . . just as I said he would . . ."*

"There they are!" A familiar voice and the noise of a number of horses reached them just as they were preparing to mount up. The sight of Michael and Simon riding through the trees, accompanied by a dozen of his men, drained the tension from his bones. "Are you all right, milord?"

"Well enough. We found the boy," he called.

Pascoe and two others arrived with torches that threw a reassuring circle of light around them. The men spotted the injuries on his shoulder and leg and, a bit further away, the carcasses lying in the small clearing. Pascoe let out a whistle of admiration.

"See there!" He slapped his thigh with a laugh. "I told ye His Lordship didn't need no help!"

They came out of the forest to find a small

crowd of people keeping watch for them. The first cries of "Lights — in the trees!" and "It's them!" created a sudden and terrible silence. Pascoe and William of Wright went first, bearing torches, and Peril and Eloise followed them out into the smoky yellow light. Not a word was spoken as the people fastened their eyes on the blood-stained bandage on their lord's shoulder and only afterward turned their attention to Eloise, on whose lap the boy was nestled.

Gasps and exclamations of wonder moved slowly through the crowd as they stopped near the center of the gathering. The others parted to give the parents access, and Dora uttered a cry and ran toward the horses.

"He's back!" she shouted. "They found my Tad!"

Peril dismounted, and a hush fell over the watchers as he handed the boy to his mother and father. Then it was as if someone struck a match to pitch; the crowed ignited with shocked cheers and shouts of celebration. Tad was hugged and jostled and patted and squeezed, then borne about the gathering on his elated father's shoulders.

As word of the rescue spread, a joyous and growing procession wound its way up the rise and through the gates of the manor —

straight into the hall. Buckets and barrels of beer were brought and people hugged and toasted and drank and — when William of Wright took up his instrument — even danced for joy.

Mary Clematis wobbled down the stairs to see what the commotion was about and gasped at the sight of Eloise's bloodstained collar and veil. She nearly fainted before Eloise could assure her that she wasn't bleeding . . . that the lost child had been found . . . that His Lordship was responsible for the boy's rescue.

The story was recounted of three wild boars and the boy up a tree. When the earl refused to say anything about his part in the story, the folk turned to Eloise for details. She related what she knew of the earl's valiant fight, trying not to embellish or diminish the danger and his courage in facing it.

Peril listened to her scrupulously fair and carefully complimentary words with mild surprise. She obviously approved of what he had done . . . counted it in his favor that he had risked so much to rescue a child he scarcely knew. For the first time in a fortnight, he felt he had some hope of passing this husband test.

He found himself returning the compliment, mentioning the sister's cool head and stout heart in the face of great danger.

Eloise listened to the earl's glowing portrayal of her deeds with surprise. He recognized her effort and her willingness to sacrifice her comfort and safety for others, speaking without flattery or cozening praises as he credited her with true valor.

In response, she blushed and stammered, and his men laughed and teased that they'd never seen her speechless before.

Then Samuel and Dora brought their son forward in the midst of the celebration to give the earl thanks. Samuel bowed and Dora knelt to kiss his hand and, overcome with emotion, gave his knees an impulsive hug. Eloise watched with a curious, sweet pain in her chest as the earl nodded with true grace, ruffled Tad's hair, and smiled.

She had never seen such a smile. It was filled with pleasure, satisfaction, and perhaps a small bit of pride. Just as she was thinking that she had never imagined seeing him so handsome and so appealing — so *happy* — he looked over at her and caught her staring at him. She looked away, certain that every bit of the admiration budding in her heart was visible on her face.

Excusing herself from the table, she

headed for the stairs. The earl intercepted her.

"Sister . . . I wanted to . . . to thank you for your help."

"I was pleased to be of service, Your Lordship." She struggled to keep her gaze near his face but not on it. "It was you who saved the boy. And me as well. I should be thanking you."

"I always keep a vow." He paused and shifted his feet. "I don't know if you understand just how important this is — finding the child, celebrating together. It's the first truly good thing that's happened in a long while. My people need this. They need hope."

Something in the tenderness of his tone melted her resistance and she lifted her gaze to his. The warmth from his tawny eyes flowed through her emotions like summer honey. Thick and sweet, it clung to the walls of her heart. Deep in the core of her, hunger and yearning opened a door she hadn't known was there. Wanting. Need. Womanly desire.

She jerked her head aside, startled by the swelling intensity of these new feelings, and her gaze fell on Mary Clematis . . . not two feet past his lordship's shoulder. Surrounded by pristine black and white, Mary

225

Clematis's face was blotched with hives that were highlighted by the sudden paling of the skin around them.

The question *What in Heaven do you think you're doing?* was suddenly visible in Mary Clematis's eyes and piercing Eloise's heart.

Shame burst over Eloise, coloring her from head to toe. What the Devil *was* she doing? She was a nun . . . about to become a bride of Christ Himself!

"Saints preserve us!" she gasped, turning frantically to scan the hall for the earl's priest. "We haven't given proper thanks!"

Before two minutes went by, Eloise, Mary Clematis, and Father Basset were on their knees, pouring out to the Almighty the company's overwhelming gratitude, and Peril was standing by with folded arms, wondering sourly what it was about him that always seemed to drive women to their everlasting knees.

Nine

Father Basset's nose was not so deep in his wine cup that he failed to see the looks that passed between the earl and the husband judge just before the sister fell to her knees, demanding to be led in prayer. It was probably a bad sign. She wouldn't be the first sister to be beguiled and led astray by a powerful nobleman. Some of the princes of the Holy Church itself behaved as if the blessed sisters were little more than sanctified concubines. Shameful business all around, this lusting and panting and pining. He halted with the cup to his lips and lowered it to stare at the earl, whose spirits had taken a tumble when the husband judge withdrew from the celebration to her chambers.

There were possibilities here. He contemplated the situation for a time, then rose and wove his way through the revelry to his lord's side.

"You know, milord," he waved at the hall with his cup, "Sister Eloise is not overly impressed with your holdings."

The earl gored him with a glance sharpened by disdain for the obvious. But when he returned determinedly to his tankard, it was clear he was listening.

"And yet, she is not entirely unaware of your own fine *manly* qualities."

That raised one of the earl's eyebrows; it appeared that his wrath might not be far behind.

"It is often said, milord, that a man catcheth more flies with honey than with vinegar," Basset said.

"God's blessed knees, Basset — I'll strangle you with your own cassock if you don't quit flogging me with your damned proverbs," Peril growled, leaning forward. "If you have something to say . . . say it plain and be done with it!"

Basset swallowed hard and resisted the urge to cross himself.

"Perhaps if you were to use a bit of persuasion . . . befriend Sister Eloise . . . you might be able to convince her to help put your hall in order. She does have a wont for giving orders and managing matters. Perhaps if you were to entreat her assistance, she would not only help right your affairs and prepare for your bride, but would also count it a virtue on your part that you humbled yourself to ask."

Hope bloomed in the priest's heart for one brief moment as the earl continued to stare straight ahead. But it died an incendiary death a moment later when the earl banged his tankard down onto the table and scorched him with a preview of Hell's fire in a glare.

"Humble myself? Humble myself?" The earl shoved to his feet and stormed past Basset, knocking him onto his rear on a nearby bench.

The little priest reeled for a moment, then took a shaky breath of relief.

Overall, the earl had taken his suggestion rather well.

Courageous. Confident. Careful . . . as in, careful to abide by his given word. Oh, and compassionate. A most important attribute in a lord. Clever? Evidence was still being gathered on that one. Chaste?

Eloise quit counting, reddened, and lowered her fingers as she sat in the sunny window of the deserted chapel. Four virtues without a single qualm, one "uncertain" and one "highly doubtful." Was she making progress or was he?

She had risen early, stepped over the bodies and barrels littering the great hall, and walked the manor's walled precincts trying to clear her head and get herself and her mission back on the proper path. As the sun climbed the eastern sky, she sought out the solitude of the neglected chapel. What better place to remind herself of the hazards of abandoning her sacred duty?

Pious? *No.* Patient? *Not really.* Persevering? *Absolutely.*

Five virtues. She held up her fingers and studied them. One hand's worth of husbandly qualifications. How many virtues did it take to make a good husband, anyway? A reasonable husband? A passable husband? A dozen? Two dozen? Three?

But there were more than just virtues to be considered here. What weight should be given to things like manly vigor and handsomeness and a broad pair of shoulders that —

Eloise shifted abruptly on her windowsill and banished that thought.

What about things like conversation and consideration and delicacy of dining and person . . . manners? Proper manners had been on the list, she was sure of it! She scowled trying to recall exactly how he ate. All she seemed to remember was the way that his lips glistened when he —

She cleared her throat and crossed her arms irritably over her chest.

What about keeping a vow and protecting the weak and attending to his duties with diligence and care? *Honor.* He was certainly honorable in the face of danger. But what about in the face of temptation? He had kissed her and touched her, and in the woods had embraced her and almost —

She slid from the window and began to pace, feeling increasingly unsettled. Well, what about honesty? He told the truth. Usually. Eventually.

Why did he have to be so difficult and contradictory? Why couldn't he at least pretend to be eager to gain a bride and a lady wife? Whatever his private feelings, why couldn't he just be pleasant and courtly and show her his best side, as men were wont to do when courting a lady fair?

She stopped dead, struck motionless by the appalling realization that she was annoyed that he wasn't "courting" her. Her *opinion,* that is.

With a quick and guilty bow toward the cross hanging in the empty chancel, she fled the chapel and headed straight for the great hall to check on Mary Clematis and see if the rest of Whitmore had roused from the aftermath of its celebration. By the time she stood inside the doors of the great hall, staring at the few souls that were stirring and at the throng that still was not, the five fingers on which she had named the earl's virtues were curled into a fist at her side.

Something good had happened on Whitmore for a change, and just look at the difference it made. Instead of a score of fighting men sleeping off a head full of ale, they now had every blessed soul on the manor snoring drunkenly in the hall! She picked her way through the heaps of revelers and stomped up the steps to her chamber.

Mary Clematis was sitting wrapped in blankets with her feet on the brazier of coals. She looked up with reddened eyes and sneezed as Eloise entered.

"Feeling any better?"

Mary Clematis shook her head, and opened her blankets to display several well-scratched bites on her bare arm and neck. "I tink . . . dis new blanket dey brought me's got fleas."

Enough, Eloise told herself as she charged across the hall and banged furiously on the earl's chamber door, was enough. The place was a shambles. There were hounds that lived cleaner, more productive lives than this. When His Lordship didn't answer, she imagined him abed and snoring in blissful drunkenness, collected her nerve, and stormed in to his chamber. The bed — and quite a bed it was, too — was empty. She stepped back out, slammed the door, and tromped down the steps to find him.

What she found, just outside the doors of the great hall, were a half dozen guardsmen arrayed behind a striking looking nobleman astride a huge chestnut horse with fancy white feet. He stared at her in surprise and then smiled.

"Good morning, Sister." He nodded gallantly. She halted, thinking of the bloodstains she hadn't entirely succeeded in removing from her wimple, and returned his greeting. "Would you do me the service of telling me where I might find the earl? I heard he was home and have brought him a piece of news."

"I was just going to look for him, myself. I shall gladly carry him news that you are here . . . sir."

"Renfrow, earl of Claxton," he offered. "One of the earl's neighbors."

She nodded respectfully. "Your Lordship."

There was one place on all of Whitmore that had managed to hold decay and disorder at bay: the stables. With a guess that the earl's attention and frequent presence had played a part in maintaining the vitality of that structure, she struck off for it. Halfway there, she realized that the earl of Claxton — a neighboring lord — was sure to dismount and likely to enter the hall, where dozens of spent revelers still sprawled over table, bench, and floor. The place was as dingy as a badger den and stunk like a slop pail. It was sure to be a humiliation to the earl.

On her way into the stable, she passed the earl's horse-master and head plowman staggering back and forth, on their feet at last, but still bound together and hissing furious. When she demanded directions, a stableboy pointed down the alley between the stalls, to a door at the far end. As she stepped into the room, filled with harness and saddles and benches for the making and repair of them, she spotted the earl and Sir Michael and Sir Simon with the boy Tad and his father. The lad was seated on a workbench, relating to the lord and his knights what he recalled of his abduction.

"I heared twigs breakin' as they snuck up, but b'fore I could get away, somebody grabbed me. I kicked an' hit" — the boy demonstrated heroically — "but they jerked me off my feet an' then it went dark, but with little square holes. It smelt like I wus inside a grain bag."

"Evil spirits," the earl declared, holding the boy's hands up to reveal the reddish marks ringing his wrists, "don't need ropes. Or grain bags."

The others nodded.

"But you weren't tied when we found you," the earl said. "How did you get free?"

"They left me somewheres on the ground. Then an old witch woman come an' pulled the bag off. Scared me proper . . . her all hairy in 'er nose an' 'er head. She cut th' ropes an' she grabbed me" — he demonstrated a tight grip on his upper arm — "and dragged me wi' 'er. Then after we walked a piece, she let me loose an' told me to run home an' not look back. I run an' I run." He looked up at his father, who clasped his shoulder and gave it a squeeze. "An' I run straight into that ol' boar."

The earl nodded, knowing what had happened from there. "Good enough, Tad. You've been a brave fellow." He squeezed the boy's shoulder and dismissed him and his father. "Thank you, Samuel."

"He truly was abducted," the earl said after they were gone. "And rescued not once, but twice."

"Rescued by a witch?" Michael said with a chuckle.

"Not likely," Simon said, stroking his chin. "But ever since the other children disappeared, parents have been keeping their children out of the trees with tales of

235

haunting and witches and demons in the forest."

"Still, someone stole him. That part is no scaring story," the earl mused aloud. "But why would someone take him and then leave him trussed like a goose on the ground?" He stroked his shoulder, wincing, as if his wound was bothering him. "There may be some truth to his story of an old woman. He was tied hand and foot . . . someone had to have freed him. But I doubt she's a witch. The boy was so frightened when we found him, he could easily have mistaken me for a bogeyman." He developed a wicked grin. "God knows what he thought of the formidable sister. A hugely annoyed raven? A great, picky crow?" The others laughed.

"A messenger, perhaps?" Her voice carried strongly into their midst.

They started and jumped up, looking all around to locate her.

"Bearing bad news," she suggested fiercely as they discovered her standing near the rear door that led into the stable. "You have a visitor, Your Lordship. One of your neighbors. The earl of Claxton, I believe. He is waiting for you in the great hall . . . along with most of your drunken and senseless villeins."

She turned and made straight for the hall to witness his humiliation.

Michael and Simon looked at each other and winced, anticipating Peril's reaction. It wasn't long in coming.

"SHIT!"

When Peril arrived in his hall, the scene was every bit as awful as the one Sister Eloise had evoked in his mind. Claxton had brought six men with him, of whom two remained mounted, two waited just outside the main doors, and two were visible at the top of the steps leading into the great hall. With a flick of a hand Michael and Simon, who strode along at the earl's back, posted men they had brought with them to watch each of Claxton's guards. Claxton himself had entered the hall and taken a seat on one of the long tables, near a pile of body parts regrettably still attached to snoring cottagers and beery, sour-smelling villeins.

Claxton was dressed, as was his custom, in a fine black velvet tunic and short cloak with a gold satin lining, black hose, and black boots embroidered with gold. The black was chosen to show his fair hair and icy gray eyes to advantage, but in truth, it made him appear colorless and shadowy instead, even in daylight. He greeted Peril with a salute, using his riding whip.

"What are you doing here?" Peril took a stand in the doorway with his legs spread and his fists at his waist. Michael and Simon stationed themselves by the guards Claxton had left at the entrance of the hall.

"Is that any way to greet your closest and most charitable neighbor?" Claxton intoned silkily. "It must have been some celebration." He smirked. "A marriage or a death?"

"Neither. It was a rescue."

"A rescue?" Surprise flitted through Claxton's expression. He scanned Peril's form and focused with interest on the bandage visible through the open neck of Peril's shirt. "Anyone I know?"

"I doubt it." Peril felt his wounds begin to throb as his blood heated.

Claxton turned aside and used his whip to tap one of the pickled heads lying on the planks beside him. "Peasants. Don't they look sweet when they're asleep?" Then he straightened and wrinkled his nose. "Too bad they smell like piss pots. Oh" — he slid from the table to his feet and looked around with feigned dismay — "or is that just your hall?"

"You're not welcome here, Claxton. I'll ask you to leave. *Now.*" Peril's muscles began to burn with the effort required to control his instinctive response.

"Such ingratitude." Claxton strolled toward him, stepping with exaggerated motions over sprawled bodies on the way. "I am beginning to regret coming to tell you that the king's treasurer, Lord Bromley, will be arriving in a fortnight to inspect your holdings and collect the taxes you've neglected to pay." He paused to let that information take effect. "It seems his agent visited Whitmore a fortnight ago, and was met by your most able steward — who, mistaking him for a peddler, insisted you needed no 'wormy warrants or other fripperish favors' and sent him packing. I know because the goodly agent came storming into my hall afterward, outraged by your man's treatment of him."

Peril's entire body flushed with humiliation. Sedgewick. Dear God. He had just gone from being no asset to being an alarming liability.

"Knowing how difficult it is to raise both crops and coin in these perilous days, I thought I would come by to renew my offer to relieve you of those forty acres along our common border."

"Go to Hell, Claxton." Peril ached with the need to wipe the smirk from Claxton's face. "I'd sooner rot in a Turkish dungeon than put anything of value into your hands."

"Don't be *stupid*, Whitmore." Claxton's courtly glaze evaporated. His features tightened into a mask of pure spite. "You can't pay the king's geld and you know it. He's furious with you already . . . he'll take those acres for payment and more. He'll wring you dry." He stalked closer to Peril, his lanky frame trembling. "Sell *me* the land. Pay your damned taxes and use what's left to clean up this stinking sewer you live in."

"Get out!" Peril gave his shoulder a shove. "Get off my lands!"

The men at the door lurched toward their lord, but were stopped instantly by Michael and Simon. The scuffle caused a reaction outside the main doors and in the courtyard, where shoulder smacked shoulder and force was met solidly with counterforce.

Claxton steadied himself and glared murderously at Peril while calculating the odds. Realizing he could never take Peril — even wounded — in his own hall with so few men, he waved his guards off and took one step back.

"You'll regret this, Whitmore."

Peril stalked toward him, forcing him back another step, then another. At the top of the steps, with his men at his back once more, Claxton paused for one last volley.

"It won't be your land much longer," he snarled. "The king will see to that. And I'll be there to see you stripped naked, landless, and penniless, with the king's heel on your neck!"

"Go to Hell, Claxton. I'm sure you know the way."

Peril watched the earl storm from his hall and give his mount a vicious lash of the whip to spur him down the path and out the gates. As his opponent withdrew, he turned the anger churning inside him on himself.

He should have seen this disaster coming . . . the taxes . . . leaving the aged Sedgewick in charge of the house in his absence. He knew the king was aware of the deterioration of Whitmore and that the king expected him to have improved things by now. It had been two full seasons now, but despite his efforts, nothing seemed to have changed. He also knew that Claxton had ties to Bromley, the king's treasurer, and that the treasurer had the king's ear.

His thoughts began to circle in an ugly and ever-tightening spiral. He should have worked night and day to see things improved . . . should have done something about Sedgewick . . . should have overseen the tares and tallies himself . . . should have kept a closer watch on his flocks at lambing

. . . should have made certain the seed was stored properly . . . should have personally selected a few horses to yoke to plows . . . should have had the hall purged of the smelly residues of winter . . . should have seen how the bowls and spoons were beginning to rot . . .

Eloise stood not far away, watching his anger dissolving into desolation, watching the rounding of his shoulders and the tightening of his jaw. She felt as if a lead weight had been dropped in her stomach and guessed that it was probably only a part of the burden the earl must be feeling.

Only now did she see the full extent of the obstacles he faced. He was in trouble with the king; totally out of coin; battling decay, decrepitude, and despondency on every front; pressed hard by a greedy, conniving neighbor; ill-served by his own feckless and fainthearted people.

Her throat tightened and her fists clenched at her sides.

Alone, overwhelmed, and struggling against enormous odds. . . . He didn't need a bride, he needed a sorcerer.

She raised her chin and blinked the mist from her eyes.

Or an abbess.

"You could have saved yourself a great

deal of trouble, Your Lordship, if you had just sold him the land and used the money to pay the king's geld and improve your hall," she said, edging into view with her hands up her sleeves.

He looked up, scowling, and braced visibly at the sight of her.

"Sell him the most productive land on all of Whitmore? You could save me a great deal of trouble, Sister — by keeping your opinions to yourself." He grappled visibly for self-control. "Especially when you don't know what you're talking about."

"Oh, but I do know. Over the last few days I've become rather well acquainted with your estate — its decrepit hall and filthy kitchen and poor larder and run-down barns and empty weaving room and cold smithy. What I am not so well acquainted with is what you are doing to remedy the sad condition of it."

He reddened furiously.

"I'm no housemaid or kitchen wench to be held accountable for —"

"Oh, but you are accountable, sir." She edged closer. "For all of it."

"I am *lord* here, not a *clerk* who must keep a tally of what every worker accomplishes."

"If you *were* a clerk, it wouldn't be much of a task. They don't accomplish much."

She held her ground as he approached. "They don't even attempt much."

"You dare call me to account for their spiritless efforts?"

"I do, indeed. For it is by your word that a steward buys, sells, and oversees production; a housekeeper orders and instructs her charges; a horse-master selects, breeds, and trades; and a weaver spins and weaves. If such things don't happen, it is because you have not given the orders."

There was a choked, bitter tenor to his laugh.

"Just give the order and it all happens?"

Her voice softened unaccountably.

"Give the order and at least it starts." She moved closer, suppressing the urge to touch him. "Your people don't need a bride, Your Lordship, half as much as they need *you*."

She wasn't at all prepared for the sudden and wrenching change in his expression. The fierce set of his features eased and his eyes grew darker and oddly luminous. It was as if his pride had proved as brittle as it was hard, and had finally snapped.

"I am a warrior, a soldier . . . not a plowman, smith, or shepherd."

As long as he believed that, she realized, he would hold himself apart from his home and the deterioration would continue.

"You will never be the true lord of Whitmore until you are all of those things and more. To be the lord of this place, you must be a part of the life of this place." Her voice lowered. "And if you expect to resurrect your fortunes here, to bring a bride into this hall and to fill this place with pride and prosperity and children, you have a great deal of work to do."

"It that an ultimatum?" He scrambled for a footing in righteous anger.

"Let us say . . . *it is very strong advice.*"

With each exchange they had moved closer together and now stood toe to toe and eye to eye. She could feel his heat all round her and see the desperation simmering in his eyes. It was all she could do to keep from reaching out to touch him. But she had to know if he would mold his great strength and determination to the tasks that lay before him, or continue to pursue the dismal course of inaction that had brought his father, his estates, and now himself such loss.

Please — she found herself beseeching the blessed saints and anyone else in Heaven who might be listening — *help him.* Somehow the words and the insight seemed to form at the same time in her mind. *Let him choose aright. Let him make Whitmore his own.*

It was, she realized, the crux of the test she had come to administer. The test of a man. The test of a heart.

She held her breath. Waiting. Hoping.

His gaze slid over her face, searching her even as she examined him. She prayed that the workings of her heart were not visible in her expression, for in that moment he needed a coolheaded abbess, not a vulnerable woman.

The silence lengthened.

"And if I were to take that advice," he said finally, in tones little more than a whisper, "where would I begin?"

She took a deep breath as her blood began to flow again in her veins.

"You would probably begin by finding a steward who knows what season of the year it is, and a keeper of the keys who can recall what they are meant to unlock."

Old Sedgewick's reaction to being replaced as steward was to promptly turn over on his bed and go back to his nap. The madame, however, speaking through her servant at the door, was reluctant to relinquish her keys. Eloise insisted upon entering the old woman's quarters to speak with her in person. Once past the door, she and His Lordship were astounded to discover that the madame lived in chambers fit for royalty. There were exquisite tapestries on the walls, carved wooden chairs and table, a gilded reclining couch, velvet cushions and comforters filled with goose down, fine carved ivory combs and brushes, a silver pitcher and goblets, and a hammered brass water pitcher and basin. The bare stone floor was immaculate, and dried roses, clover, and heliotrope set about in brass wire pomanders sweetened the air.

The madame had been dozing on her reclining couch, and after some initial confusion, recognized her lord and struggled to rise. He prevented her from standing and knelt beside the couch himself.

"Where did all of this come from, madame?" he asked the old woman.

"*Sa mère, seigneur.* She was a fine lady. Your father" — she turned aside and spat as if the mention of him fouled her mouth — "after she died, he ordered the manor stripped of her things. I brought her favorites here for keeping."

Peril looked around in discomfort. What had possessed his wretched father to purge the house of all that would make it gracious and comfortable?

"You have kept your charge well, madame," he said, his voice thick. "Now I will relieve you of the burden of the keys and you may rest."

Tears welled in her faded eyes as she stared at him. Then she waved a gnarled finger to her servant and the huge ring of keys was brought. When asked what each of the keys opened, she most often shook her head in bewilderment. The only keys that were bright from use and well remembered were the keys to the larder and smokehouse, and the "sweetest key," under which was kept the manor's store of honey and a few blocks of pressed sugar.

Peril paused outside the door, studying the huge iron ring of keys.

"Now that I have them, what do I do with them?"

"Use them, Your Lordship." Sister Eloise looked up at him and inserted her hands in her sleeves. "Learn what they unlock and take full stock of your holdings. For your next task is to find something on Whitmore that is worth a shrewd and acquisitive king's favor."

The rest of the morning they tried keys in locks and explored little-used outbuildings and the uninhabited manor house, all to no avail. Many of the storerooms had been stripped of their locks and whatever valuables they were guarding years ago. The locks that remained were often so rusted that they refused to budge with any key on the ring and had to be chiseled out of the aged planks in which they were imbedded.

After a midday pause for bread and ale, she suggested he investigate the baskets of small parchment rolls he had rescued from old Sedgewick's chambers. On those were tallied the expenditures of the estate for every necessity bought and the production of every piece of land under cultivation and of every kind of animal kept. Fortunately, the old boy had been schooled in the proper form of record-keeping and, despite his increasingly erratic penmanship, Eloise was able to make out the figures and show the earl how the records were kept and how the yields and wealth of his home had declined over the last two decades.

The outlook, they realized, was every bit as grim as Peril had supposed. Each year there were fewer lambs, fewer calves, fewer foals . . . less wool to sell, less game to hunt . . . less oats, barley, and wheat per acre.

As they pored over the scrolls, Eloise puzzled over various cryptic notes along the edges — questions old Sedgewick had for his workers, to which no answers were ever penned. It was time, Eloise declared, to get answers to those questions. They set out to see the fields and speak with some of the plowmen and sowers.

Ned, Hiram, Gilly, Hugh . . . the plowmen were a burly, wary, and naturally taciturn lot. But, responding to Eloise's knowledgeable air and occasional smile, they were soon talking openly about how difficult conditions were, about Hadric the bailiff's constant harangue, and about the gradually decreasing yields of their crops. Every year they followed prudent and time-tested practices, believing the yield should improve. Then, just before harvest, the ripening heads of grains would begin to bend and break and even disappear . . . as if some accursed spirit wandered the fields at night, blighting and stealing. They all had an opinion on the identity of that malevolent wraith, but none would speak her name above a whisper.

Mistress Ann.

Peril expelled a heavy breath and caught Eloise's narrowed eyes.

Next they mounted horses and visited the shepherds in the outlying fields. The story they encountered was of wolves frequently dragging off lambs and sometimes even the ewes themselves. When questioned carefully, however, the shepherds admitted they didn't usually see the wolves or any signs of blood or struggle . . . just awakened to find the beasts had struck in the night and their sheep were missing. Strangely, even the shepherds' dogs missed detecting them. According to the shepherds there was only one explanation for that: phantom wolves, brought by the curse.

The dairymaids and goose girls who cared for the cows and poultry were more pragmatic in identifying the source of their difficulties. The cows and poultry always produced well when given plenty of food and water, they said. Every time grain was low, the feed grain they were allotted was shorted, and milk and egg production plummeted.

As Peril and Eloise toured the dairy and buttery and checked the barns and bird coops, she evaluated the buildings and tools present. The dairy and churns and cheese troughs and metal pails were of good quality. And the stone and wooden dovecote, though empty, was well built. Those parts of the estate had readily accessible potential, but nothing to tempt a treasurer or mollify an irritable king.

As they were returning to the hall, a familiar-looking boy came running down the cart path calling frantically to the earl.

"What is it?" he caught and steadied the boy before recognizing him as the stable-boy posted by the horse-master and head plowman.

"They're pissin,' milord," the boy panted.

Eloise lifted her skirts and ran after them as they headed for the stables. There, indeed, stood the horse-master and head plowman, back to back, looking both chastened and relieved. Greatly relieved.

The earl paused beside them, looking them over, and folded his arms.

"So? Who went first?" he demanded.

"Neither of us, milord," the horse-master declared.

"We went together," the plowman said, refusing to look up at him.

Peril glanced around at the unhappy faces of the onlookers, including a number from his garrison of fighting men. Their wagering had been in vain, then. He smiled. As often happened, the men being taught a lesson had worked together to save each other's pride and to foil the onlookers' bets. He took out his dagger and cut the rope.

"Now, who gets horses?" the earl demanded.

"He does," the horse-master said, eyeing his former opponent.

"And what are you going to do with those

horses?" he asked the plowman.

"Not yoke them in with the oxen," the plowman declared. "They'll be tended and fed separate. And he'll o'ersee the breedin' still."

Eloise watched the earl clasp each man's hand, and then lead the pair into the stable to choose plow horses. As she headed back to the hall, she found herself smiling. Perhaps His stubborn, stiff-necked Lordship was just the man for these stubborn and stiff-necked people.

By the time they returned to the hall, Peril's wounds and head were aching and all he wanted was some cold beer, warm crusty bread, and squeaky fresh curds. He had to settle for sour ale, half-burned bread, and a grayish pottage that he didn't want to observe too closely. He glanced up at Eloise and found her with her arms crossed tightly over her bosom, staring at him.

"What?" he asked, feeling as if he were about to be yanked by the hair.

"A lord is known by his hospitality. If you feed your men and your guests such stuff, it is little wonder that your reputation with your neighbors suffers." She looked pointedly at the lumpy gray slurry on the table.

"I have more important things to do than —"

"Sicken on inedible pottage? Pigs would know better than to eat this, you know."

He smacked his tankard down on the table. He'd had all of the humility and instruction he could stomach for one day.

"Well, we'll see about that." He rose sharply, grabbed up her bowl, and strode for the kitchen stairs. She had to run to keep up as he strode past the stables and the dairy and down the slope to the smelliest part of Whitmore, the pigsty.

With a vengeful flourish, he emptied the pottage into an aged wooden trough filled with the remnants of things best left unidentified. Then he folded his arms smugly as several young pigs rushed to devour this bit of fortune. One by one, they sniffed and tried the addition to their feed, and one by one they drew back and left it uneaten. He paled as he absorbed the awful truth: he had just eaten something his pigs wouldn't.

She didn't feel it necessary to inform him that the little beasts were from a rare wintered sow and probably still suckling . . . unused to solid foods and more apt to be choosy. When he struck off for the kitchen, still looking a bit green, she fell in beside him. The odors of stale grease and charred food that greeted them did nothing to improve his color or his humor.

Standing in the middle of the dirty kitchen, he exploded. "Out, out!" he roared at the cooks and workers, sending them fleeing. "You're no longer a part of my household!" As they scurried out, he turned on Eloise.

"I suppose you have a bit of advice on this as well!"

"I do." She couldn't help smiling. "But I'm not certain you would want to burn it down and start over."

Ten

The kitchen remedy Eloise and the earl finally agreed upon was somewhat less extreme than a total conflagration. She suggested they throw out all of the aged wooden equipment and replace it, and that he get someone to restart the common hearth outside and oversee the baking separately. And after a quick and pungent tour of the kitchens and the chaotic larder, she suggested new irons for the hearth and a thorough cleaning of the cellars.

He folded his arms and fixed a pointed look on her. "And just who do you expect to actually *do* all of this work?"

She thought on that for a moment.

"Come with me."

She led him out the gates and down to the cottages to do a bit of scouting for kitchen help. As they passed a modest cottage at the edge of the village, someone called out to her and Eloise looked around to find the same old woman she had spoken with and prayed for two days earlier.

"Your lordship, I don't know if you know

this woman . . . she says she is your old nurse."

"My nurse? Morna?"

It was surprisingly easy to push him down to a seat on a nearby barrel. Eloise dragged a stool from inside and sat while old Morna told the earl about his mother, Lady Alicia, and about the days when she was lady of the manor.

Lady Alicia had been unable to speak much English and had been miserable at cold, colorless Whitmore from the start. She was unable to seek the heart of the earl himself, who had long since given it elsewhere, and without a command of their language, was unable to capture the hearts of the people. She was lonely and grew increasingly despondent as the time came for her first child to be born. After the babe arrived, her spirits revived and she did her best to take her place as "chatelaine."

There had indeed been wonderful banners and tapestries, rich furnishings from Italy and the East, and fine foods and wines that Lady Alicia had brought with her from her home in Burgundy. Whitmore had been on its way to becoming one of the finest castles in all of England.

Then came that stormy and fateful night when the earl's mistress breached the gates and the doors of the nearly finished tower to demand that the earl choose between her and his rich wife. The choice, however, had already been made, and the mistress was barred from the manor.

As the seasons progressed and turned into years, the old earl was filled with regret and began to pine for his lost love. He and Lady Alicia grew ever more estranged, and when she died giving birth to a stillborn child, he recalled the curse his mistress, Ann, had spoken that fateful night and began to see its effects in every misfortune that befell.

A sober silence descended for a time. Eloise watched the earl grapple with the familiar story, now told from a different perspective. She could almost feel the tragedy of his mother's unhappiness seeping into his heart, threatening his life and fortunes, and she understood how such a story could grip the hearts and minds of a simple people.

"Thank you, good mother," he said rising and turning to go.

"Wait." Eloise grabbed him by the sleeve and held him as she turned back to old Morna. "Tell us, Mother Morna, if I were to seek a good meal here in the village, to whom would I go? Who is the best cook on all of Whitmore?"

"That's easy enough," the old woman

said. "That'd be Ralph th' butcher. 'E's a right wizard with a spit o' lamb."

Ralph the butcher's name came up again and again as they strolled through the village making inquiries. Roxanne, wife of Blaine, and Johanna, widow of Micah the cooper, were named often as well, for their pies and for their delicious stews. She and the earl located all three and asked them to come to the great hall to take over the kitchen. All three said they would be honored to served their lord in such a way.

"They may not feel quite so honored," His Lordship muttered as they climbed the slope back to the great hall, "when they see the mess they're inheriting."

The next morning, Eloise met the new cooks in the kitchens and began the task of instructing them on establishing a proper hearth and kitchen in a noble household. The first task was to clear the rubbish and filth from the premises and then assess what was needed for proper cooking. Meanwhile, the folk of the hall and garrison still had to eat, so a small fire was laid in a cleared area of the huge hearth. Smoke boiled out in noxious clouds, sending them all reeling back out the open wall of the kitchen.

" 'Tis no wonder they burned ever'thin' they touched," Johanna said, grimacing.

"Who could stand to put their head in that place to tend food?"

"What we need," Ralph the former butcher declared, "is a new chimney."

There wasn't a proper mason to be found on Whitmore, and in desperation, Eloise called upon the man who knew more about fires than anyone she knew. Pascoe was reluctant at first to render service in the kitchen, but when she invoked the earl's authority, he relented. Soon he was climbing fearlessly up the stone stack and studying the problem from all angles. A clogged and filthy chimney was the verdict. And after some consultation he agreed to take a boy or two onto the roof to try to clean it.

Eloise couldn't stand the suspense of just listening to the thumping and scraping, and stuck her head into the draft box to see — just as a shower of soot and charred grease let go. She staggered from the hearth, blinking and spitting greasy ash, scarcely able to breathe. It was at that moment that the earl and Sir Michael arrived to inform her they were riding out to the north fields to see about the plowing and planting before checking on the reheating of the forge.

Peril watched her sputtering and spitting, her face now as black as her habit, and he hooted with laughter. The flustered cooks handed her a bit of linen, but, having no experience with nuns, were reluctant to make contact with her person in any way. Sensing their dilemma, he took the situation in hand himself. Still chuckling, he seized her by the wrist and dragged her, blinking and stumbling, from the kitchen to the well and trough not far outside the open wall.

"I fail to see the humor in this," Sister Eloise said irritably, swiping at her eyes and spitting out grit.

"That's because you can't see your face," he said, positioning her beside the trough, cupping his hand behind her head and pushing her down over the water. "Close your eyes."

He splashed her face again and again. At first she sputtered and resisted, but as the soot washed away, she pushed his hands aside and took over. The white underside of her veil and her wimple were sooty and water-soaked when she straightened, with her eyes squeezed shut, and groped for the linen towel. As she patted and wiped, her face emerged with a gray cast.

"Did I get it all?" she asked, pausing at the sight of him chewing his lip.

"All but the gray. Or is that blue?"

"What?" she said with alarm and tried to see her reflection in the water.

"Give me that." He pulled the linen from her hands and began to wipe and then rub her skin. For each howl of protest his brisk ministrations elicited, he paused to stroke her face gently with his fingers, soothing it. Slowly, her skin turned from gray back to healthy pink, and the touch of his fingers turned to gentle caresses. She stilled as his gaze and his hands poured over her face. When he reached the ring of gray left at the edge of her face, it seemed the most natural thing in the world for him to reach for the pins that fastened her veil.

In a few quick motions he had removed it and stuffed it into her hands. She stared at it in distracted surprise that quickly turned to disbelief.

"What are you —" She gasped as he tugged at the ties on the back of her wimple. "Wait!"

In the struggle of his trying to pull it off and her trying to keep it on, the garment slid and bared most of her head.

Eloise went utterly still. When she looked up, his gaze was not on her linen-chafed cheeks, but higher. He was staring at her hair and his eyes were alight with a certain kind of interest. . . .

Crimson with humiliation, she jerked her wimple back into place. That was when she

262

looked over and caught the new kitchen staff and Sir Michael of Dunneault staring at the earl and her in shock.

"Really, Your Lordship!" She dragged her veil back over her head. . . . askew, but at least covering her.

"I was just trying to . . . clean the rest of your . . ." He followed her gaze to their audience and muttered, "Dammit."

Red-faced, he stalked off toward the stables while she, crimson with humiliation, rushed for the entrance to the great hall.

Just what the hell had he been doing, he asked himself as he strode for the stables, pulling her garments from her, baring her head, staring at her hair? Just what he'd been itching to do for days, came the only honest answer. Pulling those damnable church weeds from her, to sink his hands into —

"I've seen you charge into the jaws of battle a hundred times, milord," Michael of Dunneault declared, falling in beside him with a genial expression. "But I've never seen you court death so openly."

"What?" Peril did not stop or even glance at him.

"I thought the good sister might go after you fang and claw."

"I was only helping her clean her face."

The earl jerked his gloves onto his hands as he went.

"Well, in *helping*, you very nearly stripped her head bare," Michael continued, weighing his words. "Women take such things rather personally."

"Women?" The earl cast a glance back over his shoulder while avoiding Michael's gaze. "She's not a woman, she's a *nun*."

"You think so?" Sir Michael asked with a twinkle in his eye.

"I know so." He turned the full force of his frustration and discomfort on Michael. "She's a nun . . . sworn to humility, piety, and obedience to God . . . and trained by the church to assess and administer estates. She has special knowledge and ability in organizing work and making land profitable. Why else would I allow her such influence and liberty with my property?"

As he stalked off toward the stables, Michael recovered his equilibrium and frowned.

"Why indeed?"

"What madness ever possessed me to do this?" Eloise said, groaning as she sank onto the edge of her narrow bed and pulled one of her aching feet up for a good rubbing. She had just spent two interminable days setting

264

the house servants and a raft of women from the village to clear and clean the great hall.

"They can't do anything without constant direction and supervision," she said. "It's like working with children. They encounter the slightest distraction or obstacle and they lose interest and revert to idleness or mischief. I've spent the last two days tromping up and down the steps between the kitchen and the great hall, dealing with one urgent dilemma or another. Where to stack the kettles . . . whether to sweep the rushes out with brooms or rake them . . . whether to use water and brushes on the stone floor. Then there is the 'Order of the Perpetual Grumblers,' who lean on their brooms and mutter that all this bother is a waste of time since it will all have to be done over next year."

She lay back on her cot, pressed her palms over her eyes, and groaned.

"If I never see another crusty iron pot or gnawed chicken bone it will be fine with me."

"Me, too," Mary Clematis said, sighing. "I got three more 'relics' today."

Eloise opened her eyes and frowned as Mary Clematis held up three nearly identical bones, one with a hunk of meat and sinew still attached. She let out a giggle as her friend opened a square of linen to reveal a sizeable pile of bones.

"It seems Saint Peter had at least fourteen fingers. And, lucky me, I've got them all."

Eloise's howl of laughter purged her tension and reclaimed some space in her crowded emotions. Mary Clematis, who was finally feeling better, rose from the chair near the window and came to sit by her.

"I'm so sorry, Elly. I've been no help to you at all." She took a resolute breath. "But starting tomorrow, I'll be at your side and doing my part." Then she frowned and began to measure her words. "Are you sure you should be helping him like this? This isn't a part of the husband test, surely."

"Actually," Eloise straightened and delivered the rationale that she had been chanting in her own mind for several days, "it's a way to learn about his character. You know, strength, perseverence, love of order . . . that sort of thing."

"Oh, I see." Mary Clematis sat back on her knees, glowing with admiration. "I never would have thought of that. When you take your vows, the abbess ought to name you Sister Mary Clevershins."

Eloise choked on an indrawn breath and came up laughing again.

"Well, I just hope she has gotten flowers and herbs out of her system by the time I return. Otherwise, knowing how well she loves me, I'll probably have to answer to 'Sister Mary Mugwort.' "

They both laughed until their stomachs hurt, and then settled slowly back to reality. As things quieted, Mary Clematis became more reflective, and she asked the question that all but stopped Eloise's heart.

"Whom do you think she'll send to be his bride?"

Eloise must have made some sound, for Mary Clematis looked over at her.

"The abbess. Whom do you think she'll send?" Then a more interesting variant occurred to her. "Whom would *you* choose to be his bride?"

Eloise felt as if she had just slammed into a wall.

"That assumes he'll get a bride," she said, grappling for balance as the world tilted crazily under her.

"Well, won't he?" Mary Clematis frowned at her. "I mean, he's working at it — and Heaven knows he needs a lady wife. So, knowing him as you do, whom would you choose? Alaina is so lovely . . . Helen is such a bright and loving spirit . . . and then there is Lissette, who seems to burn with a dark light . . ."

Eloise stood up and jammed her feet into her slippers.

"That's not my concern, Mary Clematis," she said more sharply than she would have wished. "I have absolutely no opinion on it. And I suggest you turn your mind to more productive pursuits."

Fleeing both her friend's dismay and her own jumbled and contradictory emotions, she headed for the abandoned chapel.

There, in the midst of the silence and dusty sunlight, she sank to her knees and did something she had seldom done of late. She prayed.

Since that day in the kitchen, when she got a face full of soot and his lordship bared her head and stared at her hair, she had caught him looking at her several times and it never failed to make her heart skip. Those rich golden brown eyes with their dark lashes and turbulent inner lights . . . she could almost feel them on her like a touch. Or a caress.

She moaned and squeezed her eyes tighter against the memory.

She was actively helping him resurrect his estate, preparing it for the arrival of a bride; he had no reason to ply her with charm or cozening passion. So, it must be her own stubborn womanly vanity that placed such personal interest in His Lordship's eyes. She thought she had long ago purged herself of the worldly desire for admiration that was so common in her sex. But she saw now that she hadn't overcome it at all. There were so few temptations in the cloister, she simply hadn't encountered it in a long while. Apparently vanity, like its sister sin, pride, was much harder to defeat than she had believed.

And for her to be experiencing such turmoil and temptation with regard to His Lordship, she must have strayed yet again from the true goal of her mission here. She asked the Almighty for forgiveness, for patience, for guidance, and for the proper spirit to complete her task . . . for everything, in fact, except the one thing she was coming to truly want.

The next morning, as the kitchen staff was cleaning and sorting the larder, they discovered a three-paneled screen that had been used to strengthen and brace a set of crude shelves against a wall. They called for Eloise and she examined the piece and declared it to be something of value.

Ralph and the potboys carried it out into the sunlight and dusted it off to reveal a black lacquered surface inlaid with intricate patterns of mother-of-pearl, tracery of gold, and flowers of carnelian. With a more careful cleaning, it would be breathtaking. She sent a kitchen boy for the earl, straightaway. When he arrived, he ran his hands over the screen and shook his head.

"Amazing. It looks like something from the East. I've seen such things in great houses, but never imagined anything like it here."

"More than likely, it was part of your mother's things. What if there is more?" she asked.

"More?" He straightened and tugged his tunic down in front.

"Remember that old Morna said the house was filled with rich things, and the madame said she brought your mother's *favorite* things to her chambers. That means there must have been more. What happened to the rest?"

"Probably sold off long ago," he said.

"Obviously not all of it." Her gaze flicked back and forth, as if examining an image forming in her mind. "If we could find more things like this, you might be able to sell some of them to pay your taxes."

She was already headed for the madame's door when the notion registered with him, and he had to hurry to catch up.

"If they weren't sold, they've probably long since rotted," he grumbled.

She paused with her knuckles poised at the madame's door.

"You mean, because they were *cursed?*"

He pounded on the door himself and soon they were again at the old Frenchwoman's side. She was confused by their questions at first, then sat up on her couch and gave a fatalistic wave toward the furnishings around her. "Take what you will, *seigneur.* It is all yours now."

"No, no, madame," the earl said sinking onto one knee beside her. "We only wish to know if there are more things, other things. What happened to the rest of the furnishings when the old earl stripped the hall?"

The old woman rubbed her forehead, thinking. "I took Her Ladyship's things . . . Sedgewick took the rest." She shook her head. "I do not know what he did with them. You must ask him."

A short while later, they stood in Sedgewick's disheveled chamber watching the old steward scratch his hoary head, then chin, then belly, as if the scratching might help him recall those long-ago events.

"Yea, milord." He finally tapped the side of his nose with a finger and did his best to look canny. "Squirreled it right away, I did. Knew it'd be called for someday."

"Where did you squirrel it, Sedgewick?"

the earl prompted.

"Well, it were . . . it were . . ." The old man pointed and waved in the same motion, trying to think of how to give directions. "Aw, ballocks — I mus' show ye." He heaved himself up out of his chair and shuffled for the door. Eloise and the earl followed and he led them to the kitchens.

"There were a door here," he said with bewilderment, rubbing his spotty bald pate as he stood near the pantries in the kitchen, staring at a solid stone wall. The earl took him by the shoulders and turned him around to face the doorway that led to the underground larder. "Ah . . . there 'tis." He charged through the opening, and then stood blinking and confused in the darkness. "I can't see me hand in front o' me face!"

When the earl grabbed an oil lamp, lighted it, and stepped into the larder behind him, Sedgewick brightened.

"That's better. Now where's the door?"

Bewildered themselves, Eloise and the earl turned him around and marched him back out into the kitchen. They marched him in and out of the larder door yet again before they realized that the old fellow meant another door altogether. A search of the larder, behind the stacks of barrels and the planking shelves and the hooks full of "hung" poultry in varying stages of ripeness, revealed nothing but solidly set stone walls. Then they came to the nook where Eloise and the kitchen staff had discovered the screen.

With the addition of light from a second lamp, a face of crude clay bricks was visible in the otherwise stone wall. The aged mortar was so poor that the earl was able without much effort to push one brick through into an opening on the other side. It didn't take long for the earl and the kitchen boys to dismantle the brickwork and uncover an arched doorway.

Sedgewick seemed puzzled by the newfound opening.

"The furnishings, Sedgewick. The old things you hid away," the earl prompted, giving the old boy a lamp and a nudge.

"Eh? Furnishings? What furnish— ? Oh. There was a door . . . mebbe in here . . ." Sedgewick entered the passage holding his lamp aloft and tottering along the rough-hewn floors. The earl lighted lamps for himself and Eloise, then set off after the old steward.

The passage ended abruptly in a good-sized chamber, which was empty except for a few old barrels stacked in one corner.

Sedgewick didn't stop, so they followed him through it and down another passage that developed several branches. At each junction they had to wait for Sedgewick to mumble some sort of rhyme that helped him recall the way.

"When was all this done?" the earl demanded as they checked one passage and then another. "I had no idea there were even cellars under the manor, much less a maze of them."

"Oh, but . . . t'be a proper castle, ye have to 'ave cellars an' blinds," old Sedgewick declared. "In case of a siege. A place to hide yer valuables — an' yer family. Yer father, he knowed how to build right an' proper."

"Comforting to know he was good at something," the earl muttered.

They finally came to a heavy iron door and Sedgewick gasped with recognition. Immediately he began to push and pummel the planks, and when they didn't budge, he rained blows, kicks, and curses on the massive door in a hail of frustration.

The earl handed Eloise his lamp and dragged the single-minded old retainer back bodily in order to reach the iron ring visible near the top of the door. He pulled it, the latch released, and the door swung open.

The light from their lamps flooded into a

chamber in which barrels and other shapes were outlined in layers of decayed fabric and spider webs. Eloise could scarcely contain her excitement as they made their way through the chamber, peering into barrels and wooden boxes and uncovering chests and richly made furnishings. Wiping cobwebs from a stately high-backed chair, she discovered a carved crest inlaid with familiar crimson and blue. There were at least a dozen shorter but equally beautiful chairs, several neatly carved benches stacked against a wall, and a table of sizeable proportions. Nearby barrels contained candle stands, wooden plaques bearing a number of crests used on Whitmore, and rolls of something wrapped in burlap, which turned out to be tapestries that held firm when the weave was tugged at the edge.

"There must be an entire hall's worth of furnishings here," she said, looking up at the earl. "And, given a bit of care, they're still useable." Even in the dim and flickering lamplight she was almost blinded by the earl's smile.

"We'll have to have help getting these things out of here." He charged back out the door and down the passage. It was some time before he returned, exasperated, with several kitchen boys and Michael, Pascoe, and William in tow.

"This place is a warren," he grumbled. "Damn near couldn't find my way out. We brought ropes and a pot of paint, and marked the way back to the kitchens."

Eloise wasn't certain how long he'd been gone; she was too absorbed in looking through the chests and discovering items once used in the hall. Then, as the kitchen boys and the earl's men carried things out and the room gradually cleared, she looked around for old Sedgewick to ask if they'd found everything. He wasn't anywhere in sight.

"I haven't seen him for some time," she told the earl. "You don't suppose he's gone off and . . ."

They looked at each other in alarm.

"Sedgewick!" the earl called at the entrance to each of the passages leading from the chamber. "Are you there?" There was no response from the first three passages, but at the fourth, they both heard the echoes of a voice.

"The old fool," the earl muttered as they headed together down a passage that divided several times, forcing them to halt and call out to Sedgewick again and again. "I should have known better than to let him out of my sight."

The passage slanted downward and the ceiling lowered; the earl had to bend his head as he walked. Then without warning, the passage opened abruptly into a large, vaulted chamber filled with barrels and chests and what appeared to be more rich furnishings. They had to ignore the cache and continue on toward Sedgewick's weakening voice.

They found him seated on a chest and slumped against a wall in yet a third treasure-filled chamber. He was winded and thoroughly confused, and when the earl tried to help him to his feet, he resisted and insisted on having a drink first.

"We don't have anything to drink." Eloise tried to reason with him as she took his other arm. "You have to come with us. You can't stay here."

"Just a nick of the grape," he insisted, his mouth clicking with dryness as he spoke. "Just a nick is all . . . a drop 'er two . . ."

Eloise shook her head at the earl. "It's a long way back . . . perhaps we should let him rest before we start." She patted the old man's hands as they led him back to his seat on the trunk. "Rest, Sedgewick, then we'll take you back to the kitchens for some ale."

The delay gave them time to explore the crates, barrels, and several larger items in the chamber — including what appeared to be a beautifully carved altar and chancel railing. Eloise's heart soared as she unearthed piece after piece of splendid furnishings and imagined them taking their rightful place in Whitmore's forlorn and empty chapel. While the earl was busy investigating pieces of wood that looked as though they were meant to assemble into a huge frame, she held her lamp down the passages leading from the "chapel" chamber and thought she spotted another chamber in the distance. She headed for it and was soon exploring another passage, and another . . .

Just as she was ready to turn back, she came to a chamber filled with oak barrels stacked in layers on their sides. There were rows and rows of them, nestled under a high, timber-braced ceiling. She brushed away some of the dust and cobwebs covering one barrel, squinting at the markings on the end above a heavy oak plug. *Épernay.* She skipped several barrels and then cleared another to read it. *Sancerre.* Then another nearby. *Pierrefitte.* There was no doubt she was looking at wine barrels. Dozens of them. Perhaps scores of them. From France.

She blinked, hoping the darkness and excitement of discovery wasn't playing tricks on her senses. When she knocked on the end of one barrel, it produced a dull, full-of-liquid sort of thud. Her excitement exploded and she rushed back through the passages, nearly tripping over her habit.

"Your Lordship!" She burst into the chamber where she had left him and Sedgewick. "You must come." She grabbed him by the arm and dragged him toward the passage she had just explored.

"What's gotten into you —"

"Wine!" she declared. Sedgewick's head jerked up and his eyes opened at that word. "Lots of wine. *French* wine. Come on!"

It took a heartbeat for what she had said to register, but in a trice, he and Sedgewick were jammed together in the entrance of the passage.

"I knew it were somewheres!" Sedgewick crowed as the earl grudgingly withdrew and allowed the old retainer to enter first. "Yer father — rest 'is soul — were a beer man. Didn't take to wine. So when she come with a load of it, he were fit to tie — an' stuck it away down here."

"Lady Alicia brought it with her as a part of her dower goods?" Eloise asked as they hurried along.

"That she did," Sedgewick said, suddenly

clear-eyed and lucid. As they neared the chamber, he began to rub his palms together and giggle with anticipation. "A nick o' the grape for what ails ye. Just a wee nick."

The light bloomed around the large barrel and Eloise released the breath she had held as they stepped inside the cellar. The earl went from barrel to barrel, as she had, checking the markings and sounding the ends with his knuckles. With each bit of proof his smile broadened.

"It's here . . . but is it still good?" he said, meeting Eloise's gaze with conflicting emotions visible in his eyes.

"There's naught for it, but a nick o' the grape." Sedgewick shuffled over to one of the barrels and began to tug and twist, and then to bang frantically at the wooden peg that sealed the barrel.

"Stop!" The earl looked around for something to open one of the barrels and located a mallet and dipper and several tin-lined cups hanging on pegs on one of the walls. "Let's do it right."

He turned the barrel so that it stood on end and pounded the swollen peg down into the barrel. Then he lowered the long, narrow dipper into the liquid inside. When he drew it out and poured it into one of the dusty cups, it had the clear red glint of good wine. And as the scent of it wafted up, it was like berries and spice and oak, not the sour tang of vinegar. Sedgewick smacked his lips and reached for the cup with quaking hands.

He sipped noisily, swished it around in his mouth, and for a moment Eloise thought he was going to spit it out. Instead, he swallowed, grinned his mostly toothless grin, and then buried his nose eagerly in the cup.

"It's good!" Eloise shouted, laughing. "It's good wine!" Her voice echoed back in a joyous refrain. *Wine . . . wine . . . wine . . .*

The earl threw back his head and laughed so that their echoes mingled and filled the caverns with the sounds of pleasure.

When he handed her a cup, the last thing on her mind was self-denial. She sniffed and sipped and then drank. The wine rolled like satin over her tongue . . . filled her mouth with sweetened warmth and her head with vapors so divine they brought tears to her eyes.

"It's wonderful! Of course, I'm no judge of wine —"

"Only of husbands?" the earl said, grinning.

"But I have to say" — she ignored him — "this tastes like every possible earthly rapture pressed and squeezed into a single cup."

"Every rapture?" he said with a teasing rise of one eyebrow. "And how would Sister Eloise of the Convent of the Brides of Virtue know how every possible earthly pleasure would taste? Or do you have 'standards' for that, too?"

"I . . . we . . . have good imaginations, milord," she said taking the teasing in stride. "Good enough to imagine how wonderful Whitmore will be soon, with its hall refurnished and its house and chapel cleaned and refitted. Just imagine, milord, how surprised the king's man will be when you greet him in your hall with pleasant surroundings, good food, and excellent wine . . . and send him back to his master with more of the same."

When he picked up the dipper and plunged it down into the barrel, she was right beside Sedgewick, holding out her cup for more. While the old retainer wobbled to a seat on a step beside the barrels and sank into a wine-warmed reverie, she and the earl examined the barrels. She shared with him the virtues of each region's vintages and estimated the worth of the cellar's contents. Several hundred gold pieces, at least . . . not counting a suitable tithe to the church. There was still enough wine to pay the king and to begin repairing the damage that neglect and despair had caused to Whitmore.

They strolled through the alleys between the stacks of barrels, feeling the effects of the wine and increasingly aware of each other's presence. She studied the muscular movements of his long legs as they walked; he grew engrossed with the feathery crescents of her lashes against her wine-blushed cheeks. The occasional silences became as warm as the wine in their blood and, being utterly absorbed in the moment, neither noticed when Sedgewick's lamp sputtered out.

Returning to the open barrel, if not to their better sense, they each consumed another cup. She watched the wine glistening on his lips and licked her own. He caught her expression and his smile canted to a decidedly provocative angle.

Her lamp flared as the oil was spent and the wick itself began to burn. It took a moment for her to realize what was happening, and she looked up to see Peril draining his cup and felt her throat tighten. She was having trouble thinking . . . deciding whether it mattered that their second lamp was going out. All that seemed important just now was the fact that she was here with Peril of Whitmore, celebrating something wonderful and feeling this strange and delicious surge of heat in her veins.

He started when her light died and the cellar grew noticeably darker.

"Good God — the lamps!" His eyes widened as he lifted his own lamp and discovered how little tallow was left in it. "Come on," he said, grabbing her hand and pulling her toward the door to the passage.

"But S-Sedgewick —"

"We'll come back for him."

"B-but . . . we'll never make it all the way to the kitchens."

"We can try," he said over his shoulder as he pulled her along the passage. But it was already too late. As they reached the first junction, his lamp flickered out and they were immersed in total darkness.

All she could hear at first was the pounding of her own heart and her own rapid, shallow breathing.

"What do we do?" she said, her voice constricted.

He was silent for a long moment, then moved. She could hear his hand brushing the stone of the passage wall as he turned back toward the wine cellar.

"Go back and stay with Sedgewick. When we don't return to the kitchens, Michael and the others will start a search for us. They know what a maze the place is. They'll find us. It's just a matter of time."

Moving cautiously, they felt the passage walls end and heard the sounds of their movements echoing differently in the large chamber. Sedgewick's snores helped orient them. The earl led her to the far end of that row of barrels and halted. She edged closer to him and couldn't stop herself from reaching for his arm.

"And now?" she asked, suddenly more sober and alert and needing his presence in a very direct way in the chilled darkness. She heard his rhythmic breathing and felt his arm tense with a reassuring response under her anxious touch. The darkness seemed to warm a bit as she absorbed his confidence.

"Now, we wait." His voice came low and thick.

She was startled by the feel of his hands on her shoulders. Her knees weakened as he drew her against his body and wrapped his arms around her. Then his voice rumbled intimately through her, setting her skin tingling.

"And we quit waiting."

His lips . . . wine sweet and warm and strangely soft . . . touched hers, sending pleasure trickling through her like the heat from a potent wine. Yes, she had been waiting. For this very thing. For his touch, his kiss . . . for him to turn to her with need and passion . . . for him to take her into his arms and make her feel exactly what she was feeling. Warmth. Pleasure. Connection.

She slid her arms around his waist and joined him in that kiss, imitating him at first, then improvising and exploring as her new-born desires led her. He filled her arms even as he surrounded her with warmth and strength and security. There, in the darkness, there was no world, no king, no church . . . no law but that of pleasure, no creed but that of giving in tenderness and caring.

He knelt and pulled her down beside him; she sank willingly to her knees. When he tugged her veil free, she allowed it. When he untied her wimple, she offered no resistance. The cord that bound her hair was tied in a simple bow, and in a heartbeat her hair was tumbling over her shoulders . . . then over his as he sank back to a seat on the stone floor and pulled her onto his lap.

"God, I love your hair," he murmured, burying his face in it and breathing in its mixture of linen and womanly musk. "It's like living fire. Even now I can feel its heat." He filled his hands with it and rubbed it against his cheeks, then sank his hands through it to cup her head and pull her mouth against his.

She met the hunger in that kiss and, as she ran her fingers through his hair, she searched the darkness in vain for some hint of his image. But the deprivation of one of her senses heightened the acuity of the others. She felt the moist heat of his breath on her cheek and against her mouth; tasted the salt on his lips and the winelike sweetness of his tongue. She could hear both her breathing and his quicken and could feel his hands tremble as he touched her face and hair.

When his hands wandered down her back and over her buttocks, it seemed an entirely reasonable progression of pleasure, and she began to satisfy her own curiosity about his battle-hardened frame. Slipping her hands inside his tunic and up his back, she discovered he was firm and smooth and very different from her woman's form. He tensed when she dragged her nails over his back and, dismayed, she started to withdraw. He prevented it and drew her even closer.

"Do it again," he ordered raggedly.

She dragged her fingers again and again over that spot on his back and began to understand that expressions of pleasure and pain were sometimes separated only by nuances. When she slipped her hand beneath his shirt and repeated that action, his reaction was multiplied. She had always thought of garments as a visual shield, a veil of modesty, but clearly they were a shield against the power of touch as well. Then his hand slid beneath her loosened kirtle and along her bare thigh, and she gasped at the intensity of those sensations.

She wanted to feel his bone-melting touch all over . . . wanted to explore these powerful new yearnings . . . wanted to hold him and touch him even as he was touching her. Then his fingers reached her breast and teased its tightly budded tip, and she gasped at the keenness of the pleasure that shuddered through her body. She moaned softly against his lips and then arched into his hand and into his kiss with all of the hunger his touch generated in her.

"Do you like this?" he murmured against her lips. She could barely whisper through the desire gripping her throat.

"Yes."

"Do you want more?"

Was it greedy to want more? Greed was a sin. But there was no sin here, only tenderness and pleasure.

"Yes."

"This kind of more?" His hand slid to her other breast and began to tantalize its aching tip.

She responded by pressing herself along the length of his body. She could feel herself like a vessel filling up with pleasure, expanding.

He heard it first, the faint echo of voices calling to them. "Halloooo! Are ye there, milord?" He froze, wishing he hadn't heard . . . wishing they hadn't been found yet . . . wishing they might never be found . . .

She felt the change in him and held her breath as she joined him in listening through the darkness. As the voices came clearer he started to withdraw, and she released him and slid to the floor beside him.

For a moment the only sounds were of distant movement and the quiet rasp of ties through laces. He located her wimple and veil and placed them into her hands, giving her fingers a brief squeeze. Then he shoved to his feet, closed his tunic, and called to his men.

Light burst into the chamber like the sun at dawn, blinding after such profound darkness. Blinking and shading his eyes, the earl hurried to greet their rescuers. Voices and sounds of movement and exclamations of wonder erupted and echoed through the large cellar as their rescuers discovered their find. By the time Eloise emerged from the far end of the barrels, her wimple and veil were again in place and her garments were suitably arranged. She was again the bossy but helpful sister who had come to Whitmore in place of the earl's bride.

It was only when they roused Sedgewick and started back down the passage toward the kitchens that they noticed a trail of bright hair hanging from beneath her wimple and veil down her back. Michael gallantly placed a lamp in Peril's hands and declared that he and the others would proceed ahead.

Peril delayed her in one of the chambers, on the pretext of looking at one of their finds. As the others' voices grew more distant, he looked down at her rosy cheeks and bee-stung lips, and his throat tightened.

"Your hair," he said thickly. "It's hanging down your back."

She reddened even more furiously and felt for it. He watched her remove her veil, and when he tried to help her gather her hair, she batted his hands away. Her fingers were clumsy as she twisted her tresses into a knot and tucked them into her wimple. By the time her veil was settled back into place, there were tears in her eyes and her shoulders were high and rigid.

"Eloise . . . Sister . . ."

In groping for a way to address the

woman he had encountered in the wine cellar, he spoke the one word in all of Christendom that could resurrect the barriers of the world, the church, and the sanctity of holy vows between them. She looked up through prisms of tears and self-loathing, and she drew back as if his touch burned like a foretaste of brimstone. Covering a sob with her hand, she rushed for the passage and the safety of the kitchens.

Eleven

Whispers blew like Spring's first gale through the hall the next morning: Sister Eloise had kept a vigil in the old chapel all night. Gratitude, some said, for the marvelous fortune of finding and retrieving Whitmore's treasures. Intercession, others conjectured, for Whitmore's luckless lord and for Whitmore's blighted but improving fortunes. Near a nuptial decision and seeking guidance, the few acquainted with her mission as husband judge presumed. Only one person on Whitmore had a clue as to the true state of her heart as she knelt all night in prayer: the earl himself, who was sunk into a bottomless pit of a mood and had spoken scarcely a word since the cellars.

That night, he climbed to the uncompleted top of the tower and paced in the moonlight, drinking wine from a small barrel they had hauled through the underground passages and into the kitchens.

The turmoil in his thoughts and in his blood were all but unbearable. He'd given in to the lowest and basest of human instincts and set hands to the nun sent to test and judge his character, his morality and rectitude. A holy sister. A handmaiden of the Almighty Himself.

Never mind that she hadn't resisted or even protested. He was a knight sworn to a stringent code and bound by his own word to protect her as if she were his nearest kin. And at the first flicker of a lamp, he had abandoned a lifetime of honor and sprung at her like a randy hound. He'd be fortunate if she didn't bring charges against him in the king's or church's courts.

He tossed back another whole cup of wine.

Violating a nun. It was probably grounds for going straight to Hell. Not that the Almighty needed any more grounds; his soul had been hanging by a thread for most of his life anyway. He had fought and killed in battle and lived the raw and punishing life of a soldier. He couldn't recall how long it had been since he confessed or took the Holy Eucharist, and couldn't remember a single proper prayer all the way to the end. He was damnation bound, all right.

But just now he couldn't imagine that Satan's future torments could be much worse than the agony of longing and loathing he was presently enduring.

By the next morning he was sprawled

across his bed slack-jawed and snoring, looking very much like a member of his garrison on the morning after a rout. Michael strode into his chambers with a sympathetic grimace and a bucket of water, and Peril came up sputtering, gasping, and holding his head.

"You'd better have a damned good reason for this!" he roared, though it chastened him more than Michael.

"Sister Eloise." The words tore through Peril's head like a javelin through a straw target. "She's in the hall. She wants to see you."

"I need a messenger," Sister Eloise said, rising to meet him as he strode into the bustling hall. She had been seated on one of the recently rescued chairs, directing the house women in the proper cleaning and waxing of the recovered furnishings.

"A messenger?" He was sure he paled beneath the beard-shadow gray of his face. "To whom?"

"The abbess of the Convent of the Brides of Virtue." She produced a sealed leather pouch and put it into his hands. "It must go straight away."

He stared numbly at the missive, realizing that he held the key to his future in his hands. It was her report to the abbess. The hammer and anvil pounding in his head stopped suddenly and the abrupt silence caused his head to swim and his stomach to churn. He looked up to find her moving toward the main doors of the hall. He was desperate to know the content of her message, but if he opened his mouth to ask, he was afraid he might be sick.

When she reached the doors she turned back for a moment, and from that presumably safe distance she met his gaze. He managed through his bloodshot eyes to see the strain evident in hers. But her voice came clear and strong.

"And you will need to send an escort."

Sir Michael, Sir Simon, Pascoe, William of Wright, Terrence the Bowman, and Father Basset were dispatched that very day to the convent, and whispers again flew through the manor and the village. The good sister had at last convinced the earl to marry and end the curse. The nun's vigil had resulted in her being led to a great treasure that was hidden in the tower. The earl had promised to reestablish a chapel in gratitude for finding the treasure. The earl was finally rich enough to send for a princess bride. Every rumor contained a kernel of truth that had grown through embellishment into a fanciful crop.

It was the right thing — the only thing — to do, Eloise told herself as she stood in her tower window watching the delegation leaving for the convent.

She had spent a long and painful night in the chapel on her knees, begging the Lord's forgiveness for being so unfaithful and so selfish . . . for abandoning her mission to dabble in her own shameful desires.

At first she had tried blaming it on the earl: He had grabbed and kissed and touched her, probably hoping to compromise her and force her hand. But then, he hadn't, and instead had tried to shield her from discovery and the humiliation her behavior would surely have brought down upon her. So, it hadn't been calculated or opportunistic, after all. It had just been the impulse of the moment, the prompting of the darkness and the urging of his baser desires.

But, with profuse apologies to the Almighty, she could not honestly say that his desires had seemed especially base or degrading. All he had done was touch her tenderly and passionately — she faced the bittersweet realization — the same way she had wanted to touch him for the last fortnight.

That made the situation all the more alarming. And urgent. She had to send for the earl's bride and end this test of his character — and hers — before something truly calamitous happened.

So she sat down with parchment and quill to write an earnest and positive appraisal of the earl's qualities as a man and a prospective husband. When the earl arrived in the hall later that morning, looking as if he'd been dragged through a vat of brewer's dregs, it was clear he had spent as troubled a night as she, and she knew that she was doing the right thing.

She only hoped that the sacrifice of her unruly desire in the Almighty's service would make up for the waywardness of her heart.

Later, as she was directing the men carrying the chapel furnishings from the underground cellars, she looked up to find Mary Clematis in full habit, hurrying toward her with a flushed face and widened eyes.

"I heard you sent a message to the convent!" she said in a rush, grabbing Eloise's hands. When she nodded, Mary Clematis paused to wheeze for a moment from the excitement and exertion. "Did he pass? Does he get a bride?"

Eloise forced a smile. "I had the earl send a message and an *escort*."

Mary Clematis gasped at the ramifications of that. "Really?" She squealed and threw her arms around Eloise. "How wonderful! His Lordship gets a bride . . . the people get a worthy lady . . . Whitmore gets its future back . . . and we get to go home. It couldn't have worked out better." As she caught her breath she turned to see what the workers were carrying into the manor house. "That looks like an altar!"

"It is," Eloise said, grateful that the invisible hand squeezing her chest had finally relaxed enough to allow her to breathe again. "The chapel I told you about . . . we found all sorts of things for it. Come and see."

Mary Clematis fell instantly under the spell of the neglected chapel.

"Please, Elly. I've done nothing since I've been here but lie on my cot and be a burden to you. I want to help. Let me help clean and right the chapel. Oh!" — inspiration struck — "if we work quickly enough, his lordship might even be able to say his marriage vows in it!"

Eloise clamped her jaw tight and hurried to help one of the house men who was struggling with a length of the heavy chancel railing. Mary Clematis followed eagerly, walking along with her, inspecting the freshly polished walnut.

"It's so beautiful, El— Sister Eloise." She looked up with artless excitement glowing in her face. "I'm sure Alaina will love it."

The heavy railing slipped from Eloise's fingers and landed right on her best friend's toes.

Eloise was too busy to take dinner in the hall that night; she was directing the cleaning and whitewashing of the buttery. And for the next several days she asked Roxanne and Johanna to bring her bites of food as she supervised the cleaning of the house that nestled around the base of the tower; sat with Edythe the head weaver, puzzling over the assembly of a French-made loom they had discovered in the cellars; and nursed Mary Clematis through what appeared to be a broken toe, sustained when that piece of chancel railing fell on her foot.

With a number of his men gone and a great deal to do, Peril avoided the hall in the evening as well. That first night he called for some bread and cheese to be sent to his chamber late, and the second evening he paused in the village to speak with the smith and found himself in the position of eating food produced by the two cooks he had recently exiled from his own kitchen. His patronage of their makeshift tavern had the unexpected benefit of mollifying their hurt pride and ending a stream of discontent that unsettled the villagers. While there, he noted that Tweet had something of a knack for making barley beer and, on impulse, suggested that she and Hessie return to the manor as mistresses of the brewery. They accepted with delight and, to celebrate, tapped a vat of their best brewing.

If only making amends to Sister Eloise were half so easy.

Several nights later, he walked his horse through the gates and up to the hall, noticing the red and gold streaks in the evening sky, the gentleness of the night air, and the warmth radiating from the sun-baked stones of the tower. He was not quite prepared for the bustle and busyness he encountered in the hall. There were groups of house women stitching linen and cleaning candle stands, and house men arranging furnishings and hanging yet another recently discovered banner. In the center of it all was Sister Eloise, supervising, as usual.

The smells of beeswax, fresh rushes, and dried clover caused him to take a long look at the hall he had been avoiding for the last two days. He was astonished by the changes in it. The soot had been sand-scraped from the walls, the floors had been scrubbed down to bare stone, the recovered table and chairs were freshly polished, and bright tapestries and banners hung from the rafters and on each side of the hearth. It was nothing short of handsome.

His gaze returned to Eloise.

What the devil was she doing, still overseeing and refurbishing his hall, still helping to set things right on Whitmore?

Squaring his shoulders, he headed for her, determined to say something to express his gratitude and, just perhaps, his regrets. But he reached her just as Roxanne arrived from the kitchens with a strapping young man carrying a heavy burlap bag.

"Beggin' pardon, sister," Roxanne said with an awkward half curtsey aside to her lord, "but I thought it best ye see this straight away. This is Adam, the carver's apprentice."

Young Adam bowed awkwardly and, at the cook's insistence, lowered his bag to the ground and drew out a newly carved bowl, cup, and spoon . . . then several more spoons. They were masterfully carved of finest hardwood, with designs that echoed the earl's family crest.

"Who did these?" she demanded of the youth.

"Me master told me to make spoons and I jus' . . . I thought . . . Well, I was in the hall oncet and seen His Lordship's shield —"

"You did these yourself?" It wasn't until he saw the smile dawning on her face that he nodded. "They're wonderful! Do you have other work?"

In short order, they were discussing plans for a number of other pieces to stand in the hall — including a large raised chest on legs in which to store the table linen that was being produced at that very moment, only a few feet away.

"You have a wonderful gift, young Adam," she said, putting a hand on the youth's arm. "Apply yourself with diligence to your craft, and you will bring prosperity to your family and honor to your lord."

The young woodcarver blushed and pulled his forelock, and bowed all the way to the kitchen stairs . . . which he then took in leaps of joy.

Only then did Eloise feel she had the composure required to face the earl. When she turned to him, his first words nearly unraveled her self-possession.

"You, too, have a gift, Sister Eloise." His eyes were dark with emotions she did not

302

want to see. "You manage to bring out good things in others . . . at least, most others. I myself seem to show you only my worst side."

"Please, milord —" She stiffened visibly and lowered her eyes.

"No, you must hear me out, Sister. You have been a more merciful judge than I have deserved. I would have you know . . . I will strive to be a good and worthy husband to whomever your abbess will send."

"I-I am sure the abbess will choose wisely." She forced a tight smile.

"As she did the first time," he said, taking a step backward and wishing he could do something with his hands besides long to touch her. "I only wish, Sister Eloise, that I were half as good a lord as you are a nun."

A crack appeared briefly in her composure and he couldn't help feeling a bit pleased that his words had found a tender mark.

"We must all serve God on the path we are given, milord. Even though that path may not be what we ourselves would choose." When she turned away to bury her attention in the absorbing process of hemming table linen, he could have sworn there was moisture in her eyes.

He wrestled with her statement for a moment, deciding that God, if He existed, was an unfathomably perverse being . . . to put people on paths that placed them at such odds with their own deepest natures and the desires of their hearts.

Sacrifice, they called it. According to the church, it saved and ennobled humankind.

With a huff of disgust, he headed for the comparative sanity of the stables and the company of his fellow dumb and plodding brutes.

Michael, Father Basset, and the others delivered Eloise's letter to the convent in only four days, the result of fair winds and a fiendishly fast bit of riding. The abbess, however, took her time reading it. She sat meditating in her solar, spent extra hours in the chapel, and took long walks through the lush spring fields. Clearly whatever Sister Eloise had written made her feel a great need for contemplation.

Michael and Simon went to Father Basset complaining of the delay. Father Basset went to Sister Archibald. And Sister Archibald reluctantly broached the subject with the abbess.

"It is never an easy thing, Sister Archibald, deciding a young woman's fate. But Eloise — I should have expected as much — has managed to make it even harder," the abbess declared.

"Harder?" Sister Archibald scowled. "Whatever did she write to ye?"

"She describes the man in such vivid terms . . . well, here. See for yourself." She shoved the parchment into Sister Archibald's hands and waited as the old nun read the neatly inscribed pages.

"But she clearly has tried to make a fair assessment," Sister Archibald said, before she reached the third and final page. "It's not *all* praise. She says he is stubborn an' proud an' slow to ask for help. Well, here, she does grow a bit grand an' flowery . . . 'a profound and heart-wrenching compassion as has been found only in the great saints' . . . 'feeling his people's distress most deeply and terribly, he struggles mightily under the great weight of his own sense of duty' . . . 'courageous beyond all bounds, fearing nothing, not even death itself, as he seeks to protect the small and the weak.' " Then her eyes narrowed. She shoved the page to arm's length to view it better and her eyes widened. "Oh."

The edge of the page was stained with tears.

"Oh, indeed." The abbess went to look out her solar window and stood drinking in the sun on her face for a moment. Then she turned to Sister Archibald. "You know how you've always spoken of making a pilgrimage to Canterbury before you die? Well, I think now would be the perfect time for it." She slipped her hands up her sleeves and summoned her most beatific expression. "And on the way you can deliver His Lordship's bride."

"Whom are ye going to send?" Archibald asked.

The abbess disappeared into the adjoining bedchamber and returned with a small wooden box. When she placed it in Sister Archibald's hands the elder nun opened it with a quizzical expression and stared at the contents. Then the sense of it struck her and she looked up with alarm.

"Are ye certain about this?"

"Absolutely." The abbess produced a most satisfied smile.

Sister Archibald sighed.

"Oh, dear."

Spring finally arrived at Whitmore with a series of warm rains that brought both banes and blessings. Mud covered the village paths, but well-watered crops sprouted vigorously in newly planted fields. The whitewash applied to the dairy ran in streams down the path, but the dirt and grime on the other work houses was rinsed away as well. The stream and pond overflowed, but so did the fresh water in the rain barrels and cisterns. Then the rain stopped, the sun came out, and everything on Whitmore seemed renewed.

Except Eloise's spirits.

She worked hard from dawn to dusk each day; directing, overseeing, arranging, and establishing. Everywhere she went, people greeted her warmly and spoke enthusiastically about their lord's upcoming marriage and the lifting of the "curse." Whenever the subject came up, she would shut her eyes and think of the convent and of how much easier life would be when she had turned her stubborn will and wayward heart, not to mention her troublesome mass of hair, over to the Almighty.

Peril suffered the same litany of inquiry and expectation wherever he went on Whitmore, with a strangely similar discomfort. And it was all but intolerable, each evening, when he sat at his newly refurbished table with Sister Eloise and pretended to be interested in her flat-to-the-point-of-toneless reports on some aspect of the estate's progress.

He would unfocus his eyes and try to

imagine some meek, biddable young thing in her place, staring up at him with limpid brown eyes filled with wifely adoration. Then he would shift uncomfortably and try imagining some lithe, nubile young temptress in that chair, looking at him with sly, womanly hunger. It was a measure of his discontent that he fled that one to conjure a prim, elegant young princess of a girl who continually sniffed at him, as if she believed that he had a penchant for stepping in dog piles.

When his horse-master rushed into the hall, more than a week later, with news that three newborn foals from their best mares were missing from the north pasture, his first response was relief that he finally had a problem that involved four-legged females instead of the two-legged variety.

His second and somewhat belated response was chagrin that he had been so focused on reviving his property and preparing for his bride that he had let the matter of the boy Tad's abduction languish. Only now, when there was yet another serious loss, did he move to lead a mounted contingent of his men out to the pasture and the surrounding forest to conduct a thorough search. If only he could get this marriage business over and done with, so that he could get back to the simpler and infinitely more satisfying duties of being a leader of men.

He was still out with his men the next morning, when Michael and his bridal escort rode through the village, into the gates, and up the knoll leading to the hall.

"Elly!" Mary Clematis hobbled on her makeshift crutch all the way from the herb gardens to the weavers' house to bring Eloise word of their arrival. "They're here! Sir Michael and the escort — the bride is here!"

Eloise stood with her hands full of carded wool and a spindle slowly spinning to a stop at the end of a newly wound strand of yarn. Her heart slowed like the spindle and stopped as well.

The bride was here.

She grabbed up the skirt of her habit and ran to the front of the hall, where a large donkey cart sat just outside the doors. The sight of three black habits clustered together in the hall sent waves of recognition and longing through her. She halted in the doorway to absorb the fact of their presence and brace for what lay ahead. Sir Michael first heard and then spotted her. The delegation followed his gaze and turned to greet her.

"Sister Archibald!" She flew to embrace the old nun, who laughed and endured her enthusiasm with good grace. "And Sister Mary Montpellier. And Sister Rosemary." She hugged each of them in turn, and then looked past them and all around them. "What are you doing here?"

"Well, my child," Sister Archibald said, giving her cheek an affectionate pat, "ye know I've always wanted to make a pilgrimage to Canterbury. Our good abbess thought now would be a good time, seeing that ye made yer report an' there was a timely escort to see to our safety."

"How thoughtful of her. And the earl's bride, where is she?" Eloise looked around. "You did bring her, did you not?"

The old nun folded her hands around the cross hanging from her waist.

"If we might see you in private, Eloise," she said with a calm that might have meant anything, but combined with a furtive glance toward Michael could only mean that there was something she preferred he did not hear. With a feeling of growing dread, Eloise led them first to the newly refurbished chapel — which was occupied by Father Basset, engaged in a loud and earnest prayer vigil of thanksgiving for his restored sanctuary.

They finally found the solitude they sought in one of the refurnished chambers in the manor house.

"What's happened? Where is the earl's bride?" she blurted out the minute the door closed behind them. "I sent my report of the husband test to the abbess, along with a recommendation that he be given a bride."

"Yes, yes, my dear. The abbess was much impressed with yer report. It was clear that ye had made a thorough study of the man's character, habits, an' nuptial potential." Sister Archibald came to take her by the hand and pat it reassuringly. "And the abbess has indeed sent him a bride."

"Well, who is she? Where is she?" Eloise was annoyed by the old nun's cryptic manner.

Sister Archibald turned to Sister Rosemary, who produced from under the surplice of her habit a small wooden box and handed it to her. And with that same calm smile, Sister Archibald put it in Eloise's hands.

"She is here."

Scowling, Eloise flipped the metal latch and opened the box. Inside there was a small silver disk on a handle, similar to a hairbrush. But when she lifted and turned it, the other side of the disk was a mirror of highly polished metal. She stared at it, then at the trio of elder sisters in confusion.

"She is here?" She looked into the empty box again, then beneath it, certain she was missing something. Then she grew agitated. "What game is this? I sent for a bride . . . for the earl and you bring me a . . ." She paled as the first hint of its meaning bloomed in her mind. Then Mother Archibald confirmed it.

"Look into th' mirror, Eloise. Ye will see the earl's bride."

Knowing what she would see and hoping against all odds that it would be a trick or that the laws of nature would have somehow changed . . . she did look. And there was her own face. Plain as day. Her eyes wide with horror. Her skin pale with disbelief.

"Me?"

"Yes, you."

Her knees buckled. They led her to a seat on a bench beneath a large window, and one fanned her while another produced a vial of foul-smelling salts and waved it under her nose. Her dizziness was soon replaced by a rush of heat.

"But that's preposterous — absurd. I'm a nun. I cannot marry anybody!"

"You're a novice, Eloise. You have not taken your vows, nor have you made the final sacrifice of your worldly life to God," Mary Montpellier said.

"But I'm the convent's husband judge. I'm an official of the convent. I'm due to take my vows when I return . . . the abbess said so."

"I know this comes as a shock, Eloise," Sister Archibald said settling onto the window seat beside her. "But the abbess spent three days in prayer and supplication and this was the answer the Lord provided. Ye are to marry th' earl. That is the abbess's order."

The finality of it was crushing.

"But I'm a *nun*. Almost. I've promised my heart and hands to the church and to God. It was long ago decided that my vocation was inside the convent." She trembled and her hands grew clammy. "I know I have not always been the most exemplary of novices, but my efforts to improve things have yielded at least *some* good things." Panic crept into her voice and she grabbed Sister Archibald's knotty hands. "I know that the abbess would find me changed by this experience. I have learned much in my time here, and I promise that if I am allowed to return to the convent —"

"Eloise!" Archibald interrupted her rising plea and turned to the other sisters. "If ye would leave us for a few moments, Sisters." When the door closed and they were alone the old nun freed her hands and took Eloise's face between them. "Ye must hear me, Eloise. The decision is made and will not be undone. If ye value yer devotion to our order and our convent, ye must submit to our direction and marry th' earl."

"But I'm a *nun*," Eloise repeated, feeling the words resonate without finding a mark and return to her an empty echo. "I was never a maiden meant for marriage. I'm going to be an abbess someday. The convent is where I *belong*."

"Listen to me, child," Archibald said, mirroring Eloise's misery in her own sad expression. "The abbess would never have allowed ye to take vows as a nun. Ye are too stubborn and inquisitive and restless to ever make a nun. Ye are too bright and earnest and impetuous to ever be bound by our ancient rules. Ye are of th' world, child. It has been plain to us for some time now."

Her life with the sisters . . . her growth, her struggles, and her dreams . . . opened before Eloise in her memory. The censure that had followed her attempts to improve the convent's workings, the disapproval in the older sisters' faces, and the times she had felt merely tolerated . . . she had thought they were just the difficulties that accompanied being a novice. Had each, instead, been a sign of their growing judgment that she didn't have the heart of a nun? That she didn't belong with them?

The possibility took up residence so quickly in her that she could not properly defend against it. The possibility that she had never belonged in the place she had always thought of as her home was unbearable. The weight of it descended on her and she had to move or be crushed by it.

Pulling away from the old nun, she rushed out the door and down the steps and around the hall. When she reached the gates, she began to run. When she reached the fields, she kept running. When she reached the woods, she kept going. But the fire consuming the old dreams and expectations in her heart slowly ran out of fuel, and she finally sank onto a tree trunk beside a small stream. The soothing sounds of the water gurgling nearby released the tears she had been holding back. They came with huge, wrenching sobs that purged the tension of years of needing and trying to remake herself into what she and others both expected she should be.

When the last of her sobs died away, she lay on the tree trunk looking up through the tiny new leaves of the trees. The blue of the sky overhead was deepening; the sun was beginning to set.

She had no idea where she was, but for the moment it didn't seem to matter that she was lost in the woods. It couldn't compare with the horror of being so lost inside.

If she wasn't a nun, who was she? If God didn't want her, who did? That, she couldn't help feeling, was the key to it all. God hadn't accepted her apology . . . was punishing her for her grievous lapse of steadfastness and purity of heart. They said they had known she wasn't suitable for some time now. But if she hadn't allowed Peril of Whitmore to steal away some of her devotion to her calling, would she be going home to take her vows anyway?

Her thoughts turned to the earl, who was forced to share her punishment. He had come to the Brides of Virtue seeking a bride filled with the highest virtue, and now was being assigned a wife so lacking in obedience, respect, and humility that she was considered unfit to give her life in service to God. She could just imagine his reaction to that.

He had humbled himself to accept her counsel and guidance believing she was a nun, thinking she was the convent's — thus,

God's — capable representative in his life. What would he think when he learned she was really just God's hanger-on?

She didn't ever want to see that anger and disappointment in his eyes.

As the shadows lengthened and began to join, she heard sounds of movement in the forest nearby and froze. Locating the source and watching from behind a tree, she made out several horsemen and shrank back, thinking they were the earl's men, sent to bring her back to face his ire. She slipped backward through the old leaves and underbrush, trying to make as little sound as possible. But her foot snapped a small branch and the sound resonated through the trees.

Clutching her veil together beneath her chin to cover the white of her wimple, she turned and ran. Behind her, the voices and the sounds of horses crashing through the underbrush grew steadily louder. As the riders closed in on her, she was suddenly grabbed and dragged and stuffed bodily into a large, hollow tree. A hand clamped tightly over her mouth, and though she struggled, she was pinned too tightly into the crevice to resist.

"Hush!" came a fierce whisper. "These aren't the kind of men a woman should be caught by in the woods!"

Twelve

Something in the voice and in the dark eyes staring into hers caused her to quiet and still. As her eyes adjusted, the light coming through the narrow opening in the tree trunk allowed her to see more of her captor. There was a halo of wispy graying hair around a set of decidedly feminine features. It was a woman!

They stayed in the hollow for some minutes, listening, waiting for the horsemen to leave. Several moments after the last sounds outside died away, the older woman removed her hand from Eloise's mouth and backed out of the tree.

"Shhh." She pressed a hand to her own lips as Eloise emerged into the lowering daylight. "They'll not be far away. Come with me."

Eloise scowled, uncertain, but then picked up her skirts and followed the retreating form, imitating her caution. Her rescuer had long graying hair hanging free down her back and moved with more subtlety and grace than Eloise would have expected in one so much older. After a while, they emerged into a small clearing and the old woman straightened, stretched, and paused to wait for her.

"We're safe enough now. They don't come this far north in the woods." She flashed a grin and Eloise noticed a healthy set of teeth. "It's haunted here, you know."

"It is?" Eloise looked around warily. "By what?"

"Me, of course. At least that's what they think. It causes them to stay well away and leave me alone, so I am content to let them think me a ghost or spirit." She smoothed back her hair and produced a cord to tie it into a bundle at the nape of her neck. "Well, at least my hair is dry."

"Your hair?" Puzzled, Eloise fell in beside her as she walked.

"I had bathed in the stream and was walking back with my hair down, letting it dry. Though in truth, I like to let it free whenever I'm in the woods. What is it about women's hair that terrifies men and little boys so? One glimpse and it's 'Sweet Mother Mary — it's a ghost!' "

Eloise shook her head, hoping to clear it. Surely she was dazed and was hearing things.

"What was it that set you flying? A molestation, a beating, or a betrayal?"

"What?" Eloise stopped and looked at the woman.

"From your habit, I can tell you're a sister of the Roman church. You were in the woods . . . terrified of being discovered . . . and bearing the tracks of tears on your face. Something bad must have happened."

"You are the most plainspoken ghost I've ever encountered," Eloise said, tightening her mouth as if to keep her secret inside.

The woman's quiet laugh was no hallucination.

"I probably am, at that," the woman said, studying her and her reluctance to speak of whatever it was that had set her fleeing. "You're running from something." Her smile became compassion itself. "I ran once. To Paris and Rome and Athens . . . even Jerusalem. In the end I came home. Problems don't disappear when you run, you know. You carry them with you wherever you go." She tapped Eloise's chest, above her heart. "In here." She tilted her head and watched those words find fertile ground in Eloise's heart.

Eloise's shoulders drooped as she weighed the woman's wise words and the heaviness of her conscience against her sorrow over her rejection and her fear of the future. How far would she have to run to escape the painful memories of her convent days . . . the serenity of the cloister, the holy aura of the chapel, the lively chatter of the girls as they passed along the cloister walk? Where could she go to forget the stubborn, brave-hearted earl, with his magical kisses that set her lips tingling and his touch that set her skin aflame?

"Where is it you want to go, little sister?"

"I want . . . I should . . . I don't know. I don't know where I belong."

"Well, everyone belongs somewhere." The woman dipped her head to collect Eloise's gaze in hers. "Creation is so great and so varied that there is a place in it for everything and everyone." Again she smiled. "The hardest part of living, I have discovered, is learning where you truly belong and finding the courage to live there."

Eloise studied the woman's sun-weathered face and thoughtful expression. How could this strange woman in the woods know the exact words that would both guide and comfort her aching heart? Angels, she had heard it said, often appeared to people in unlikely guises.

Some of the weight on her shoulders and chest began to lift.

"You're right. Running away won't solve anything. I must go back to the manor. I must see it through. Can you direct me toward Whitmore?"

"Whitmore?" The woman searched her face for a moment, then grew solemn. "That is where your trouble lies?" When Eloise nodded, the woman studied her and sighed. "Then it is on Whitmore that you must seek your answers." She looked around to orient herself and then pointed out the way.

Eloise struck off in the indicated direction, then turned to thank her guide and ask her name. The woman was already gone.

She walked for some time, her eyes adjusting to the deepening darkness, hoping she was headed in the right direction. After a time, she heard the sounds of movement all around her and tried running first one direction, then another. Each way was blocked by men on horseback emerging from the trees. She froze, her pulse pounding.

"What the Devil?" came a familiar voice.

She whirled and found the earl moving up behind her in the dim light.

"What are you doing out here?" he demanded.

"I was just taking a walk . . . in contemplation . . . and lost my way," she said as more familiar faces emerged from the darkness.

"We found a camp, recently abandoned,

not far from here," he declared irritably. "There are thieves camped in these woods. What if they had found you first?" He edged closer, removed his foot from his stirrup and lowered a gauntlet-clad arm, indicating that she should climb up. When she hesitated, his scowl deepened. "Well, are you going to ride back or do you insist on walking?"

Sir Ethan dismounted to give her a knee up and, unable to refuse, she climbed aboard. As the earl kicked his mount into motion, she had to grab him to keep from tumbling off. He chuckled as she fumbled for a secure hold on his mail tunic and belt.

"Already forgotten how to ride double?" He seized her hands and pulled them around his waist on each side, letting his hand linger over hers.

She hadn't forgotten. From the sudden warming of her body wherever they touched and the ache of longing in her middle, she hadn't forgotten any part of being close to him, of having her arms around him, of wanting him. Even knowing that this unexpected taste of closeness to him was probably a part of her punishment, she laid her cheek against his broad back and allowed herself to drink in the fleeting pleasure of his presence.

And while she was being wanton and

wicked and selfish, an even more dissolute part of her felt glad that the fair but haughty Alaina would never be able to put her arms around him like this. Or the sweet, dark-eyed Helen of Ghent. Or sultry, raven-haired Lissette de Mornay. She felt a defiant surge of pleasure at the thought that none of the precious maidens groomed by her convent would ever have him or hold him or . . .

She didn't want anyone to marry him — the admission dealt the finishing blow to her cloister-centered ambitions — *except her.*

The sight of an empty donkey cart in front of the hall jolted Peril as he rode up the path toward the tower and house. The escort he sent to the convent . . . they were back with the bride he was promised. Until that moment, he hadn't reckoned with the fact that he would soon stand face to face with a stranger, a young and sheltered girl who would speak vows with him and from that day forward would share his bed and board, his triumphs and difficulties . . . his very life. He fought a brief and shameful urge to flee. Instead, he glanced over his shoulder at Sister Eloise.

"They're here." He beckoned to Sir Ethan to come and help her down. "What were you doing out wandering around in the woods?

Why weren't you here to greet them when they came?"

She waited until she was on the ground and halfway through the doors to answer.

"I was."

He dismounted and handed his horse off to a stable-boy, glowering at her retreating form, astounded by her silence on so important a matter. She might have at least said something, warned him that he was riding into his first glimpse of — He rubbed his chin irritably and groaned as he realized he was bearing four days of beard and three days of sweat, smoke, and horse into his first meeting with his bride. There was no way to reach his chamber and bathe and prepare himself without going through the hall.

He removed his gauntlets and tucked them into his belt, then raked his hands back through his hair. He was as presentable as he would be. . . .

But then he paused inside the door, at the foot of the steps. His mouth was suddenly dry and his heart was pounding as it did the night before a battle. Each of the steps before him looked like a wall that had to be scaled. . . .

Michael appeared at the top of the stairs and hurried down to take him by the arm and pull him back outside. By the light of the torches set in brackets outside the doors, his second in command didn't look pleased.

"I'm sorry, milord. I didn't know what to do. She said to bring them, so, I brought them."

"*Them?*" Peril glanced back through the doors.

"The nuns, milord. Three of 'em." He scratched his ear, clearly bewildered. "None of them looked young enough or spry enough to be a bride, but you had given orders . . ."

Peril groaned. More nuns. And no bride. Something had gone wrong; he could feel it in his bones. And he had a fair notion of who was responsible. Giving Michael an absolving clap on the shoulder, he took a deep breath and strode for the hall.

The delegation from the convent was gathered with Sister Eloise and Sister Mary Clematis, seated on a bench beside the hearth at the far end of the hall and looking like a solemn row of blackbirds perched on a gable. Father Basset hovered behind them with a look that might have been either anxiety or the onset of the ague. As Peril approached, he was somewhat relieved to recognize one of the three nuns; Sister Archibald had been his chaperon at the convent. The others were, as Michael had observed, neither young enough nor spry enough to be a bride in disguise.

He turned a questioning look on Sister Eloise, but she avoided his gaze.

"Welcome, Sister Archibald, Sisters," he said springing up onto the dais and making straight for the leader of the contingent. "I wasn't aware you had arrived until this very moment. I was out in the forest chasing down a pack of thieves when I happened upon Sister Eloise. My apologies that I was not here to greet you. I hope my servants have made you comfortable." When they nodded and murmured thanks and were properly introduced, he braced himself and looked all around. "Now, where is my 'bride of virtue'?"

Sister Archibald glanced at Sister Eloise, who still refused to look up.

"Sister Eloise did not tell ye?" she asked.

"Tell me what?" He felt a sense of doom creeping over him and turned to Sister Eloise. "Tell me *what*, Sister?"

"Yer Lordship, is there somewhere we might speak in private?" the old nun asked with a lowered voice.

Privacy. It was the death knell of his hopes for a quick and painless wedding. He gave the order, and as Michael and Simon cleared the hall of everyone, except the nuns, the earl, and Father Basset, a hot spot developed in the pit of his stomach. He fixed a glare on Eloise that was so intense that she couldn't help but lift her head. As the main doors banged shut, she went to stand beside Sister Archibald. And she did not look happy.

"Where is my bride?" he demanded growing louder with each word. "I complied with your damnable requirements . . . submitted to your husband test and passed it. Where is she?"

"She is here, Your Lordship." Eloise retrieved a wooden box from one of the other nuns and thrust it into his hands.

He opened it and scowled at the small silver mirror. "What is this?" He picked it up and held it up into the light.

"That was not meant for ye, Yer Lordship. 'Twas meant for Sister Eloise," Sister Archibald said, taking the mirror from him and handing it to Sister Eloise, who held it up and looked into it so that Peril could also see her reflection. "So that *she* would see yer bride."

His expression went blank for a moment as he struggled both to reach and to avoid the obvious conclusion. His fists clenched.

"Dammit, sister, the only thing I hate

worse than proverbs is riddles. Tell me whatever the Devil you mean to say in plain language."

"It is me," Sister Eloise said with strain evident in her voice. "The abbess said *I* am to marry you."

The drop of a feather could have been heard all over the hall.

Peril stared at her anguished eyes and bitten lip and realized she was serious. Here in front of God and Father Basset — who sat down with a thud — she was declaring that he had to marry *her*.

"But you're a nun. You can't marry. In fact, you're already supposed to *be* married, to God Himself!"

"Please, Yer Lordship," Sister Archibald said, seizing both his and Eloise's arms. "If ye will but hear my explanation. I know this comes as a shock — it . . . always does. But 'tis by far th' best way to both test an unknown candidate's suitability for marriage and to supply him th' proper bride. The husband judge is always a novice, a special young woman who has not yet taken her final vows. If the candidate can win the favor of th' husband judge, then she is given to him as his bride."

"But th-that is . . . trickery!" he sputtered.

"No, Yer Lordship, it is common sense.

Who better to wed a man than a woman who already sees and appreciates his finer qualities and has pleaded his case to the abbess of our convent?"

"It is dishonest to send out a woman under the pretense of — it's an outright lie." He turned on Eloise. "I thought you were a real nun, promised to God."

"I was." Eloise said, her eyes stinging. "At least *I* thought I was."

"But you knew you hadn't taken vows." Then he turned on Sister Archibald with his temper rising. "You sent a green, unsworn girl to sit in judgment over me?"

"The abbess sent th' best person for the task, Yer Lordship. Eloise of Argent may be a novice, but she is hardly a green girl. She is one-and-twenty years of age. She has studied agriculture and husbandry and estate management, and is well lettered and skilled at record-keeping. From what I have seen and heard, both ye and yer estate have already benefited from her varied talents."

She released the earl to put an arm around Eloise.

"The abbess believed, after reading Eloise's report and seeking our dear Lord's will, that there was but one woman in our convent fit to serve as yer bride. Thus, her order to Sis— I mean, *Eloise* — to marry ye."

"Her order?" This new wrinkle sent him staggering back. He looked at Eloise's pale face in dismay. "You've been ordered to marry me?"

"I have," she said quietly.

"And you would com— ply with this order?" His voice cracked mid-statement.

Eloise looked up, her expression guarded but somehow still vulnerable, her blue eyes dark with turbulent emotion. He couldn't help thinking that she spoke the truth; she hadn't known she was intended as his bride. She had honestly come to judge him and had found him worthy. And in pleading his case she had managed to seal her own fate as well as his.

"Answer me. Would you obey your abbess and marry me?"

She looked to Sister Archibald and then to the other nuns, as if hoping for a reprieve. When none came, she took a deep, shuddering breath and nodded.

"Yes."

He couldn't fathom it. Marrying Sister Eloise. Who wasn't actually *Sister Eloise* after all. And if she wasn't a nun, who was she? An ordinary female? He fell back a step, then another, staring at her. All of this time he'd been bullied and ordered about by a mere maid? He turned on Sister Archibald.

"I came to your convent for a bride filled with the highest virtue, and this is what I get? An apprentice nun who has to be ordered to marry me?"

"But, don't you see, milord? She is perfect." Father Basset was suddenly on his feet, miraculously recovered from his initial shock. "Who could be more virtuous than a young sister of the church, one whose heart is pledged to God's holy work? And what holier work could there be than ridding a whole estate and village of the specter of a foul curse?" With his hands clasped in eager supplication, he came to stand beside the mortified Eloise. "Just think, milord, of how much she has already done to lift the people's spirits. Only imagine their joy when they learn she is to be their lady."

Peril glanced from the eager Basset to Sister Archibald to the nuns now standing behind Eloise in a show of support.

"In order to be *their* lady, she has to be *my* wife!" he declared with rising alarm. "What assurance do I have that she could ever be a proper wife?"

Sister Archibald seemed stunned by the question, then recovered and folded her arms with a stern expression. "Ye agreed to abide by the abbess's choice for yer bride.

We expect, Yer Lordship, that ye will honor that word."

"And your abbess agreed to send me one of the maidens that were present that morning . . . one of the ones who helped to —" He suffered a cold shower of insight. That witch abbess. That scourge on the male half of humanity! Basset had warned him about her kind.

He turned away, struggling to master his chaotic feelings, and spotted Michael and Simon standing nearby, guarding the kitchen stairs, their arms crossed and their faces carefully blank. As he glowered at them, Michael's mouth quirked up on one side. The more his irritation showed, the broader and more insinuating Michael's grin grew. The wretch clearly relished the notion of his lord having to marry the bossy little nun. A moment later that same grin appeared on Simon's angular face.

Dammit, a man should be able to expect better loyalty from the men sworn to protect him with their very lives!

He grabbed his bride by the arm and dragged her toward the tower steps. "I want a word with you, *Sister* Eloise."

She tried to resist, but he pulled her up the steps and into his darkened chamber. For a long, volatile moment he towered over her, smelling the wool and linen scent of her, feeling her warmth in the cool chamber.

"Tell me you didn't know," he demanded.

She shook her head slowly. "I *didn't* know."

Her face was taut with emotion, and now that she was looking directly at him he could see that her eyes were red and her nose was swollen. She apparently hadn't taken the news much better than he had. The thought was anything but comforting. If she and the old nun were to be believed, she had expected that when his bride arrived, she would journey back to the convent and take her vows. She wanted to be a nun. And he wanted a wife, not a permanently installed judge of every aspect of his life!

"But now that you do know, you're willing to sacrifice yourself on the altar of holy obedience." He stuck his face close to hers. "Well, thank you, Sister Judge, but no thank you."

"What are you saying?" She staggered back a step.

"I asked for and was promised a bride filled with the highest virtue. You may qualify on the 'virtue' part, but I have serious doubts about your suitability as a 'bride.'"

"But, I — I —"

"What do you know about being a wife?" He didn't wait for an answer. "Don't tell me, let me guess: You've made a thorough study of it."

She looked as if she'd been slapped. For an unsettling moment, he could see hurt warring with outrage in her response. To his relief, her anger won.

"You have already seen my character and my abilities," she declared.

"I've seen proud, headstrong, all-knowing 'Sister Eloise' at work. She's used to having her say and then having her way. But I've never seen this 'Eloise' who has been ordered to become my bride." He knew the instant he said it that it wasn't quite true. He had indeed glimpsed another young woman . . . that night in her chamber . . . that day in the wine cellar . . .

"They are one and the same." Her voice thickened and her eyes suddenly glistened with moisture.

"Are they indeed?"

He edged closer and boldly looked her over, recalling the color of her hair and the softness of her lips and wishing those memories weren't inserting themselves into the decision he was making just now. He had to marry her or not marry her; there was nothing in between.

"Would you willingly fulfill *all* the duties of a wife? Before you answer, I would have you know that I intend to have a cooperative bride in my bed and I intend to have children. Can you do that?"

She looked away for a moment and he saw her cheeks redden.

"I don't know, Your Lordship."

It was as honest an answer as he had ever heard.

"Would you try . . . in good faith?" he demanded.

"I would try."

God's teeth! What was he getting himself into?

"I'm not a religious man. I won't attend mass every damned day. And I won't have you dropping to your knees to sob on Heaven's shoulder every time I look at you crossways. Can you live with that?"

To her credit, she thought about it for a moment.

"May I celebrate special holy days like Easter and Christ Mass?"

It was his turn to think. "I suppose there would be no harm in that."

"Then I would learn to live with it."

"Then you'll see to my hall and house and not bother me with trifles. You'll accept my word as your law and you'll obey me" — inspiration struck — "as you've obeyed your blessed abbess. Can you do that?"

She hesitated, blinked, then seemed to resign herself.

"I believe I can obey you as if you were my abbess."

He watched her shoulders begin to sag under the weight he had just placed on them, and something in him balked at the notion of burdening them further. There would be time in the days ahead for teaching her the finer points of wifery. Right now he had a more important test to perform.

He reached for her veil and she shrank back. He engaged her eyes and narrowed his, giving her to understand that her promise of obedience began now. She swallowed hard and submitted as he found the pins holding her veil and removed them.

She watched her veil as it slid away, but made no move to halt or touch it. Then he reached for the ties of her wimple and undid them, pulling the garment from her. She bit her lip and looked down. As he tossed it aside, her gaze followed it to the dark puddle her veil had made on the floor. When he untied her hair and let it fall down her back, she tensed. He lifted her chin to search her reaction and was disarmed by

337

the tears in her eyes.

There was only one way to know if those tears were caused by sadness at the passing of her old life or by a genuine dread of marrying him.

He took her face between his hands and lowered his lips to hers.

Eloise's senses reeled. A part of her long-trusted defenses had slid away with each convent garment he pulled from her. He had bared her head, but in reality he had also bared her bruised and tender soul. She stood before him naked now, revealed and vulnerable in a way she never imagined. She no longer had the protection or the guidance of church and convent. There was no saintly example, no prescribed churchly formula to help her deal with the approaches of a man who would soon claim her future, her being, and her body as his right.

She was just Eloise.

A woman. Alone.

Then his lips covered hers and his arms wrapped around her and his body infused hers with sensual warmth. She opened to his kiss, drinking in the assurance of his movements, his confidence, his hunger. She slid her arms around him and felt the soundless sigh of approval that vibrated through his body in response. He wanted her willingness in this most intimate of encounters just as she wanted, needed, to feel his desire for her. It began to fill the empty place in her heart.

She was indeed just a woman. But no longer quite so alone.

When he released her, she nearly collapsed. Her bones had all but melted under the heat of his kisses. She struggled to focus her eyes and found him staring at her with an intensity that took what was left of her breath. She saw him turn, adjust his tunic, and take a deep, determined breath. Then he opened the door, grabbed her by the wrist, and pulled her back down the stairs and into the start of a very different life.

Most noble marriages occurred after lengthy negotiations in which property settlements were the main focus. The marriages of the penniless but worthy Brides of Virtue were also subject to certain "agreements," as Peril learned the moment he descended the stairs with Eloise in tow and announced to the hushed hall: "I have decided to marry Sis— Eloise."

While the other sisters recovered from the shock of seeing Eloise's hair so blatantly displayed and flocked around her with outstretched arms, Sister Archibald pulled a small sheaf of documents from under her apronlike surplice.

"Excellent. Just excellent." She leveled an authoritative look on Peril. "We have enough people present to hear the words of betrothal an' witness th' settlement."

"Settlement?" Peril felt as if he'd been blindsided. *Again.*

"The little matter of Eloise's dower settlement and yer donation to the convent." Archibald smiled beatifically. "Formalities, really."

"But I have already given my word that —"

"The abbess took th' liberty of drafting an agreement." Sister Archibald opened the parchment and perused the writing. "Just a simple signature or two."

"What sort of settlement could the abbess expect His Lordship to make . . ." Eloise hurried to the table to scrutinize the documents, and there it was: one third of his property and chattels were to go to her. And one tenth of the manor's income was pledged to the convent for the next ten years! "But this is —"

"Not your concern." Peril grabbed the documents from her.

"But a tithe from the estate's income for ten years . . ." She scowled at Sister Archibald and then at him. "The amount surely must be adjusted."

"I said, this is none of your business. As my bride you will have to learn to *listen* better."

"But as your bride, milord, is it not my duty to help guard and conserve your resources and to see that you don't pay exorbitant sums for things that —"

"No sum would be exorbitant for a suitably virtuous and *obedient* bride," he declared, with a glare that warned her to amend her willful behavior.

She took his point and drew in her chin. Her guilt at costing him so much of his substance had just been countered by his arrogance. If he refused to listen to her, then he deserved to suffer the consequences.

Ignoring the documents in his hands, he looked her over instead.

"Rest assured, Eloise, I intend to get full measure for my money." Amidst muffled chuckles from Michael and Simon, he turned to Sister Archibald. "Where do I sign?"

Then came the matter of the nuptials themselves.

"When, milord?" Father Basset's voice cut through the excited group. "It is still Lent, and soon it will be Holy Week, and then Easter. And of course we will need time for the banns —"

"Two days," Peril declared.

"Two *days?* But, milord, that is impossible." Basset began to wring his hands. "The church —"

"Can damned well make accommodations in special circumstances!"

"Special circumstances? Yes. Well." Father Basset leaned back to avoid Peril's jutting chin. "I suppose there is always room for a dispensation . . ."

Then Sister Archibald presented Peril with a copy of the documents and a smile that bordered on the cherubic. "I wonder if we might impose upon ye yet again, Yer Lordship . . . for another kindness?"

He took a breath and braced.

"What more would you have of me?"

"We must leave for Canterbury a day or so after th' wedding. I was hoping ye would be so kind as to provide us an escort."

"An escort to speed you on your way?" He smiled fiercely. "It would be my pleasure."

Sister Mary Clematis and Sister Archibald and her delegation, who were the only family Eloise had, were put to work overseeing the wedding dinner and the readying of the hall. They eagerly took stock of the manor's food stores and planned stew, pies, pasties, special breads, and puddings. Then they set the householders to cleaning and preparing the hall and the bridal chamber. The one real difficulty they encountered was the matter of Eloise's wedding garments. There was no fabric, and certainly no time for stitching something new. It was late on the eve before the wedding that Madame Fleurmort emerged from her chamber with one of Lady Alicia's favorite gowns, a pale blue velvet, complemented by a dark blue velvet circlet, and an embroidered silk veil.

That night, the women gathered in Eloise's tower chamber to bathe her and prepare her for the following morning. They scented the water with wild violets, and afterward, a tearful Mary Clematis brushed her hair until it was dry.

"Oh, Elly, I don't know what I'll do without you."

"It will be all right, Clemmie." Eloise swallowed against the lump in her throat. "Perhaps if we ask, the abbess will allow you to stay here with me."

Later, in the dark of night and in the solitary vigil of her sleepless mind, Eloise wondered if this felt like the vigil she might have kept as a novice taking final vows. As she lay listening to the old sisters snore on their pallets around the chamber, tears trickled from the corners of her eyes back into her hair.

This was her last night as Eloise of Argent. By tomorrow's None, she would be Eloise of Whitmore, and would continue to bear that name until death parted her from her earthly lord and husband.

The next morning, Peril stood on the dais of his newly refurbished hall, flanked by his knights and priest, waiting for his bride and feeling that he had forgotten something. He fidgeted with his slashed velvet sleeves, then adjusted his gold-trimmed belt and squashed the urge to run a hand over his still damp hair. It didn't matter how he looked, he told himself. His reluctant bride would hardly be impressed.

Still, he continued to make minor adjustments until he glanced over his shoulder and found his knights smiling knowingly at him. He jerked his gaze away to look out over the rest of the sizeable crowd of villeins and cottagers gathered in the hall.

He *wasn't* nervous, dammit. Just eager to have it done.

Then the sounds of women singing issued from the tower stairs, followed a moment later by the nuns, walking two by two. They bore lighted candles and sang so sweetly of

"Maria Dolce" that the entire assembly, some of whom had already imbibed a good bit of beer, fell quiet. Then *she* appeared, wearing a pale blue gown that bared much of her throat, and a veil so fine and delicate that it looked as if it must be made of spider webs into which tiny violets had fallen.

But what captured and held his gaze, as she followed the nuns on a circuit of the hall, was the river of bright hair flowing over her shoulders and down her back. It shimmered like spun gold as she moved.

When she came down the center of the hall toward him, his mouth went dry. Her eyes and dress were the same glorious blue, her cheeks were blushing a maidenly pink, and her skin was smooth and clear. He was momentarily thunderstruck. She was nothing short of beautiful.

He couldn't recall later what Basset had said or what he had agreed to do as her husband. He vaguely remembered her promising to love, honor, and obey him . . . which seemed strangely irrelevant just now. But he would always remember that moment of acute embarrassment when Basset asked him for a ring to bless, and he realized that a ring was the thing he had forgotten.

From behind him came the sound of a clearing throat. Michael of Dunneault stepped up and placed a golden ring set with a pale sapphire in his hand. Mortified, he nearly refused it, until the old housekeeper said plainly: "It was your mother's, *seigneur.* At her vows."

With a grateful nod to the old woman, Peril took it from Michael and placed it over the end of each finger of Eloise's left hand before returning it to her third finger to stay. She looked up at him with those beautiful eyes . . . so feminine . . . so utterly alluring . . . and he felt his chest suddenly constricting and his lungs being squeezed in his chest.

Who the Devil was she?

He had never seen this woman before in his life!

His blood drained from his head as Father Basset pronounced them man and wife and conferred a blessing for long life and many children upon them. Then a cheer went up, led by his men, and she looked up at him. With dismay he realized he was supposed to kiss her. Here. Now. He almost groaned aloud.

Eloise, standing on the dais, face to face with him, was having a very similar reaction. The man she had just promised to love, honor, and obey loomed over her, filling her sight, her head, her heart, and her future. As she watched him bending to give her a perfunctory kiss on the lips, she couldn't find a single familiar aspect in the face she had seen daily for more than six weeks.

Who was this man who had just become her master?

And how was she ever going to share a home and a life with him?

But it wasn't a home or a life she was required to share with him that night, it was a bed. And though she drank several cups of excellent wine over the course of the celebration, she was utterly sober when the nuns and the house women came to escort her to her bridal chamber.

The earl's chamber was larger and better furnished than the one she had shared with Mary Clematis across the landing. In the center of it stood his massive, paneled bed, and nearby sat a pair of large chairs fitted with down pillows, a heavy table strewn with documents and rolls of parchment, and a pair of iron-bound chests for linens and clothing. Three of the recently rescued tapestries hung on the walls, and the bed was draped with heavy silk damask. But the chamber's most arresting feature was the hearth built into one wall between two glazed windows. In front of it were two pierced-metal folding screens that could be adjusted to direct the flow of the warmed air.

The nuns had asked the house women to air the chamber and the bed furs, to wash the sheets, and to have the kitchen boys collect daffodils and wild hyacinth to set in baskets around the chamber. By the time they escorted Eloise to her bed, the chamber was lighted softly with beeswax candles and the air was warm and sweet. They smiled covertly at each other as they dismissed the house women and began to remove Eloise's veil and gown from her stiff form.

"Now, Eloise," Sister Archibald said as they unlaced her sleeves and the gusset at the back of her gown, "yer training has not included matters of th' bedchamber. But ye need only remember that there is nothing in all of human experience that is not covered by the Golden Rule: 'Do unto others as ye would have them do unto ye.' "

Sister Rosemary giggled and Sister Mary Montpellier groaned.

"Sisters!" Mary Clematis blanched as white as her wimple. "Will you be all right, Elly? I mean, His Lordship is such a great, strapping beast of a man . . ."

"Well, if you find yourself in difficulty," Sister Mary Montpellier said in compressed tones, "just close your eyes and think of Heaven."

"Oh, lovely." Sister Rosemary rolled her eyes. "A marriage-bed martyr in the making." She seized Eloise's hand and gave it a comforting pat. "The Almighty decreed man and woman should be one. How could they possibly become 'one' if the joining was so horribly unpleasant?"

Then Sister Archibald stepped in to pinch Eloise's cheeks and turn her toward the bed.

"There must be something in th' man to admire, my girl, else our good abbess wouldn't have given him such an excellent bride." The old nun's eyes crinkled. "Focus on that tonight, Eloise: th' goodness in th' man."

By the time the calls and pounding came at the door, Eloise was tucked, naked, into the bed, with her hair drawn around her shoulders to shield her from curious eyes. Sister Archibald answered, and when the door swung open, there stood red-faced Peril of Whitmore, with his wine-warmed knights at his back offering advice on the night's endeavor and offering — should he require assistance — to stand in for him with his bride. The nuns refused to admit any but the earl himself, and exited themselves as soon as the revelers departed.

Mary Clematis was the last to leave. She looked at Eloise with her eyes brimming with tears, then lowered her head and slipped out the door.

Eloise had never felt so alone or so uncomfortable inside her own skin. Her nakedness seemed more pronounced against the soft linen; every inch of her skin was alive with awareness of what lay ahead. It would change her, she knew. She would never be the same.

She wasn't aware that she had squeezed her eyes shut until he spoke from just in front of her, startling her into opening them.

"Are you naked under there?" he demanded.

"Yes." Her voice sounded pitifully small in her own ears.

She was not at all prepared for his response.

"Damn."

Thirteen

Peril stood in the center of the chamber, taking his bearings and wishing he were either a lot more sober or a lot more drunk. He was sauced enough to be randy as hell, and clear-headed enough to understand the importance of this night and to perceive the dread in Eloise's face. It had taken him a moment to spot her in the bed; she was so pale that she blended alarmingly with the bed linen. But then, there she was, all flaming hair and enormous eyes, braced and waiting for him to come and ravish her.

He stalked closer and saw her slam her eyes shut and drag the cover up under her chin. Leaning over, he asked his question and she answered.

"Damned meddling nuns." He sank down on the edge of the bed, feeling grossly annoyed. "Always so infernally *helpful*. Did it never occur to them that I might enjoy stripping you of clothes myself?"

She stared at him in disbelief.

He left the bed and began rummaging through the trunks. With a huff of disgust, he threw open the door, charged across the landing, and burst through the nuns' door demanding Eloise's trunk. There were squeals of terror and scrambling; anyone would have thought he was a marauding army the way they clung to each other and pointed at the small trunk with trembling fingers.

He carried the chest back across the landing, into his chamber, and kicked the door shut behind him. He set it on the table, threw it open, and located her habit, which he carried to her in the bed.

"Oh, but . . . I didn't . . . They didn't mean . . ." The anxiety in her eyes astonished him. Sister Eloise would never have looked at him like that. She'd have told him to turn his back and behave himself.

"Put it on, for God's sake. So I can look at you without feeling like a bloody lecherous heathen." He turned his back and folded his arms.

"But I — I th-thought . . ." Sister Eloise never stammered. Eloise apparently did little else. "I thought y-you . . . y-you would . . ."

"Well, yes. We'll get around to that sooner or later. But there's a whole night ahead, and it occurred to me, Sis— *Eloise,* that I don't even know where you come from or who your family is."

He heard the slide of fabric and the subtle rasp of laces and wondered if he'd lost every last scrap of his sanity. She was naked and in his bed . . . why hadn't he just pounced on her and gotten the ruckus over with? But just as he was wavering, she said "all right" and he turned.

A bolt of desire shot straight to his loins. He wasn't mad, he was brilliant! She was standing there in her kirtle . . . laced up the front . . . with no shift to fill in the gaps. Her arms were bare and her hair was pulled to one side and hanging over her shoulder.

"There wasn't a proper shift," she said, folding her arms under her breasts, which only pushed them higher. He took a hot breath and answered through the desire searing its way up the back of his throat.

"I believe we can make do." He spotted the pitcher of wine and pair of silver goblets someone — *blessed, thoughtful nuns!* — had left on the table, and he poured himself a cup and tossed it down. When he looked up, she was staring at him and the cup in his hand and he thought to offer her one. She nodded and he poured. Wine. Of course. That would warm her up. He watched her take a sip and saw her shoulders relax.

He dragged the two large chairs together before the hearth and waved her into one.

She sank nervously onto it and sipped her wine, staring straight ahead. On his way by the candle stand, he wetted his fingers and doused two of the four wicks.

"Your family?" he prompted, settling into the chair beside hers.

"Harold of Argent. My unlucky father. Margarete of Ghent, my more unlucky mother. My father had been knighted under the Duke of Norfolk and received a barony for his service. It was a poor, rocky, ill-starred place. My mother buried two sons before they reached fostering age. I was her third child, and she died not long after I was born. My father placed me in fosterage in an old knight's household, and they raised me with loving care . . . until I was twelve years old and Mistress Maude died and Sir Markum soon followed. They tried to find my father, only to learn that he had been killed in battle two years before. There were debts, and only an aged uncle to plead my case. The duke seized the land to grant to another of his vassals, and had me sent to the convent."

"Greedy bastard," he said, scowling.

She seemed to relax more at that and mustered a smile. "It worked out for the best. I truly loved the convent. The order. The wisdom of the elder sisters. If only the abbess had loved —" She halted and buried the rest of that thought in her wine. "And you, milord? You were fostered early yourself."

He nodded. "My father sent me to Northumbria's house when I was but three years, and then he crossed the channel to make war for whoever had need of his services. I grew up in the company of knights-at-arms, and became squire to a bluff old Scot, Sir Angus, who was half warrior and half priest. He was a bold and unrepentant skeptic." He raised his hand. "I swear, he had to count his own toes before he'd believe there were ten."

She smiled.

"Which explains your distrust of the church," she said.

"Which explains the start of it. My own encounters with clerics and church workings only proved Angus's mistrust. I've seen too much wrong wrought in the name of 'the faithful' to put much trust in the church or God."

"You don't *trust* God?" she asked, alarm rising.

"Let's say . . . I'm willing to reserve judgment on Him, if He's willing to reserve judgment on me." He watched her wrestling with that statement and counted it strongly in her favor that she didn't try to "enlighten" him.

"You've traveled much," she said, after a brief silence, watching him with growing curiosity. "Tell me where you've been."

He rose to refill her goblet and pinched a third candlewick. When he returned, she had drawn her legs up onto the chair and tucked them to one side. Her head rested against the tall back of the chair and her hair had slid from her shoulder into a red-gold stream down the side of the chair. As she reached for the goblet, he had to steel himself to ignore the fact that she looked like the ripest, most ravishable little nun in all of Christendom. Many a promising campaign, he reminded himself, had been lost due to an ill-timed or overeager advance.

Instead of resuming his seat, he sat down on the fur rug in front of her chair and began to speak of the cities he had seen. He told her of Rome and Florence and Venice with their palaces and markets and merchants ... of Constantinople with its great cathedral and Hippodrome . . . of Spain with its strange blend of Christian and Moor. He spoke of Alexandria in Egypt and of Cypress and the cities of old Greece and Macedonia. She sipped her wine and devoured every word.

When he finally set his cup aside and reached for her, she was lost in wonder. She stiffened briefly as he drew her down onto his lap, but relaxed again when his arms merely wrapped around her and pulled her close. It was quiet, and the wine had clearly gone to the head that she was now laying on his shoulder.

He removed one of her slippers and aimed it at the last remaining candle. The flame went out as the candle turned over, and suddenly the chamber was lighted only by the dim glow of the coals left in the hearth. He watched her luminous eyes focus on his mouth and her full, moist lips part in invitation. He lowered his mouth to hers and she sighed as if utterly satisfied by the result.

When he reached for her laces, her hand closed on his wrist and he opened his eyes into her questioning gaze.

"Close your eyes," he whispered, and was gratified when she obeyed. "Pretend we're in the cellar again. It was cold down there, but we made our own warmth. Remember how it felt when we touched?" It was a risk, recalling that volatile event, but soon her hand fell away and he untied her uppermost laces and slipped his hand inside her kirtle. Bare skin. Cool breasts with warm, tightly budded nipples. The risk had paid off.

She met his next kiss with a growing eagerness that connected every sensitive spot on his body into a web of sexual need. With trembling hands he loosened more of her laces and paused to look at her. Her eyes were closed, her lips were thick and moist from their kisses, and her kirtle was open to her waist. Inside that erotic black sheath was a wedge of creamy skin and two bare breasts with darkened nipples. She shifted sensuously on his lap, rubbing his swollen flesh in the process, then with her eyes still closed, pulled his head toward hers.

It was indeed like that time in the cellar, Eloise realized dimly . . . as if those days and weeks of anxiety and regret had never intervened. Had their passion, once interrupted, worked a spell on events and people to bring them back to this very point? They were once again kissing, touching, caressing. And this time, it didn't have to end. This time it had been authorized and sanctioned — was positively encouraged by the powers of earth and heaven.

As he loosened the rest of her laces and pushed her kirtle from her breasts and down over her shoulders, she lay back over his arm and offered him what seemed to fascinate him. The warm tugs and wet velvety strokes of his tongue against the tips of her breasts vibrated intimate chords within her body. She held her breath, concentrating on those sublime sensations, feeling herself paradoxically both expanding and contracting inside.

Her woman's flesh began to burn strangely, anticipating him, empty and hungry for him. She wanted his hands on her everywhere at once. Every inch of her skin yearned for contact with his.

When his lips slid from hers as he rose and carried her to the bed, she made a sound of distress deep in her throat. Then the earth tilted, or they tilted . . . she didn't care which. All she knew was that she was now on her back with his body covering hers, and that this divinely thorough contact somehow assuaged the hunger in her skin. When she pushed him back from her and started to remove her woolen kirtle, he prevented it.

"Leave it on," he murmured, taking her lower lip between his teeth. Then he pushed up to his knees, dragged his shirt off over his head, and paused to stare down at her as she lay between his knees. Her dark habit with its devastated lacing framed her pale breasts and exposed curves. Over the pillows, around her head and beneath her shoulders, lay a torrent of bright hair that glowed softly in the dim light.

"You look like the most decadent female in all of England."

"I assure you, milord, I am not," she said, her voice breathless. "I am a proper bride. You, on the other hand, look like a great barbarian bent on having his way with whatever maiden is fortunate enough to fall into your hands."

"Don't you mean *un*fortunate?"

She blushed at her slip of the tongue, then rebounded on a shockingly devilish impulse to meet his gaze and smile without a trace of repentance.

"No maiden seeing what I am seeing at this moment could ever call herself *unfortunate,* milord."

Surprised by her boldness, he threw back his head and laughed.

"Eloise," he said, his voice low, "you never cease to surprise me."

She drew air between her teeth as he settled slowly over her, starting with her legs and then covering her pelvis, her stomach, and her breasts. When his wine-spiced breath again bathed her face, she curled her fingers through his soft, dark hair and pulled his mouth to hers.

"All I can bring to your bed is willingness,

milord. Make me a wife."

Her black kirtle quickly joined his garments on the floor.

When he fitted himself against her and began to move, she met his thrusts . . . tentatively at first, then with shuddering pleasure as he rasped a sensitive point that sent pulses of pleasure through the deep core of her body.

She held him tightly, straining closer, uncertain what would satisfy this craving for stronger and deeper sensation. Reading her desires with his own, he began the joining of their bodies and absorbed her gasps of both pain and pleasure with his mouth on hers.

It felt foreign and yet, to her body's wisdom, felt right. This was the tantalizing pleasure that drove men and women together and fused them into one flesh for all time. The idea now made perfect sense. This pleasure was utterly irresistible. As he threaded his hands through hers and braced above her, she felt a rush of heat and a hunger for more, and still more.

His eyes were black with desire and shot through with golden sparks of pleasure, and his body was covered with a sheen of moisture in the golden light. His every motion created a lush wave of new sensation in her and, from his expression, within him as well.

She writhed and arched beneath him, glorying in that driving erotic heat and divinely focused pressure. Her every moan and motion demanded more.

Suddenly she felt herself rising and crashing through some unknown barrier, shattering into shards of white-hot pleasure. Then, as her response calmed, he sank into her depths to find his own release and she felt it as if it were happening to her again.

For a time, as they lay together joined and spent, she could not have said where her body ended and his began. They were well and truly joined. They were one body, one heart, one spirit.

It was all so overwhelming that her emotions overflowed in tears. As he nuzzled her temple and encountered the salty wetness, he slid to the bed beside her and pulled her into the curve of his body to hold and comfort her. The storm of passion and emotion subsided, leaving her exhausted but content to be lying in the circle of his arms.

Fatigue claimed her, but not before the habit of nine long years asserted itself in the act that now ended each of her days. She looked heavenward and offered one terse, heartfelt prayer.

"Thank you."

It was not meant for him, but his answer might easily have been divinely inspired.

"You're most welcome."

In the early dawn hours, she awakened to the feel of his body curled around her. There was enough light coming through the glazed windows for her to see clearly the rather startling sight of their bodies pressed intimately together. His breathing was slow and even; he didn't stir when she peeled her skin from his, pulled the sheet up and over her, and sat looking at him.

His ruggedly handsome face and expressive eyes . . . his broad shoulders and powerful chest . . . his thickly muscled arms that seemed equally at home holding a sword or a woman . . . the pale scars on his shoulders, thigh, and arms . . . each part of him told a different story. He was powerful and decisive, courageous and unstinting, by turns hard and tender. He was definitely mortal and perhaps more vulnerable than he would have others suspect.

Then it struck her that he was one more thing: he was *hers*. Her husband. The other half of her earthly flesh. The companion of her soul. What would it have been like to watch another maiden arrive and stand with him before the priest and ascend the steps to this bridal bed? As irritating as it was to admit, the abbess had made the right choice. How had she known?

Smiling, she bent to drop a kiss on his eyelid and it popped open.

"Oh!" She jerked back, blushing from head to toe.

"Are you all right?" he asked, pushing up onto one elbow to make a languid assessment of her bare shoulders and wildly tousled hair.

"Of course." She pulled the sheet higher. "Why wouldn't I be?"

"No splinters?"

"Splinters?" She gave a start. "Where would I have gotten —"

"No blisters?"

"I —" She glanced at her shoulders and arms. "— I don't think so."

"No sudden swellings" — he looked pointedly at her bottom half — "or unusual knots, masses, kernels, or lumps? No raw or broken skin?"

"No, *nothing* like that." But the way she bit the inside of her lip betrayed her burgeoning worry and she finally gave in to the urge to look inside the sheet at herself with alarm.

He sat up with a laugh.

"Then it would appear you've survived your wedding night, wife."

She gasped as he wrapped her in his arms and carried her down to the bed with him. They lay face to face, gazing at each other as her indignation and his laughter both faded and the moment between them warmed.

"I did more than just survive, milord," she said, tracing his cheek and his lips with her fingertips.

"I'm glad, Eloise of Argent. I would not have you lie in my arms and pine for a pallet in a convent."

She chuckled. "I think you overestimate the charms of a convent's accommodations. This" — she shifted closer, so that their bodies touched in strategic places — "is much better." Then another thought occurred to her. "You know, I really must write the abbess."

"Sending her your thanks?" he said, nuzzling her ear.

"About the husband test."

He drew back with a scowl. "To demand she cease using it, I hope."

"No. To tell her it's woefully incomplete. There was nothing in the standards about *this*." She gave him a short, soft kiss. "Or this." She urged his hand over her breast and then sighed with pleasure. "And there was definitely nothing in the standards to gauge a man's response to this."

She raised her knee so that it skimmed the outer edge of his thigh and then propped it provocatively atop his hip. It was brazen of her to flaunt her womanliness in such a shameless fashion. But her sense of it was new and powerful and so very enticing . . . she couldn't resist.

"But how could one ever report such findings? 'Lord Peril is a very manly fellow in his personal parts,' " she boomed in an official-sounding voice.

He stared at her in disbelief and she wondered if she had gone too far until he broke into a grin.

" 'He employs a firm but pleasing touch," she continued, " 'and has remarkable endurance. Furthermore, he is not one to hog the covers afterward or to roll over and snore as if he's imbibed a snoot full of wine.' "

He pulled her tight against him so that his laughter migrated into her chest, and soon both were weak with mirth. Then he shifted over her and lay cradled between her thighs. As he began to move, invading her silken heat, she wrapped her limbs around him.

"And how would you report *this*, Husband Judge?" he demanded, his voice hoarse and his eyes darkening with rekindled desire.

"I suppose I would have to say," she said,

tilting her hips to bring him to the place where her yearning both began and ended, "that milord was quite a missionary."

"A what?" He stilled and looked down at her in dismay.

Her eyes twinkled.

"Since, in your arms, a woman can glimpse Heaven itself."

It was well past dawn before Eloise roused again. She moved languidly and felt an ache spreading through her lower half . . . as if she had ridden horseback for too long. Biting her lip, she slid from the bed, stretched gingerly, and went to wash. After brushing her hair and rubbing her teeth with salt, she padded back to the bed and stood admiring the curve of Peril's lashes against his sun-bronzed cheeks. Who would have imagined when she entered the convent as an awkward twelve-year-old that she would one day wed a nobleman and spend her first night with him discovering a host of lush and enthralling . . .

Pleasures. *Carnal* pleasures. Delights of the flesh.

She jerked her gaze from her husband's sprawled form and suddenly saw the heated events of the night just past very differently in the cool, clear light of day. Her skin heated with chagrin. All of that moaning and writhing and clutching and panting — dearest Heaven, had she really done such things?

She looked at the bed beside him, at the impression her body had made beside his in the feather ticking. With only the slightest turn of thought she could feel again his body pressed hard against hers. She had indeed done those things. And with more eagerness than was strictly required.

She fell back a step and steadied herself against the bed. The ache that spread through her lower body seemed both a confirmation and a remonstrance.

She had expected that there would be some changes in her, some differences after so momentous an occasion, but suddenly she felt so vulnerable, so uncertain . . . so unlike herself.

Trembling, she located her simple black kirtle on the floor and halted, unable to pick it up. It belonged to a novice, a young, inexperienced maid. With tears springing to her eyes, she turned instead to the wedding clothes hanging on the pegs near the door. As she donned the silk shift and the blue velvet kirtle and fumbled with the ties, she grew steadily more anxious. The stiffness and weight of the garments felt unfamiliar, the aches of her body felt shamefully specific, and her thoughts were jumbled by conflicting emotions. Every element of her surroundings seemed foreign and unreal.

She looked at the window and realized the sun was already high in the sky. Desperate for reassurance, she turned to the comfort of a long-standing habit of holy duty. She sank to her knees beside the bed, clasped her hands, and threw herself into her morning prayers.

It was the emptiness of the bed that awakened him, Peril realized. He rolled over expecting to feel warm skin, but found only cool linen. He raised his head and spotted her red-gold hair at the edge of the bed. He grinned to himself, closed his eyes, and stretched thoroughly, luxuriating in the ache of every passion-strained muscle.

A wedding night, he thought to himself, wasn't all that different from a good hard day on the practice field. Except — he had never been this eager to have another go at setting a quintain spinning.

"Good morning, wife," he murmured in a tone laden with the anticipation of pleasure. But as the moments dragged by uninterrupted, he opened one eye and found that she hadn't moved. He sat up and stared at her, first with growing confusion, then with growing comprehension.

Humble posture . . . folded hands . . . closed eyes . . . He nearly choked.

She was *praying!*

His morning-spawned surge of desire fled as surely as if it had been doused with icy water.

But last night she had welcomed his every desire! She had been eager, sensual, and surprisingly responsive. He glared at her penitent pose. No doubt she had been shocked by her responses, too. And being a nun — or having wanted to be one — the guilt of such indulgence must have driven her to her knees.

The thought skewered him in an unexpectedly vulnerable place. He thought of all of the times he had lusted after a glimpse of her hair and had mentally stripped her of those damnable church weeds. He knew he was lustful and half heathen and — as Basset was wont to say — probably doomed to sweat throughout eternity. But it never occurred to him that she might feel tainted by his desire for her and by the performance of her marital duty to him.

He rolled from the bed and paced back and forth, quietly, feeling steadily more coarse and accused. She was his wife, dammit. What was he supposed to do on his wedding night? A man had to have some relief from the strain of morality and self-discipline. Wasn't that what wives were for?

He relieved himself in the chamber pot, splashed his face with water, and stuffed himself into his hose, shirt, tunic, and belt . . . heedless of the noise he was making. When she still didn't acknowledge his presence, he snatched up his snug-fitting boots and began to jerk them on.

The pacing, the muttering, and even the splashes from the chamber pot Eloise might have withstood with a modicum of grace. But the willful and determined stomping was just too much. She looked up — having completely lost her place somewhere in the Psalms — and found him sitting, drawing on his tall boots, and stomping to settle his feet in them. He finished, looked up to see her watching him, and leveled a penetrating look on her.

"If you're finished, my lady" — he rose and headed for the door — "I think it's time we appeared together in the hall." He lifted the latch, swung the door back, and curtly waved her through the portal. At a loss to explain his sudden irritation, she complied with his order. As she passed by, she heard him mutter: "To prove to the good sisters that you survived the night."

★ ★ ★

The house had been slow to stir that morning. Heads were woolly, tongues were thick, and bodies were sluggish from the long night's celebration. Even so, most of Whitmore was up and abroad by the time Peril and Eloise emerged from their bridal chamber into the hall. A rousing cheer went up from Peril's men, and she halted, feeling positively naked under their eager scrutiny without her wimple and veil.

Soon the rest of his garrison arrived. Michael, Simon, and Ethan greeted their lord with the report that all had been quiet in the night . . . at least *outside* the nuptial chamber. Peril's black look only seemed to encourage their jocular behavior.

"Sweet mercy, the howls and shrieks." Michael clasped his hands and knelt nearby in mock supplication. "Spare the spurs, milady, we beg of you!"

"Spurs?" Simon, the eldest and most courtly knight, gave Michael a cuff on the shoulder. "She's a lady, you dolt. She'd use a crop at most."

"He does look a mite winded, though," Ethan called from the midst of Peril's men. "He's new to saddle and bit, milady. Ye must go easy on him at first. He'll soon make ye a proper palfrey."

Eloise knew that Peril's men were given to teasing, and had she been her old self she might have seized one of their jibes and sharpened it for her own use. But she was now their lady and had no idea how she was expected to deal with such raucous behavior. She looked to Peril, whose attention was suddenly buried in his food.

"Well, now, milady." Large, bluff William of Wright rose, stretching and rubbing his stomach. "Where do we start today? Jousting, sword practice, or the quintain?" There was a roar of laughter from the rest of the men. When she looked at Sister Archibald and Father Basset, they were laughing and seemed to be very much into the spirit of the teasing. The scowl reappeared on Peril's face, however, and quickly developed into a full glower.

"Here's to Lady Eloise!" Michael's shout drew an echoing salute from every man in the hall except the earl, who was caught mid-bite and sat with a mouthful of food and a darkening countenance. "As good a general as ever waged a campaign!"

She groaned silently as she felt Peril's distemper focusing on her.

"General?" She paused in the midst of reaching for the pitcher of ale. "I am no soldier, Sir Michael. Nor have I mounted any sort of campaign."

"Too modest by half, my lady," Simon declared. "When you've fought so valiantly and conquered the heart of 'the spur of Northumbria.' "

She blushed violently and looked to Peril. Even embattled by their laughter, he seemed anything but conquered or subdued.

"It is not fighting that wins a heart, Sir Simon."

"No, milady? Then what does?" he asked, winking at his comrades.

She scrambled to come up with a plausible answer and put an end to this excruciating exchange.

"Honesty, sir" was the best she could do. "And earnestness and heartfelt devotion to duty and the welfare of others. Such things, Sir Simon, are what truly captures a heart."

"A grandmother's heart, perhaps," William of Wright called out, grinning from ear to ear. "But a warrior's heart requires capturing by something a good bit softer and a great deal warmer." There was considerable laughter at that, and a number of wicked murmurs she was grateful not to be able to understand.

"Something like . . . a fall of hair the color of a heartwood fire," Pascoe declared boldly. "Is that not so, Your Lordship?"

Peril's eyes glinted as he glanced at the bright tresses flowing down her back. He paused to finish his morning ale before answering.

"If I meet a true warrior on the practice field today, I'll ask him." He tossed his napkin down and rose.

"Meanwhile, we still have thieves to catch. Simon, you'll take out the next patrol and set men to watch in the areas we agreed upon. Ethan, you'll take the garrison out to the practice field for the day. William, have the horse-master bring out the two new mounts to begin their training. Terrence — you're needed in the smithy, helping to train the farrier's new apprentices."

"And you, milord?" Eloise asked as his men quitted the table in a far more subdued manner than that in which they had arrived. "Where will you be?"

"I need not account to you for my time," he said irritably.

"No, milord," she said, her face heating. "But, in case you should be needed . . ."

He eased and studied her before answering.

"On the field with my men. And you, lady?"

"With your permission, I will look for some cloth to furnish myself with garments more suited to my new vocation. The sisters have agreed to help me."

He paused and nodded.

"I have no objection. Except" — he looked her up and down with an embarrassingly thorough gaze — "I will not have you trussed up inside one of those head cloths that nuns and old women are wont to wear. I want no one mistaking my bride for a *nun*."

Fourteen

The earl of Claxton sat astride his horse with a number of his mounted men-at-arms in the midst of a copse that overlooked several newly planted fields. He could see a figure making its way stealthily toward him, using the hedges at the far end of the little valley as cover. He shifted in his saddle and expelled an impatient breath. While he waited, he surveyed the fields below and assessed their vigorous new crops of oats and barley.

"I believe I may leave this grain," he said to himself, as much as to his minions. "By harvest, these fields will be mine. And it would be a shame to destroy so many of my own crops." His comment drew desultory laughter from his men. "What about those foals?" he asked the captain of his guard. "Are they as good as you thought?"

"Excellent, milord," came the reply. "Deep chests, powerful legs, fine heads . . . not at all afraid of a bit of noise. They'll be fine battle mounts by the time we're through with them."

A chuckle issued from the depths of Claxton's throat. "Whitmore always has

377

supplied us with the finest of horseflesh. I really should tell the bastard about it someday."

The bushes nearby rustled, and a crouching figure charged across the open turf to Claxton's well-hidden party. The man, dressed in simple yeoman's garb, made straight for the earl and either bowed with respect or bent to catch his breath — it was difficult to say which.

"Well?" Claxton demanded irritably.

"The news is . . . the earl was just married . . . yesterday."

"Married?" Claxton was stunned but only for a moment. "To whom? Who would marry that penniless bastard?"

"A nun," his informant said, still catching his breath. "From France."

Claxton burst into harsh laughter. "A nun? I know the wretch is desperate for a bride to counter his 'curse,' but I doubt he's stupid enough to try to wed a nun." He fixed the fellow on a threatening glare. "What is her name?"

"E-Eloise, milord. That's what they call her. Sister Eloise."

"And you say she's from France?"

The fellow nodded.

"Ugly as sin, no doubt. Some pockmarked chit he got paid to take off some fat

378

merchant's hands," he declared. The fellow didn't nod this time. "Well? Is she a drab or isn't she?" The fellow looked uncertain if he should answer, then decided to brave it.

"Isn't."

"Dammit to Hell!" Claxton shouted. "Where did the bastard find someone to marry him?" When the fellow didn't answer, he shouted, *"Where?"*

"France, milord." The fellow frowned, confused by the question he had already answered. "She were a nun. In a convent."

Claxton groaned with frustration, dismissing the details because they'd been carried in and were probably tainted by so deficient a wit.

"He was gone, and I heard he had crossed the Channel," he mused irritably, "but I didn't think anyone would have little enough sense to pay him a dowry and give him a bride." He ground his teeth at the thought of Whitmore finding a source of finance at the last hour . . . when he had spent the last five years patiently draining everything of worth from the estate under the guise of a "curse."

Annoyed beyond bearing he turned on the messenger again.

"What has my trusted agent been able to

pry loose from Whitmore's stores this time?"

"Had t'leave it in the trees, milord. It were too heavy on th' soft ground."

"Fetch it," he ordered his commander. His captain motioned two men to follow and spurred his mount in the direction the peasant indicated.

While he waited, Claxton stewed and considered ways to hasten the process of Whitmore's demise.

"A new wife could either prove to be a disastrously wicked distraction or a spur to Whitmore's efforts to rescue his estates. I can take no chances with victory so close. We'll step up our raids on Whitmore." His pale eyes darted over a scene forming in his mind, and he began to smile.

"Married," he muttered, more to himself than his companions. "And the bastard didn't even invite his neighbors to the wedding. Well, we must overlook his loutish manners and acquaint ourselves with this 'lady' of his. And what better occasion to unmask Whitmore for the pauper we have made him than when the king's purse keeper comes to call?"

He looked up to see his captain riding hard for him, and came to attention.

"Wine, milord," the captain reined up in

front of him with a huge grin. "And plenty of it!"

Eloise's day was spent with the sisters, exploring ways to provide herself with garments that did not look as though they came from a convent. They discovered some bolts of sound and pleasantly supple woolens in one of the housekeeper's wardrobes, and gathered in Eloise's old upstairs chamber to plan some garments. As they talked and worked, Eloise began to count the hours until the following morning, when the sisters would depart to celebrate Easter at Canterbury Cathedral and then return home.

"I wish you could stay," Eloise told them, reaching for Sister Archibald's hand and already feeling the loss yet to come. "But at least you can leave Clemmie with me for a while longer. I'm sure the abbess wouldn't mind."

Sister Archibald wagged her head sadly and looked to Mary Clematis, who raised her chin, trying to be brave.

"Oh, Elly, I've been nothing but a burden to you. I — I need to go home." Her courage melted and she looked down at her tightly clasped hands through prisms of sudden tears. "Look at me . . . I'm a disaster."

Her habit, once black and handsome, was now faded and stained around the bottom from her desperate efforts to clean it. Her wimple was frayed and her veil had shrunk unevenly from repeated wetting and drying. Her face was pale behind the reddish patches and freckles caused by sun and dust and who knew what other agents of misery. Her hands were red, cracked, and sore from her scrubbing in the chapel, and her foot was still bandaged to protect her healing toe. Most alarming, her habit now hung loosely from her shoulders. Eloise hadn't noticed just how much she had dwindled until now.

"Ye're wedded now, Eloise," Sister Archibald said with a sympathetic smile. "Ye need a lady's maid and companion, not a chaperon from a convent." She stroked Eloise's cheek.

"Mary Clematis was not meant for life in th' world," she continued. "She belongs in a cloister, where everything is calm and ordered and always the same from day to day. Ye were meant for the world, Eloise. Ye've blossomed here. Ye thrive on the challenge presented by this man and this place. Ye grow lovelier every day ye're here."

Tears began to spill down Eloise's face, and in a moment there wasn't a dry eye in the chamber. They hugged and patted her and said fond farewells. In their good wishes was such an air of confidence and admiration that Eloise held back the feelings that clamored in her heart for expression.

She wanted desperately to go with them to Canterbury and then to return to the safety and sameness of the convent. But that was impossible. Even if she could somehow undo her vows and convince the abbess to take her back . . . how could she ever purge herself of the passion for Peril of Whitmore that seemed to have risen out of her very bones? How could she abandon the connection that had been formed between them as they joined in that Heaven-ordained pleasure?

What had been done, she realized as she and the sisters comforted each other, could not be undone. To voice her distress would only burden Mary Clematis and the others as they left the next morning.

She dried her tears and theirs and hid her aching heart in a show of determined productivity. The rest of the day the nuns helped her work on her garments, met with the cooks to plan for the upcoming Easter celebration, and toured the manor to see what would be Eloise's new home.

As the sun was lowering, she led them into

the weavers' house, where she showed them the work their head weaver had begun on the new French loom. There they met Edythe's plainspoken daughter, Rose, who was of marriageable age, but less than enthusiastic about the matches available for her on the manor.

"She has no desire to work at th' loom, either," Edythe declared. "But she's good-natured and handy wi' a needle. An' she knows how to keep order."

Mother Archibald settled a critical look on Eloise's stunningly prominent tresses and asked: "By any chance, does your daughter know how to bring order to a woman's hair?"

That evening, the men of Whitmore's garrison straggled into the hall after dark, looking exhausted. The sisters and Father Basset had eaten earlier at Eloise's insistence, but she had waited to take her supper with her husband. When he strode through the door, looking dusty, disheveled, and out of sorts, she rose from her seat by the hearth and sent immediately for his food.

"Good evening, my lord," she greeted him, holding out her hands for his sword. He tossed it onto the great table with a clang.

"No, it is not a good evening. Which is probably only fitting, since it was a wretched and trying day." The practice field had not improved his humor. "My cup, woman," he declared irritably.

Woman? As she bristled, she felt his men's eyes on her.

"It must have been a strenuous day indeed," she said as she brought the pitcher of wine to fill his cup, "to have knocked my name from your head altogether."

He scowled as he reached for the wine she had poured.

"Eloise, milord." She prodded his memory. "I am your wife." She glanced down the hall at his men slumped over and around the planking tables below them . . . watching. "You were late coming from the field, and we —"

"You need not remind me of the hour," he said shortly. "We keep no bells here, nor do we have need of them."

She paused, quelled her indignation, and completed her statement. "We wanted to be certain your food was hot."

He reddened and sat down hard in his chair.

Platters of bread and wheels of soft cheese were brought around. He seemed to be far away in his thoughts as she served his portion of the savory stew from the large iron pot carried on poles by the kitchen boys, and then dismissed them to serve Peril's men.

As Eloise settled on the edge of the chair beside the earl's, Clemmie hurried over from the nuns gathered with Father Basset on benches at one side of the hall.

"Father agrees it is a wonderful idea, El—" She caught sight of Peril's glower and amended her address. "Lady Eloise."

"What is a wonderful idea?" Peril demanded with a suspicious squint.

"Since there is no church on Whitmore," Eloise responded, "I had an idea to invite the manor and the village to hear mass in our chapel. I asked Father Basset if he might agree to say an additional mass or two."

"More masses?" Peril reddened. "That won't be necessary."

He waved Mary Clematis off to deliver that message, but Eloise raised a hand to halt her.

"And," she continued determinedly, "afterward I want to provide a small meal for the people to break their Easter fast . . . pies and cold smoked meats, hot cross buns, sweet wafers, and ale. And eggs for the children."

"Too much work and expense," he declared with a dismissive wave that roused every fighting instinct she possessed. "It's not necessary."

"Milord." She turned her back to the sisters gathered nearby and lowered her voice to a fierce whisper. "There are many things that are not necessary to existence, but lend life great richness and meaning. You said yourself that your people need a sense of hope and good things to celebrate. A bit of solemn ceremony followed by a joyful celebration will help to bring order into their year and into their lives." When he still looked unconvinced, she crossed her arms and channeled all of her determination into one last volley.

"Besides, you promised that I might celebrate holy days as I see fit."

She had him there and they both knew it.

There were times that being a man of his word was damned infuriating. Peril gave a snort of disgust, but after a brief wrestle with his conscience, he nodded and gave a dismissing wave, ceding her the right to make such plans.

As he turned back to his food, he saw Michael, Simon, and Ethan watching the exchange closely. They might not have heard what she said, but they had certainly guessed she was taking him to task and getting the better of him. When they caught his glower, they looked away, exchanging covert smirks and winks.

Too often that afternoon he had overheard jests and insinuating comments about sharp-tongued women and henpecked men. They recalled his earlier confrontations with her, when she was his husband judge, and had already crowned her with victory laurels in the eternal battle for control in a marriage.

The burly William of Wright had held up a small set of leather hose worn under armor, as the men were equipping themselves for practice in the armory, and announced that they were just about Lady Eloise's size. Peril called him out on the first round of jousting and unseated him fully. That ended William's comments about who "wore the breeches" in Whitmore's hall.

But, Peril knew, it also revealed how tender his pride was on the subject. And his men, sensing there was fresh sport to be had in their otherwise tame and even boring existence, continued the game covertly. God's teeth, what he wouldn't give for a good hard skirmish of some kind, to snap both himself and his garrison back into order!

As he finished his food, his men's humor revived, as did their intense scrutiny of both him and Eloise. His gaze warmed as it followed theirs to her curvaceous figure, moving about the hall. He couldn't blame them for watching her; she was altogether appealing. He began to think about unraveling the hair that lay coiled at the back of her head. . . .

Some of his men abandoned the hall, and others began to collect at the far end of the hall for a game of quoits. He gave a yawn and called for Eloise.

"Yes, milord?" She arrived at his chair from the side of the hearth, where she sat with the sisters, who were mending linen.

"I had a hard day of training and would retire to our chamber."

The look he gave her made plain his expectation that she would join him.

Conversation among the knights and men seated nearby paused as they listened for her response.

"I am not tired, milord. And the sisters are helping me . . . mending linen."

"It will wait until tomorrow." His tone sharpened. "Retire with me."

Her eyes were filled with emotion as she looked up. He braced for a hot response, but after a moment she glanced back at the sober-faced sisters, who were watching them intently, and then nodded.

Moments later he found himself being swept up the stairs in a wave of femininity. The sisters had decided to retire at the same time and, as they engulfed him on the steps, he found himself pressed on all sides by what felt like resentment. He took Eloise by the elbow and would have pulled her straight into their chamber, but she resisted long enough to give each of the sisters a brief hug. Sister Archibald was last in the group and, over Eloise's shoulder, gave him a dark look.

By the time the door closed behind them, his jaw was set with irritation. Clearly, they believed he was bent on devouring their poor little sister. He wasn't a beast, dammit. And she wasn't their "little sister" anymore.

He removed his garments with brusque movements while watching her from the corner of his eye. She removed her gown and hung it on a peg, then went to splash her face, rub her teeth, and brush her hair. He climbed into the bed and watched her drawing the brush through her hair, feeling each stroke as if it were being made across his belly.

She approached the bed, and he was about to remind her she wouldn't need the shift she was wearing, when she went down on her knees and folded her hands.

Ahhhh!

He jolted upright, staring at her with disbelief. Again! How dare she do this to him? Did she hope to anger or convict him so that he wouldn't try to take her tonight? His feet hit the floor with a thud and he paced, watching her fingers turning white and the furrows in her brow deepening . . . sensing that she knew he was watching and was determined to continue in spite of him.

She murmured a scarcely audible "amen," rose, and was startled by the sight of him standing nearby wearing only a fearsome glower.

"What the blazes was that all about?" he demanded.

"What do you mean?" She retreated a step.

"*Praying*. I told you before we spoke vows that I'd not have you dropping to your knees every time I look crossways at you." His eyes narrowed. "That includes you praying at me every time I insist you join me for a bit of pleasure. I'll not be harangued by holiness in my own damned bed!"

She seemed genuinely shocked by his outburst, which was only to be expected, he told himself. Pious sorts always pretended to be innocent when called on their sanctimonious behavior.

"You think I was praying in order to avoid — ?"

"You wouldn't be the first to try to use prayers as a shield, or a *weapon*."

"A weapon?" The heightened color drained from her face. "Why would I try to wield a weapon against you?" As the rest of his statement registered, she looked at him as if scarcely able to believe he would accuse her of something so vile and hypocritical. "You — you think of everything in terms of battles and fighting. Did it never occur to you that I might pray because it settles my mind and heart and gives me strength and solace? Did it never occur to you that my prayers might have nothing to do with *you?*"

No, it bloody well hadn't. His face began to heat and his body began to feel a good bit more exposed.

"Well, what were you doing praying when you knew I was waiting to . . . What the devil were you praying about?"

"Do I now answer to you for my soul and the content of my prayers?" she said with a choked quality that teetered between outrage and anguish. Guilt crept up his spine as he watched the sparks in her eyes glistening behind rising tears.

Prayers and now tears. It just went from bad to worse.

"I wouldn't have a clue what to do with them," he declared, trying for a tone of disdain and failing. "All I want is your . . . your . . ." The word *body* refused to come out, and there was no other way to say it without sounding appallingly crass. What had he done to send her flying into the Almighty's arms instead of his? "Did I hurt or frighten you somehow? Is that why you . . . why you threw yourself into . . ."

"Prayer?" She melted with sudden understanding and those tears finally began to roll down her cheeks. "It isn't that. It isn't *you*." She bit her lip and then revealed miserably: "It's them. They're leaving tomorrow."

"Them?" Her answer totally disarmed him. The sisters? This was about *their* leaving? She was praying because . . . Well, of course she was. They were the only family she had, and after tomorrow morning there was a good chance she might never see them again. "Ohhhh."

Insight struck: this was the second huge change in her life in as many days. No wonder she felt unsettled and needed comfort. Then a second, broader insight hit. She had turned to the solace of prayer because it was something she had spent most of her life doing. Vows or not, she had lived and practiced as a nun. And prayers had been a big part of that. Regular prayers. Morning and evening.

Sweet Jesus. He was practically giddy with relief. So unburdened that his embarrassment over his asinine behavior seemed somehow irrelevant. All that mattered was the sight of her standing there in her undergown, wiping her tears, struggling to hold back her sobs.

He closed the distance between them and stood for a moment without touching her, aware of his nakedness and, for the first time in many years, uncomfortable with it. Just as he was deciding to retreat and pull on a shirt, she hurled herself against him and buried her face in his chest. He blinked, uncertain quite what to do as she clung to him, sobbing, and he felt her warm tears running down his bare skin.

Following a seldom-used instinct, he wrapped his arms around her and let her cry. Gradually he began stroking her hair and make soothing, shushing sounds. As he held her close to his heart, some of the ache in her breast began to migrate into his. He winced as he shared the pain of this unsought passage. To be left alone in a strange place . . . he knew too well what that was like.

Before long, he was adding "It's all right," "Don't cry, Eloise" and "You won't be alone, here."

Slowly, the emotional tempest subsided and she leaned closer to him. Then closer still.

The uncertainty lodged in her heart ached for the reassurance of his presence . . . his hands, his lips, his body pressed against hers. Now, more than ever before, she needed passion to rise and fill her heart and her senses, to soothe the aching void in the core of her. Lifting her face, she drew him into a kiss that was intensified by despair and seasoned with the salt of her tears. She slipped her knee between his and molded against him, coaxing, demanding a response.

He told himself it didn't matter why she was so eager to lose herself in a storm of passion; it was enough that she wanted him in this way. But he took extra care to cover every inch of her face with the most tender and healing of kisses, ending with the press of his lips against her closed eyelids. He felt a powerful and compelling desire to kiss away every bit of sadness in her, to surround her with pleasure and happiness and the joyful reassurance of being wanted. And when they joined, he spent every ounce of his self-control in seeing that their passions soared and spent together.

Afterward, she curled against him and fell

into an exhausted slumber, but he found himself strangely sleepless. He propped himself up on an elbow and watched her breathing. He became aware of a tender spot in the middle of him, something like a bruise, but one that — when he sought to touch it — had no physical dimension. That feeling grew into a poignant ache that took on a pleasurable aspect as he thought of the way she had turned to him to comfort her and to turn her grief into a sweeter passion.

Smiling, he sank back onto the bolster and wondered at the pleasure he took in that quiet, intimate moment and in the realization that whatever else Eloise was, she was *his*.

The next morning, Peril was gone when Eloise rose, dressed, and said her morning prayers. Her eyes felt scratchy and a bit swollen from last night's tears, but otherwise she felt curiously at peace. Thus, it was something of a surprise when she stepped out onto the landing and Mary Clematis dragged her into their old chamber and shut the door quickly. Sister Archibald was pacing and wringing her hands, and Sisters Rosemary and Mary Montpellier were on their knees in frantic supplication.

"Ye're all right!" Sister Archibald hurried

to put her arms around Eloise. "We were worried that — have ye been crying?"

"His Lordship can be such a beast," Mary Clematis said with distress that was echoed in the others' expressions. "We've sent up a fleet of novenas."

They'd been praying for her! Eloise reddened. While she was lying naked and well comforted in his arms, they had been praying that she wouldn't be devoured by "the beast." That was what they thought of him. It appalled her to realize that it was what *she* had thought of him, too, at one time . . . before she had come to know him . . . before she experienced his gentle kisses, his teasing, and his concern for her . . . before he had absorbed her fear and loss and replaced them with longing and pleasure.

When the sisters saw him, they saw only his public face, his proud and authoritative and even domineering side. By virtue of their oath of chastity and their cloistered existence, they would never see the gentler, more intimate, more human side of him . . . or indeed of any man. She could suddenly feel her mind, her horizons, her whole world broadening. For the sisters, men would always be the forceful, power-hungry, controlling creatures they were in the world.

For the first time in her life, she saw her

beloved sisters as more than sheltered; she saw them as limited in their view of the world and of life. When she assured them that all was well and told them that Peril had not only treated her well but had comforted her tears, she could see they did not truly believe her.

And she realized with a certainty as deep as her sadness: It was indeed time for them to go.

Generosity and compassion might someday be rewarded in Heaven, Peril thought to himself as he watched Michael and three of his men escort the old nuns' cart out the main gate at dawn the next morning, but they definitely had earthly benefits. He glanced down at Eloise, who was standing not far away, waving and calling to her departing friends. Beneath the mist in her eyes was the residue of a long night of tender comfort and pleasure. She had surprised him by turning to him in her distress last night, and he had consoled her in the most direct manner possible. Then he had consoled her again just before dawn. He smiled to himself. He was getting to be quite a compassionate fellow. . . .

"Milord!" His man Richard came rushing up from the direction of the stables. From the soldier's tired face and damp shoulders, it was clear he had been one of the men out on patrol last night. "We found them, milord," he panted out. "We almost had them."

"Where?"

"Upstream . . . near Edwin the Cottar's fields . . . an' we gave chase . . ."

"Wait —" Peril turned to Terrence, who was just entering the hall, and sent him for Michael, Simon, and Ethan. Then he ushered Richard back into the hall and went down the benches, rousing the men dozing there as he headed for the great table. He didn't see Eloise follow him into the hall and then stand for a moment watching him reach for his maps. He did, however, look up just in time to see her striding back out the door without so much as a by-your-leave.

Michael, Simon, and Ethan came on the run, and soon there were a dozen men assembled around the table, listening to Richard's report and poring over the map of the estate.

"It would be the far west fields . . . closest to Claxton land," Peril declared, tracing with his finger the line representing the boundary between his land and Claxton's, letting it come to rest on a part covered with forest. "From what Richard says, there are almost a dozen of them."

"You think Claxton's harboring them, milord?" Ethan asked.

"There are too many of them for him not to know they're there. And even if he were beyond setting them to raid my lands — which he is not — then at the very least he does nothing to stop their raids on my lands. Either way . . . hell, yes, he's harboring them."

The impact of that conclusion sobered them all. There was only so much provocation a lord could tolerate, and Claxton was pushing him ever closer to the point of retaliation.

"Why not just take a force out and hunt them down, milord?" Simon asked. "Once we have them in hand, they'll give us proof of Claxton's treachery."

"Claxton has a sizeable force himself. If I charge onto his land, on any pretext, he'll scream that it is an act of war. In fact, it may be just what he hopes for." He left unsaid the fact that he was not on favorable footing with the king, just now, and that the king took a dim view of costly wars between his vassals.

Just then the serving women arrived on the kitchen stairs with platters of bread and cheese and pitchers of sweet ale. When he looked at them with dim surprise, the one called Faye explained: "Her Ladyship sent us, milord. She knew ye'd be wantin' to break yer fast."

Peril nodded and motioned to his men to eat. They grabbed at the fresh baked bread, boiled eggs, and rich cheese like greedy boys, and soon their mouths were stuffed and cheeks were bulging. The food and ale, and his men's reaction to it, reminded him that there were other aspects to the problem — conditions that needed to be met before fighting broke out. Until he had secured the manor's food supply and water . . . until he had laid some plans for Eloise's safety in case of a siege or a burning . . . he could not just charge into an armed conflict.

"We'll have to bide our time until after Bromley's visit and I've sent the king his tax. Then, when it comes to blows with Claxton, the king may hear the reports of it without prejudice."

Peril took a drink of ale and, over the rim of his tankard, spotted a young man standing not far away with an arm full of roughly planed wood and eyes the size of goose eggs.

"Who the hell — what do you want?" he barked, furious that he hadn't seen the boy straightaway and that his plans might have easily been overheard.

The fellow — the young woodcarver, he

recognized belatedly — swallowed so hard they could see his throat bob.

"I come to see the little nun, milord."

Twice more, as he and his men made plans for laying in food and stores and increasing patrols in the west and south, along Whitmore's border with Claxton land, they were interrupted by craftsmen asking to see the "little nun." The newly installed baker brought her a sample of bread that was baked with water in the oven, as she had apparently suggested. And an itinerant patching tailor had learned in the village of her call for a tailor or seamstress, and had brought "the little nun" a sample of his and his wife's stitchery.

"How many times do I have to tell them?" he said to his men, then turned to roar at the unfortunate tailor: "There is no more *nun!*"

The man bolted for the door, where he ran straight into Eloise as she was entering the hall with Edythe the head weaver and two of her women. As they sorted themselves out, she learned what he wanted and directed him to the kitchens for a bite to eat while she studied the samples of handiwork. When she approached Peril and his group of men, she was nearly bowled over again.

"Where the Devil have you been all morning?"

Fifteen

Peril stood with his feet spread and his fists propped on his hips. She glanced at the men around the table, who were watching the exchange between him and her with amused interest, and had the disconcerting feeling that this show of ire had as much to do with their presence as with her absence from the hall.

"In the weavers' house, milord. The loom we discovered in the cellars has been wound and is finally producing —"

"In future, stay closer to the hall, wife," he said gruffly, "and save me from the pestering of hordes of people looking for 'the little nun.' "

"I am sorry you were interrupted, milord, but Edythe and the others could hardly bring their loom to the hall to show me their work. Come with me to the weaving house and see —"

"I am occupied with more pressing matters."

She glanced at the empty platters and tankards on the table and at the relaxed posture of the men with whom he was sharing those "pressing matters," and drew a different conclusion.

"You really must see, my lord. You will be astonished at the —"

"The only thing that would astonish me this morning, my very persistent bride, would be a bit of peace in my own hall," he said. Unfortunately for him, his sharp words struck her substantial backbone instead of a more tender part.

"I have a proposal, milord, for something that may enlarge both your peace and your purse." She squared her shoulders and joined him on the dais, beckoning the weavers to join her. They approached, but seeing his irritation, stopped at the edge of the step.

"I will hear you later, milady," he said glowering.

"This will only take a moment, milord. Shearing is beginning, and we wish to petition you to reserve a portion — perhaps one tenth — of the shearing for Edythe and her weavers to make into a new kind of cloth." Mention of the upcoming shearing had clearly gotten his attention, so she continued. "You see, the French loom makes it possible to add depth to a cloth — to produce patterns unlike anything woven in this region. It could be a lucrative bit of income for Whitmore." His air of disinterest only made her more determined. "Instead of selling the wool to Paris and Brussels and then buying back it back as cloth, at outrageous prices, we could weave our own woolens. You must know, Your Lordship, that your sheep produce a very long and fine-gauged wool. Only imagine what sort of cloth it could make."

It made no sense to her that his countenance was darkening and his shoulders seemed to be swelling. It was such a marvelous idea, and such a splendid stroke of fortune to have found the loom his mother had brought from France, that it never occurred to her that he would be just as pigheaded as his father and dismiss it.

"I don't need to think about it, wife, and neither do you," he declared in fiercely clipped tones. "This is not your concern any more than it is mine."

"Then whose is it, my lord?"

"It is the proper charge of the steward of Whitmore."

"May I remind your lordship that you have not yet appointed a new steward. And until you do, *someone* must continue to make decisions and see to the health and prosperity of the estate." She knew the instant the words left her mouth that she had gone too far.

"That someone, lady, will not be *you!*" he declared. "It will be the steward of Whitmore. For this very day I am appointing a new steward to oversee the business and prosperity of Whitmore. You need no longer trouble your head with such weighty matters."

"Even so . . . most noble ladies see to the making of cloth on their —" She stretched to her fullest height to meet his temper squarely. "I have every right and duty to suggest things that will benefit the people of Whitmore."

Infuriated by her continued obstinance, he resorted to raw intimidation, looming over her, using his height to reinforce his power and authority.

"Fine. Make your suggestion. To the new steward. It is he who will make the final decision."

"And who is this paragon of diplomacy, administration, and husbandry?" she demanded, unable to think of one viable candidate on all of Whitmore.

"Hadric of Hyde."

"Hadric the bailiff?"

"One and the same." He stalked forward and she edged back.

"But he's . . . just a bailiff." She could tell

from the murmurs the news unleashed among his men that they were hearing it for the first time as well.

"As bailiff, he has worked with the plowmen, the shepherds, and the cowherds and dairymaids, and he has had responsibility for the barns and tools."

"But he has not —" She halted, knowing she had to choose her words carefully. "He knows nothing about many aspects of the estate, including the hall, the kitchens, the weavers' house, the smithy, the carpentry . . . overseeing purchasing and record-keeping. Are you certain he can even read?"

"He is my choice!" Peril roared, with enough heat to scorch her eyebrows. "And as such, you will give him your respect and cooperation. You will take your notions about this weaving to him and you will abide by his decision. Is that clear?"

She stood trembling, praying that her anger and humiliation weren't as evident to everyone else as they felt to her. He was, by this very public action, putting a minor official of the estate between them. He was declaring that, from this time on, she would have to approach him on such matters through a third party or not at all.

"Yes, my lord earl. You are perfectly clear to me."

She ushered the stunned Edythe and her weavers out the doors of the hall, where she did her best to reassure them that their idea would eventually find acceptance and sent them back their looms. As she stood on the steps, Peril's men came out of the hall behind her and, to a man, they slowed and looked at her with regret or sympathy or outright apology.

She headed for the herb garden, where amongst the fragrant green she could reassemble her shattered composure. There, she sank onto a stone seat and struggled with both the pain of his dismissal and the feeling that she had just goaded him into making a decision that he would come to regret.

Hadric was a lean and hungry sort, with small eyes that were forever darting past whomever he was speaking with, always looking for something or someone of greater benefit to him. Even in her short time on the estate, she had learned how much the tenants and villeins who worked under him mistrusted his direction. Surely Peril knew as well.

Then why had he done it? To have the decision done? To get rid of unwanted responsibility? Her heart skipped several beats. To demonstrate the force of his will and bend her to it?

She heard movement nearby and looked up to find Peril looming above her, his face dark and jaw set in a mode she recognized all too clearly.

"I would have a word with you, wife," he said irritably, pulling her to her feet. He glanced around to find them alone and then pierced her with a stare. "What the hell were you doing in there?"

"Just what it appeared, milord." She raised her chin, refusing to submit.

"Flouting my will before my men . . . ignoring my orders . . ."

"Trying to help you and Whitmore."

"Disregarding my authority . . . forgetting your place . . ."

"My place?" Anger and hurt battled visibly for expression in her. "I don't have a 'place' here. There is no prescribed set of duties for me to assume. There hasn't been a lady of the manor on Whitmore for a score of years. Tell me what you expect of me, milord. Do you even know?"

That set him back on his heels for a moment.

"A lady sees to the house and the food . . . and she stitches a lot . . . sews things. She watches the servants to see that they work properly. She waits patiently for her lord husband to come home and she sees to his needs in bed and at board." He seemed a bit more confident with each duty named. "And she sure as blazes doesn't stick her nose in where it's not wanted or needed."

His notion of a proper and compliant wife sounded more and more like the convent's ideal of a submissive and obedient nun. And just think how miserable she had been at that!

"Well if that is truly what you expect of me, milord, then you'd best brace for a disappointment." She drew herself up straight. "I neither 'watch' nor 'wait' well, and I'm terrible at both 'sewing' and 'sitting.' And as to not sticking my nose in . . . I assume you mean I should never try to change or improve things . . . that you would rather have an impoverished estate and miserable people —"

"What I would rather have" — he stalked closer, looming over her — "is a modest and obedient wife!"

"I *am* obedient," she said thrusting her chin up.

"The hell you are. You're always butting in, trying to change things, issuing orders thither and yon, and defying my wishes in my own house and before my men. You're arrogant, immodest of speech and glance, and unwomanly in pride and attitude. You fail to give your lord and husband proper respect, and you regularly overstep your authority. You swore to me that first night that you would obey me as you did your blasted abbess, and I've yet to see the first bit of it."

"Oh, but I do obey you as I obeyed my abbess," she declared, too angry to consider the consequences of her words. "Why do you think she ordered me to marry *you?*"

Her vengeful pleasure at having shocked him was short-lived. He grabbed her by the shoulders and pulled her hard against him, staring down into her face. For a long moment she wondered if he meant to kiss her and prepared to resist the melting she knew would occur in her resolve. But then he released her abruptly and took a step back, looking at her as if seeing her and the reason for the abbess's choice of her as his bride in a very different light.

Once again, she realized, she had pushed too far.

He drew himself up to his full height, retreated into his coldest, most impenetrable mien, and stalked off toward the stables.

Eloise fled to the chapel where she sank on a kneeler, squeezed her eyes shut, and waited for the hammering of her heart to ease.

What had she done? The horror in his

face had been like a knife in her heart. She had been barred from taking a nun's vows because she was deemed too disobedient and outspoken to ever be a proper nun. Now it seemed she had not only perfected those flaws, she had added to them arrogance, immodesty, and unwomanliness.

Was there any part of her he didn't dislike?

If only she could change. If only she could somehow bridle her tongue and subdue her spirit.

Her throat tightened . . . her stomach wrenched . . . her entire being rebelled at the thought. If she constantly bit her tongue, she would soon lose the ability to speak at all. If she continually suppressed and denied her spirit, how long would it be before she was only an empty shell?

She could never change that much, she realized with deepening despair. If she could have, she would have done so long ago. She would never be that pale, biddable creature whose saintly presence alone was enough to please her lord husband and heal an entire manor's broken hopes and spirit. Wherever she was, whatever her title . . . she was stuck being Eloise. Prideful, headstrong, disobedient Eloise. Vulnerable, softhearted, temptation-prone Eloise. The Eloise who had never really fit in a sister's sober habit. The Eloise who might never truly fit in a lady's delicate gown.

Work, the sisters had often said, was the best remedy for an unsettled heart. Upon leaving the chapel, Eloise immersed herself in productive activity. She made visits to the weavers' house, the bread ovens, the dairy, the carding house, the chandlery, the brewery, the newly stocked dovecote, and finally the cottages in the village outside the gates. At every stop, there was ample evidence of her "unwomanly" activities and interference.

It was no small consolation that everywhere she went people stopped in the midst of whatever they were doing to greet her . . . some with "miladys" and awkward bows and curtseys, others with "Sister's," head-scratching, and a confused bit of cross-making. A few expressed pleasure that their lord had "gone an' married a nun." Who better to break a curse, they said, than a holy woman?

After her first two or three attempts to explain that she was not now and never had been a true nun, she merely nodded and accepted their bizarre notions and heartfelt congratulations with as much grace as she could summon. She had begun to feel she was coming to terms with their confusion when she paused to admire a well-cured fleece hanging on an open cottage door.

It was the home of Whitmore's head shearer, who was at that moment sharpening one of several pairs of shears laid out on a bench in front of the cottage. She inquired about the ongoing wool harvest, and he seemed surprised and rattled on self-importantly, making it clear he expected her, as a lady, to know nothing at all about sheep or shearing. Then came the offhand question that pierced her to the quick.

"Say, milady, what'e'er happened to that lil' nun?"

Eloise stared at him, at a loss for an answer. With the act of changing garments she seemed to have become an entirely different person to him.

"She were a sharp one," he continued. "Knowed her way around a sheepfold, all right. Ol' Hadric could'ave learnt a thing or two from 'er."

The morning's painful encounter with her husband came back to her with vengeance, wounding her anew. Peril had placed that same sheep-ignorant Hadric in charge of Whitmore's assets just to show her that she wasn't in charge.

She quitted the shearer and the other cottagers who had been following her through the lanes, and headed back through the gates and across the manor.

If it weren't for the pain in her heart she would have felt completely hollow inside. How could he treat her so, after all she had done to help him with his estate? After all they had shared together in their bed? Did he believe that the mere fact of receiving pleasure had somehow scrambled her wits?

He had listened to her and given her his respect and cooperation when she wore a habit. It seemed in changing garments she had changed in his eyes, too, and not for the better.

"Lady Eloise!" An unfamiliar voice stopped her an she looked up to find that she had blown well past the weavers' house and was now all the way down the other side of the manor hill, near the barns. Hadric of Hyde was hurrying toward her while waving sharply to a pair of men standing in the barn door, ordering them to close it. She saw the men scowl, and she glimpsed a covered cart inside before the door slammed.

The jangle of the chain of Hadric's new office brought her attention back to him. She stared at the heavy silver links and medallion. It was Sedgewick's chain, the one the old steward had worn so faithfully and well.

Hadric's usually sallow complexion was an odd, ruddy color that spoke of his excitement.

"Milady! I have just been made steward!"

"So I heard. I wish you well in your new task, Hadric." The words left a bitter tang on the back of her tongue.

"Thank you, milady." The man positively preened with self-satisfaction. "I understood from the earl that you wish to see me about the shearing."

He was the last person in the world she wanted to see, about anything. But in the interests of her weavers' pride and Whitmore's future income, she asked him to accompany her to see some samples of cloth being made on the French loom. He was reluctant at first, but went with her to the weavers' house.

It was clear from his comments and his air of distraction that he knew little about spinning and weaving and was loath to concern himself with them. But when they asked for a portion of the shearing to be set aside for their use, he quickly became more attentive to their request and declared he would give it his utmost consideration. Milady would have his decision, he said — with a manner so ingratiating that it could only have been false — in a day or two.

Edythe stood beside Eloise in the doorway watching the new steward scurry back to his barns. The weaver winced and rubbed her sleeves vigorously over her arms.

"Ooh. I feel like I may 'ave to 'ave me bath a month early."

The next morning, Peril stood on the large boulders beside the mill stream, staring at the wreckage of a water wheel lying on the bank of the stream. He picked up pieces of shattered wood and studied them, then handed them off to Simon and William.

"I just come to begin work at daybreak," the miller was saying for the tenth time, wiping his nose on his sleeve, "an' there she was . . . all broke up and just lyin' there. That were me pa's wheel. An' his pa's afore him." He buried his face in his hands and for a moment gave himself over to the consolation of his good wife, two apprentices, and a number of patrons. From the group came murmurs that were all too familiar.

"The curse . . ."

"Evil spirits . . ."

"Mistress Ann . . ."

"It was *not* that damnable curse!" Peril

417

declared furiously, striding into the middle of the startled group. "It was smashed deliberately — by human hands. Can't you see that?"

"But who would do such a thing to my wheel?" the miller said with disbelief. "What would it profit?"

"In my experience, every bit of destruction benefits *someone*," Peril declared, scanning the nearby trees and thinking of the thieves being harbored on Claxton's land. They must have seen — or been warned of — the patrols his men had been riding to the west and south, and the wretches had swung around to plunder and destroy his northern holdings instead.

"Then we must ask ourselves who would profit from Whitmore's lack of a mill wheel and lack of rolled oats for feed and flour for bread," Simon offered, coming up from the stream bank with William of Wright.

"Who would wish to see Whitmore barren an' hungry?" William added.

"Only one person," Peril said, his stance hardening as Claxton's snarling face rose in his mind. "There is no need to blame spirits and curses when the earl of Claxton lies in wait along our borders." He turned to Simon and William and lowered his voice. "His henchmen grow bolder. And so must we."

The miller followed anxiously as Peril headed for his horse.

"What do we do, milord? We must have a mill to grind grain."

"We'll build another. I'll send the carpenter and the cooper out to look at the old wheel and housing. Meanwhile, I'll have Hadric find the smaller grindstone my father kept as a part of his siege works."

"While you're at it, milord, you might want to consider cleaning out that silted pond and making some improvements to the mill," came an all too familiar voice. Peril looked up to find that Eloise had just arrived, astride old Sir Arthur.

"What are you doing out here?" he demanded, looking around to see who had escorted her and finding her alarmingly alone.

"I heard of the damage to the wheel and wanted to see if I could help. I've heard of a new arrangement . . . an overshot wheel, where the water pours down over the top. It would prove far more —"

"You're needed in the hall, lady, not out here," he declared, still smarting from the fact that she had shunned him last night . . . presenting herself in their chamber with a young girl she identified as her new lady's maid, and effectively ignoring his presence as she taught the girl her duties. Then she had spent an inordinately long time on her knees at evening prayers . . . long enough to disgust him and send him from the chamber to check on the night watch. Now here she was, inflicting herself on him and his decisions this morning. "You're never to be out riding alone, *ever*."

"I just thought —"

"No, you didn't think," he said shortly. "And that, lady, could prove disastrous."

"I simply wanted to —"

"You know, milord," Simon interjected, drawing Peril's ire on himself. When Peril looked daggers at him, he seemed remarkably unconcerned. "If it would be more productive than the old wheel, perhaps you should consider —"

"I'm certain Hadric will take all of that into consideration in making his decision," he growled at Simon.

"Then, at least insist that Hadric consult with Sir Simon to learn something about this new wheel arrangement before he makes up his mind," she said, causing him to turn back to her.

"Whom he consults and whether he consults are none of your concern, milady." He stalked over to her and stood up into her face. "I thought I had made that clear to you."

"Very clear, Your Lordship." Her face flamed and she turned Sir Arthur sharply to set off for the manor. She barely heard Peril order William to escort her back to the hall.

She had hoped to be of some help, but the minute he heard her voice, he had braced to resist whatever she said. She had watched him do it, feeling helpless to prevent it. He was determined to make her into a nameless, faceless vessel of virtue by day and lust by night . . . of no more value to him than the average rabbit's foot. Or serving wench.

Things were deteriorating between them at a heartbreaking pace. He had scarcely spoken three words to her at supper last evening. He had just eaten and then retired to their chamber for the rest of the evening. When she mounted the steps to her bed, with young Rose to attend her, he had stood glaring at her as she instructed the girl, then had stalked out of the chamber. He demanded she behave in a more womanly fashion and when she did, he seemed to hate that even more. From the sounds she heard coming from the stairwell, he had mounted the stairs to the unfinished tower above and paced well into the night. When he did come to bed, she refused to let him see how his absence had upset her; she feigned a deep and untroubled sleep.

Cresting the last rise before the village, she paused to let William of Wright catch up. They rode in silence for a few moments before she asked if he would help her dismount and then take her horse back to the stable, saying that she wanted to walk the rest of the way.

"His Lordship ordered me to escort you to the hall," he reminded her.

"But we're so close . . ." When she looked up into his broad, sympathetic face, tears pricked the corners of her eyes and she looked quickly away. He must have seen them, for he dismounted and came around the horses to help her down. She watched him disappear through the manor gates, and was overcome with a sudden dread of returning, of facing the same impossible situation with the same useless solutions. She veered to the west, skirting the village and heading for the edge of the forest.

But she had scarcely entered the trees when she heard someone moving nearby and slid to the shelter of a nearby trunk. As she peered around it, she spotted a curious bloom of color — purple — and then a flash of silver.

A woman with long, unbound hair stepped out into a shaft of dappled sunlight and called to her.

"Are you there, little sister?"

It was the woman who had helped her the day she learned she was never to be a nun. She stepped cautiously out into the open.

"Who are you?" She examined the woman. "What are you doing here?"

"I suppose we haven't exactly been introduced." The woman chuckled. As she came forward, Eloise saw that she wore a vivid purple gown and hoops of gold in her ears. "Many people have called me Hildegarde. As to what I am doing here" — her smile had an element of irony to it — "I've grown tired of living alone and thought perhaps I could find a place in the village." She looked Eloise over carefully and noticed both the tracks of tears and the bright halo of burnished hair.

"You no longer wear a veil," Hildegarde observed.

"I am no longer a novice. I am now a wife and a lady. Lady Eloise."

"And you are not happy with that," the woman concluded.

"I would be much happier . . . if my husband wanted me." Tears sprang again to Eloise's eyes. Why was it she could say things to this strange old woman she could say to no one else on earth?

"Is the man blind and daft?" Hildegarde

came to put an arm around her. "A maid as lovely as you? I should think he would delight to make you his."

"Oh, he *wants* me." Eloise had to force the words past the lump in her throat. "He just doesn't want *me*." The difference in emphasis bespoke a world of meaning. Hildegarde seemed to understand the distinction. She shook her head in sympathy, and that was all it took to unleash Eloise's tears.

She made her way with Hildegarde back to the stream bank and sat down on a stump. There she told the story of her coming to the manor, her task as the convent's "husband judge," and the abbess's order that she marry the earl.

"I'm headstrong," Eloise declared, wiping her eyes on her sleeves. "And I'm bold and outspoken and disobedient. I made a terrible novice, I know. I probably would have made a terrible nun.

"But it seems I've made an even worse bride. I'm always sticking my nose in where it's not wanted. I don't seem to be capable of being modest or silent." She looked up with the desolation of her heart visible in her eyes. "And that's what he wants. A rabbit's foot of a bride. Someone who is virtuous and simple and content.

"I don't belong here." She stared off into the spring green of the newly leafed forest. "I feel like I don't belong anywhere . . . not in the convent, not on Whitmore. I don't belong to Christ and I certainly don't belong to the earl." The pain of that admission was so awful that she couldn't believe her ears when she heard what sounded like a laugh.

"Oh, my girl . . . there are so many things for you to learn." Hildegarde's eyes were brimming with compassion; it was impossible not to believe her. "Come with me. Let me help you learn the first and most basic lesson of all."

"What?" Eloise asked, as Hildegarde pulled her to her feet and dragged her along a well-disguised path in the woods. "Wait — where are you taking me?"

"To a place where the earth and heaven meet. Where the sunshine turns to sky." She paused and gave Eloise an eye-twinkling smile. "Where you will learn where you belong."

Wary, but driven by a need to ease her aching heart, Eloise followed her. They walked for what seemed like miles, and finally came to a hill so steep that they had to tuck their skirts to climb. Hildegarde, despite her age, reached the top first and when Eloise joined her, they stood together at the

425

edge of the forest, overlooking a pristine valley filled with meadows and pasture.

The sun was so bright and the sky so blue that they almost hurt Eloise's eyes. The greens were delicate and tinged with yellow . . . spring's color. She took a deep breath and smells of moist earth and new grass filled her head.

"Let down your hair," Hildegarde told her. After a moment of uncertainty, she removed the pins and cord and handed them to Hildegarde. Next came her blue gown and her shoes, and she shook her hair out around her shoulders. With some prompting, she opened her arms to let the breeze fill her shift. It felt strange, almost indecent . . . the slide and billow of her shift over her bare skin. It was almost like the earl's — she shoved that thought away.

Hildegarde told her to close her eyes and she did. She could feel Hildegarde come to stand beside her, speaking in soft, even tones.

"Do you feel the sun on your face, Eloise? It is a caress from your mother, the mother of all life, the source of all light. Do you feel the wind in your hair? It greets you as your sister. Do you smell the spring awakening in the soil and the herbs and the green wood? It awakens in you as well. You are a part of this new birth, this spring. Where do you belong, Eloise?"

"I don't know," Eloise whispered, feeling a deep ache opening inside her.

"Look up and see the sky. The blue that wraps the earth like a warm, protective blanket." The voice continued, soft and earnest, wrapping like a balm around Eloise's battered heart. "Look at the swaying grasses in the meadow below. They are nourished by the sun and share that nourishment with all who seek it. Feel the earth cradling you . . . holding you up . . . eager to greet your every step. Where do you belong, Eloise?"

"I'm . . . not sure." Something began welling up inside her empty heart.

"Can you feel the moist earth beneath and around your feet? You are made of clay borrowed from the earth, and so you will always be a part of the earth . . . of all things created and good. God moves and breathes and is revealed in creation. And the creation is always still unfolding around us." She paused for a moment. "How many shades of blue are there in the world, Eloise?"

"I don't know . . . a dozen, I suppose . . . perhaps more." It was hard to speak for the lump in her throat and hard to see for the tears pricking her eyes.

"Hundreds, Eloise. There are hundreds

of shades of blue. Why is that?"

"I'm not sure."

"Why do you think?"

"Because . . . things were created that way . . ."

"And why would the Creator take the trouble to make so many shades of blue?"

"Because . . . because . . . I don't know . . . because He wanted to?"

"Ah. You understand more than you think. You see, the Creator loves to create. Loves to make things new and different. Takes delight in the variety and uniqueness of each part of this world. The Creator made you, Eloise. Made you lovely and stubborn and bright and bold and passionate . . . all the delightful and contradictory things you are. And the Creator set you here in the midst of the rest of this wonderful creation to grow and to learn. Where do you belong, Eloise?"

The sensation of the coolness of the earth faded, and it felt as if her feet and the earth were somehow blending. As the sun warmed her face and chest, she lost track of where the sunbeams ended and her skin began. She breathed in the scents of the new grass and moist earth and held them inside her . . . feeling them becoming a part of her and herself becoming a part of them. The tears in her eyes began to fall.

"I feel like I belong *here*," she said holding her arms out to the breeze.

Then it came to her. God wasn't mad at her. Hildegarde's words rang true: God had made her the way she was, with strengths and weaknesses, with hopes and dreams and a heart filled with emotions to explore. Why would He expect her to deny and denounce everything he had put inside her . . . including her desire for Peril of Whitmore? It was as if a locked door in her heart swung open and a great wave of peace flooded in through it.

"I think I must belong wherever there is sky and land and greenness . . . wherever I can feel the warmth of the sun and the wetness of the rain."

"You are indeed learning." There was a smile in Hildegarde's voice. "The Creator has steered you to this man and into this marriage to be who you are and to do what you are good at doing . . . not to make you into something strange and foreign to your nature. Your lord husband may not want a willful and determined and strong-minded wife — but he must need one, else the Creator would not have brought you to him."

Those words stirred a host of memories and thoughts in Eloise.

He needed her? The good she had done on Whitmore would never have happened if she had been the meek, biddable, compliant creature Peril claimed to want. He *had* needed her. Stubborn, disobedient, and opinionated her. He needed her to meet him toe to toe and nose to nose and tell him the truth. He needed her to make him dig deep into his heart and strength in order to lead his people, to make him live up to the potential inside him. Her heart began to pound. She needed him too, to challenge her, to make her grow, to call her beyond the limitations of her experience into a new way of life.

"Where do you belong, Eloise?"

She raised her arms and began spinning around and around, laughing joyfully through her tears.

"Here! I belong right here!"

They stayed on that hilltop much of the day, basking in the sun, sometimes talking, sometimes in silence. When the sun began to sink in the sky, Eloise donned her kirtle and tied her hair back into its sober knot. But she knew as she did it that she would never again be quite as tucked and pinned and tightly wound as she had been before this afternoon on a hilltop.

As they made their way around a ridge

and through a small stretch of woods to a rise overlooking Whitmore, Eloise was loath to let Hildegarde leave.

"You were coming to seek a place on Whitmore . . . Why not come with me to the manor? You said you've studied all about herbs and healing. We could use someone to tend the herb garden and create an apothecary."

"Do you truly want me?" Hildegarde said with a pensive look.

"I can never repay the gift you gave me this afternoon. But I can offer you a home and a place to practice your skills as a healer."

"But what about the earl?"

"He is a good man, Hildegarde. He is gruff and stubborn and pigheaded at times, but he truly wants to do what is best for his people. He will want you to come and be part of Whitmore." She could have sworn there were tears in Hildegarde's eyes.

"Then I'll come." She put her arm through Eloise's. "And I will be more than pleased to serve you and the people of Whitmore."

Sixteen

"Where the blazes is she?" Peril scanned the faces of the house servants and men of the garrison who were gathered in the hall. He didn't expect an answer; they had already reported the results of their fruitless search for Eloise.

"She didn't say where she was going, and no one has seen her since she came back from the mill?" The nods and shakes of heads all meant the same thing: no one had seen her or had any idea where she might be. It was dark outside and she was missing. The fact of it hit him like a fist in the gut.

Missing.

Dear God . . . if anything had happened to her . . .

"We'll widen the search," he declared, feeling something in the deep fabric of his being rip as he struggled to separate his churning emotions from his duty to remain clearheaded and in control. "Michael — you take half a dozen men out to the north. Ethan — half a dozen to the south. Simon — you go to the east, and I'll take the west." He beckoned his knights over and drew a diagram in the ashes of the cold hearth. "Start just outside the walls and work your way out like the spokes of a wheel. Stay within sight of each other and call out frequently, until you reach the trees. Go all the way to Whitmore's border . . . no exceptions."

Then he turned to William, whose burly frame was weighed down by his sense of guilt. "*You* . . . you'll take the rest of the men into the village and leave no stone unturned. I want every shed, crate, and barrel checked."

"Yea, milord. If she's there, I'll find 'er." The big man's misery was so evident that Peril was almost tempted to feel sorry for him. Then another voice spoke up.

"Yea, milord, we'll find our lady and bring 'er back to you!" There was a chorus of agreement, out of which one voice — Pascoe's — stood out.

"Even if it means we have to ride down the gates of Heaven itself!"

Another roar of determination.

Their lady. To a man, his garrison were taking the loss of her personally. They liked her, he realized. And more. They admired her strength and many abilities and fiery spirit, and if truth be told, they enjoyed the way she often got the better of him. At that moment, looking into their faces, he realized Pascoe's boast was not an idle one. They would ride down the gates of Heaven to bring her back. As would he. The lump in his throat he had been fighting for the last half hour settled in and would not be dislodged.

"Let's go." He ordered his men out to their horses with a sweep of his hand. As they hurried out the door, Michael and Simon lagged behind to clap him on the shoulder.

"We'll find her, milord," Michael said, studying the anxiety etching new lines into Peril's face. "She's strong and has a sound head on her shoulders. If Claxton has her, he'll soon learn he's bitten off more than he can chew."

Simon, who had been with Peril the longest and always seemed to see to the heart of his moods, simply grasped the top of his shoulder plate and rocked him. "The Almighty won't let milady come to any harm." His forced smile was a reflection of Peril's own misery. "It took Him too long to find a woman who could put up with you."

Peril raked his hawk-shaped helm off the great table and strode out into the chaotic courtyard.

It was past sunset when Eloise entered the

hall through the kitchens, where she found the cooks and kitchen servants so frantic over her absence that they had removed the smoked fish pasties from the oven and the lentil stew from the fire while they awaited to see what would happen. She reassured them she was all right and ordered the serving women and potboys up to the hall with the food. Following them up, she found it empty except for Father Basset, who was pacing and wringing his hands as he muttered what were probably prayers. When he looked up and saw her he all but fainted with relief.

"Where is everyone?" she asked. The little priest sank onto a bench, clutching his heart, and pointed wordlessly to the main doors. Through them she could see torches and hear horses and raised voices. "What's happened?"

She ran for the door with a dozen awful possibilities springing to mind: an accident of some sort, another missing child, the arrival of the king's treasurer. With her heart pounding, she paused on the steps, squinting into the torchlit yard, looking for Peril among the men already mounted and the men still preparing to ride.

"There she is!" someone shouted. "On the steps!"

There was a rush of movement toward her, and suddenly Peril was there, grabbing her by the upper arms and squeezing as if he was afraid she wasn't real.

"Are you all right?" He looked her over frantically and when she nodded, confirming what his eyes told him, his reined anxiety gave way to an explosion of anger. "Where the hell have you been?"

"I just wanted to walk as I came back from the mill," she said, trying to wrest her arms from his ironlike grip. "And I came across a —"

"A walk?" He gave her a small shake. "With thieves and raiding parties rampaging all over?"

"I am perfectly capable of — What raiding parties?" The depth of the concern beneath his anger finally registered. "What's happened?"

"If you had stayed in the hall as I ordered, you would have known," he said furiously. "We found a cottage burned and a dozen sheep killed in the east pasture this afternoon."

"Killed?" She saw relief in the faces of the men collected around them.

"Slaughtered and just left," Michael supplied from nearby, where he was holding his and Peril's horses.

She gasped. "The tenants?"

"Escaped. Barely." Peril released her and straightened. "It was mindless destruction, like the wheel this morning. It would have been even worse if the shepherds' dogs hadn't raised an alarm. No place in the forest or the outlying pastures is safe" — he grabbed one of her arms again — "and I won't have you putting your life in jeopardy and forcing me and my men to spend hours and hours searching for you!"

She looked up into his eyes and saw tension around them and the darkness visible at their centers. He truly had been worried about her. And the men . . . She looked around at what she now realized was a search party. The knowledge both heartened and chastened her.

"If I had known, milord, I wouldn't have gone out."

"You saw the wheel, and I told you this morning never to go out without an escort." He released her and jerked his gauntlets from his hands. "What more do I have to do? Tie you to a bedpost?"

There were snickers and mutters at that and he lashed a glare at his men, who looked quickly away.

"All you have to do, milord," she replied with adamant dignity, "is to treat me as if I have wits enough to understand, and tell me about the dangers in a reasonable manner. I am, after all, a reasonable woman."

A murmur rippled up the steps and around them.

"That, milady, is open to debate."

She lifted her chin. This was no time or place to discuss that.

"What is not open to debate, milord, is the fact that your supper is now ready and waiting. After such a trying day, I'm sure you and your men must be starving." She lifted her skirt and reentered the hall.

He watched her moving up the steps, skirts swaying, then jerked his attention back to the men staring expectantly between him and the open doors.

"Leave the horses saddled," he ordered, waving them into the hall. "We still have to ride patrol tonight, after we've eaten."

The food was tasty and the ale and bread plentiful. Peril watched Eloise directing the servants and pouring ale, and felt his anxiety receding now that she was safe and home where she belonged.

As he combed the manor looking for her, he had felt a strange, empty feeling opening at the bottom of his chest . . . something like a longing, an ache, a desire to pull her into his very body where he could have her with him always and protect her. It was an unsettling sensation that he attributed to fear that something had happened to her. But that didn't explain why, now that she was here and safe, he was still feeling that volatile ache inside. Or why it got even worse when he saw the anger evident in the rigid set of her shoulders.

"Wine, milord?" She brought the pitcher to the table and filled his goblet before taking her place beside him. He buried his attention in his food and tried not to look at her.

"While I was out and abroad today I found someone to tend the herb gardens and serve as apothecary and physician for the manor," she said in a determinedly civil manner.

"Oh? Where is this learned marvel? Where did you find him?"

"*She* is there, milord." She pointed to a strange-looking older woman standing near the kitchen steps and then beckoned to her.

Peril stopped mid-sip of wine, staring at the woman's plentiful gray-streaked hair, golden earrings, and startling purple garment.

"This is Hildegarde," Eloise said as the woman approached and bowed her head. "She has traveled much and has studied healing with the Moors of Spain, and herbs and medicines with the physicians of Paris."

"A woman?" He scowled.

"Who better to tend a garden, milord, than a woman?" Hildegarde spoke for herself, her dark eyes twinkling. "And who better to tend the sick and the injured than one who was once at death's door and was given back her life?"

The woman's lively gaze and nimble turn of phrase left him only one objection: "You should have consulted me before appointing her."

Eloise bristled with the urge to say that he hadn't bothered to consult her or apparently anyone else in his choice of Hadric, but she held it in check.

"Such matters are well within a lady's usual duties. If you don't wish her to live in the house, I will certainly find a place for her in the village."

"Can you set broken limbs?" he asked Hildegarde.

"I have restored many arms and legs, milord."

"If it comes to that, can you remove a shattered limb?"

"Sadly" — she gave a rueful nod — "I have also had to perform that surgery."

He studied them both for a moment, then

440

nodded and returned to his supper. A physician would have been far down on his list of things to acquire for Whitmore, but when fighting broke out with Claxton, they would need someone to tend the injured. He watched Eloise send Hildegarde to a seat on the far side of the great table, opposite Hadric and Father Basset, and he grabbed her by the elbow.

"She sits above the salt?"

"She is more than a servant, milord." Eloise removed her arm from his grip. "She is educated and occupies a position of trust. Your knights and steward sit at our table. As one of my women, she is entitled to eat with us."

"One of your women?"

"As you know, milord, I have recently acquired a lady's maid, Rose. The lady of a manor needs help, just as the lord does."

He buried his response in his cup of wine.

When Eloise sat down to her own supper, beside him, she felt his gaze coming back to her again and again. Each time she felt a deepening indignation.

Nothing had changed, she thought. Then she realized that wasn't true. Something within her had changed. Something important. She turned her thoughts to Hildegarde and the powerful events of the day. She belonged here, on Whitmore; she believed that now.

As she sat looking out over the hall and thinking of the conditions here when she arrived, it struck her that this was indeed the path she was meant to walk. She was meant to live among these people and help resurrect this hall and land. She was meant to marry this man. She looked at him and felt her anger melting into a dangerously potent longing. If only she and Peril could somehow make peace. If only he could come to accept and respect her for who she was, instead of who he wanted her to be.

Later, when Peril had led the men out to their horses, she asked Hildegarde and Rose to join her and several of the house women as they gathered by the hearth to make plans for the next day's work. She looked up from the slate she used to record the next day's tasks to find Hadric approaching their small circle with a condescending smile.

"If I might have a word, Lady Eloise." He gave an exaggerated bow.

Was it her imagination, Eloise thought, that put a hint of a sneer into his use of that address?

"Yes, Hadric." She turned on her chair to face him.

"You had lodged a request with me that a

442

part of the shearing be held back for the weavers here on Whitmore. It grieves me, milady, to tell you that there has been such a woeful shearing, such a terrible shortfall of wool, that we will have none to spare." His smile of sympathy caused her to stiffen as if she'd just heard the unexpected screech of a rusty hinge. "Perhaps next year."

"Perhaps." She forced a polite smile. "Thank you."

As he departed, she had some difficulty concentrating again on the slate she was using to list the next day's plans. Wretched creature. Was the flaw in him or in her that made her distrust every word he spoke? She looked up to find Hildegarde watching him with an intent frown as he departed. Later, when she showed Hildegarde to her new chamber in the manor house, the healer finally shared her concern.

"Who was that man, milady? The one who spoke with you by the hearth. He wears a chain of office. . . ."

Eloise sighed.

"That is our steward, Hadric of Hyde." She worked to keep her distaste for him from showing, and so was surprised to see the puzzlement deepening to distress on Hildegarde's face. "Why?"

"Because . . ." Hildegarde seemed to

wrestle with the revelation she was about to make. "I have seen him before."

"He does travel all over the manor, seeing to His Lordship's business."

"In the forest." Hildegarde winced as if the memory pained her.

"Well, he was bailiff until recently. I'm sure he had to check which trees were to be cut and whether or not there had been poaching —"

"He was not alone," Hildegarde said, engaging her eyes.

Eloise went still, sensing something important was coming.

"He was with that band of thieves."

That same moment, in the barns on Claxton's estate, the earl of Claxton and his henchmen were receiving a cart that had just arrived from Whitmore via the forest that lay along their common border.

"Open it. Let's see what he's sent this time," he ordered the thatch-headed fellow who had driven the cart.

When the felt cover was thrown back and Claxton discovered the cart contained only bales of raw, freshly sheared wool, his face reddened.

"No wine? I sent word I wanted more of the wine," he snarled, striding around the cart, searching it, as if certain there must be something more.

"This were all 'e could send, jus' now." The messenger crouched back. "What wi' the raid an' all, the earl's men is everywhere."

Claxton uttered an oath and strode back to the rear of the cart, glaring at the bales. "So he's finally stirring himself, is he? Well, let him make his precious patrols. It's too little, too late."

There was a muffled sound from the middle of the bales and he turned a scowl on the driver, who winced and pulled a bale down to reveal a young boy, bound hand and foot, his mouth stuffed with rags.

"Kitchen boy, milord." The cart driver winced. "Hadric said he had to be got rid of."

Claxton heaved a disgusted breath and pulled the terrified child from the cart. Thrusting the wriggling form at one of his guardsmen, he ordered: "Take this to the cellars and see it gets fitted with some iron." Then he turned on the driver again and jabbed a finger at him.

"You tell Hadric I want that wine."

"He said 'soon,' milord. It'll be easier now 'at he's been made steward."

"What?" Claxton was knocked back on

his heels by the news. "Hadric? Whitmore's steward? When?"

"A few days past."

"My Hadric . . . my greedy, duplicitous agent of disruption . . . *steward* in charge of all of Whitmore's property? He's robbed Whitmore blind as bailiff and is rewarded by elevation to steward. This is too good!" Claxton laughed with an edge that was imitated by the men around him. "Too good by half. I'm almost tempted to feel sorry for Whitmore."

He glanced over at his captain, who gave him a quizzical look.

"I said *almost.*"

Still chuckling, he folded his arms and then reached up to trace his smirk with one gloved finger. "I've had word that Bromley is on his way, already south of London. Perhaps I should send him another urgent letter. The sooner the Lord Treasurer learns what a sty Whitmore has made of his estate and samples the hospitality of mine — especially my new wine — the sooner Whitmore will be added to my holdings."

Eloise waited up in their chamber for Peril to return. The empty hours lengthened and she finally curled up on the bed to stay warm. She was awakened by Rose the next

446

morning just as she had fallen asleep: in a ball under a fur cover on the bed, her head on the bolster that Peril always used.

Rose brought word that Peril and his men had not yet returned from their patrols. Eloise hurried through her morning prayers and then rushed down to the kitchens to make certain that food and drink would be ready for them when they returned. She was surprised to find that the food for breaking fast was late and the usually pleasant cooks were in a testy mood.

"Wretched pot boy let the fire go out," Ralph declared, irritably. "Little bugger. Wait 'til I get my hands on 'im."

Eloise frowned and looked to Johanna, who explained, "The boy we call 'Gravy' was supposed to keep the fire last night, but he let it go out. And he wasn't sleeping by the hearth this morning. They alwus do that when they're tendin' the fire. We haven't seen hide nor hair of 'im."

For some reason, the news lodged in Eloise's mind. It was just a kitchen boy's mistake, she told herself. He was probably off dallying somewhere, or hiding to escape a well-deserved cuffing. But she thought of the boy Tad and the other missing children, and a shiver went through her.

"Send me word as soon as you've found

him," she told Johanna and Ralph. "If His Lordship returns before the food is done, serve bread and baked cheese and ale. They won't object to simple fare."

It wasn't long before Peril and the first group of his men came rumbling into the hall, saddle-worn and fatigued, mail rattling and boots clomping. Peril dropped his sword, gauntlets, and helm on the table and then peeled his mail shirt from his shoulders. She called for food and ale and had a houseboy build up the fire in the hearth. Then she came to stand beside him with prominently folded hands.

"You were out all night."

"Another cottage burned." He rubbed the corners of his eyes, which were red from smoke. "We found the tenants hiding in the woods. They didn't see or hear anything, so they're certain it was 'Mistress Ann.' I told them about the other cottage and the dead sheep and they still insisted it was the curse."

"And what do you think it was?" she asked, thinking of the poor tenants and of Hildegarde's revelation.

"Claxton and the thieves he's been harboring on his land. I'd stake my life on it. But I can't appeal to the king or charge into a fight, until I have proof he's involved." He studied the surface of the ale in his tankard as if it might help him divine his best course of action.

"A fight? Surely not, milord." She braced for a hot reply, but what came was surprisingly reasoned and personal.

"It is not by my choice," he said gravely. "Warring is costly and wasteful. But I will not shrink from it. I cannot allow my possession of Whitmore to be questioned . . . or the security of my people and property to be threatened."

The idea of war and fighting rattled her. There had to be a better way than bloodshed to resolve this enmity.

"I have learned something. I don't know if it will help," she said, steeling herself as she settled on the edge of the chair beside his. He had to know. Especially now. "Last night, after you left the hall, Hadric came to tell me that the season's shearing has been bad, and he cannot allow our weavers to keep a portion of it." He scowled and she hurried on. "Hildegarde saw him speaking to me and asked who he was. She said she had seen him in the forest . . . in the company of the thieves who have been stealing from Whitmore."

Peril stared at her for a long moment and she held her breath. Then his features hardened.

"What is this? Hadric denies you a bit of wool and now you accuse him of thievery and betrayal?"

"I do not accuse him of anything," she said, straightening her shoulders. "I am only reporting to you what Hildegarde observed."

"Hildegarde?" It took him a moment to recall who that was. "You accuse my steward on the word of an old woman you met yesterday in the woods?"

"I have good reason to trust her. She was reluctant to tell me what she had seen, and only did so out of concern for us and our household. She has no reason to bear Hadric malice."

He let his gaze travel pointedly over her. He may as well have said aloud that *she* did.

"I have been nothing but honest and forthright with you, milord." She rose, unable to endure his open distrust a moment longer. "And the undeniable truth is that Hadric is seldom where he should be — including at this table during meals — and he is not liked nor trusted by those who have worked most closely under him. With all of the losses Whitmore has suffered, is it so beyond your imagining that someone in your own household could be helping these thieves you chase?"

She felt her eyes pricking and throat tightening and paused for a moment before issuing one last volley.

"If you won't take my word or Hildegarde's, then at least have the good sense to watch the man and see for yourself."

Peril scowled after her as she whirled away and strode for the kitchen steps. He knew Hadric was a sore point with her. He also knew that Hadric was all she had said and probably more — unreliable, disliked, and often inexplicably absent. And it wasn't beyond the pale of possibility that someone had been helping the thieves; he had discussed that very possibility with Michael and Simon just last night. If everything she said made so much sense, then why was he still so damned reluctant to credit her and her source?

He gulped down the rest of his morning ale, wishing he wasn't having these second thoughts. He wore the breeches on Whitmore, dammit. He made the decisions and he stuck by them. If he didn't, he would lose the respect of his men and his enemies alike. He was the lord here and she was his wife. She had to learn to give him the respect and the obedience she had promised him.

But as he stared at the kitchen steps, where she had disappeared, the hurt and anger in her tone came back to him. For a moment he wished he could recall those last few exchanges between them and soften his words. He hadn't meant to . . . He rubbed that troublesome tender spot at the bottom of his chest.

Whatever her flaws, she had always been forthright with him. She had given far more of her time and energy and abilities than he had a right to expect, and had never been vain or duplicitous or — he groaned to admit it — vengeful. She never asked for anything for herself. And even now, when she was obstinate and interfering, it was on behalf of an idea meant to benefit him and his people.

He looked up to find Michael and Simon watching him. He waved them over for a word and scanned the hall as they reached his side and bent to listen.

"Find Hadric," he said, his voice lowered. "He has been far too difficult to locate in recent days. Report to me on where he is and what he is doing."

Michael nodded, reading the gravity of the order in his face.

"And, Michael . . ."

"Yes, milord?"

"Don't let him know he's being watched."

What followed was the longest day Eloise had spent since coming to Whitmore. Peril sent his men to escort the rest of his outlying tenants back to the manor for protection, and as they and their animals, their carts, and their children began to arrive, arrangements had to be made for their lodging, food, and provender. Peril dozed for a while in the hall, then mounted and rode out with another party of men to see that the remaining livestock was secured, apparently without a thought as to how the growing influx of people would be handled — or by whom.

"It would have been nice," Eloise told Sir Ethan irritably as she stood in a muddle of overloaded donkey carts, separated families, and squawking poultry, "if His Lordship had mentioned he was bringing his tenants inside the walls. That way we might have prepared."

"There was no time for plans, milady. With two cottages burned, His Lordship would not take the chance of losing more than just wattle and daub."

That sounded noble and generous enough, she said to herself. But Peril wasn't the one who had to deal with the messy situation his nobility and generosity generated. She gave Ethan a disgusted look and gestured to the chaos around her.

"Where is the esteemed Hadric, now that all of this needs managing?"

He gave her a sympathetic shrug.

She took charge and threw herself into assigning and organizing the refugees. For most of the morning, she held court on the steps of the weaver's house, mediating arguments over assigned lodgings and shortages of straw and firewood, and conflicts involving space, children, and the common use of various individuals' household goods. By the time the sun started to slide down the western sky, Eloise was ready to pull out her hair.

How could these people be so cross and contentious with each other when they'd just been given safe haven inside their lord's gates?

When she had the chance, she broke away and posed that question to Hildegarde as they stood together on the path overlooking the slope where most of the resettled tenants were camped.

"I think it can be only one thing." The healer frowned thoughtfully. "Fear. Whenever people are difficult or greedy or angry or combative or even just plain selfish . . . it's usually because down deep they are afraid."

Eloise thought on that for a moment and the observation rang true. "This morning, as I tried to help them, I kept hearing mutters of 'the curse.' They're determined to believe that everything bad that happens on Whitmore is the result of angry words spoken a score of years ago."

"And what do you think?" Hildegarde searched her intently.

"Me?" Eloise shook her head. "There may indeed be such things as curses. But I believe that this particular 'curse' gets credit for a lot of things caused by far more earthly forces — such as bad husbandry and simple laziness." She looked up and found Hildegarde wearing a sober expression. "The earl is convinced that the earl of Claxton's henchmen are responsible for much of the loss on Whitmore. But the people seem to fear the curse more than the threat of going to war with a neighboring lord."

Hildegarde nodded and squeezed Eloise's hand.

"People always prefer the devil they know to the one they don't," Hildegarde said, wagging her head. "They fear what they cannot see more than what they can . . . even if the greater threat is right before their

455

noses. It's just in the nature of mankind."

And in the nature of a man, Eloise thought. Peril of Whitmore would rather have a thieving and untrustworthy steward rob him blind than risk trusting her judgment and word. It struck her: did that mean he was afraid, too? Of what? Her? What about her could possibly strike such fear into the heart of the "spur of Northumbria"?

Hildegarde watched Eloise's spirits droop and saw her wander over to a large tree stump that sat just off the path, near the herb garden.

"What's the matter?" she asked, following her young mistress.

Eloise expelled a heavy sigh as she sat down. "You remember what you told me last night about Hadric? I told the earl this morning."

"But he didn't believe you," Hildegarde completed it for her.

Eloise nodded and looked down the hill toward the stables, where the growing sounds of men and horses indicated that Peril was probably back with his patrol. As she shaded her gaze and searched him out, she saw that the rest of his men were collecting around him for the latest report.

Hildegarde sank down on the stump beside Eloise and watched longing bloom in her face as she caught a glimpse of him.

"It is a hard thing to find yourself yoked to someone and pulling in opposite directions," Hildegarde observed.

"That sounds perilously close to a proverb. Don't let the earl hear you say such things. He hates proverbs." Despair tinged her words, prompting Hildegarde to reach for her hand.

"Well, he doesn't hate you, Eloise."

"I'm not so sure about that."

"Aren't you?" Hildegarde gave her a rueful smile. "After only one evening in the hall with the pair of you, it's clear as Venetian glass to me. He looks at you as though you're a feast and he is a starving man."

Eloise was unconvinced. "All I ever see is frowns and glowers."

"Well, I suspect he's not especially pleased to be wanting you with every fiber of his being, when he can't seem to figure out what to do with you."

"Every fiber of his being? If that were true he wouldn't treat me so high-handedly."

"Still thinking like a nun." Hildegarde gave several "tsk's." "This is what comes of living tucked away in a convent for years. He's a man, Eloise, and you're a lovely and passionate young woman. He wants you so much he's practically blue all over. But he probably knows more about horseshoes than he knows about women. And, truth be told, you're not the sort of 'wed-her-bed-her-and-forget-her' bride he had expected. He hasn't the faintest notion how to have you without giving up some of his hard-won control."

"You make it sound so encouraging," Eloise said miserably.

Hildegarde smiled at her response. "You know . . . you and His Lordship are not so different. You both long for more, but are so afraid of giving up some precious part of you to the other. Did it never occur to you that what you gain can more than make up for what you give away?"

Eloise opened her mouth to protest, but closed it without speaking. Of course it had occurred to her. She was willing to give . . . she didn't withhold . . .

"You said all you see on him are frowns and glowers," Hildegarde said. "What do you think he sees from you? You know, Eloise, you catch more flies with honey than with vinegar."

After a moment Hildegarde patted her hand, rose, and returned to her weeding in the herb garden. Eloise watched her, feeling the healer's insightful words working on her heart.

Peril was afraid, that much was clear. Of what? Giving himself to her? Afraid she would take things he didn't want to give: his authority as lord of the manor . . . his role as a warrior and a leader of men . . . his independence and sense of control over his own life?

Didn't he know? Couldn't he see — in her face every time she looked at him or slipped into his arms in their bed — that she didn't want to take anything from him? If anything, she wanted to give him things. Her willingness. Her help. Her support. Her admiration and respect. Her —

She swayed on her seat.

Her love.

She loved Peril of Whitmore.

She steadied herself and pushed her thinking further still.

If he couldn't see that love . . . and from all appearances, he couldn't . . . what was standing in the way? Her own fear? Her pride? Her determination to control her own life and destiny? Her refusal to temper her will and her ways, to be the first one to "give"?

She felt the world shifting beneath her feet, taking on a different shape altogether. What had felt like mountains suddenly seemed like molehills.

What victory could there be in withholding herself from the possibilities of love and caring and pleasure and devotion? What did it matter who gave first . . . as long as there was mutual giving?

Where did she start?

She caught sight of Hildegarde sitting back on her heels, smelling a small flower she had just uprooted.

Well, vinegar hadn't worked. Perhaps it was time she tried honey.

Seventeen

Peril saw her coming down the path toward the stables with her hair uncoiled and shining and her skirts swaying, and he felt that annoying ache begin again in the bottom of his chest. He rubbed the spot where his ribs joined his breastbone, and considered ducking back into the stables and slipping out through the harness shed. But she hailed him with a wave and he realized it was too late. She knew he had seen her.

As he watched her approach, he detected a certainty in her step that drew his eye and alerted his finely honed sense of danger. He hated it when she was collected, composed, and sure of herself.

"Milord, I wonder if you would tell me where to find our esteemed steward," she said crisply, her eyes bright and cheeks rosy from her brisk walk. "I have a number of things to discuss with him."

It took him a moment to register what she had said; he was stuck like a fly in honey on the berry-colored ripeness of her lips.

"I have more important things to do than keep track of Hadric." He snapped back to

461

attention. "What kind of things?"

"The need for more firewood and more felt for tents and more straw and hay for the cottagers that you and your men brought inside the walls. And the fact that the small millstone still hasn't been set up and the cooks and baker will soon be out of flour, and the fact that one of the kitchen boys seems to be missing. And if the king's treasurer arrives anytime soon, we'll have nowhere to put him, with all of these extra people and animals. And we'll have used up all of the special foods and baking that was done for the celebration of Easter —"

"Enough!" He brought up both hands, feeling overwhelmed. "Send a runner to find — A boy is missing?"

"One of the kitchen boys, the one they call Gravy, hasn't been seen since yesterday. He let the hearth fire go out during the night, and when they went to look for him, he wasn't to be found. And I *sent* a runner to find Hadric. He came back saying the steward wasn't to be found, either."

"Why wasn't I told about the boy?"

"He's an orphan. If it weren't for the cooks, no one would know or care that he is missing. He may just be hiding to avoid a good cuffing."

"And he may not." Peril's rising irritation

was weighted with an equally heavy sense of responsibility. "Another missing child. At the worst possible time." He beckoned to a few of the men loitering around the stable doors and sent them off to check the stables and garrison. Young boys with time on their hands often gravitated to the stables or the men's lodgings to watch and listen to the seasoned warriors.

"I have spent much of my time, this day, doing things that were rightly Hadric's responsibility. If you don't know where he is and what he is doing, either, then perhaps you should come with me to search for him."

There had been no word from Michael or Simon regarding their observation of the man, and it occurred to Peril that he had seen neither of them since last night. It was time for him to find out firsthand where and how the elusive steward spent his time. He nodded and she straightened, pleased.

"I suggest we head for the sheep pens. We can check the barns along the way." She took two steps, then found herself halted by his grip on her elbow.

"Sheep pens?" He knew where this was headed now. "It's that damned wool again, isn't it? Cottages have been burned and livestock slaughtered. The thieves in our forest

463

grow bolder by the hour, and you harangue me about a few bags of wool?"

"Hadric has been overseeing the shearing and tallying the wool crop, and last night told me the crop was too poor to allow my weavers to keep any."

He gave her a look of disbelief.

"If there isn't sufficient wool, woman, then there isn't sufficient wool. The man can't spin it out of thin air!"

"But what if the man has made it disappear into thin air?" she said, brazenly engaging his gaze. He felt a traitorous rush of heat. "If he was meeting with the thieves, it wasn't to *get* something from them, it was to *give* them something. Is that so beyond the pale of possibility? Or do you distrust the idea only because it comes from me?"

"All right — fine! We'll settle this matter of Hadric once and for all. I'll see the shearers and hear what they have to say." He grabbed her by the wrist and struck off toward the sheepfold at a purposeful pace. Behind them, a few of his men peeled away from the stables to follow at a discreet distance.

When they arrived at the sheep pens, they found the shearers' helpers marking the sheep with a special dye pot, separating them according to age and breeding, and then herding them into pens beside each shearer's station. For a few moments, Eloise and Peril watched ewes being upended and relieved of their thick winter coats. Then Peril beckoned to the head shearer, and the man turned his shears over to another man and came to speak to his lord.

Looking at the piles of wool being clipped from the sheep, Peril asked what the shearer thought had caused such a short crop.

"Short?" the man said with a laugh. "It's as good a shearing as we've had in ten years, milord. Good strong wool and plenty of it. Mistress Ann didn't get none o' this crop."

"Strange, don't you think?" Eloise turned to him with crossed arms. "The shearers say it's a fine crop, but Hadric said it was dismal."

"A question I'll put to Hadric when I find him," he said. Half of his brain was struggling to decide what to do with this disturbing bit of evidence, while the other half was starting to smolder like a bog fire.

They headed for the barns and sheds, where Hadric had spent much of his time as bailiff and by all accounts continued to spend most of his time.

The first barn was filled with the scents of hay and grain and old wood. Sunlight coming in between the vertical boards sliced through the dimness at regular intervals, illuminating her hair in brilliant flashes as she walked ahead of him. He was struck by the sight and found himself watching for the next flash of fiery color and appalled at himself for doing so.

"What is usually kept in this barn?" she asked.

He jerked his head up and looked around.

"Grain and feed . . . oats, millet, and barley that don't fit in the granary . . . flax, seed of various kinds, tools, drying racks . . ."

But there was almost nothing in the barn; a few frayed bits of rope coiled on pegs, an old cart wheel, a broken willow poultry rick, and sundry old burlap sacks tossed into one corner. The dirt floor was bare from wall to wall, except for an occasional pile of old straw.

"No Hadric," she observed. "Not much of anything else, either."

Scowling, he turned on his heel and headed out the door and for the second barn, across the way. He stepped inside with his heart beginning to thud and called to the steward. He was answered by an echo from a large, dark, and empty space.

"What is usually kept here?" Eloise asked, looking up at him.

He swung back out the door without answering. His jaw was set and his fists were clenching at his sides. She repeated the question, but he ignored it as he swung through the plow shed, the farrier's hut, and the toolshed and the carpenter's shop, calling for Hadric and demanding the steward's whereabouts of everyone he encountered.

One by one, the workers left their tasks to follow their lord and lady at a distance. The prospect of watching the earl dress down the irksome Hadric was alluring enough, but there was the added fascination of watching the sparks beginning to fly between the earl and his bride.

"Wait —" She caught him by the arm just outside the third and final barn. "Surely those barns aren't supposed to be that empty, even in the spring season."

"No." He clamped his jaw shut, refusing to say more.

"Then what's happened to the things that were stored there?"

"How would I know?" he barked, raising his hands and letting them fall. "I know, according to you, I'm supposed to know everything, to oversee everything, and to inspect everything. But, unlike you, I can't be everyplace at once and do everything by myself. I am forced to rely on others."

"I never said — Of course you have to rely on others."

"Generous of you, milady."

"When they are worthy," she added.

It was like a blade between his ribs. An indictment of his discernment, a condemnation of his judgment. She had questioned his leadership before, but never armed with such incriminating evidence.

He looked up to find a growing clutch of people watching them. With a growl, he grabbed her by the arm and dragged her into the barn with him.

The door banged shut behind them and he pulled her around to face him, dragging her close in the dappled light coming through the open loft overhead.

"And just who is worthy, Lady Eloise?" he demanded, his voice rising. "Not my cooks . . . not my shepherds . . . nor my plowmen . . . nor my smith's apprentices . . . nor my housemaids, my housekeeper, my steward, or my guardsmen. Does anyone on Whitmore pass your test?"

He held her hard in his grip, his chest heaving and his eyes burning rings of amber. Eloise stared at him, seeing in him the anguish, uncertainty, and self-doubt she herself had wrestled with for weeks. And she understood. He no longer needed an abbess, he need a woman . . . a woman willing to give . . . first.

"Yes," she said as calmly as she could.

"Who?" His eyes narrowed and she felt him bracing for an attack.

She launched her most potent weapon, and it struck without his realizing he was hit.

"You."

It took a moment to register; it wasn't at all what he had expected.

"Me?" He loosened his grip on her shoulders as he scrambled to understand what she meant.

"You passed the test long ago, Peril. I think the one who is being tested here is *me*."

"What?"

"You don't trust me," she said tautly, feeling her entire plan veering off course. "You never have. Starting with that day, two months past, that I shaved you in front of the abbess and all of the sisters. You didn't trust my judgment then and, despite all that has happened and all I have done to help you and Whitmore, you still don't trust me." In spite of her determination, emotion boiled up hot and thick in her. "And, frankly, I've had enough of it."

He released her and stepped back.

"Well, you did come here *pretending* to be

469

a nun," he said caustically.

"I was not pretending. I *was* a nun, for all relevant purposes. I had lived and worked and practiced the disciplines of the convent for most of my life."

"Except when you chose not to," he charged.

She stiffened, realizing that he used her own words, spoken under duress, against her.

"Except when I believed there were better ways to do things and tried to help my fellow sisters. The same way I've tried to help you and the people of Whitmore."

"By passing judgment, interfering, and refusing to obey?"

She gasped. She had intended to provoke a clearing of the air and then apply a bit of honey . . . but this . . . It was all getting out of hand!

"Yes. I must 'pass judgment' daily in the course of my duties as lady of this house and manor. If I didn't, how long do you think it would be before things returned to the dismal state they were in when I came? And as to interfering . . . if I hadn't, you would still be sitting in a filthy, crumbling hall with no hope of a marriage, an heir, or a way to pay your blessed taxes! I have worked tirelessly on your behalf and you still treat me as if I were an enemy hostage in your camp."

"I treat you like the headstrong, disobedient woman you are."

"Very well. I'll grant you that I am on occasion disobedient. Let the heavens resound. Such news!" She took a step closer to him and shoved her chin up. "And just how has that inconvenienced you, milord? What great wrong have I done you or your people with my hideous disobedience? I took a walk and worried you."

"You — you speak to me without proper respect."

"I do not coat my words with honey and feed them to you only at your command?" She drew back in mock horror. "I should be drawn and quartered. Sent to the stocks. Clapped in irons at the very least. But only after you have done so to Hadric — whose cozening words have cloaked despicable actions, and have done you far more harm than my poor tongue."

"You assume authority that by rights . . . belongs elsewhere."

"I've usurped another's place? Whose? Do you have another wife tucked away somewhere?" She advanced on him and he fell back a step. "All I can claim is what others give me, milord. That is the only authority a woman ever has. And if others on

471

Whitmore give me their cooperation, their allegiance, and their assistance, it can only be because they see something of value in me. Something that you, apparently, do not see."

Those words caused her throat to tighten and her eyes to burn. She wanted to stare him down, to make him turn away first . . . to make him yield to her. But she felt tears pricking the corners of her eyes and lowered her lashes first, furious with herself for being so weak.

"Yes, I have faults. Plenty of them." Her voice thickened tellingly. "But surely they must be weighed against my strengths and graces . . . the good I do and the good I try so hard to do." She made herself look up and he was glowering at her. Glowering!

"Well, you have faults as well, milord." Angry tears began to burn her eyes. "You're pigheaded and irascible and impossible to fathom. You hold me in your arms at night and then keep me at arm's length by day." She looked away, unable to look at him as the secrets of her heart leaked out. "You refuse to speak to me, except when you're giving orders or chastising me. You tease me with glimpses of the warmth and the humor inside you, and then lock it away like the worst of misers. You consult with your men

472

and give them your counsel . . . but I, who share your bed, must learn that we are on the brink of war from the bits and pieces of news you flog me with!" Surges of hurt and anger struck, catching her squarely between them. "Why is it you can trust a wretch like Hadric with your entire estate, and you cannot trust me with even the smallest part of —"

"Of what?" He grabbed her by the wrists to keep her from fleeing. "What have I withheld from you? I've given you my name and a third of my property" — when she looked up, his scowl deepened — "oh, yes, I finally read that damnable settlement . . ."

"I tried to tell you. You wouldn't listen."

"I've been patient and understanding with you — more than most men would be. I've given you the reins of the house and most everything you've asked of me —"

"Except the one thing that would make all the rest seem like mere details."

"And what is that?" he demanded, straightening.

She could feel him bracing and knew there was no going back. She had to say this and to face him when she did.

"Your heart."

He stiffened and released her. As he stared at her, some of the ruddy color drained from his face.

"Don't be ridiculous."

Of all the things he could have said to her . . .

"Ridiculous?" The pain of realizing that he didn't value something that meant so much to her was overwhelming. For a moment she grappled openly with it. Then she staggered back, turned, and quickly fled a few paces, bumping into an old cart bed that was missing wheels. She heard movement behind her and when she turned back, he was standing just behind her with a dark expression.

"Ridiculous?" She shook her head. "The highest virtue, the noblest emotion . . . the giving of love is ridiculous?" She teetered on the brink of an explosion, and until her hand found the aged rope hanging on the post beside her, not even she had a notion of what expression her hurt and anger would take.

She pulled the rope off the peg and flung it at him, the entire coil. It caught him squarely in the chest and he gave a surprised "oof."

"And I suppose it's ridiculous that I've turned myself inside out over these last few days trying to figure out what was wrong between us and how it could be fixed. I suppose it's ridiculous that I hardly slept the last two nights without you beside me." Her foot raked part of an old bucket and she picked it up and hurled it at him.

He ducked.

"What's really ridiculous is the fact that I can't help watching you when you eat . . . watching you as you move and mount a horse . . . watching the way you rub the table with your fingertips when you're thinking." She reached for a willow poultry rick and heaved it at him.

He ducked again.

"Itching to correct my table manners, no doubt . . . worrying that I'll mar the wax on the table."

"Wishing I could trade places with the table," she said, now backed into a corner with a broken wooden handle in her hand. Those wretched tears that had been burning her eyes finally began to sear tracks down her cheeks. "Wishing I could make you look at me and see something — anything — good in me. Wishing I could touch your heart the way you have touched mine."

She could hear her own breathing, loud and fast, and his, equally fraught. The entire universe narrowed down to just one moment, just one breath, just one impulse.

He sprang at her, catching her off guard and sending her stumbling backward into some felt-draped bales stacked in the darkened corner. Dust billowed and aged haystraws launched into the air as they came down on top of the stack. She pushed and writhed, struggling to get free and finding herself wedged ever more securely in a crack between the bales of whatever they were on. He had managed to get a leg over her and to pin her chest with his, and now seized her face and turned it toward him.

"Eloise — stop! Eloise —"

Tears were rolling back toward her hair and her nose was red and she was biting her lip savagely. He took a long look and then covered her lips with his.

She tried to push him away, tried to get some distance, some sanity. But he was so hot and so heavy and so filled with the passion she had ignited in him. In a heartbeat, without conscious decision, she quit pushing against his chest and instead clamped her arms around his neck and pulled him hard against her.

His kiss was ravenous, panting, searing, possessing . . . and she met every ounce of force and desire with a hunger that she had never fully expressed before. This, this explosion of desire was what he wanted . . . what she wanted . . . what was inevitable between them. And just when she thought she might expire from lack of air, he lifted his head to stare down at her and she gasped for breath and stared dizzily up at him.

"Are you" — he glanced over his shoulder at the broken wooden handle she still held, which was digging into his back — "going to use that?"

"That depends. Are you going to let me up and leave me alone?"

"Hell, no," he declared, his eyes glittering. "I may never let you up. I may keep you here until the barn falls down around our heads."

"Well, then it appears I won't be needing it after all," she said, tossing it away.

He stared at her with a tangle of emotions in his face . . . things she sensed he was having trouble sorting out, things she needed to hear. Someone always had to be the first to give. . . .

"I know I'm difficult at times and proud and stubborn and all the rest," she said. "But there is one thing I pray that you not forget or discount as you tally my worth. I have a deep and earnest heart, milord. Peril. And it is wholly, unreservedly yours. I only pray it will be enough."

He stopped the rest with his lips on hers, and after a long and exquisitely tender kiss, he raised his head. "It is more than enough,

Eloise. More than enough."

Another kiss led to a caress, which led to more caresses, which led to the discarding of clothes. He made love to her there, in that dark private corner of Whitmore. Her garments and his were spread for a bed and they came together, again and again, holding each other tightly, completing a joining that had begun months ago. They teased and kissed and stroked until their passions crested and they were left cooling, their desire banked for another time.

She lay cradled in his arms as he stroked her hair.

"It's not true, you know. That I don't like you. I like all kinds of things about you, Eloise. Not the least of which is what you just did to me. It's just — I've never been given to fine and pretty words with women. It's hard for me to speak about these things. But that does not mean I care for you any less." He stroked the side of her face. "You are my world, Eloise. Since I met you, I have not gone to sleep a single night without your name on my lips and a vision of your face in my mind." He stared into her deeply luminous eyes. "You shame me with your courage . . . I would not have been able to say to you the things you just said to me."

She put her fingers over his mouth and smiled.

"I love you, Peril of Whitmore. Accept that as my gift to you. And give me your trust in return. For I will guard it well and will spend my life, if need be, to honor it."

They lay together for a few moments, savoring the warmth and new sense of closeness between them. For the first time in her life, Eloise felt as if she were truly at home. She was searching for words to say that to him, when they became aware of voices outside, not far away. They looked at each other ruefully, wishing duty wasn't always so present and demanding. Peril kissed each of her closed eyelids and rose, and when Eloise finally struggled up, she looked at their makeshift bed.

"What *are* we lying on?" she said, looking over her shoulder and then around her. She tested it with her hands. "It feels like there must be a pile of old horseshoes in the middle of it." She flipped up the felt covering the pile and, instead of straw, she discovered wool — bales of bound shearing.

She looked up at Peril, who was sorting garments, his and hers.

"What do you suppose this is doing here?" she asked, feeling herself coming more alert and not especially pleased by it. "Is wool usually tucked away in the corner of this barn?"

Peril looked around the straw-littered floor of the barn and scowled. "It's usually . . . I believe so." He reached for her hand and pulled her to her feet so he could throw back the covering.

There were half a dozen bales, and in the middle, two had slid apart to permit something underneath to show through. Something dark, wooden.

"What's that?" she asked, pointing even as she reached for the edge of one bale and pulled. Peril dragged the other bale away and they stood together, staring at a familiar-looking barrel. A wine barrel.

Together, they began to drag the rest of the wool away and discovered a second barrel. Peril stooped and read the name scorched into the end of one.

"Pierrefitte." He rose, staring in horror at the evidence he had demanded only an hour before. "What the Devil are these doing here?"

"Hidden away with bales of wool," she added, coming to the same conclusion he was reaching. "The day I talked to Hadric about the wool and took him to the weavers' house —" The memory of his waving the barn door shut behind him came back to her. "He came out of this barn and, behind him, I saw a cart. It was piled high with something and was covered."

Peril was in motion, stalking out to the center of the barn to study the dirt floor, which still bore the deep tracks of wheels that had been laden with a great deal of something. He looked around the dimly lit barn, taking in every heap and bulge and shadow. It wasn't difficult. The place was almost as empty as the others.

Alarm rippled through him and he strode over to Eloise, his face scarlet with equal parts of anger and humiliation.

"You were right about him." He strode over and took her by the shoulders, staring down into her passion-flushed face. "There is only one explanation for this being here. He intended to take it somewhere. And it doesn't take much to guess just where and to whom he was taking it."

Her pleasure and relief at having him finally see the proof of Hadric's treachery was balanced by her dismay at knowing that the man with access to every bit of value left on Whitmore had indeed betrayed them. And his betrayal had been deeper and broader than — an even worse possibility struck her.

"Peril, what about the rest of the wine?"

He gripped her arms harder. "I told him

to have the house men help him move it up to the first chamber or two of the cellars, so that it would be easy to transport when Bromley got here. If he managed to bring these barrels out here . . ." He couldn't even say the rest. "Come on."

He grabbed her by the hand and hurried for the door. When the great rusty hinges screeched and the planking door swung open, they stepped out into the rosy, late evening sun and into the stares of a small crowd made up of Peril's men, displaced tenants, craftsmen, shearers, dairymaids, weavers, apprentices, stablemen, and housemaids.

They stopped dead under that eager scrutiny. Grins appeared and chuckles and jocular comments wafted through the crowd. Mortified, Eloise looked down at herself and found her gown rumpled and hair tousled . . . both littered with haystraws. It couldn't have been any clearer what they had been doing in the barn. Then someone started a rowdy cheer that quickly grew to engulf them. She blushed crimson and for a moment, buried her hot face in Peril's sleeve.

Peril released her hand to slip an arm around her and pull her tight against his side and she looked up, smiling through her embarrassment . . . to find his gaze riveted on several men on horseback, sitting to one side of the crowd.

At their head was a stout, florid-faced man in a heavy velvet tunic and a gold collar from which hung a seal of office. With him were a handful of men in light armor, two wearing helmets and crests on their chests and displaying knightly colors on their horses. How long they had been waiting outside the barn she could only guess, but some were leaning on the pommels of their saddles with expressions that said it had been long enough for them to have inquired what was happening and to perceive the vigor and thoroughness with which it must be taking place.

"Whitmore!" the man at the head of the delegation addressed him.

Peril nodded and then urged her along with him as he strode over to face the mounted contingent. By the time Peril greeted the man, she had already guessed who it was.

"Lord Bromley!" Peril loosened his grip on her enough to make a slight but entirely proper bow. "You surprised me, my lord treasurer. I had no word of your arrival, otherwise I would have arranged a more suitable welcome."

Bromley motioned to his men and dismounted, handing off his reins to one of the men who hurried forward to attend him.

"More suitable, perhaps. But you would be hard pressed to offer me a more memorable arrival." Bromley focused on Eloise as he came forward, causing her to send a trembling hand to her messy hair. "Let us hope that whatever prompted your 'discussion' in the barn ended well."

"Amicably, sir." Peril sounded as though he spoke through his teeth. She decided not to look up at him. "May I present my bride, Eloise of Argent."

"Pleased to meet you, my dear." Bromley reached for her hand and she felt her knees weaken as she stepped forward and dropped into a proper curtsey. Keeping her hand trapped in his, he looked to Peril. "I was given to believe you were not married, Whitmore."

"It was a quite recent event," Peril said tautly.

Bromley's fleshy face warmed slightly with the suggestion of a grin. "No doubt still *adjusting* daily."

"Twice daily!" came a jocular voice from the crowd. There was no mistaking what was meant.

Eloise wished the ground would open and

swallow her. But with miracles being so rare of late, she sensed she would have to rescue herself.

"Have you ridden far today, milord?" she asked, wishing he would quit looking at her as if imagining her performance in the barn. "Where have you come from?"

"Hathersby," he answered. "Been riding all damned day."

"Then you must be ready for some food and drink." She withdrew her hand from Bromley's and looked to Peril with a confidence she wasn't certain was justifiable. "I shall see that arrangements are made."

Behind her, as she fled up the hill to the house and hall, she could hear Peril dispersing the crowd and sending them back to their duties. Her mind was awhirl by the time she reached the kitchens, and it took a moment for her to settle her thoughts enough to explain to Ralph, Johanna, and Roxanne that Lord Bromley and his men had arrived and needed drink immediately. Their best ale, she ordered, then she sent two house men back down to the barn to rescue the barrels of wine she and Peril had uncovered and to bring them to the kitchens.

"How many to feed?" Johanna asked anxiously.

Eloise was about to say a half dozen, when two of her housemaids came rushing down the kitchen steps with alarm.

"There's soldiers in the court, milady!" Milla gasped out.

"Twoscore or more," Kate added, nodding anxiously.

Eloise groaned. Priorities. What came first? Keeping Lord Bromley satisfied until they could discover how much of their wine Hadric had stolen.

"Those must be Lord Bromley's men. Most of them will camp outside the gates . . . hopefully we shall only have to feed and house a dozen or so."

In moments she was handing out orders like the general Peril's men had dubbed her. Shortly, ticking was being stuffed with fresh straw and beds were being set up in the barren rooms of the manor house, linens and furnishings were being ferried from the tower chambers to furnish Bromley's quarters, and water was being drawn in quantity, to be heated for the lord treasurer. All the while she was thinking about the barrels of wine in the cellars below and praying that Hadric hadn't been able to remove much of it. How could he, with the kitchens tended day and night?

She had no more time to think; Peril was

suddenly escorting Bromley and his party into the hall and calling for ale to wash the dust from their throats. Rose hurriedly brushed Eloise's hair, twisted it into a rope, and coiled it into a crespine. While she changed her slippers, Rose brushed her green woolen and plucked the hay sprigs from the sleeves of her golden yellow undergown. Eloise was on her way down the steps when she heard Bromley pronouncing judgment on the hall that lay at the heart of Peril's holdings.

"Damned fine hall you have here, Whitmore," he declared. "I confess it exceeds my expectations. I was led to believe that the estate had foundered and fallen into disrepair."

"I must also confess, my lord," Peril said, with a heartfelt smile at Eloise as she exited the stairs, "if you had come three months back, you would have seen a very different place."

"Then there have been a number of changes at Whitmore," Bromley declared, eyeing Eloise as she settled against Peril's side. "For the better. And to what do you owe this turn of fortunes?"

Peril didn't need to craft a reply; the truth served quite well.

"To the inspiration of my new wife,

milord. It can be nothing else." As he looked at Eloise, he felt his heart doing strange gyrations in his chest. She appeared sweet and fresh and deliciously maidenly as she blushed becomingly and lowered her eyes.

Bromley watched between them, his gaze slowly warming. "It is a canny fellow indeed who remembers that the wife he compliments in the morning is the same wife he will meet in his bed that night."

When Eloise sent Peril a covert wink, he felt the knot in his middle begin to loosen. He wasn't in this alone. And if Eloise thought they could make it work, then perhaps they could. He searched her pleasure-blushed face as she poured ale, and smiled ruefully at the way the sight of her lively blue eyes lingered in his vision after he turned his gaze back to the lord treasurer.

Stubborn, disobedient, impulsive Eloise. Bright, generous, and capable Eloise. Passionate, generous, true-hearted Eloise. What had he ever done to deserve something as wonderful as she?

Bromley drank deeply and his eyes flew wide. He peered into the brew with astonishment. "I say. Damned excellent ale, Whitmore. Sweet as an ale can be."

Peril nodded numbly, feeling at a loss for

talk of such matters when all he wanted to do was grab Eloise by the hand and rush down to the cellars and see if the wine he intended for the king was still there.

"My husband was quite clever about finding and employing the best possible brewers, Your Lordship." Eloise stepped neatly into the silence. "But as you know, it is said that 'the garrison is no better than the beer.' " Bromley, his secretary, and his captain laughed, apparently well acquainted with the dictum that the battlefield performance of men-at-arms was directly related to the quality of the beer they were provided.

"This ale was brewed by two sisters." She leaned closer and adopted a confidential tone. "Quite a pair they are. Some say they use a bit of wheat in their mash . . . that it makes for the sweetness of the ale. But they refuse to speak a word about their brewing secrets."

"A friendly warning, my lord Whitmore." Sir Stephen, Bromley's captain, a weathered, hard-eyed veteran of the king's own guard, spoke with an alarmingly straight face. Peril's heart stopped momentarily. "Keep these brewing marvels locked up whilst His Lordship is here. He's not above a bit of poaching from time to time." A smile creased the man's weathered face around the eyes and mouth, and Peril sent Eloise a tense smile.

There was not a spare moment for Peril to consult with Eloise in private; both of them had to be in constant attendance on Bromley until it was almost time for supper to be served. Ethan arrived with his patrol, just in time for supper, and as they sat down to dine, Peril was able to take him aside and send him down into the cellars to check on the wine. Eloise watched him with Ethan, sensing what was happening, and redoubled her efforts at making the treasurer comfortable.

The food Eloise had arranged was simple but pleasing and plentiful, and when she poured wine for Lord Bromley his approval turned to abrupt praise.

"Marvelous!" He sipped and savored yet again. "So rich and flavorful. Where the devil did you come by such exquisite grape?"

"It's French, Your Lordship," Eloise said, with a look at Peril. "My lord's mother brought it with her from France. It's from a vintner called Pierrefitte. Perhaps you have heard of —"

"*Pierrefitte?*" Bromley nearly choked. "Surely you jest."

"I do not, my lord treasurer." She answered Peril's frown with a pleading look. While Bromley was absorbed in the wine, Peril shook his head, warning her not to say another word. She gave him a determined frown, and behind her wine cup mouthed the words "trust me."

He wanted to trust her . . . he planned to trust her . . . he did trust her. But why did he have to prove it right now? He groaned as he heard her say:

"In fact, it is this very wine that milord intends to send to London with you." Then her eyes flew wide and she gave a rather ingenuous gasp. "Oh, my." She looked up in dismay. "I suppose I've let the cat out of the bag."

Bromley's humor quickly faded. "Don't tell me, let me guess." He leveled a sharp look on Peril. "You intend to send wine to the king in lieu of coin for your tax. Do you have any idea how much watered-down grape squeezing I have to sample and reject in the king's name each year? This had better be damned exceptional wine."

"I believe you just declared it so, milord," Eloise said gently. When Bromley looked at her she gave him a faintly mischievous smile.

"So I did." He looked at Peril with narrowed eyes and gestured to Eloise. "Doesn't miss much, does she?"

"No, Your Lordship. Not much indeed." Peril sent her a small but genuine smile.

There was talk of London and new treaties and the king's summer progress in the west. As the dinner was being cleared away and some of the tables were being dismantled, Eloise prevailed upon William of Wright to play for them. Soon torchlight and sweet music, as well as the rich wine, were casting a spell of geniality over the hall. It was then that Ethan reappeared on the kitchen steps, looking strained. Peril and Eloise both watched with sinking hearts as he shook his head.

It was all Peril could do to remain seated there, with Bromley and his retinue rambling on about the various wines they had sampled, knowing that the wine they had just promised him had been stolen from the cellars. What was he going to do?

Three of his men appeared in the doors of the hall, looking worn and saddle weary. They steered a course for Peril, and by the time they reached him, had caused a ripple of rising attention through the men-at-arms relaxing in the hall below the dais.

"Milord," Richard declared, doffing his helm and executing a stiff bow. "Sir Michael sends word that he's found Hadric. Out at Edwin the cottar's. He has some of the thieves with him — and two wagons loaded with barrels. Wine, milord. He's got two wagons loaded with your wine."

"What are they doing?" Peril shoved to his feet in the silence that ensued.

"Camped in the ruins. Waiting for cover of darkness and to head through the forest for Claxton land."

Peril looked to Eloise, who rushed to his side, and then Bromley, who sat forward with a scowl.

"What is this about Claxton?" the lord treasurer demanded.

"My neighbor, the earl of Claxton, has been harboring a band of thieves that prey on my lands and people," Peril said tautly, fixing Eloise with a tumultuous look. She squeezed his hand and met his gaze with unwavering support. Who knew how Bromley would receive the news?

"Harboring criminals is a serious charge, Whitmore." Bromley drew himself up, instantly the hard-eyed royal councilor once again. "You'd better be able to prove it."

"I'll prove it," Peril said, then looked down at Eloise. "I need my sword and helm." As she bit her lip and pulled away to hurry up the stairs, he turned back to the treasurer. "A few days ago, I set men to watch my newly appointed steward. He has been hard to find of late, and my wife and I were checking the barns when you arrived. He has cleared them of everything of value. And now my men report that they have found him in the ruins of a cottage that his thieving cohorts burned to the ground two nights ago . . . driving wagons loaded with the wine I intended to send with you to London. Clearly, he has been in league with the thieves and their master, the earl of Claxton."

"The old earl — Claxton's father — was a good and honorable man, a friend of mine. It will take more than your word to convince me, Whitmore," Bromley declared.

"You are welcome to come along and see for yourself, Your Lordship," Peril said, reaching for his sword and helm as Eloise came running back into the hall with them. "Once we have Hadric and his cohorts in hand, they'll tell us who has aided them in hopes of saving their own hides."

Bromley studied him for a moment, then smacked the table with a fist.

"By damn, I will go along. See for myself. You, too, Stephen," he ordered his captain. "It's been too blasted long since we've seen a proper fight."

Shortly the hall was ringing with orders. Peril chose a dozen men to ride with him. Bromley called for his squire, his secretary, and his armor — though not in that order — and he chose his captain and one other soldier from the king's column to accompany him.

When Bromley's squire tried to settle the lord treasurer's embroidered colors and crest over his head and onto his chest armor, Bromley prevented him. From the corner of his eye, Peril saw Bromley order Sir Stephen to remove his own emblazoned surplice and leave it in the squire's keeping as well.

The three visitors, then, intended to ride under Peril's banner and authority. Peril understood: Bromley would not charge into a fight wearing his own colors until he knew for certain who and what he was fighting. It was a prudent measure for a man who carried the king's authority with him as he traveled about the countryside. The king could not afford to be caught on the wrong side of a conflict between his nobles.

When the horses were brought around, Eloise slipped her arm through Peril's and accompanied him to the doors. Then she pulled him aside for a moment, into the shadows.

"Be careful, milord," she said, feathering

her fingers gingerly over his face, as if committing the feel of it to memory. "I love you. Come back to me well and whole."

"I will, wife." He pulled her hard against him and into a deeply passionate kiss. When it ended, he pressed her forehead with his cheek, absorbing her warmth and her love, storing it in his heart. "I'm leaving a score of men here with Ethan. And there are twoscore more of Bromley's men. You'll be safe."

"I'm not worried about *us*. I'm worried about *you*." With her heart drumming rapidly, she accompanied him outside. "I'm issuing fair warning," she said. "If you're not back by dawn, I intend to start *praying* for you."

"You do that," he said with a chuckle. Then he gave her one last squeeze before leaving her there on the steps.

She stood watching Peril leading his men and the king's treasurer off into the night. She had faith in Peril's ability as a soldier and in his men's loyalty and fighting prowess. But beneath that confidence was a recognition that there was no guarantee that some of the blood that would be shed would not be Peril's. She might lose him, she understood, just as she was finding him.

Eighteen

Peril led his party quickly along the grassy tracks between the fields until they reached the rolling land used for pasture. There, they left the road and kept to the shadows at the edges of the trees. As they neared the ruins of the tenant's burned cottage, Peril halted the column, had them dismount, and led them through a stand of young trees to a place overlooking the clearing. Through the ghostly black ribs of the burned cottage they could see there were no wagons or thieves nearby. Peril gave a low whistle that was answered by another . . . and a familiar form stepped out into the moonlit clearing.

Michael greeted Peril with news that the wagons had left an hour before, rolling west, toward Claxton's estate. He had sent two of his men ahead to track the wagons and scout out the best place for an attack. After a few moments to agree on a strategy, they moved off on foot to follow the wagons.

Bromley proved to be an experienced and tenacious campaigner. He and his captain stayed close to Peril, made little noise, and followed Peril's hand signals ordering them to fan out from the path. They were so adept at staying hidden in the shadows that Peril sometimes had difficulty keeping track of them.

In the darkness and quiet of the forest, Peril steeled himself for the coming confrontation and tried not to think about what would follow. After he had Hadric and the wine in hand, he would still have to deal with Claxton. He couldn't help wondering if he had done the right thing, charging off after the wine and leaving Whitmore without a leader. What if he was playing into Claxton's hands?

A familiar owl hoot indicated they had made contact with their forward scouts. Terrence stepped out of the gloom to tell them that the wagons were just ahead and would soon reach a small clearing. The perfect time for the attack was as they emerged into the open, Peril declared. They moved up cautiously in single file on either side of the weedy trail. Through the dimness came the rhythmic creak of wooden wheels and the thud of hooves. A moment later, they caught sight of Whitmore's two largest hay wagons, piled high with barrels.

Peril's heart began to pound, and his senses began to narrow and concentrate on the details of the situation: the six or so thieves visible on the wagons themselves, the three men on horses out in front, the place where the tree cover ended, and the relative location of his men to the wagons' course. The only thing he didn't see was Hadric. It was a small detail, but lodged in his mind all the same and gave him a moment's pause. He needed Hadric as well as the stolen wine to prove Claxton's treachery.

He delayed giving the signal to overtake the wagons, watching, continuing to stalk the precious contraband. Then the wagons rumbled toward the cover of the trees again; if they didn't strike soon, the opportunity would be lost. He had to attack and hope that Hadric was somewhere at the front.

He raised his sword and by the time it slashed downward again, the air was filled with battle cries. Surprise provided Peril and his men a decided advantage. As the wagon drivers were pulled from their seats, they put up a surprisingly effective resistance. The sounds of blades clanging and grunts and bellows reverberated all through the clearing. Peril charged to the front of the fracas, looking for Hadric and finding only his unknown accomplices.

He dragged one of the men on horseback to the ground and dealt him a blow with the hilt of his blade. The man plowed into him and knocked him back enough to escape toward the trees. Peril plunged into the undergrowth after him and had almost caught him when a low rumble arose around them . . . like thunder at first . . . then a growing roar. Confusion caused him to falter, and his opponent took advantage of the moment to scramble away into the shadows.

Horses . . . it was the sound of horses. . . .

"Back! Fall back to the wagons! Horsemen!" He charged back out into the clearing, waving his men back just as the first horsemen appeared, riding straight for him.

Suddenly the clearing was filled with armored soldiers on horseback. Several of Peril's men climbed up onto the wagons and stood their ground with blade and axe. The others were left afoot to deflect the blows of experienced warriors still on horseback. The screams of horses and the clang of steel on steel merged into a frenzy of sound and fury. The skills forged in the heat of a hundred battles suddenly took over, and Peril lost all but the most necessary of awareness. Through instinct, everything became line and motion, balancing point and trajectory. His entire world narrowed to the edges of his opponents' blades and the movements of their eyes. His chest heaved, his arms flexed and contracted again and again as he wielded his blade. His legs braced for impact one moment and then flexed sharply, launching him out of harm's way the next.

When he had a moment to look around, he found the odds now three to one. He and his men had faced worse and lived to tell the tale. And they were fighting valiantly — even Lord Bromley. Then, in the blink of an eye, as the lord treasurer defended himself ably from the front, a second attacker reached him from behind and thrust a blade into him. A bolt of horror shot through Peril as Bromley crumpled to his knees. He surged in to take a stand over the older man and was charged by no less than four swordsmen. He was suddenly fighting on all sides, fighting for his life as well as Bromley's.

Above the melee someone began to shout: "There he is! Get him!" The four became six, and without someone to cover his back —

A loud cracking sound exploded and his head snapped forward. His vision exploded in shards of light that within seconds were snuffed by utter blackness.

Cut off from the rest of his men, Peril fell under that savage and ruthlessly concentrated attack. Michael and Sir Stephen redoubled their efforts to reach him and Lord Bromley, only to have their attackers draw back suddenly.

"Hold! You — Whitmore's men — hold or they die!" There was a stunned moment of confusion in which they located the speaker. He was holding Peril's slumped form up by the arm and had a sword pressed hard against his neck. Another soldier was just laying his blade to Bromley's throat.

Terrence and Richard lunged to their lord's rescue, but ran into Michael, who held them and snarled for them to stand down. A moment later, a figure on horseback at the edge of the trees rode forward. It was Hadric.

"I'd like nothing better than to provide milord Claxton with Peril of Whitmore's head. But right now, I want that wine even more. You'll give ground," the traitorous steward declared, "and let us take the wagons, or Whitmore and his man here will die." There was a moment's hesitation and his thin voice grew more shrill as it grew more adamant. "Give way or have their blood on your heads!"

There was no room in that ultimatum for either subtlety or heroics. With his body screaming against this unnatural restraint,

Michael ordered Peril's men back. When some didn't obey straight away, he caught them bodily and shoved them back, snarling into their fury-blackened eyes and blood-hot faces: "This is not the time or place! They'll kill the both of them."

Some of Claxton's men rushed to retake the wagons and, as Peril's men stood aside, trembling with barely contained violence, drove them across the clearing and into the trees.

Just as abruptly as they had come, Claxton's guardsmen began to retreat into the forest. They seized their horses and mounted up . . . but not before collecting Peril and Bromley and hoisting their limp forms up onto the wagons.

"They go with us," the leader of Claxton's soldiers declared. "If you try to stop us before we reach Claxton's keep . . . they'll *die.*"

Panting, steaming, holding their blades at the ready, Peril's men watched Claxton's guard melt into the forest with their hostages.

"We have to follow them," Sir Stephen said, pacing toward the place they had disappeared. "See where they take them."

"You heard what they said," Michael said, following, pacing furiously. "They're headed for Claxton's keep. There's no need

503

to hide their greed and treachery any longer
. . . not if they have Lord Peril in their
power."

The captain looked at Michael with har-
nessed anger burning in his eyes.

"This Claxton has finally bitten off more
than he can chew. He not only holds your
lord, he holds the wounded Lord Treasurer
of England. If milord Bromley dies while in
his hands" — his voice grew low and chilling
— "there won't be a rock in England big
enough for the wretch to hide under."

The earl of Claxton's men, bearing two
wagons of precious French wine and two
hostages, rode as hard as they dared for
Claxton's manor and keep. Hadric, at the
front of the contingent, congratulated himself on his quick thinking . . . figuring out a
way to rescue the wine *and* deliver a helpless Peril of Whitmore to his master in
chains. It was a good thing he had decided
to ride ahead and bring back an armed
guard to escort the wine. He had felt uneasy for the last day or so, as if someone was
watching him. . . .

He couldn't wait to see Claxton's face
when he returned from paying calls on
Whitmore's neighbors, where he intended
to sow distrust and outrage regarding

Whitmore's blasphemous marriage to a "nun." He smirked to himself. The time for shaming and tarnishing reputations was past. Action was what was needed now. He thought of how decisive he had been, and how readily Claxton's men had obeyed him. Everyone had always underestimated him . . . even Claxton. He was a force to be reckoned with now, Hadric of Hyde.

"Get those barrels down to the cellars, straight away," Hadric ordered the servants who came out to meet them as they entered the main gates of Claxton's castle. As the servants climbed up to take the place of the soldiers on the wagons, they spotted Peril and Bromley and asked what should be done with them. Hadric turned to the lieutenant who had led the party of soldiers and ordered: "Take them down to the dungeons."

It was nearly daylight when Peril's men returned to Whitmore, bearing wounded men and devastating news. The lookout on the tower called down the news that they were approaching, and most of the household and the balance of the garrison were there to greet them.

"We were outnumbered — the bandits took Lord Peril!"

Their words wafted to the steps of the hall where Eloise, Hildegarde, and the house-holders waited anxiously. Eloise felt a wave of sickness. She swayed, and had to be steadied by Rose and Hildegarde as she watched the men helping the wounded from their horses. As Hildegarde rushed to see to the injured, Eloise hurried to Michael to learn what had happened.

"Is it true? They seized Peril?"

"They have him, milady." Michael doffed his helm and went down on one knee before her, clearly agonized by the report he had to give.

"Was he hurt?"

"I didn't see any blood. They had a blade to his throat and Lord Bromley's — there was nothing we could do."

She turned to the captain of Bromley's guards. "Did you see Lord Bromley fall? Was he badly hurt?"

"He was cut . . . bleeding," Sir Stephen said grimly.

"As are you, sir." The trickle of red con-gealing on his thigh jolted her from the numbness that had overtaken her. She took him by the arm and helped him into the hall.

As she and Hildegarde saw to the wounded, Michael and Sir Stephen told her of finding the wine barrels and of the cannily timed attack. Michael identified the leader of the soldiers as none other than Hadric. They had taken Peril and Lord Bromley to ensure themselves safe passage back to Claxton's keep.

"And once they're safe," Eloise said, her throat constricting, "what use will they have for two hostages?"

"Our only hope is that they didn't know who Lord Bromley was," Sir Stephen put in, "and that when they find out, they'll be willing to release him."

"But what of Peril?" she asked, her fears making her eyes dark and luminous. "Claxton hates him . . . has coveted his lands and holdings for years."

Michael's genial face tightened with contained anguish. "Claxton will never release him, milady. Why would he free a man whose death could only benefit him?"

"Peril's . . . death." Eloise's heart seemed to stop.

All of that strength and vitality, that powerful force of being, stilled and silenced? Was it possible that she would never see her husband again, would never touch him or feel his arms around her? Was she never to see the love she craved filling those warm amber eyes . . . never to finish the journey that she had only just begun with him? She was suddenly swamped by memories of his big powerful body, his agile movements, his deep voice and gentle hands. Their loving, their arguments, their ever-growing respect for each other . . . all to end now and here? It was impossible even to imagine life going on if he died. Just thinking of life without him was physically painful. She closed her eyes, forcing herself to breathe, forcing herself past the desire to die, too, if . . .

"We have to do something," she said, opening her eyes.

"I say we ride down Claxton's gates and take the place apart stone by stone." Ethan smacked the table with a fist.

"The first casualties of any battle would be milord Peril and Bromley," Michael said, grasping Ethan's shoulder.

"Surely not. When he finds he's taken Lord Bromley" — Bromley's Sir Stephen raised the hope — "perhaps he will realize the danger he is in and will be willing to negotiate their release. He cannot be stupid enough to try to dispose of the king's treasurer."

"Claxton is a clever and ruthless man," Simon declared. "He could say Bromley died of his wounds, and who could contest it?"

"Wounds his own men inflicted," Sir Stephen countered.

"Without his knowledge, he could say," Simon answered. "His men had thought they were fighting off a band of thieves known to haunt the forest."

There was no satisfactory rebuttal to that; it was all too plausible.

"Whatever happens," Ethan said, staring into an increasingly bleak set of options, "Claxton cannot allow Lord Peril to leave his dungeon alive."

There it was. The raw truth of the matter. Peril was in Claxton's power, and Claxton was not a man to ignore such an opportunity.

"We have to do something," Eloise said, wringing her hands, struggling to rise above the fear and despair threatening to overwhelm her. "There has to be a way to get them out."

"We would have to act fast . . . send in someone to free them . . ." Michael began to strategize. "We'd have to distract Claxton — make him think he's about to be attacked — while someone was bringing Peril and Lord Bromley out."

"But how would we get someone in?" Simon scowled. "Is there a way under his walls, a separate gate, a weakness in his defenses?"

There, the promise of a plan would have

stopped if Hildegarde hadn't come to take Eloise's hands.

"Please, milady . . ." Sympathy and determination vied in the healer's dark eyes. "Do you trust me? Would you come with me, asking no questions? Would you trust me to lead you into the heart of the earl of Claxton's castle?"

Eloise and the others turned to Hildegarde in surprise.

"How would you know about Claxton's home?" Eloise searched her friend's fierce determination.

"It is a long story, milady . . . If you will just accept that I lived there as a young girl and know every inch of the cellars and blinds built under that keep, I can help you get them out."

Eloise didn't allow her astonishment to delay her response.

"Of course I would trust you."

"Then I can lead you in and help you bring Lord Peril and Lord Bromley out." She looked at the startled expressions on the men's faces. "Meanwhile, you gentlemen must somehow hold Claxton's attention on his front gates."

Arguments broke out. Too dangerous for women, they said.

"Exactly why it would work," Eloise argued with a revived spark in her eyes. "After all, who notices a woman?"

"Especially an *old* woman," Hildegarde added with a sardonic smile.

Too risky, they countered.

"No more risky than doing nothing," Eloise declared. "You've said that Peril will never be allowed to leave Claxton's dungeon alive."

No matter how they argued she went them one better and, in the end, Lady Eloise called on all her authority and stubborn determination and prevailed.

The decisions that followed were less contentious. It was a straightforward campaign: Peril's garrison and Lord Bromley's twoscore men would combine in a display of might and menace. They would call Claxton to parlay . . . issue demands . . . listen to Claxton's explanations and offers. If through such tactics they could buy Eloise and Hildegarde an hour or two, Hildegarde seemed certain, then they could have Lord Peril and Lord Bromley free.

It was a desperate solution, but it was also a desperate situation.

"You know, of course," Simon said to Eloise that evening at sunset, as he helped her onto old Sir Arthur's back, "that Lord Peril would have our guts for garters for letting you do this."

She smiled down into his long, angular face that was so filled with concern for both her and Peril.

"If this works, my dear Simon, His Lordship will be too grateful to care who turned the key to release him."

The earl of Claxton had stridden into his finely furnished hall that morning, knocking feet from tables and dumping drunken soldiers out of chairs and half-dressed serving maids off benches and onto the rush-covered floor. He kicked a metal tankard across the floor where it clanked into a stone step.

"What the hell is going on here?" he shouted. Then he spotted the figure slumped casually in his own chair, at the head of his large, rectangular table. Hadric of Hyde.

"There you are, milord." Hadric pushed to his feet, squinting as if the light hurt his eyes, clearly still suffering the effects of too much drink.

"What the devil are you doing here?" As Claxton approached, he motioned to his captain to remove Hadric. Instantly, two of the soldiers at his back descended on the traitorous steward and dragged him from Claxton's chair.

"Is that any way to treat th' man who brought you the head of your archenemy?" Hadric said, wrenching his arms free and straightening his tunic and silver chain of office.

"What are you talking about?" Claxton demanded, picking up the silver goblet Hadric had used and catching the scent of wine in it. "How dare you enter my hall in my absence and help yourself to my chair and my wine."

"Wine I brought you, my lord earl."

"My wine all the sa—" He realized Hadric was behaving with a confidence that bordered on smugness. "You brought the rest of it? Whitmore's wine?"

"Much of it, milord." Hadric strolled around the head of the table toward him. "The rest is still on Whitmore . . . but hidden so well that it might as well be in your cellars, for all the good it will do Lord Peril."

Claxton relaxed a bit, eyeing the cocky retainer. "What did you mean about bringing me Whitmore's head?"

"What would you give to have Peril of Whitmore in your hands, in your dungeon, this very moment?"

Claxton's face colored beyond its customary pallor.

"Good God." He stared at Hadric as if seeing him anew. "He's here?"

"In your dungeon as we speak, milord." Hadric waved grandly to the men struggling to their senses around the hall. "Thus, this modest celebration."

Claxton headed for the stairs with his captain and Hadric hurrying along in his wake. "How?" he demanded, his face beginning to glow with anticipation. "How did it happen?"

"I came ahead of the wagons to get some men to escort them. When we returned, Whitmore and his men had found the wagons and all but recaptured them. We surprised them, and in the fray, Whitmore was bashed in the head. I wasn't about to leave without the wine, so I seized Whitmore and ordered his men back. They stood by, helpless as babes, while we took the wine and him."

Claxton flew down the spiral steps two at a time in his eagerness to reach the dungeons. When they reached the heavy oak door, he pounded with an impatient fist and called for the gaoler. An aged man-at-arms met them at the door and held a lantern up to see them.

"It's me, you half-wit. Open the damned door!" Claxton growled.

Claxton surged into the depths of his prison, ignoring the faces and hoarse pleas of prisoners in cells along the way. Ducking his head, he followed the gaoler down one last narrow and labyrinthine set of steps. The gaoler held his lantern up to the crude iron bars that covered the opening at the top of the door.

There, on the floor of the damp cell sat Peril of Whitmore, blinking and shielding his eyes from the light.

"Well, well, well." Claxton oozed an ugly pleasure. "Whitmore. Welcome to Hell . . . as it is affectionately known amongst my imprisoned population."

"You won't get away with this, Claxton," Peril said flatly. "Even you can't be this stupid."

"Stupid? My dear fellow . . . I'm not the one locked in a cell in the bowels of my enemy's castle. How careless of you to let yourself be captured alive. I should have thought you'd have preferred to fall on your blade rather than endure the humiliation — not to mention the torture — I have in mind for you."

"Whatever you do to me, Claxton . . . it won't last long." Peril lurched to his knees and then his feet, having to bend his head in order to stand in what was little more than a damp, airless cave. "Even now, my men are planning an attack. And if Bromley dies, the king will come down on you and crush you as if you were a fly."

"Without their fearless leader, your men will be easy targets for my archers. And they'll make better practice than a quintain for my —" The mention of Bromley's name halted him. "When you die, the king will receive word from his loyal and trusted treasurer that it was in a skirmish along our common border. You see, Lord Bromley is —"

"Dying in this cell . . . beside me . . . as you stand gloating," Peril said. "He came with me to catch my thieving steward and your henchmen as they tried to move stolen wine from my house to yours."

"Don't be absurd. Bromley is due here in a day or two — he's to be my guest." But something in the defiant certainty of Peril's voice made him seize the gaoler's lantern and hold it up against the bars. He spotted the body lying on the stone ledge beside Peril . . . the graying hair, the broad girth . . . the profusion of scarlet stains on its tunic and sleeve. The sight bled the taunt from his voice. "It can't be!"

"But it is." Peril delivered each word with relish. "And when the king learns that you injured his trusted councilor and held him prisoner while he died, you'll be dead as well in less than a fortnight."

"I'd listen to him, if I were you, Renfrow," came a weakened but still commanding voice from that cold stone bed.

"Milord!" The voice shattered Claxton's malicious hauteur. "I had no idea . . . no way of knowing . . ." His eyes flitted frantically over the treasurer's prostrate form as he tried to think what to do. "Of course I mean you no harm . . . I can arrange for a doctor . . . see to your wounds. This has all been an appalling error." He turned on Hadric, who had begun to slink back up the passage.

"You idiot!" He struck Hadric and sent him slamming into the rough rock wall. "You kidnapped the Lord Treasurer of England and threw him in my dungeon!"

"I didn't know who he was!" Hadric tried to shield himself from Claxton's repeated blows. "Your soldiers — it was them — they grabbed him up when I ordered them to get Whitmore! Please, milord" — he scrambled back, trying to make it to his feet — "after all I've done for you —"

"You idiot — you've ruined me!" Blind fury seized Claxton and he reached for his captain's sword and plunged it hard into Hadric's back as he tried to escape up the passage. Hadric gurgled and choked as he slid slowly down the wall and lay crumpled in a spreading puddle of red.

The shedding of blood vented Claxton's rage enough to clear his head. He pushed his captain aside and came back to the window.

"I'll take you upstairs, milord . . . see to your wounds and make you comfortable." He stared anxiously at Bromley's inert form. "*You* needn't suffer simply because of Whitmore's arrogance and imprudence."

It was the unspoken condition of that offer that Bromley heard the loudest.

"I have always cherished the memory of my friendship with your father," Bromley said, shifting slightly, raising his head to peer up at the light. "It grieves me to see what a coward and a backstabber his son has become. But then, even as a child you were pale as a grub . . . wet and nauseating."

"Don't say things you will surely come to regret, milord treasurer," Claxton said, his tone, like his countenance, hardening.

"Your letters to me regarding Whitmore . . . Did you honestly think I would accept such venomous accusations at face value . . . without seeing conditions on the estate for myself? I hate to disappoint you, my boy, but people at court are not nearly as corrupt or stupid as you seem to think." The lord trea-surer lowered his head and closed his eyes as if dismissing Claxton. "If I am to die now, Renfrow, I prefer to do it right here. I am certain there is a better class of people in your dungeons than above them."

"You stupid old fool. You will die here, all right. I'll see to that." He looked at Peril. "And you, Whitmore . . . when you're dead I'll level that monstrosity you call a hall and see to it that my men keep your widow too busy on her back to mourn you."

Peril lunged at the door, his face mur-derous, his eyes burning with hatred. It was a measure of his intensity that Claxton lurched back to avoid him, even with six inches of oak and fat iron bars between them.

"Go to Hell, Claxton," Peril snarled.

Claxton met his fury with cold malice.

"You first, Whitmore."

When the light faded and the cell was once again shrouded in blackness, Peril felt his way over to Bromley and laid a hand on the older man's head.

"I'm sorry, milord," Peril said thickly. "This was not your fight."

"I have a few regrets, Whitmore. Coming to your estate, seeking the truth of your character and situation for myself, is not one of them." He paused for a moment and his voice sounded strained when he spoke again. "Is it bad?"

"I've stanched the bleeding as best I can. There are two wounds . . . your shoulder and your back. But you're awake, and at least you're not lying in a pool of blood."

"And you? Are you wounded?"

"A bad crack over the head. The damnedest thing is . . . I'm seeing two of everything. Two cell doors . . . two lanterns . . . even two Claxtons."

Bromley managed a raspy chuckle.

"Now that's torture."

Somewhere in the next few minutes Bromley lapsed again into unconsciousness, leaving Peril alone to face the unending blackness and the torment of his throbbing head and his own desperate thoughts.

To have allowed himself to be captured . . . to have underestimated the situation so . . . it had never occurred to him that he might encounter soldiers from Claxton's garrison. It was supposed to be just a skirmish with thieves, and the element of surprise was on his side. Until that awful moment when he looked up and saw them riding in with blades drawn, he hadn't really come to terms with what war with Claxton would truly mean.

Always before when he fought it had been on someone else's lands, around some stranger's walls and bailey and tenants and livestock. Always before, it was someone else's house and buildings that burned and the soil of someone else's homeland that absorbed the blood that was spilled. But this was Whitmore. His house. His land. His people who would struggle and suffer and even die in the contest over property rights and vain grudges that seemed to have no beginning and no end.

Whitmore, he realized with a flood of emotion long denied, was his home. It was the one place on earth where he belonged.

Was that why it had taken him a moment too long to seize the fact that he had plunged into battle with armored and well-seasoned opponents? Was that why he had discounted the potential dangers they would face?

As the hours dragged by, he listened to Bromley's troubled breathing and went over every decision, every clash of will and interest that had led him to this disastrous point. If only he had listened to Eloise earlier . . . watched Hadric more closely . . . acted more decisively on his conviction that Whitmore's troubles came from all-too-earthly sources.

It seemed all he had now was time to think. To remember.

And the one thing he wanted to remember most of all was Eloise. The way her hair seemed to burn with unearthly fire that first night by the campfire. The way her hair had wrapped around his wrist the night her friend was ill. The way she looked up at him through those lashes . . . the way she licked her lips when she was thinking . . . the way she crossed her arms and glared at him . . . the scent of her face when it was warmed by the sun . . . the taste of her kisses as she yielded to him in their bed. He had wanted her to distraction even when he thought she was a nun. And for a brief time — all too brief a time — she had been his.

What was it she had said about paths? People were set on one by the Almighty and had to learn to accept it. If that was true, what was his path? A lifelong trail of wars and conflict that led him to a nasty death at the hands of a man whom he despised? Was God that vengeful and uncaring? Or was God merely using Claxton to mete out justice on a life ill-lived . . . wasted?

And what about Eloise? What part did her strong and vital spirit play in his life? What was he to make of her passionate, loving heart and her courageous declaration of love for him?

In the dark and pain and despair of his enemy's prison, he recalled again her face, her smile, her determination to tear down the walls he tried to build around her. She was his one bit of light and warmth and hope. She was, he realized with no small anguish, the kiss of pure grace upon his life. Unsought. Undeserved. Something good and loving . . . given to him . . . to show him a new way . . . to crack open the husk around his battle-hardened heart.

He felt the center of his chest and found the slow, regular beating of his heart. She filled every chamber. She filled every breath with the desire to live . . . to see her again . . . to tell her the one thing he knew she wanted and needed to hear.

He loved her. With all his heart. That was what this was, this sweet pain that lodged in the bottom of his chest . . . this ache, this longing. It was love. For her. And she might never know.

As he lay in the blackness of Claxton's dungeon, on that filthy ill-hewn floor, with the sands of his life running through the hourglass . . . tears formed and began to trail along the creases around his eyes. The pain in his head was excruciating, and the squeezing in his chest made him feel as if his heart might stop.

As a sob rose up his throat he covered his face with his battered hands.

"Oh, God, please" — he prayed for the first time in memory — "don't let me die before I see her again."

Nineteen

No one seemed to notice Eloise and Hildegarde making their way along the cart road that followed the stream beside Claxton's walled castle. Most of the people on Claxton's estates wore ragged clothes, and women — especially old ones — were never a threat. Nor were the things they carried — leather bags slung over their shoulders — remarkable in any way. Women were always carrying such things to and fro. Truth be told, the sentries on the ramparts of the castle walls were too busy watching for a plume of dust, the sound of horses, or the glint of metal in the dying sunlight . . . evidence of an armed force approaching.

Eloise and Hildegarde kept their heads down as they met workers coming in from the fields. As soon as they reached the back side of the castle, they left the path and cut across an overgrazed pasture to a copse left uncut in the clearing that had taken place around the castle. There, Hildegarde paused in the middle of the trees to stare at the walls of the castle and compare them to memory.

"Do you still recall where it is?" Eloise prompted, thinking that the walls looked daunting and impenetrable. "What if it's been filled in?"

"I doubt it's been tampered with," Hildegarde said, winding around through the trees, reacquainting herself with them, seeing them as they were more than twenty years before. "Every castle needs a secret entrance . . . and exit."

Just as Eloise was ready to say she couldn't see anything resembling an opening, Hildegarde stared intently at the ground, knelt, and threaded her hand down between the grasses. She straightened with a smile.

"It's here. Roots and weeds have all but covered it over." Her smile broadened. "It can't have been used of late. I doubt the current earl even knows it is here."

Eloise knelt beside her and produced large knives from the leather satchel she wore. Together they cleared the weeds, roots, and debris from the opening. With her heart pounding, Eloise looked up at the castle and estimated the length of the passage they would have to traverse. Too long, she thought to herself.

Moments later she was slithering through the opening, headfirst, plunging into darkness and into a damp, earthy-smelling tunnel that was not quite tall enough to allow her to stand. Tucking her skirts up out of the way, she accepted the bags Hildegarde handed down to her, and then helped the older woman climb through the opening as well.

Their fragile flame, brought in a small lantern, now spread to the wicks of two small lamps and it was clear from the slope of the tunnel that their course would take them down. Hildegarde took the lead, feeling her way along the packed rock and brick walls.

"You lived here, on Claxton's manor?"

"Until I was fourteen. My father was the old earl's head clerk. Kept most of his records and oversaw his tenants' accounts."

"What caused you to leave?" Eloise asked, trying in vain to take her mind off the damp, treacherous slope and off the dangers that lay at the end of it.

"A man. Two men, really. One I wanted. The other wanted me."

The tunnel dropped so steeply that their feet slipped and they slid all the way to a much taller and more level bit of tunnel. Picking herself up, Eloise looked back at the rising slope behind them in horror.

"How will we ever get Lord Bromley out through here?"

Hildegarde stroked the side of the bag she carried and scowled. "I may have to tend him where he is and wait for rescue."

Eloise understood that meant she would have to lead Peril out and trust that he and his men could fight their way through the walls to rescue Bromley and Hildegarde. That assumed that Peril was not badly injured, and . . .

She wouldn't think it, couldn't think it. He was all right. They would find him and bring him out to safety, she told herself.

The passage deepened, allowing them to stand, and progress was easier. The walls were now cut stone, and the dank air gradually gave way to a drier, clearer atmosphere. Eloise's hopes rose as they began to climb an occasional step and encounter an occasional side tunnel.

Hildegarde paused at each to chart the way. True to her word, she brought them at last to what appeared to be a storeroom filled with old barrels and crates and cobwebs. Eloise looked around as they passed through the chamber.

"This looks just like the cellars beneath Whitmore," she said.

"It is just like the cellars beneath Whitmore," Hildegarde said. "The same stonecutters and masons that did these tunnels went to work for the old earl of Whitmore after they left here."

Soon they ran into their first obstacle, a large, aged oak door that looked as if it hadn't been opened in a decade. Wiping dust and spiderwebs aside, they searched for a latch and finally found one. It still took both of their strength to pull the door open, and the sound the rusted hinges made was piercing. Hildegarde grabbed her by the wrist and dragged her quickly down the passage and into a side tunnel, where they waited with pounding hearts to see if the noise had drawn attention. After a while, they crept out of hiding and continued on.

It was taking longer than Eloise imagined. She began to worry that whatever negotiations had begun might not hold Claxton's interest long enough to give them time to find Peril and Bromley and to escape.

Then they came to a passage that caused Hildegarde to pause and scowl. She closed her eyes, recalling images of long ago, and finally shared her dilemma.

"One of these leads through the cellars to the kitchens . . . the other to the dungeons." After a moment, she pointed to the left. "This way. I think."

Something darted furtively in the passage off to their right, and they both gasped and shrank back against the wall. After a moment, Hildegarde took a deep breath and stepped out into the passage holding her lamp high.

"Please tell me it's just rats," Eloise whispered.

Another spurt of scurrying occurred and this time Hildegarde lurched after it and a chase ensued. Suddenly there was squealing and howling and the lamp dropped and everything went dim. Eloise rushed after her and found her on the floor of the passage, with her arms around a wiggling bundle of rags.

"Lemme go!" came a small, shrill voice as the struggle slowed.

It took her a moment to realize that Hildegarde was holding a child . . . a very small and very dirty child. When Eloise thrust Hildegarde's lamp closer to him, she found herself looking at a disturbingly familiar face.

"Gravy?" She put out a hand to touch him and he cried out in terror. "Gravy, it's me . . . Lady Eloise. Of Whitmore."

He quit struggling and blinked up at her as if seeing her for the first time.

"M'laidy Elleweese?" he said, as if it were too much to hope for. A moment later, she opened her arms and he scrambled into them.

"How did you get here?" she asked.

"Hadric — he brung me. I didn't run away, I swear."

"I believe you. But why would Hadric bring you here?" He shook his head and she had to force his chin up.

"I was jus' tendin' the fire when some men come into the kitchen an' they grabbed me. The next thing I knowed, I was here an' they beat me an' made me work. I come down here to hide from 'em."

It was then that Eloise's fingers touched the iron collar around his neck. She stooped down and held him out to look at him. He had a black and swollen eye and a cut lip . . . and wore a heavy iron collar around his thin neck.

She looked up at Hildegarde with anguish in her eyes.

"We can't leave him here."

Hildegarde nodded and knelt to ask the boy which way to the kitchens. He wiped his eyes and pointed. When they asked if he was sure, he nodded.

"Please, don' make me go back there!"

Eloise laid her hand along his cheek. "You'll come with us, Gravy, and we'll take you home with us. But you'll have to be quick and quiet."

The boy wiped his nose on his sleeve and nodded.

The three of them pushed on toward the dungeon. The walls narrowed so much that it was almost hard to breathe, and suddenly the passage floor became a series of crude steps that wound up and down, seemingly without rhyme or reason. Then they came across a large stone niche carved into the side of the passage, covered with fat iron bars. When Eloise held her lamp closer, she and Gravy both were jolted back by the sight of a human skull and bones.

The horrific image would not leave Eloise's mind. Was Peril even now lying in some cramped, black niche, waiting for death to come and claim him?

"Hold on, my love," she whispered desperately. "Hold on."

Moments later, they were flattened against the walls at the end of the narrow passage, staring at the dim light coming from a place where the passage widened into a stonewalled chamber . . . beyond which was a heavy oak door inset with those same thick iron bars. It was the entrance to the dungeons.

"In my day, it didn't have a door," Hildegarde whispered irritably.

"We have to find a way in," Eloise said on a groan.

"There is no other way in," Hildegarde

said. "We'll have to make whoever is in charge open the door for us." She thought for a moment. "Gaolers only open doors if they see something they want — usually something edible."

Eloise looked at Gravy. "Do you think you could find us a basket and some bread? Or a tray with a cloth on it?"

It took forever for them to make their way back toward the kitchens. From their hiding place in the cellars, Gravy darted out to grab bread and an earthen jug of ale. They found an old basket and Hildegard put a piece of the linen she had brought for bandages over it.

When Gravy pounded on the dungeon door, the gaoler stuck his lantern up to the bars and glowered down at him. "Whadda ye want?"

"Th' earl, he sent this fer the lord." Gravy was convincing in the part of the beleaguered kitchen boy, down to his very cuts and bruises.

The gaoler grumbled, but keys clanked in the lock and the door creaked open. When the gaoler grabbed at the basket, the boy protested, saying he'd get "beat" if he didn't deliver it properly. A tussle ensued, and Eloise and Hildegarde were able to slip through the door and around the chamber to the steps that led down to the cells. The sound of a fist smacking flesh stopped Eloise in her tracks, and Hildegarde had to drag her on down the steps.

"Ain't nobody gets nothin' down here 'less I get my share," the gaoler growled as he trudged down the steps.

Eloise and Hildegarde fled ahead of the gaoler's lantern, past barred doors and cells little more than the size of coffins. The passage abruptly stopped, and in a panic, they flattened against the wall. Fortunately, the gaoler stopped just around a slight curve in the wall.

"You in there" — he banged on the door — "His Lardship sent ye a last meal."

"Take it away," came a familiar voice.

Eloise grabbed Hildegarde's wrist. It was Peril. She lifted her head from the wall to see the gaoler pushing a hunk of bread through the bars and Peril pushing it right out again.

"Keep your rotten food," Peril growled.

"Ye'll come around." The gaoler picked up the bread and bit into it himself. "They alwus do."

Suddenly there was a jingle and the sound of running feet in the passage, and the gaoler yelled, "Hey, you li'l shit — git back here wi' them keys!"

But as soon as Gravy reached the upper

chamber, he darted this way and that and snatched up a three-legged stool to fend off the ham-fisted gaoler. Cornered, the boy charged back down the steps, still holding the keys and the stool.

The gaoler charged after him. Gravy ran until he banged into the end of the passage and then whirled, and as Eloise grabbed him to pull him back against the wall with her, it was clear their presence was about to be discovered. Instinctively, she seized the stool, and as the gaoler came around the bend, she raised it and brought it down on him with all her might. The thickheaded gaoler roared with pain and stumbled against the wall, bent over. Eloise hit him again with the stool, but it was Hildegarde who finally sent him sprawling — with several whacks from the heavy tool bag.

For a moment the three stood panting, staring at each other. Then Eloise hurried up the steps between the cells calling softly to Peril.

"Peril, where are you? Are you all right?"

"Eloise?"

Peril's head pounded continuously, and if he turned his neck a certain way, he seemed to see flashes of light. But that voice . . . it was so real . . . He gritted his teeth and shoved to his feet again, heading for the door. There, outlined by the dim light, was a head, a face. He blinked, shading his light-sensitive eyes. Then he caught a flash of flame-colored hair and realized it was no dream.

"Eloise?"

"Yes, it's me!" she said, trying to keep her voice low. "We're here to get you out. Is Lord Bromley all right?"

He put his hands over hers as they clasped the iron bars. It was all he could do to get his breath. His mind and heart both began to race. She was here!

"He needs help. He's lost some blood, and — How the hell did you get in here?"

"Hildegarde brought me," she said as she took the keys from Gravy and began to try them in the crude iron lock.

"Michael, Simon — those idiots let you come?"

"They couldn't have stopped me from coming. We have a plan . . ." Her hands trembled so badly it was difficult to find the right key.

"Let me." Hildegarde stepped in and found a likely match for the lock. Two tries and the latch clicked and the door swung open.

Eloise nearly bowled him over as she threw her arms around him and held him as tightly as she could. He wrapped his arms around her, holding her, absorbing some of the warmth and vitality he had thought might be lost to him forever. When he could bear to loosen his grasp, she pulled back to touch him all over, demanding to know if he was injured.

"A knock on the head," he said, seizing her quaking hands and pressing desperately grateful kisses on her fingers. "I'll live."

"I'll hold you to that," she said, wiping tears. Then she sank her arms around his waist, hugging him again. Then together they turned to Hildegarde, who was kneeling beside Lord Bromley examining him by the light of the lantern Gravy was holding.

"Who's this?" Peril asked, looking at the boy.

"One of our kitchen boys . . . the one who was missing," Eloise said. "We're rescuing him, too." She smiled at Gravy and he smiled back through his battered face. Then she turned to Hildegarde. "What do you think?"

"His Lordship is in no condition to walk, and we cannot carry him. He'll have to stay here —"

"The hell I will," came a graveled voice from the figure on the ledge. Bromley opened his eyes and struggled to rise. "I'm coming with you."

"No, Your Lordship." Hildegarde tried to push him back down onto the pallet. "You mustn't move."

"I won't stay here and rot in this cell," Bromley growled, shoving her hands from his shoulders and pushing up. "If I have to die today, I intend to do it aboveground."

Amazingly, the lord treasurer could stand. Peril took one side and Eloise the other, and together they helped Lord Bromley up the passage toward the gaoler's chamber. There, they paused to let him rest and have Hildegarde take Peril's place. Suddenly there was a flurry of feet on the stairs coming from the castle above.

"This wasn't part of our plan!" Eloise said in a frantic whisper. She tossed the leather tool bag to Peril and told him to look inside. Then she and Hildegarde staggered into the passage with Lord Bromley.

"Exactly what was your plan?" Peril asked, holding up the hammer and chisel before dropping them.

"Does it matter?" She ducked under Lord Bromley's arm again.

Tucking the two long daggers into his belt, he tested the grip of the short sword they had brought and then hurried after them. The steps up and down seemed to take forever. Lord Bromley was weakening, and the red stains on his bandages were spreading. By the time they reached the first storeroom, they knew they would have to make yet another unexpected change in plans.

"That way leads to the kitchens," Eloise told Peril. "We could go that way and out through the yard. Hopefully there will be enough confusion at the gates that they won't notice a few more frantic people running."

There was no time to argue. With Gravy as their guide, they wound their way through the cellars and up into the pantry. Then they heard a voice that made their blood chill in their veins.

"I don't care if they did see me leave — I'm not staying there to get killed on my own doorstep!" Claxton bellowed.

"But milord, they're coming over the wall. My men can't hold them without —"

"They'd better hold it! You'd better hold it. Give me that! Now get back up there and save my house from being fired!" Claxton parted the curtain and charged into the pantry with a pair of armed guards. He paused long enough to shift the leather money bags he held in his arms. "There's a passage down here somewhere that leads out under the walls. You find it for me, and I'll make you rich men."

The two soldiers headed into the passage. As Claxton halted to tie the two bags together and sling them over his shoulders, Peril stepped out into the middle of the pantry.

"Well, well, Renfrow. Isn't this just like you?" His voice was as hard as blue Damascus steel. "Running away and leaving someone else to do your fighting for you."

Claxton whirled and, at the sight of Peril, blanched visibly.

"What the hell? Who let you out?"

"That would be me," Eloise said, stepping forward. When Claxton looked confused, she smiled. "I'm Lady Eloise, Lord Peril's wife."

"The nun," Claxton said without thinking.

"Not exactly," Peril said, circling the tip of his blade toward the sword that hung from Claxton's belt. "Fill your hand with steel, Claxton. So I can kill you honestly."

Claxton dropped the bags from his shoulder and lunged for the kitchen door in the same instant. Peril raced after him, dead set on finishing the conflict between them once and for all.

Claxton raced up the steps from the kitchen and into the great hall, where a dozen soldiers were frantically trying to hold the great doors shut against Peril's and Bromley's men. Claxton's captain whirled and saw him, and saw Peril behind him, advancing.

"Don't just stand there, you dolt — kill him!" Claxton shouted at his captain.

With a look of contempt for his master, the captain raised his blade and charged Peril. Steel rang as blade met blade again and again. The captain's longer blade gave him the initial advantage, but as he tired, it also meant he had more weight to lift and swing. Soon his hacks and cuts grew slower and brought him closer to Peril. And closer. Then too close. With one hand, Peril blocked a chop from his blade, and with the other, sent a dagger up under his opponent's ribs. It was a desperate battlefield technique, the sort of thing a man had to learn in order to survive during war. The captain, schooled in knightly skills but never having experienced the crucible of real combat, had never before encountered it. Both the captain's and Claxton's eyes were wide with surprise as he crumpled and fell.

A pair of men pulled away from their defense of the door to go to Claxton's aid, but the craven earl was already fleeing again up the steps to the tower rooms in the keep. Peril raced after him, and two soldiers raced after Peril. He soon sent them careening back down the steps. The sounds from the hall below made it clear the doors had been breached. Blades clanged; there were shouts and roars, grunts and cries of pain.

All of that faded in Peril's consciousness as he shed all but the most essential of perceptions. There were two men in that upstairs chamber. Only one would emerge alive.

Claxton, cornered, drew his blade. He snarled and feinted a lunge, laughing when Peril braced for a charge that never came.

"This . . . this is what I wanted all along," Claxton declared. "You and me. Settling old scores. The winner take all."

Peril watched Claxton cutting the air with his blade.

"Liar."

Claxton charged him with a roar of pure bloodlust. Peril met his blow, but was driven backward and barely had time to recover and meet the second blow. Claxton was surprisingly strong, for one so tall and reedy, but his swings were erratic and left him open to quick backhand cuts. Soon Claxton had several trickles of red pouring down his black tunic.

Peril watched the desperation rising in Claxton, saw the realization dawning that he could not win against Peril's superior strength and experience. It was a dangerous moment, Peril knew. Men who saw death in their opponent's eyes did desperate and unpredictable things.

When Claxton feinted with his shoulder and brought his blade straight up, Peril felt it slice into his arm. Buoyed by the sight of blood, Claxton rolled to the side, intending to pivot and bring his blade around to catch Peril in the back. But Peril instinctively ducked and rammed his sword upward, catching Claxton square in the gut as he turned.

Claxton fell with a thud, and the chamber fell eerily silent. Everything in Peril's vision seemed to swim, as if he were underwater. He looked down at his arm and realized with a curious sense of detachment that blood was pouring from it. He dropped his sword to clamp his hand over the wound, and he headed for the spiral stairs. The rough stone of the wall scraped his shoulder as he descended, and when he reached the bottom he realized all was strangely quiet. There seemed to be bodies everywhere. He remembered stepping over one . . . and then there was Eloise . . . running toward him.

He opened his arms and felt her warmth enfolding him as he collapsed. The last thing he recalled was looking up into her tear-filled eyes and wanting to tell her . . . tell her . . .

He awoke more than a day later, in his own bed, in his own house, on his own estate. That was his first thought as he looked up at the bed drapes and around a familiar room. He was home.

He struggled up onto his elbows and felt a stabbing pain his left forearm. He looked down and saw a bandage, then felt his head and realized it was bandaged as well. His mouth felt like the bottom of a fish barrel and his head was beginning to pound anew.

"Don't you dare try to get out of that bed." Eloise appeared at the foot of the bed with a tray in her hands. "Hildegarde says you nearly cracked your head open and that you're not to get out of bed for two more days."

"How long have I been asleep?"

"Not nearly long enough," she said, pushing him back down.

"What happened? Is Bromley —"

"He is across the hall, being cranky and demanding." She settled beside him on the bed and balanced the tray on her lap.

"Hildegarde is having a bit of a time with him."

"What about my men?"

"Hildegarde's patched them up. Very few have serious injuries. It seems Claxton wasn't nearly as keen on keeping his garrison in fighting trim as you were. And his men didn't relish laying down their lives for a man who saw the enemy at his gates and ran. Now open up."

"What's that?" he demanded, peering into the bowl.

"My famous Flemish broth. You love it, remember? Open up."

"You came for me," he said, seizing her hand and holding it, spoon and all. "I remember now . . . in the dungeon . . . you came for me." The wonder in his eyes changed abruptly. "Don't you ever do anything like that again!"

"I won't," she said with a canny look. "If you won't."

The defiant glint in her eye and set of her jaw said she was deadly serious.

"You're a hard woman, Eloise of Whitmore," he said.

"I can be. When the occasion calls for it."

Tough as iron, his Eloise. With the heart of a lion. Exactly the sort of woman a stubborn, prideful, and overbearing man needed. And the most miraculous thing was — his chest developed that ache again — she loved him.

"Kiss me," he said, pulling her closer, "and prove to me I'm still alive."

She smiled, dropped the spoon into the dish, and leaned down to kiss him. He wrapped his arms around her and she didn't care that the broth tipped and spilled onto the tray.

"I love you," he said, looking deeply into her eyes.

"I know." She smiled, stroking the side of his face.

"You do?"

"You told me."

"I did?" He tucked his chin. "When?"

"When you came rushing down Claxton's stairs and threw your arms around me, saying, 'I love you, Eloise — I love you with all my heart!' " She smiled, clearly pleased with the timing and manner of his announcement.

Just then Michael, Simon, and Ethan peered around the door and, seeing him awake, came in to make reports.

"Fie, milord, you're looking better already!" Michael declared.

"How many of us do you see?" Ethan asked as they paused by the foot of the bed.

"Six," Peril said sourly.

"You see," — Ethan gave Simon an elbow — "I told you he would be fine."

"All is secure, milord," Simon assured Peril. "We've found your missing wine and a good bit more . . . wool from this year's shearing, grain, sheep, cattle, and those three foals that disappeared. Claxton's thieves had taken them all. Better still, we found the two missing children."

Peril sat up sharply, looking from Simon to Eloise.

"Molly Bane's and Ellis the tanner's boys? They've been found?"

"It's true," she said, her eyes glowing through a mist. "Like the boy Gravy, they had seen Hadric and his accomplices loading and removing things bound for Claxton's estate. So he took them prisoner and sent them along . . . made them work in Claxton's household."

He let out a whoop and flung his arms out, then quickly winced. But no amount of discomfort could remove the joy from his face.

"You should have seen Molly Bane's face when she saw her boy running toward her," Michael said, still clearly under the spell of that moment. "And Ellis's wife, Ardith — I bet she's still hugging and crying."

"There was celebrating in the village last night, I tell you," Simon added.

"They're home, Peril," Eloise said, putting her hands over his. "Safe and sound."

It was a moment before anyone in the room could speak again.

"Bromley's captain has taken charge of Claxton's castle," Simon continued, "pending word from the king, and he helped us to search and uncover the truth."

"That bastard Claxton. *He* was Whitmore's curse." Peril tested the bandage on his head and then pulled it off. When Eloise tried to keep him in bed, he glowered at her and said the only way he would stay there was if she joined him. She flushed crimson at the knights' laughter and brought him his hose and a tunic.

He wanted to see his home, wanted to explore this odd new sense of well-being, of being renewed, almost reborn. He dressed and, with some help, descended the stairs to his hall, where the men present sent up a cheer to greet him.

He called for food, real food, and finally submitted to Eloise's demand that he eat lightly and drink only sweetened barley water. Then, as Eloise settled beside him and held his hand, gazing fondly at him, a boy came running into the hall and made straight for Peril.

"Milord! Milord — they're gonna burn 'er!" the boy shouted. "Come quick!"

It was Tad, the beekeeper's son. Peril rose, grabbed the child by the shoulders, and bent to look him in the eyes.

"Whoa — what is this about, boy? Burn who?"

"That hairy old witch woman . . . the one in the forest . . . the one I got away from. She come back to get me!"

"Old witch woman?" He scowled and looked at Eloise in confusion.

"A *hairy* old witch woman?" Her eyes widened. The coincidence was too great to ignore. "Hildegarde. It must be Hildegarde!"

Peril headed for the door with Eloise at his side, reminding him to take care and mind his head and arm. When they reached the open air, they spotted people running down the path toward the manor gates and across the cleared land to the middle of the village. She picked up her skirts and ran.

A crowd of people had gathered on the main road at the edge of the village. As Eloise pushed their way to the front, she heard the word "witch" used in various fearful combinations. At the center of the throng stood Hildegarde, held fast by two of the village's strongest men.

Eloise groaned. Hildegarde's costume alone was probably enough to make her suspect in the village; that vivid purple kirtle and the large gold hoops in her ears. Even worse, her graying hair now hung loose about her shoulders again and her dark eyes fairly crackled with indignation.

"This is Hildegarde, our physician," Eloise declared for all to hear. "You must release her!"

The men holding Hildegarde protested, charging her with stalking through the village casting spells, giving women and nursing babies the evil eye. Worse yet, she had frightened young Tad the beekeeper's boy right out of his wits. The lad had run through the village, screaming that the witch he escaped in the woods had come to get him back.

"Listen to me!" Eloise held up her hands for quiet, and the crowd quieted enough for most to hear her. "This woman is a healer and an apothecary who has just come to live and work on the manor. She did not snatch young Tad in the woods. Hadric and the thieves in the forest did that — we have proof now. In fact, I believe she was the one who freed him from those who had taken him. Is that not right?"

"It is." Hildegarde nodded. "I found a boy tied hand and foot in the woods, some time back. I freed him and walked him a ways through the woods."

Disbelief roiled through the crowd.

"She'll say anything to save her evil hide!"

"But I won't!" Eloise turned instantly on the part of the crowd where that voice originated. "And I'm telling you that this woman is not an evil witch. She is the very opposite — a Good Samaritan!"

The reference seemed to be lost on them, but Peril picked it up as he thrust through the crowd with the boy Tad in tow.

"Is this the woman who helped you, after you were taken in the woods?" the earl demanded, his voice calling the attention of the crowd to his presence and authority. Taking Tad by the wrist, he dragged the boy to the center of the circle to see the woman against whom he had leveled the charge. "Think carefully, boy. These are serious matters."

The boy shrank back and lowered his eyes. " 'At's her, I guess."

"Discovering and untying a boy that's bound hand and foot is not evidence of witchcraft," he said, glowering at the lad, then at the men holding Hildegarde. With a motion of his hand, they released her.

"Tell us who you really are," he ordered her, "and where you come from."

"I am now known as Hildegarde." She stepped forward, addressing the villagers several of whom skittered back behind their lord. "For the past two years, I have lived in an old cottage in the forest. Some distance away."

"And what were you doing in the village today?" Peril asked.

"Not souring mothers' milk or casting evil eyes, if that is what you want to know. I came to see the children who had been returned to their families . . . to see if they needed any care. On the way I saw a woman nursing a child that looked yellowed and bilious, and asked if I might help. I know healing arts."

"Black arts, she means!" came a voice from the crowd. Peril located the man at the rear, and his glower caused the wretch to redden guiltily.

"Are you a witch?" He continued the questioning.

"I am not," she said evenly, with a direct and untroubled gaze. Peril felt the knot in his gut loosen. That major hurdle was successfully crossed.

"And you have never cast a spell or curse on man or beast?"

He was not at all prepared for her answer. "Unfortunately, Your Lordship . . . I have."

A wave of reaction swept the crowd and he looked at Eloise with a blend of alarm and outrage.

"I did not mean to do so," Hildegarde continued above the murmurs of her audience. "I was young and foolish and very, very angry. I uttered hateful words, not knowing how potent they would be. They became a curse that to this day has haunted a whole manor and village."

Peril felt the hair prickling on the back of his neck.

"What manor?" he demanded, bracing. "What village?"

"This one, Your Lordship."

For a moment Peril could scarcely speak. What sort of madness was this? He looked at Eloise, who shook her head in disbelief, seeming just as shocked as he was.

"Explain yourself," he ordered, stalking closer to Hildegarde, searching the weathered lines of her face and her vivid brown eyes.

"Once, I lived here." She pointed up the hill. "In the same hall where I now reside. In those days I was known by the name of Ann of Levenger."

That claim ignited a small explosion in

the crowd. Everyone began to speak at once and every utterance contained the same ominous words: "Mistress Ann."

Peril felt his blood draining from his head. Here, before him, was the fabled cause of his parents' enmity for each other, the origin of his people's belief in that damnable "curse," and the source of the discord that had nearly ruined a once-proud estate.

A ragged, knotty figure pushed through the crowd to reach the front, demanding, "Lemme through, lemme see 'er. I'll know if it be her!"

Old Morna halted a few steps from Hildegarde and then tottered forward, squinting. She touched Hildegarde cautiously, then drew back abruptly.

"It be Mistress Ann, all right."

The people's reaction to that was so unsettled that Peril feared they might do violence to the woman.

"This is no place to speak of this," he said, lifting his head to look around for his knights, who had followed him from the hall. "Take Hildegarde up to the hall," he ordered.

"Please, milord." Eloise caught his arm. When he looked down, her eyes were huge and earnest in a way that unexpectedly disarmed him. "This is the *best* place to speak of this. Your people have labored for years under the specter of a curse supposedly uttered by her. They need to hear how it came about in order to understand it and overcome it."

He searched the quiet wisdom evident in every aspect of her face. She was probably right. She was, after all his "bride of virtue." She was the one who had journeyed from the safety and comfort of her cloistered world and plunged heart-first into the midst of his crumbling estate and stubborn, superstitious people. This, of all things, she had a right to decide.

He turned to Hildegarde.

"Speak, then, Hildegarde. Explain yourself."

"I was raised on the earl of Claxton's estate — my father was the old earl's head clerk, many years ago. The earl saw me and wanted me for his mistress, but I had already fallen in love . . . with Raymond, earl of Whitmore. I ran from my home and came to live at Whitmore with him. I believed he meant to marry me." She shook her head ruefully. "Young women in love are seldom the wisest judges of character. However much he loved me" — she looked at Peril — "your father loved another thing more: his ambitions. He wanted Whitmore to be the finest castle in the south of England and spent all of his coin in building what you see there."

All followed her pointing finger to the sight of the unfinished tower.

"He needed more money, more workmen, and more stone . . . so he did what most noblemen do for money: he contracted a marriage. And he moved me out into a cottage of my own.

"It shames me to confess that even after his bride arrived and they spoke vows, he still came to me. When I learned I was with child, I begged him to annul his marriage and make my child his heir. He refused. When I confronted him and demanded he choose, he turned me out and told me never to return.

"That was when I said those words of portent. And I repeated them in the village with great bitterness and malice in my heart. There was no excuse for what I did. I was hurt, and I wanted to hurt him back."

The quiet was so intense, they could hear the new leaves rustling in the bushes nearby.

"And you ran away," Eloise said, remembering Hildegarde's words to her that day in the forest. Hildegarde nodded.

"Being here was too painful. I blamed him, his greed, and his treachery. When I

lost
that
Hea
running
healing an
world, and I lea
keep. Then, when
the flame in my heart ha
realized I had to come home this is
where I truly belong."

"That was it?" Peril asked both himself
and her. "No black magic, no seething caul-
drons, spider venom, or eyes of newt Just a
few words?"

"Just words, milord." Her eyes glistened
with moisture as she met his gaze "But
words can be powerful things." She looked
sadly at the faces of Whitmore's people.
"Look at all of the pain and despair and confusion my few hateful words have caused."

"There must have been much pain, to
cause so much hurt," Eloise said.
Hildegarde's wistful smile bore traces of a
heart much broken and much mended.

"When I returned, I heard of the 'curse'
and what happened to the old earl and to
Whitmore. I was distraught when I realized
how my words had traveled down through
the years and brought pain and suffering to
others, but I didn't know how to set things

"I sub myself to your judgment, my lord, and whatever punishment you think fitting. if there is any mercy in your heart, beg you to let me serve you and these pple as my penance. I will promise to car for their injuries and tend them throug their ills for as many days as the Almight sees fit to grant me."

Peri looked at her graying head, thinking of his father, wishing he had known his mother . . . angry, and yet unwilling to deal out more pain to a woman who had already suffered much at his family's hands. Then he felt Eloise's hand on his and he looked up.

The little nun in the woods. His bride of virtue. In fleeing him, she had run into the woods and in coming back to him, she had unwittingly brought the cause and the remedy of Whitmore's "curse" with her.

"If what you say is true, you have suffered enough punishment," he said to Hildegarde.

"And you have already rendered much true and faithful service. If you would stay here and practice your healing arts, I welcome you to do so."

"Thank you, milord." She took his hand and kissed his ring. There were tears in her eyes as she rose. "And thank you, Lady Eloise, for your faith and your protection. I will serve you well."

There were tears in Eloise's eyes as well.

"You already have, Hildegarde." Eloise embraced her warmly. "You already have."

That evening, just after sunset, as Peril stood on the rampart of the unfinished tower looking down over the village, Eloise gathered the courage to climb the stairs to find him. He seemed troubled and she went to stand beside him, letting the silence draw to the surface the words that needed to be spoken.

"I thought they would be happier," he said after a few moments. "I expected they would be celebrating their freedom. But it's so quiet in the village, it's almost eerie."

"Give them time. It was the belief of their own minds and hearts that held them prisoner, and it was struck down before their eyes today. It may take a while for them to come to terms with that and with the freedom it gives them."

She looked up and found Peril watching her with a strange expression.

"I thought I would hate her," he said slowly. "I probably *should* hate her for all the pain and suffering she's caused. But when I looked into her eyes, I couldn't. She is so different from what I would have expected. So filled with care and regret and forgiveness." He rubbed the center of his chest as if it ached. "In some ways, we're very much alike."

"You are?" She searched his dark centered eyes. "How?"

"Both of us have lived lives filled with conflict and destruction. Both of us have made the decision to change our lives, to make something good come from all of the pain and despair we have felt. She is, at long last, where she belongs. And so am I."

"And where is that, milord?" Eloise began to tremble as he pulled her into his arms.

"In your arms," he said smiling. His eyes began to glow like polished amber in the warm light of the setting sun. "And in your heart. As I lay in that dark prison cell, I realized that the thing I had searched my whole life for was finally in my hands. And I damned near let it slip from my grasp. I love you, Eloise . . . my bride of virtue. Wherever you are . . . that's where I belong."

She felt as if a blindfold had just fallen from her eyes. In one breathtakingly lucid instant, she understood the conflict he had carried inside and guarded so carefully from others. Peril had felt like a stranger here, too — on his own estates, in his own home. And from there it wasn't hard to see that he probably had always felt like a stranger, wherever he went. He had been fostered too early, separated forever from what little family he had, and plunged into a hard and violent life that forbade attachments of almost every kind. After years of wandering in strange lands and fighting enemies he barely knew, he came home to a place he barely knew and a people that needed things he could not give them . . . his heart, his strength, his passion.

But it was not just Whitmore's people that had needed and wanted those things; she needed them, too. Now that he had learned that he belonged here and with her . . . and gave of himself willingly . . . there could be peace in his heart and in their life together.

She ran her hands up his back, melting and molding eagerly against him.

"Welcome home, milord."

And she kissed him.

The next day, Easter Sunday, Father

Basset said several masses of celebration and thanksgiving for the new life blooming everywhere on Whitmore. No one in the last morning mass was more surprised than Eloise to see the lord of Whitmore enter the chapel and stride down to the front to bend a knee beside her. Through her tears, she saw him take her hand and hold it between his big callused ones. And when she looked up, there were tears in Father Basset's eyes as well. And she knew then that Father Basset had spoken the truth, those months ago. Peril had wanted a wife . . . a partner to his heart and life. He simply hadn't known it.

The people of Whitmore celebrated Easter with a feast, sweet buns and eggs, and plenty of ale . . . with egg hunts, wrestling and foot races, and singing and dancing. By the time the cottars and villagers straggled back to their homes that night and poured themselves onto their pallets, there was an entirely new feeling in the air over Whitmore.

And in more than one cottage, the children were put to bed with a new story that was to become their favorite for generations to come.

It began with a curse . . . dark days . . . a wicked neighbor . . . dastardly deeds. Then a courageous lord crossed the sea to find a bride of virtue to break the curse. And she came and she lived among the people and worked her good magic on the lord and the land. And when the lord was captured, the courageous lady went to rescue him. And from that day on . . . Whitmore enjoyed nothing but blessings . . .

Which explained the bountiful harvests on Whitmore, the beautiful countryside, the health of the people . . . and the surprising number of Whitmore sons who won the king's favor and were granted estates of their own.

About the Author

Betina Krahn — having successfully launched two sons into lives of their own and still working on launching her pesky pet schnauzer *anywhere* — divides her time between homes in Minnesota and Florida. Her undergraduate degree in biology and graduate degree in counseling, along with a lifetime of learning and observation, provide a broad background for her character-centered novels. She has worked in teaching, personnel management, and mental health . . . despite which she remains incurably optimistic about the human race. She believes the world needs a bit more truth, a lot more justice, and a whole lot more love and laughter. And she attributes her stubbornly sunny outlook to having married an unflinching optimist and to having two great-grandmothers actually named Pollyanna.